AN IMPRINT OF THOMAS H

This novel is entirely a work of fiction.
The work includes certain historical facts. Other than that, the names, characters and incidents portrayed in it are the work of the author's imagination. Any resemblance to actual persons, living or dead; events; organizations; or localities is entirely coincidental.

First published in Great Britain 1986
Bryce Thomas

Cover illustrations by Amazon

A CIP catalogue record of this book is
available from The British Library

ISBN: Paperback Book: 978-1-907696-35-0

Printed and bound by
Amazon

FORWARD

The Vlatsov Plot is an entirely fictional story about events leading up to and after the assassination of Mrs. Indira Gandhi. As far as the author knows, no such plot actually existed.

But it could have.

It must be noted that many of the events in this story relating to the assassination of Mrs. Indira Gandhi and her funeral are purely historical fact and did happen. The plot to kill Mrs. Gandhi developed over several years with large sums of money exchanging hands but THE VLATSOV PLOT is just one scenario of what might have been behind the plot to kill her. It is an entirely fictional figment of the author's imagination.

For clarification, therefore, below is a list of names of only some of people that took part in the assassination of Mrs. Gandhi. Any other names bear no relationship to any other person who actually exists or existed and any similarity is purely coincidental.

BALBIR SINGH was a Delhi police sub-inspector, arrested December 4th 1984. He stated that there were at least two plots that he knew of. He was convicted of plotting to kill The Premier on 21/1/86 and Condemned to death.

KEHAR SINGH. Was an assistant in the Directorate General of Supply and Distribution. He was arrested November 30th and convicted of plotting to kill The Premier on 21/1/86 and Condemned to death.

BEANT SINGH was the 36 year old bodyguard that shot Mrs. Gandhi with along with Satwant. He was killed after his arrest. He and several others received large sums of money in the three years prior to the assassination.

SATWANT SINGH was the second bodyguard involved in the assassination. He was wounded after the arrest and later implicated the men named above. He was convicted of murder of Mrs. Gandhi, 21/1/86 and Condemned to death.

*****

The following names are of persons connected with the unrest in India around the time of Indira Gandhi's death.

JASBIR SINGH is a nephew of Sant Jarnail Bhindranwale. Refused entry into Britain, eventually arrested in the Philippines and escorted back to India.

SANT JARNAIL BHINDRANWALE was a Sikh extremist and a terrorist. He was killed in the Golden Temple at Amritsar.

SANT HARCHAND SINGH LONGOWAL was leader of Akali Dal. He was an agitant, organizing demonstrations and disruption, but was not an advocate of terrorism.

MAGBOOL BOOT was leader of the Kashmir Liberation Front.

MAJOR GENERAL SHUBEGH SINGH was an ex-soldier, and a terrorist, killed along with Bhindranwale at the Golden Temple.

*

Many thousands of innocent Sikhs died as a result of the death of the Indian Premier.

PREFACE.

To average people in the street, there are things that just do not happen.

One might presume that a story about the covert activities of the world's leading intelligence services is inopportune. Some of the most devious and treacherous acts of subterfuge and assassination have taken place by the true professionals of the game during periods when the major powers are supposedly establishing agreements to try and agree.

Although this book is

AN ENTIRE FIGMENT OF MY IMAGINATION,

many actual acts by opposed governments are and were not recognised at the time to be what they really were. Murders are cloaked in the guise of natural death through illness, as with the death of Sir Hugh Gaitskell; assassinations or attempted assassinations are put down to mindless terrorism, such as the Brighton Bomb, Kennedy, Pope John Paul II, Indira Gandhi, despite the fact that such terrorist organisations are funded through governments; and through disinformation is put down to the over zealous efforts of unbiased reporters to establish the truth. I don't believe that people should be carried along with the tide of complacency. Most governments are involved in these kinds of acts to some extent, mainly carried out under the definition of defense of their own political system. Several governments and several terrorist organizations are mentioned in the book. I do realise that some governments are worse than others, and therefore this story does display a certain political leaning.

CHAPTER 1.

10.30 p.m. 31st July 1984.

This was going to be the pay-off for all that work. It no longer mattered about recognition or promotion.

After tonight he would never have to work in a laboratory again; those unsociable hours; having to have permission to go out; the inaccessible place in the middle of a desert; the top men pushing, always pushing, never happy with today's results, always wanting more. "Stuff the lot of them," the grey haired, wiry framed man whispered to himself as he drove the jeep up to the main gate. "Now I'll be able to go for a piss without asking them first."

"Good night Mr. Taylor," the guard, a young military police officer, said cheerfully as Edward waved his pass at him from the open side of the Jeep. He stopped the engine as if he had all night for the search procedures to be carried out by the young guard.

"Good night," he replied. His leg trembled as he glanced at the armed military policemen standing outside the fourteen foot high perimeter fence. A fence topped by six thousand volts. It wasn't a research station, it was a prison camp. He knew, as did all the people working at the centre that the fence and the guards were there to keep people in, not out. Anyone wanting to get in from the outside would have sixty miles of desert to cross without being detected on the electronic scanners. The five heavily armed Sioux Scout fighter helicopters that could be scrambled in the space of three minutes at any time, day or night, were ready, and would have intercepted them before anyone got within fifty miles of the Research Centre. The whole place was surrounded by a security cordon of radar, electronic sensors and closed circuit television cameras backed up with anti-aircraft and anti-missile missiles. They didn't trust their own scientists, their own laboratory technicians or even their own resident cleaners. Even the rubbish was incinerated in the Centre's own waste disposal unit. Nothing escaped. Normally the high security just made Edward angry. The top government officials had asked him, no begged him to join their team of elite brains; and for what; life in an inaccessible prison camp in the desert, as if scientific research was the only thing he lived for. But today he wasn't angry, he was afraid. The nerve in his right leg quivered. It hadn't shook that badly since he was a child, when it had trembled uncontrollably whenever he had been frightened by bullies or angry teachers. He had hated this weakness in himself as much as he had hated the people who brought the condition upon him. Now he hated the guards and the controllers of the Research Centre, and he hated the U.S. government for ever having bribed him to go there with gestures of patriotism in the first place. He was scared and he hated them for that as well.

"Having a few days off sir?" the military policeman enquired cordially, as he placed the pass in a slot in a machine.

Edward held his breath and said a silent prayer. After a couple of seconds which seemed like minutes it slid back out. He breathed an inaudible sigh of relief. The beads of sweat on his nose evaporated in the cooling night air. "Got to have a break from this place some time, or we'd all go completely mad," he said with a grin, trying to keep his voice as steady as he could. His mouth was as dry as the arid desert outside the gates. He pressed his right knee against the steering wheel to control his shaking limb.

"You're right there sir," the guard replied as he signed the pass. "I see you were issued a pass from 18.00 hours." He checked his watch and wrote the time on the clip-board. It was now 22.31.

Edward smiled. "Damned controllers," he said convincingly. "Issue you with a pass and then call you to a goddamned meeting. I'll be driving all night now."

"I see. Well take care sir," the guard said, handing back the pass and looking in the back of the Jeep. "Enjoy your leave," he said cordially and waved him through without any further inquiry.

Edward smiled a genuine smile. The young guard didn't like the place any more than he did. He withdrew his hand, threw over the starter and drove casually out into the cold desert breeze and away from the Research Centre. Only he knew it would be for the last time.

*****

Edward looked at least fifteen years older than his forty five years. Life had taken a heavy toll on him. His grey hair and heavily lined face were not hereditary. Things hadn't been easy, that's all. His benign character had undermined his genius. He had never fitted in at school because he asked questions when he should have been taking in what the teachers wanted him to know. Their tunnel vision had never allowed him to explore the frontiers of the sciences, only the well grazed enclosures. He got first grades in his exams effortlessly, and despite the fact that he'd struggled hard against the background of poverty into which he had been born he eventually won a scholarship to the University of Boston, first to take a degree in Chemistry and then, at last, to undertake research, the thing he'd most wanted to do since he was fourteen. He'd been engrossed in his research work for so long he'd had little time for the more earthly things. He'd been married once to a shapely and quite attractive young girl called Rosita, but they had nothing in common after the initial sexual attraction, and as the years passed he had found himself drifting away from his partner as he spent every waking hour, every waking minute thinking about his work. Finally after three and a half years he came home to find her in their bedroom, screwing hard down on a young undergraduate from the same campus. She turned her head with a little gasp of surprise as she heard him enter the room. Edward just walked out and left them to get on with it. He'd never seen her since. He took an occasional trip to the local brothel when the urge got the better of him, but apart from that his needs were frugal, somewhere to work, somewhere to read, somewhere to sleep. He was just ripe for the high-powered patriotic sales talk of the men who were recruiting for the new Government Research Centre, set up by President Kennedy for research into alternative defense systems to the nuclear bomb. He was well suited to the isolation of the centre at first, but gradually he began to miss his freedom. No holidays without somebody tailing him, no freedom to come and go as he pleased, and worst of all no brothel. It was the latter that he started to miss the most. The only red light he saw was in the photographic laboratory where he occasionally went to see frames of his experimental work taken with a high speed camera. He tried to chat to the female scientists, but he was an ineffectual suitor, and they treated him like a scientist, not a man. He tried to concentrate on his work, but eventually, with the little time given him on leave when he could indulge himself in his one weakness, he did a vault face, turning from a dedicated research scientist into a dedicated lecher. God how he was dying to make up for those wasted years!

*****

In his rear view mirror he could make out the lights of the Research Centre dwindling into the distance. He put his foot hard down on the accelerator. The road was a straight strip of concrete stretching far into the darkness, no bends, and no stopping places. The cool wind flapped at his jacket sleeves as he kept his foot hard to the floor, not to stop his leg shaking now, but to distance himself from the hell and fury that would be released in the next two hours. The open-topped Jeep was ideal for this kind of monotonous driving, the wind sweeping into his face, keeping his mind alert as the adrenalin began to dissipate from his bloodstream. And it was ideal for what he had done. He had one major obstacle ahead. As always he was tailed when he left the centre, an indignity suffered by all the personnel. They couldn't do anything that the government didn't know about it. He thought about many Russians who were treated exactly the same, but his society denounced the Soviet system, and they in turn denounced capitalism. What a cockeyed cocked up world he thought to himself. All in the name of freedom! All as bloody bad!

The obstacle still lay ahead. As he joined the main highway and turned north he glanced in his rear view mirror. There it was, an unmistakable dot of light in the distance, perhaps a mile back, perhaps two. The headlights gave it away, but it would be in no hurry to catch up. There was another hundred miles of empty road ahead, and plainly his was the only pair of headlights on it ahead of the tail. But then if he pulled over and turned his headlamps off, he wouldn't have fooled them. There would be a homing device on his jeep that couldn't be removed without a thorough search, and he hadn't the time. He glanced at his watch as he pressed the button to make the liquid crystal display light up. It was already 11.40. He'd cut it close, perhaps too close, to fit in with the rest of the plan. He'd lied to the young guard about the meeting. He'd picked up his Jeep from the vehicle compound at exactly 18.00 hours. When computer operator ran the late concurrence program and checked the times he would have to report a lapse of four and a half hours and nothing on the report sheet to say what Edward had been doing during that time. But he'd needed it, every minute. And he needed the darkness now, but had he cut it too fine? There would be search helicopters out within fifteen minutes of the alarm being raised. He would know exactly when that was. The tail car would receive a radio message to overtake and arrest him, or in a chase give his exact location. He kept one eye fixed on the mirror. If that light behind got any closer he'd know they'd got the call.

He checked the watch again. Five minutes past midnight and he'd still got twenty miles to go. His leg began to shake again, making the Jeep kangaroo. He pulled his body under control only with the maximum of effort. He would have liked to slow down but he had to go faster. Then he heard it. First he thought it was the wind about his ears, but gradually it became a sound of its own. It was the beating sound of rotor blades up above and behind him. He looked in his mirror. Still the dot of light was in relentless pursuit, not losing ground, but making no effort to flag him down. "Jesus," he squawked up at the sky. "That bastard's got here quick!" They must have found out earlier than he'd calculated. He looked around in the blackness but all he could hear was the beating of the rotor blades above his head. "Why the hell don't they stop me and get it over with?" he said between clenched teeth. Panic began to well up in him. He was going to spend the rest of his life in a cell, and he hadn't even had the chance to visit a brothel. He couldn't stand that. He wasn't going to be taken alive. "What a shitting cock-up!" he shouted to vent his exasperation. "Ten more minutes and I'd have made it."

He kept his foot hard to the floor of the Jeep. Miraculously his leg wasn't shaking anymore. His body had passed through the barrier of fear. Now all that remained in the pit of his stomach was the dull pain of defeat, but that in itself was enough to enable him to channel his energy. No longer was it dissipated throughout his body, but flowed to his brain. His mind became sharpened with increased supply of adrenalin, more alert as he decided what he should do to take his pursuers with him. It calmed him to know that they would lose as well. "Come on then you bastards!" he bellowed, and gave out a hideous laugh. He didn't care now that the rotors beat directly overhead, getting lower every second. He reached into his right hand pocket and took out a thin cylindrical piece of metal. He'd planned for this, but had prayed not to have to use it. A thin wire dangled from the detonator, and at the end of it swung a vehicle's cigarette lighter. He lifted the passenger seat of the Jeep forward and opened the lid of the auxiliary fuel tank. He dropped the detonator inside and re-screwed the cap tightly. Still the helicopter hovered over his head, out of sight in the blackness of the night. Then, as he pulled out the Jeep's own cigarette lighter, letting it drop to the floor, and plugged in the one from his pocket, he saw the shadow of the hovering death as it blacked out the belt of Orion. One push was all that it would need now. He slowed down in the middle of the road. Why be polite and pull over? He was going to burn the bastards anyway. He stopped and left the engine idling. In his rear view mirror he watched the speck of light coming closer. Or was it? It seemed to have stopped as well.

The helicopter still hung ominously overhead like some apparition, not coming down, not going away, and not even putting on the searchlight. He relaxed and took his hand from the lighter. He'd have plenty of time to reach for it when the vultures came in. He checked his mirror again. Yes, the tail car had stopped as well. He saw the headlights fade out as they sat and waited for his next move. "Jesus!" he panted. He hated people they were so illogical. "Well," he shouted. "What are you bastards waiting for? I can sit here all night if I have to."

It was then that Edward was glad he'd taken his hand away from the cigarette lighter. His body lurched forward uncontrollably as a loud-hailer burst its sound down upon him. "What the hell are you playing at?" the voice demanded, and then straight away gave an order. "Keep going to the rendezvous point. Everything is all right, repeat all right."

Edward couldn't see the helicopter, but with the sound of his racing Jeep engine abated, the noise above him, somehow didn't sound the same as the heavily armed fighters from the Research Centre. It sounded to be a lighter machine altogether. Quickly he pushed the gear lever forward and gunned down the road. He yanked out the wires of his home-made bomb and the lighter plug fell harmlessly to the floor. He glanced at his watch and saw that only three minutes had passed. It had seemed like an eternity in hell, but at least the helicopter with its un-nerving beat had gone, and so had the light from the following car. He drove the Jeep to its limit, and fifteen minutes later he reached his destination. He could see the first gleam of moonlight pushing the blanket of darkness off the horizon as he swung behind a derelict gas station, and out of view of the main highway. His headlights' beam glared back at him from the dormant headlights of another vehicle, until he'd pulled alongside, leaving the back of his Jeep level with the back door of what appeared to be a hearse.

Two tall, smartly dressed men came out of the wooden building. "Hello, Mr. Taylor I presume?" asked one of them.

"Thought I'd never get here," replied Edward. "Won't be long before they start missing it."

"They already have, but don't worry about a thing," the other replied. "Your job's over. Now it's up to us."

"But the tail?"

"You're a worrier Mr. Taylor. We jammed his radio as soon as the alarm went out.

"When?"

"Ten minutes ago."

"Then they'll be here in less than thirty minutes. All they have to do is follow the road to the tail car and pick me up from there. They'll know I've stopped even if you have jammed the homer because my lights are out."

"Then I would be obliged if you'd leave the panicking to me," the man said and held out his hand. Edward got out and handed over the keys. He watched as the two men diligently unloaded the two spare petrol cans from the sides of Jeep into a large coffin in the back of the hearse. Then they went to work on the spare tank.

"Careful," Edward said as he watched them go to it. He went over and unfastened the cap, pulling out the detonator by the dangling wire. He fastened the cap back on firmly.

"That near was it?" the second of the two men chuckled. It seemed like a game to them. To Edward the next hour or so was a matter of life or death, but their calm was euphoric. It took only a couple of minutes before the first of the two men had unfastened the one remaining bolt that Edward had left to hold the auxiliary tank in place. He pulled it forward and together the two of them eased it down to the ground beneath the Jeep. They slid it out and heaved it into the coffin. One of the men jumped into the Jeep, started it and by vision of moonlight only skillfully drove it under the narrow lean-to. Then both men went into the station and carefully carried out, under the cover of a white sheet, something no bigger than a suitcase, which they painstakingly positioned in the coffin. They closed the lid, clamping it firm with six large brass butterfly nuts, and finally closed and locked the back door of the hearse.

Edward watched in silence as the two undertakers went to get in their vehicle to drive away. Suddenly he began to wonder if he hadn't trusted the people he was dealing with too much. They looked like they were going to abandon him there. But then the first of the undertakers picked up a flashlight from the dashboard of the hearse, gave a brief signal and then slammed the door as the driver revved the engine ready to speed away.

Instantly there was a sound in the distance as the Allison turbine of a Spitfire helicopter fired, and the rotors began to swish through the still desert air. A moment later it loomed overhead, its searchlight blinding Edward momentarily. Dust flew all around him as it settled on the sand thirty yards away. "Go on, get in," said the undertaker, and drove off around the same side of the gas station to which Edward had approached. The tyres squealed above the noise of the rotors as they hit the hard surface of the highway.

Edward did as he was told. He shielded his eyes as he walked towards the helicopter, and a hand stretched out, grabbing him by the upper arm. "Come on, we don't have much time," the gruff voice of the pilot shouted in his ear. "We've less than half an hour before the place is swarming."

The pilot released Edward's arm as he climbed into the seat, and began to lift his machine off the ground. He circled low over the area following the path of the hearse to the road. When he was satisfied that the wheel marks had been obliterated, he swung away to the north and the cover of the hills, away from the searching radar beams of their pursuers.

*****

The strict security at the Research Centre was difficult to transgress. Everybody had to sign for their car from the car compound immediately before they left. The cars were fueled and maintained by staff on the site. Any luggage had to be checked and loaded by the duty officers in the main residential block. Even then, personnel had to be watched outside the Centre. Few had full security clearance. They were followed for their own safety from kidnapping, as well as the inevitable microfilm or defection reasons.

When the timesheet printouts were checked at midnight there was some doubt as to Edward's activities in the five hours before he'd left. Every guard station had a remote terminal into which the electronically pre-coded passes were fed. Normally the computer would raise any discrepancy in the central control room in a fraction of a second at the time it was entered at the remote terminal. A discrepancy would result in the terminal retaining the pass. It hadn't happened and the discrepancy had only been picked up on the secondary checking procedure which was run through the computer at the end of each shift in a form of double entry book-keeping. The mainframe operations night manager called the Centre Controller and Head of Security, Colonel Adam Felspars. "I'm sorry to bother you sir, but there is a query."

That was all it needed. The Colonel had the printouts in his hand in under a minute. Felspars was the fifty-eight year old, tall, thin Security Chief with slate grey hair, a reputation of being meaner than a starving grizzly, and a vulpine resolve in, expending his duties. He had been head of the security team since the Centre had opened and knew the place and its procedures backwards. He had built up a formidable screen of security systems and equipment, was briefed each day on the research in progress in all the different departments, and held supreme authority over all inside the boundary fence, being answerable only to the Secretary of Defense and the President. His whole manner exuded authority effortlessly and no one ever questioned him of his actions for he captained the place like a ship on the high seas, his own ship in the desert. With a workforce of over three thousand, and double that in security men both plain clothed and in uniform, he commanded a very big ship indeed, and controlled and monitored the crew both on board and wherever they went on the mainland.

He called the section in which Edward worked, and had the men in it survey the stock and check against the computer printout. Everything seemed in order. Edward had covered his tracks well. The survey had taken ten minutes. The Colonel gave a sigh of relief, and then asked for the copy of the gate sheet printout just to put his mind at rest. When it arrived he swore. "Get that damned guard in here at once," he commanded. Within two minutes the young military policeman, who had just finished his watch, was standing in front of the Colonel's desk. Calmly the Colonel asked him why he'd not reported the difference in the pass time and the time Edward left the Centre.

"Said he'd been called to a meeting, sir, and the terminal accepted the pass."

"Then what the hell's has gone wrong? The times on the printout don't tally." The colonel turned to the VDU operator. "Check the meetings," he ordered.

The computer man punched the keyboard of the VDU which listed all the meetings held that day in chronological order. Two more minutes passed before the answer came back. "No meetings with Taylor this afternoon sir," the officer announced, after reading through the list twice to make sure.

The colonel picked up the telephone receiver. "Scramble, repeat scramble. This is not an exercise, repeat this is not an exercise. Stop and apprehend one Edward Taylor, heading west to main highway." He paused for a moment. "Who's on Taylor's back?" he asked.

The young operator consulted a VDU. "Barking and Orgreave," he announced.

"Right, get a call to them to overtake and hold him till this matter is cleared up."

"What if he is clean, sir?" the guard asked.

"He knows the rules and so should you. You're a new recruit, I can understand you not picking up on it. He's a top scientist, and it is hard to be firm with someone like that until you get to know them. But he knows the rules backwards. If he's clean then it's his own damned fault if he gets brought back here for questioning." He gave the guard a stern look. "As for you, you won't do this again in a hurry. I hope as much as you do that it'll sort itself out this time, but there'll be a full inquiry and it won't go easy on you."

"Yes I understand sir,"

The colonel turned away. "You'd better get out," he said gruffly.

00.30 a.m. 1st August.

"Sir, I've just received a report from Taylor's section," James Bradbury had entered Colonel Felspars' office without knocking, his normally white chubby face flushed pink with the effort of urgency. "Something is missing." He placed a single sheet of paper on the desk in front of the Colonel.

Felspars read it through quickly. "What the hell! This is top secret stuff and he's just driven away with it in his suitcase?"

"Not sure sir, but the guard says he checked his hand baggage and it was just the usual hand stuff, you know, a couple of shirts..."

"I know what hand luggage usually consists of Bradbury, thank you all the same," Felspars interrupted. He picked up the phone and dialed. "What sort of vehicle was he driving?"

"A Jeep sir," Bradbury answered.

"Huh. Oh, hello Bill," said the Colonel as he diverted his attention to speaking into the phone. Can you come down straight away? I have an emergency and I need your brain."

"I'll be with you in five minutes," Bill Pointer answered and hung up. He was the person Felspars turned to for calculations on hypothetical questions of security and defense. A physics scientist first, a consultant strategist second, Felspars knew he had the analytical mind necessary to state all his options immediately and clearly. He'd spotted the young scientist at a Research Centre dinner, which he held every fortnight, inviting different people each time so that he could get to know who they were and subtly tease from them their ambitions, attitudes and intentions. Bill had been given auxiliary duties as a member of his security council ever since. Three and a half minutes later he knocked on the Colonel's door and put his head into the room. It was a bony head with a long face and a long thin jaw, and the pallor of a reclusive office worker. "What is it sir?" he asked with an injection of urgency into his voice.

"Hah Bill," Felspars said, turning from a large map on the wall behind his desk. "We've got a man who's done a runner; driven out of here in a Jeep at," he consulted a printout, "er, 22.30 hours last night."

Pointer just stood and listened, his gaunt pale face lifeless against a bush of frizzy red hair. He knew the colonel would ask the questions when he'd finished his explanation. "Nothing in his luggage. Pass issued for 18.00 hours wasn't thrown out by the computer at time of his leaving, only on shift end run. Managed to cover up a theft of top secret material by preventing it being thrown up on the printout, until it was rechecked manually. Radar scan showed him moving to main highway followed by the usual car full of agents, in this case two, and then out of range at approximately 11.50. Lost contact with the tail who never radioed in to say what was happening." He looked straight at Pointer.

"Yes sir."

"How, who, where, when, and how many?"

Bill Pointer didn't need to be asked why. Everybody knew the answer to that already. "How," Bill said as he took out a pair of half moon spectacles from the top pocket of his grey tweed jacket and placed them on the tip of his aquiline nose. "It's relatively difficult I should imagine. I'd need time to see how the magnetic strip on the pass had been altered and what with. Also,

I wouldn't be surprised if he hadn't tampered with the program. He was a brilliant man you know."

"Was?"

"Well he's gone now. If he ever comes back it won't be voluntarily."

"That's why you're here. I want him back with everything he's taken."

"Quite," Bill placated. "However, that takes me to the next question, who." He readjusted his spectacles and glanced over the printouts. "You see, whoever's helping him probably doesn't want to lose him. They won't be after just what he took with him. What he has in his head is worth many times more than that. Having said that, they must want what he's taken as well or he wouldn't have left this way. He would have disappeared while on leave. They, and there will be quite a few involved, will have had his escape organised on the outside ready for when he'd finished setting up his own plan of escape from the inside."

The Colonel ignored the use of the word 'escape.' Now wasn't the time to justify his prison camp approach to security at the Centre, the 'why' that could motivate fifty percent of the personnel at the Research Centre to do the same as Edward Taylor given the right incentives. "Go on," he said calmly.

"Once they have it, then the chances are Taylor will be whisked out of the country. So we must see where he's going next." He regarded the map for only a few seconds. "I presume you have helicopters going out to intercept?"

"Left here at 00.15 hours."

"We must presume the people helping him have a helicopter as well. They can travel in a straight line, and I'd plunk for one of those to a car any day if I were being pursued."

"Why not a light aircraft?"

"More visible. Got to have a lighted airstrip for take off and landing."

"Right, a helicopter it is."

"North to the cover of the hills then east." He ran his bony finger over the map. "They have to keep out of sight of the pursuing radar that our choppers carry. At a cruising speed of a hundred and sixty miles per hour, their relative gain on a small chopper cruising at say a hundred and thirty is only going to be thirty miles per hour. With at least a start of seventy miles in a straight line, that will mean that Taylor will be in the hills before your choppers pick up a bleep if he keeps in their shadow." He thought for a moment and pushed his spectacles back up the bridge of his nose. "They don't have infra red scan do they?"

"No."

"An oversight that. Instead of just armed helicopters you'd be better with Sikorskys." The Colonel ignored him. Bill had suggested that to him before, but after an up-hill struggle to get the helicopters he had, he'd had little chance of exchanging them when Bill later joined the team and suggested it. It had seemed like a good deal at the time, five modified Sioux Scouts, originally experimental helicopters with two 7.62mm cannon in a twin turret and anti-tank missiles. All were going to be superseded after 1963 in the U.S. Armed Forces by the faster and better equipped all purpose fighters, the Huey Cobras. The manufacturers, Bell, in order to place their prototype machines, as good as they were, had sold them at a price that was more than favourably tailored to his budget. His had been a policy of deterrence, not solution.

"Where can we get a Sikorsky at short notice?"

"No use now. The range to cover will be too great."

"So?"

"So I suggest you contact the Air Force Chief of Staff and get something with the proper equipment. Infra Red is all right, but ideally you need pulse-doppler as well. You need it within the next couple of hours, or the quarry will have escaped, for once they stop the sound scan will be ineffective, and when the engines have cooled it will be more difficult to pick them out in a large mountainous area with infra red."

"What makes you think they'll stop?"

"Two things; first, Taylor's a brilliant man, and he knows just how important he is. I know him and he doesn't overlook any possibility in the laboratory. He's unlikely to overlook the likelihood of an infra red or a sound scan."

"And?"

"And there's a likely chance that the pilot of the chopper, not being able to fly over the high land, will not want to fly the valleys at night. In that case they'll sit back and wait till daylight when there's so much stuff flying about that we'll have little chance of picking them up."

"Which aircraft would be best for the search?"

"Hawkeye if they have it in the Nevada desert ready to go. But it's essentially a navy plane and if they haven't one nearby, it wouldn't get here quickly enough even with a cruise speed of around three hundred miles per hour."

Colonel Felspars picked up the phone again. "As fast as you can, get me Washington, Secretary of Defense, and get me plugged into the choppers direct." He held the hand-piece to his chest. "We'll try for anything they've got," he frowned.

"Hello," came a sleepy voice on the other end of the line. "Can I help you?"

"Who's that?"

"The Secretary's secretary."

"Put me through to him."

"It's very late sir."

"I know what the time is. I don't make social calls through my operator. I wish to speak to The Secretary direct on a matter of national security."

"Hold on sir."

Colonel Felspars turned aside to speak to Bill. "Got to go to the fountain head in these matters. Takes time to get through the drips, but it's worth the struggle. Get on the other line and make sure all the roads have road blocks will you."

A couple of minutes later he heard the voice of The Secretary of Defense on the other end of the line as he grumbled down the phone. "What is it Colonel," he said with a resigned sigh of indignation.

The Colonel explained as quickly as possible what had happened, being careful not to state exactly what had gone missing, and then explained what he wanted. "Can you get the Air force to do a reconnaissance?"

"When?"

"Now, before air traffic begins to build up. We've a rough idea where to look."

"What do you want me to do?"

"There are air bases all around here, Idaho, California, Nevada. Somebody must be able to help. I'd like you to get the word out to Mountain Home, Watersdown Strip and Beale. I know Beale has SR-71s stacked up just waiting to be used. They only use them for training flights now. They could reach here in half an hour from take off in California."

"They aren't going to like using them for your searches. It costs an arm and a leg just to get them off the ground."

"Only you can prevent Taylor getting away with top security classified equipment, sir."

"I'll see what I can do. Do you want to hold?"

"No sir, I'll wait for them to contact me, but believe me, I wouldn't ask you to do it if it wasn't in the interest of our own national defense."

"All right," was the reply before they both hung up.

*****

Edward held tightly to his seat as the Spitfire Mark 2 helicopter drove fast and hard into the darkness that lay ahead. It consoled him to think that the pilot must have flown the course in a daylight rehearsal in order to assure that nothing was going to loom up in front of them and swat them like a fly hitting a car windscreen.

"Chris," announced the pilot as he peered at a tiny screen above his head and held out his hand. From the light of the dials Edward could just make out his negroid features and the thick heavy forearm extending towards him.

"Eddy," replied Edward, holding his breath as he left go of the seat with his right hand. Chris's grip was strong and steady, and it exuded confidence. Edward leaned back in his seat and relaxed.

"Gum?" The pilot handed him some Wrigley's.

"Oh, thanks." Edward took the packet and unwrapped two pieces. He put one in his mouth and handed the other to Chris. He took it without saying another word, his attention firmly on a floating compass above their heads.

"Not a lot of light tonight," Edward said to try and keep the conversation going.

"Haw, don't you worry about that, Eddy. This bird knows her way home all right." He glanced at the clock and chewed avidly.

"Thirty four minutes," he stated. "Got a bit of a head wind so I reckon it'll slow us down a mite."

"What when we reach the high ground?"

Chris chuckled. "Now don't go worrying yourself about that. The moon is up now. We'll manage all right."

"They'll pick us up on their radar if we don't get to the cover of the hills soon. They'll have aircraft heading out already to intercept us."

"We'll soon be there." He pointed ahead into a black empty space. It was impossible to see the division between land and sky.

"Damnation!" Edward swore as the moon disappeared and then reappeared just as suddenly.

"What's the matter?"

"It's cloud cover."

"That should help us if it's thick enough," Chris said eventually.

"Oh yeah?"

"Their choppers won't be able to see us through it."

"Those valleys are dangerous even in daylight. Without the full moon we'll be grounded unless you use your searchlight."

"Won't be using it."

"They are cumulus clouds. They wouldn't see your light even if you directed it straight at them."

Chris chuckled. "Will you shut up you dumb scientist?"

"Is that what you think of us, dumb and useless, can't change a fuse, all brains and no sense?"

"Well, it must take a special kind of person to lock themselves away in the middle of a desert for the sheer fun of banging their heads together."

"Why do you think I got out?"

"Sorry Eddy, you can't be such a bad guy," Chris conceded. "But the fact is I can see perfectly well, see." He pointed to the little green screen above his head. "You scientists aren't the only ones with new gadgets."

The moon and the stars disappeared for good as the helicopter swooped beneath a thick, heavy layer of vapour. Chris checked the compass, the altimeter and the clock. Two minutes and they would be onto the high land. "Let's hope the cloud isn't too low to fly under," Chris said and then banked the machine suddenly as the land seemed to come up to meet them. "Christ, we made better time than I thought." He adjusted the screen so that it was directly in front of his face. The land below was rising steeply. He climbed with it until the cloud began to envelope them, turned the helicopter due east, adjusted his altitude to stay beneath the cloud, and followed the range of mountains. He checked his clock again and then stared at the screen in front of him, swinging the craft from side to side. "Can you see a damned canyon?"

Edward strained his eyes. There was no light beneath the black blanket of cloud. They were driving ahead in what seemed to him a vast canopy of darkness. "Are there any landmarks?" he asked sarcastically.

"Yeah, but a pointed ridge is no goddamned good stuck up in the sky this sort of weather."

"Doubt if I'd notice it in passing anyway."

Edward pointed to the green screen. "What the hell is it?"

"A Condor night sight. Marvin had it shipped from Britain especially for me."

Edward undid his safety harness and leaned over Chris's shoulder.

"Hell it's like daylight. They've got passive night vision devices guarding the Research Centre, but I never realised they were that good."

"They aren't. This one's even better with some light from the stars or the moon, but it's the best there is," Chris chuckled. "Thanks to Her Majesty's army."

"British?"

"Sure is."

"Stolen?"

"Doesn't bother you does it? I mean stealing off some other government."

"Not bothered who you got it off if it gets us out of range of that lot behind us."

"They're made for use on the Shir main battle tanks. I bet the fella that stole this from Pilkingtons daren't go back either." He laughed out loud.

"Great," Edward giggled. It shocked him for a moment that he could take it so lightly, but his mind, his most used limb, was beginning to function logically again. Now he wasn't so afraid.

"How long were we supposed to fly east?" he asked.

"Five and a half minutes exactly."

"Well, give it another minute and then backtrack. We've been going for six and a half now. I think we've missed it."

"I don't think we have. What's the cruising speed of this thing?"

"About a hundred and thirty."

"Not been making anything like that in this black hole."

"You're right," shouted Chris. "There it is." He swung the helicopter north-east and followed a thin winding dry river bed. Both men seemed more relaxed now, knowing that the radar scanners could no longer pick them up. The going was slower than either would have liked, but whatever space they could put between themselves and the Research Centre was worth the effort to make the progress. "I didn't expect to be making such damned poor time," Chris complained.

"How far are we going?"

The west coast, would you believe?" Even he sounded less sure of himself.

"You do realise that they'll scan the area with everything they've got, don't you? They'll stop at nothing to get me back with what I have taken."

"That's what Marvin told me you'd say," Chris said with a laugh that carried more doubt than humour.

"The best time to travel is in daytime when there are hundreds of birds and aircraft in the sky."

Chris shook his head. "Not for us it ain't." He patted the night scope like a pet dog. "We'll get through, don't you worry."

"No, but when they realise that we are under cloud cover they can use other things to pick up our movement."

"Such as?"

"Such as spy planes."

"Bullshit!"

"No, AWACS."

"Marvin never mentioned anything about that to me. You know, I think you have what we ordinary folk call a pulled muscle, only yours is in your damned head."

Edward ignored the repartee. "The Airborne Early Warning Aircraft have powerful surveillance radar capable of scanning low flying aircraft close to the ground," he stated. "From five miles up they can achieve a three hundred and sixty degree azimuth scan by rotating the radar dome. They can detect clusters of falling leaves within a range of two hundred and thirty miles."

"Yeah but can they pick up a tiny chopper in a valley?" Chris said deliberately. These scientists sure had the gift of the gab.

"Over a shorter range they can use a pulse doppler elevation scan."

"What the hell are you talking about?" This old devil hadn't kissed the Blarney Stone, he'd been hit with it!

"A method of using the Doppler Effect in sound, you know, approaching train whistles have an increasing pitch and disappearing ones have a decreasing one. Understand?"

"Nope," Chris humoured him.

"Huh, well anyway, it's called a doppler shift, and they receive it in frequencies caused by the relative motion of the target plane and the radar rotordome. That cuts out unwanted reflections and pinpoints us or any other moving object." He tried to explain it as simply and as quickly as he could.

"You really think you're that important to them that they'd go to all that trouble?" Chris laughed at the poor demented scientist. He sure had spent enough time in the desert. The whole thing was turning him mad. "They say there's only a thin thread that stops a genius from being an idiot," Chris said unkindly. "I think the thread has snapped in your case."

"You'd better believe it."

Chris sat silently for the next five minutes. Edward had planted the seed of doubt in his mind, and as his eyes followed the beam of infra red light into the darkness, that seed began to germinate. He knew about such aircraft, they'd been used over Vietnam, but would the defection of one screwed up old scientist warrant an operation like he had mentioned? "How long before they can get one of those planes in?" he asked as casually as he could.

"All depends if they've got one handy. There's one up there somewhere. NORAD surveys all North America perpetually. There could be one anywhere between here and Alaska, possibly two, and the navy has them as well." He thought for a moment before continuing. "But they could probably bring one in from an air base quicker. I know they have them grounded at Air Force Base Tinker."

"So what're you saying?"

"What I'm saying is that they will probably fly something in either from Oklahoma, or elsewhere within another two hours. They'll scan the helicopter almost immediately at night. There won't be many idiots squirming up and down these dry valleys in a tiny chopper in pitch darkness."

"If they go to all that trouble they must want you back pretty bad."

"Just my brain. They couldn't give a shit about the rest of me."

They both laughed.

"I have my orders to get you to the coast in one piece, brain and all," Chris stated after recovering his chewing action. "What do you suggest?"

"I suggest," Edward said, scratching the back of his ear, "that you do just that. Personally I'd prefer it."

"Damn it man, I'm serious."

"So am I." They fell silent for a while and then, after considering the situation again, Edward spoke. "I suggest we stop until daylight."

"Don't like it," Chris replied. "My orders are definite."

"Okay. how about this. Drop me off and go ahead alone. You're in no danger if I'm not with you. Without me you can come and go as you please. They might stop you, but so long as your pilot's license is in good shape they'll let you go on."

"Somehow I don't see Marvin being too pleased at my turning up empty handed. I think he would rather I didn't turn up at all, and I'm damned sure I wouldn't."

"Drop me off and come back later then."

"Forget it. From now on we are Siamese twins, like it or not. I have precise instructions and I intend keeping to them."

For the next fifteen minutes neither spoke. The strain on them was telling on their reflexes. It took Chris all his time to spot the turns and the bends in the valleys as the cliffs and rocks grabbed out at them like hidden spectres. Time and again they would sweep over the brow of an escarpment and drop into what seemed yet another dark bottomless pit as the ground dipped away from them below the field of elevation of the night scope. The cloud was beginning to suck at the rotors as they climbed each steep valley floor. Then suddenly and without warning all sense of bearing was lost. The thick cloud had come from nowhere.

"Holy ssshit," Chris exclaimed, his voice building up to a crescendo. Edward felt himself tossed back against his seat as the helicopter veered upwards, twisted around and stalled. The tips of the rotors swept by a cliff face and blasted a spray of sand all around them, blacking out their visibility. They spun around and around out of control as the helicopter lost height. Chris clung onto the controls, his eyes wide with the fear of imminent death.

"Aaah, my god!" Edward shouted as he covered his face. Just when there had been a trickle of hope injected into his weakening resolve he was to meet his end, a violent end, in a plummeting helicopter. Chris put all his strength and concentration into pulling the machine to a halt. Sweat ran down his face as the helicopter fought against him, and then, suddenly, as if becalmed, it stopped spinning and hovered like a warble fly against a horse's side, facing the great jaws of rock that had been waiting to swallow it up. Chris gently spun it around a couple more times until he had orientated himself, and then he pointed the nose downwards to give himself more vertical vision.

"That does it, I'm having a rest."

"Phew, that was close!" Edward puffed as his heart rate slowed down to a hundred and twenty.

Chris didn't say a word. He landed his machine, unfastened his safety belt and stopped the engine.

Edward did the same, and followed the pilot out into the chilled air. His clothes were sticking to him with the wet perspiration of tension and shock. He shivered with the sudden coldness, took a few deep breaths, and climbed back in. Chris stayed out longer. Edward couldn't see in the darkness but he suspected that his pilot was emptying his bowels.

"What now?" Edward asked as Chris climbed in and slammed the door.

"What now? I'll tell you what now" He turned around and reached behind him. "I'm having a drink. D'ya want one?"

"Thought you'd never ask," Edward beamed as he imagined the sweet feeling of best imported Scotch whiskey burning his parched throat, as he smelt its fumes clearing his sinuses, as it washed down into his stomach and, like a hot cinder, radiated warmth through his entire body.

"Coffee?" asked Chris, handing him a Thermos flask.

"Huh, anything wet I suppose."

They sat surrounded by silence and sipped at their hot drinks and felt the anxiety and tension ebb away from their minds. Edward had forgotten how good a drop of hot liquid caffeine could be. Back at the Research centre he'd taken to having a glass of Scotch every night to anaesthetize his mind in order to let his body sleep. He'd spent weeks on planning and scheming to get his brainchild out of the heavily guarded compound. Marvin Belk had asked him for it. He'd offered him a million dollars for as many containers as he could bring with him, and he'd persuaded Edward that he could get both him and his goods out of the Research Centre safely. Edward had told him about the Airborne Early Warning Aircraft that could scan nearly a thousand square miles at a time, and he still assured him he could get him out. It worried him that Belk hadn't mentioned it to Chris. It was important. A sudden doubt emerged from the back of his mind, a doubt he had tried to suppress for so long that it hurt to refute it, but he couldn't have planned for them to be caught, surely. It had taken six long months of brief meetings behind the closed doors of a Portland brothel to co-ordinate the plan. A plan to steal what he considered was his already. He'd paid for it by being subjected to a life of a prisoner. He was determined never to live like that again. He had a brilliant brain, and because it had yearned for some exercise to stretch it he had forsaken all his other needs and ambitions. And what for? “Peanuts and bullshit," he blurted out loudly, making Chris pour the last of his coffee on his crotch and not in the cup he was aiming at.

"Jesus!" Chris yelled as he unfastened his belt and eased his trousers off his skin.

Edward was laughing. Not a chuckle, not even an ordinary laugh, but a trickle of mirth that fermented in his toes and bubbled up inside him, getting bigger and more out of control as the pressure of his insides weakened, and it finally burst out like the foam out of a champagne bottle. He was still free. Up to now he'd beaten the bastards. And he laughed with a mixture of relief and despair.

"Blasted wizened old coot!" Chris shouted at the top of his voice. "You damned stupid jackass! you...you..." He looked at the lined face of the scientist and the tears of laughter streaming down his face. Edward tried to control his mirth in the light of Chris's plight. He sniffled and looked at the pilot's face. It was an angry face, a puzzled face. A smile was escaping from the corner of its lips, and as it escaped, it flowed faster, soon filling the whole mouth with a grin, then a chuckle, and then, infected by the contagious noises from Edward, it cracked into the same raucous sound.

01.05 a.m. 1st August.

The Colonel picked up the phone and before he could speak a voice came over to him. "Hello Colonel, Air Force Base Beale here. We're sending out a SR-71. Estimated time of take off 01.40. It will be with you by 02.00. Please establish and maintain a radio link with our ground control, giving details of co-ordinates to be scanned and all known air traffic there."

"Thank you; will do." He hung up. "Right, let's get down to the radio room."

*****

The stop had done them good. They were both relaxed and more alert. Chris fired the Allison turbine and took the helicopter forward slowly, hovering only twenty or thirty feet above the ground. He took his time to search the wide valley floor for a way over the next escarpment without going into another bank of cloud. It hung over them, grey and lifeless, waiting to grab them again, but Chris was in control again. This time he wasn't travelling at ninety miles per hour up the gradual incline, he was going at a quarter of that speed. Slowly he moved into the cloud and edged over the top of the ridge, pointing the nose down to angle his vision beyond the ten degrees below horizontal that he achieved when travelling level. "That's it," he shouted as he opened the throttle. "We've got over the highest part, now we're going home."

Edward could only take Chris's word for it. He was blind in the darkness. He could only see the shadow of his hand in front of his face because of the faint glow from the cockpit dials. He had no idea where they were or where Chris was taking him. But Chris seemed confident, and, apart from the few minor insults that he'd thrown at him, he seemed to be friendly enough, and he was nothing if not determined. He sat back and tried to relax the best he could. The blackness seemed as endless as the time that dragged by, but then, suddenly and without warning, he felt the helicopter slow to a hover. Over the sound of the engines he heard Chris's voice.

"Here we are, our stop for the night," he said and landed his helicopter.

*****

"We're picking up a few charted flights, one or two that have to be checked out, but one positive signal has just disappeared," reported Ground Control. The voice on the other end of the line read out the co-ordinates for the Research Centre's helicopters to close in. The Colonel was checking the map.

"Not made such good time if that's them," he said to the wall.

*****

Chris relaxed as the silence drummed in his ears. A welcome silence while he considered his situation. What Edward had said was preying on his mind. Perhaps he was as important as he said he was. Perhaps they would pull out all the stops to find them. What a job! An ailing charter business, up to his eyes in debt because his old chopper had burned in a fire, and then this, a chance he'd had to take, an opportunity he couldn't turn away from, the one offer that he couldn't refuse, an offer to pay off all his creditors. An offer made in exchange for just one measly job, and it was a cock-up. He was sitting in the middle of nowhere with a cracked scientist, being pursued by the whole formidable U.S. Air Force. He'd faced danger before many times in Vietnam, but the odds had been on his side then. He sighed, a long frustrated sigh.

Edward leaned back and rested his eyes after the strain of looking into a black chasm. His body was steaming with perspiration. The lines on his face channeled the sweat to his neck like tributaries to the confluence of an estuary. "Why have we stopped now?" he asked. "If they're going to spot us they'll have already done so by now."

"Just following orders Eddy old boy, just working as planned."

"I still think we'd be better keeping going now," Edward complained as he wiped his neck with his handkerchief. Chris switched on the cockpit light and went into the rear compartment.

"Since we're stopped, you don't mind if I have a bit of shut-eye, do you?" Edward asked him.

"Not in the least," Chris replied and threw him a blanket.

"Just thought I'd make sure," Edward asked sarcastically. He realised that his pilot could have kept going. He wondered if it was the near fatal accident that had made him stop, or if there was a plan. It didn't seem to fit. They would have been better stopping before there was any chance of being spotted. But, whichever way he looked at it, they'd come close to death once. Now there seemed little point in making sure of it.

It was peaceful, and they soon lapsed into sleep. Chris had made himself a passable bed with blankets on the floor, while Edward wrapped his blanket around himself and leaned his head against the cockpit window. It was cold but they were both too tired to notice the gradual decline in the temperature until Edward began to stir. At first he heard nothing. His nervous energy had been spent, his adrenalin burned up. His sleep was as deep as any he'd sunk into for months and that was without the help of his usual dram. It wasn't a noise, so much as a vibration against his temple. He felt stiff and cold as he lifted his head and shook himself awake. Chris was snoring in the back, each breath regular, deep and vibrating against his throat. He smiled and relaxed, but as he leaned his head back against the glass, his eyes became alert. He could feel the sound from outside, feel the vibration of it, a droning sound, not unlike that made by a helicopter. "Bloody shit!" he shouted and jumped forward to reach for the light switch. His seat belt brought him to an abrupt halt. "Damn it all!" he gesticulated as he struggled with the release button.

"What's the matter?" asked Chris, jumping up and hitting his head on the roof.

"They've found us!" Edward's belt let go of him and he threw himself on the switch. The blackness that ensued seemed to bring its own chill to their bodies.

"What'yer talking about?" Chris complained after standing motionless and holding his breath for an eternal half minute.

"Can't you hear them? They're here?"

"Ah ah ah," Chris laughed. "Godammit, you're even dreaming about them now."

"Quiet!" Edward's tone was emphatic.

Chris held his breath again. He couldn't hear anything. "Nope, you're definitely going over the edge. That tiny thread of sanity has finally snapped."

"Listen will you, you loaf head. There's a chopper out there. I heard it." He opened the door and shivered as the still chilled air drifted over his already hypotherming body. He pulled the blanket close around his shoulders and stepped out into the blackness. The cloud had closed in on them deadening all sound as well as the light of the moon. But it was there, as sure as the moon was up above the cloud, it was there, only very faint, but there all the same, a beating of the air which had caused gentle shock waves to vibrate against the glass of the cockpit; a beating, that had brought him out of his deep sleep. It was there and getting louder.

"Jesus Christ, you're right!" Chris shouted as he peered out of the cockpit.

Edward dived back inside and sat in his seat. "They must have scanned us. There's no way they could have found us otherwise," he stated despondently. "Come on man, get going!" he shouted at Chris.

"It's no use running, they have at least five to our one, and each one can out run us."

"Then what?"

"Wait," Chris ordered. "They haven't found us yet. What time is it?"

Edward put on the cockpit light. "Three fifty."

"Then they must have picked up our movement over an hour and a half ago when we parked this thing. That means they have some co-ordinates but can't spot us. They'll be flying high hoping to flush us from under the low cloud. They haven't got us yet," Chris shouted as he looked out through his night scope. "I'll see them before they see me, and then they won't see me for dust."

"No!" Edward shouted and grabbed his arm desperately. "They are armed. Lets get out of here now man."

"I'm not moving until I have to, and then they'll have to catch me first," Chris replied pulling his arm free, and placing the radio headphones around his neck.

Edward lunged at Chris, placing himself between him the control panel. "Now you're going to listen you flea bitten no good pilot," he shouted.

Chris, with the effort that a bull uses to swish off a pestering fly, pulled him to the floor and pinned him down against the control panel with his forearm. "They've been searching for more than three hours, possibly three and a half," he shouted angrily. "They'll be reaching the stage where they have to return to base for re-fuelling soon, or they'll not make it back. If they can't find us they might all go home and wait for daylight."

"And what if they don't?"

"Well we can hope they at least take it in shifts. That way there might only be one to avoid at a time."

Edward sat for a moment with the palm of his hand on the crown of his head. He took a deep breath and expelled the air from his lungs. "You could out-maneuver one or perhaps two, given an even chance."

"You what! There is no even chance. Never was. They've each got sixteen air to air missiles. I've always considered myself a good pilot, but not that damned good!"

Edward groaned as the panel began to dig into his back. He realised he was panicking and Chris was talking sense. "Oh, you're right of course," he conceded. "The longer you wait the less chance they have of keeping their numbers together. Who knows, they might think they're chasing a shadow and all go home."

"That's what we're all hoping for you crackpot."

"Sorry," Edward said meekly. "I'm not using my head."

"You don't have to tell me that."

"I'm shit scared, don't you understand?" Edward protested.

"So am I, Eddy old pal, so am I." He gave his passenger a casual grin. "Get off my godammed foot will you." He released his arm from Edward's throat and got out his packet of chewing gum.

"We're staying put then?" Edward asked as he took a peace offering.

“I'll give you plenty of notice when I decide to make a run for it," Chris said, prodding his chest with his finger.

"Promise?"

"Jesus! Okay." He turned off the light and Edward got up and fumbled his way back to his seat. "We'll freeze to death before we're spotted, perhaps," Edward said as he tried to hold his moral up and his jaw closed. It still rattled with the shivers that were shaking his body, half shivers of cold, half shivers of fear.

"Here, grab these blankets," said Chris as he reached back and tossed them to the poor old scientist. "When we have to fly it might help if you can move your limbs." He placed the headphones over his ears and tuned in the radio.

Time seemed not to pass, their bodies metamorphosed like a living sperm cell in a deep freeze. Each time Edward asked the time, and each time Chris flicked on the light, hardly a few minutes had passed them by. Gradually the sound of helicopters faded into the distance and eventually died out altogether. There was a faint hint of daylight lessening the blackness in the distance. The low cloud cover seemed to lift like a Persian flying carpet and hover high on the distant rocky tree painted peaks. And with the daylight came a flowing warmth that made Edward slip without a struggle into a deathlike sleep.

6.00 am 1st August.

The road blocks were already up when James Dawlish and Andy Turner reached the Oregon State boundary nearly six hours later. They'd made good time with a well planned detour, but as they neared the state boundary they overtook a Toyota pick-up and then kept a few hundred yards in front of it.

A large truck came on behind from nowhere. Captain Brian Hollins, a soldier armed with a sub machinegun held up his hand for them to stop at the road barrier. Six other soldiers stood with firearm at the ready in case they should try to drive straight through without stopping. James wound down his window as the soldier bowed his head to see inside. Without saying a word, he looked at James and Andy closely, and then straightened up to look at the photograph in his hand. Neither man resembled Edward Taylor in the least way. James was broad shouldered, with short jet black hair and dark bottomless eyes. Andy, slightly less well built, in complete contrast, was almost an albino blond, except for his pale blue eyes.

"Business good is it?" Captain Hollins asked James.

"Not a dying trade," he replied with a rueful smile.

The soldier's face remained glum. "What's in the coffin?" he demanded.

"How many guesses do you want?" asked James.

The soldier half smiled. "Then you won't mind if we take a look, will you?"

"Please yourself," said Andy. "Are you going to open it or shall we."

"Just you," Captain Hollins instructed him. "The driver stays here." He waved one of the privates over and nodded towards James. He stood with his Colt XM sub-machinegun pointing at the car door, while the captain went around the back. Andy took the keys from James, got out, and unlocked the back door of the hearse.

"Won't take long," Andy said as he unfastened the first two butterfly nuts. Then he climbed in along side the coffin and unfastened the other four. "It's a transport coffin," he explained. "Makes it easy to reopen when we get the body where we want it."

"Stand out," the soldier instructed."

Andy stepped out and stood to one side as the captain eased opened the coffin lid. As the light broke into the dark interior, the captain dropped the lid, and stood back. "Godammit!" he swore as a stomach-wrenching smell hit him in the face. For a moment he fought hard to control the involuntary spasms of his stomach as it heaved. "Lift that fucking lid back," he shouted at Andy.

Andy did as he was told, and lifted the lid up while the captain, now holding a handkerchief to his face, glanced at the face of a corpse. Peering through the shroud, the face of the dead man was worse than he'd expected. The gaping mouth with a trickle of stale fluid emanating from the corner of the lips, the dark sunken eye sockets, the leathery-looking skin with grey whiskers beginning to grow again, and a face that didn't look at peace even in death, was worse than he could have possibly imagined on a battlefield, and that was somewhere he had never been. He motioned for Andy to seal the lid and went to the front of the car where he could breathe. "Do they always smell as bad as that?" he asked James.

"Not if we can get them embalmed quick enough," he replied. "The trouble is, this guy had been dead for four days before anyone found him. Heart attack in his chair. Well in this sort of heat it doesn't take long..."

"I get the picture," Hollins interrupted. "Where are you taking him?"

"Portland. His daughter wants him buried back home where he should have been in the first place, instead of living in a shack out in the middle of nowhere.

"He probably enjoyed it," the captain argued.

Andy locked the back door and got back in the passenger seat.

"Okay." said Captain Hollins. "You can go." He waved them through as the barrier was lifted. He waved the Toyota forward and signaled for it to pull up. The truck pulled up close behind. They couldn't be as bad as a hearse to search.

The two undertakers didn't look back as they drove away.

6.30 a.m. 1st August.

"We've located his vehicle. No sign of him anywhere. His car was driven into a dilapidated old gas station approximately a hundred miles due west of the base, and left there. No sign of Taylor, the missing goods, or how he got away from here. We can only presume there was a car or a helicopter waiting for him," Arnold Hickman, a military policeman advised Colonel Felspars over the radio. He took off his helmet and padded his forehead with a non service issue red and yellow polka-dot bandanna. The desert air was already reaching for higher temperatures.

"What about the tail?"

"Nowhere, no signal, no men, no car, nothing."

"An air search has already been launched and road blocks have been put up. That's all we can do," came back the reply. "A chopper will be with you in forty minutes. I'll be in it to take control of the search. Over and out." Hickman replaced the radio receiver in his Jeep and loosened his collar. This was going to be a bastard of a hot day, a real tester.

*****

"Besides what's missing from the Research Centre, Taylor is missing and so are the two men detailed to follow him," Colonel Felspars explained over the telephone to the United States Security officials in Washington D.C.

"So it's definitely missing?" came back a reply.

"Checked and double checked. No doubt about it."

"Was the SR-71 any use?"

"Thought we had him cold. Picked up a chopper in the mountains and followed it. It stopped a couple of times, but when we finally caught up with it, it turned out to be a commercial crop sprayer. Travelling home by all accounts. We're still holding him for questioning; though I have a feeling we're wasting our time. He seems to have a reason for all his movements."

"Even at night?"

"That's what the F.B.I. has said. I haven't questioned him myself."

"What are the chances of finding Taylor with what is missing?"

Felspars hesitated. "By the looks of it, it was organised and carefully planned. Taylor went to a great deal of trouble to short circuit our checking procedures. Somehow he altered his magnetic pass and our data files. I can only presume that whoever it was that helped Taylor will have been just as well prepared and will already have it stored away somewhere. Taylor might be dead now for all we know. He will have outlived his usefulness."

"Not necessarily. He has a great deal to offer to a foreign power. Much more than he took in his Jeep. What he has in his head is worth millions."

"What are you suggesting?"

"I'm making the point that he's got to be stored away himself until he can be smuggled out of the country. Have you any idea where he might want to go before he leaves?"

"Only his Mother's in Medford," Colonel Felspars suggested. "Unless," he said and then paused. "Unless he goes looking for a woman."

"What woman?"

"Any woman," Felspars said firmly. "Whenever he went on leave he spent most of it in a brothel."

"Not much to go on," said the man in Washington. "I'll get the F.B.I. onto it straight away. It's a long shot, but until you have anything better it'll have to do."

"Good,"

"Let me know when you find those other two men."

"Will do." Felspars hung up. He had a gut feeling about the two men that were detailed to follow Edward. He had a feeling he was going to come up empty handed on all counts today.

*****

Well, shall we give it a try?" Chris asked. "I've got a time table to keep to you know." He was sitting in his seat with the headphones on his knee.

Edward looked around him. The helicopter was under a canopy of enormous sequoia. The cockpit faced out towards the mountain peaks that he had just been able to make out in the grey light of dawn. What time is it?" he asked.

"Nearly mid-day."

"Have you been asleep as well?"

Chris gave out a chuckle. "Not until I knew for sure that they'd gone. I listened in on the conversation. Seems like they had a wild goose chase."

"How do you mean?"

"They went after the wrong chopper, that's what I mean. Might as well get going then," he yawned. "They're either gone home or waiting for us." He fired the engine, put on his headphones and tuned his radio in again. "If they do spot us now they'll challenge us first," he said. "That's one chance we never got in 'Nam."

"Are you sure?"

"Hell yeah. They'll have a hell of a lot of dead choppers by the end of the day if they don't." He let the turbines warm up well and then let the warm air blast into the cockpit. It was a warm welcome blast. Too much would possibly make them sleepy, but for a while anyway, it revived them and made them more alert.

*****

James Dawlish reversed the hearse into the back entrance of the building. It was a large monolithic structure standing in its own ground. To the front, with the smell of freshly cut grass lay a large velvet lawn, and a sign announcing it to be Poulson's Funeral Parlour. Andy Turner closed the back gate and joined his partner. He unlocked the back door of the vehicle, opened it, and together they slid the coffin out onto a nearby trolley. Coffins were easier to move that way without a small army of men. They wheeled it into the building with little endeavour. Once inside, they both assiduously attended to the unscrewing of the six brass butterfly nuts that clamped the lid to the container.

"Right," said Andy as he released the last one. Taking one end each, they lifted the lid clear and placed it to one side, being careful not to mark it. Coffins could be used many times by undertakers, sold to the bereaved and salvaged behind the curtain that led to the furnaces of the crematorium. The bodies were removed and the coffins recycled to be sold again. A common practice, and seldom queried by mourners. It had become a practice to handle them diligently. Neither man took the least bit of notice of the smell of the decomposing corpse. The white shroud had covered all but the face. Beneath it were just the head and shoulders of an old tramp. He'd been the unfortunate one to wander past the railway siding on the day that the two undertakers needed a body of an old man. He had worked well for them. His last job. "Can you help me," James had said quietly to him from the window of a rented van.

"If I can," the tramp had replied. He could and he did. His remains were placed in the bottom of a plain coffin with the parts that had been left behind. The lid was sealed. There would be no problem getting rid of that. It was their trade after all.

They turned to the more important matter. Three metal containers were lifted out of the foot of the coffin and placed into a crate marked 'Crankshafts'. The lid of the crate was nailed down firmly and the coffin was tidied away for the next time. The contents of the crate had one last journey to make before being delivered to the shipper. Tests had to be done to make sure it was what it was supposed to be. That was a job for the experts.

CHAPTER 2.

2nd August 1984.

New York was having its usual skin-baking summer. Not that anyone seemed to have the time to doff their clothes and fry their flesh in The Big Apple. The incessant throb of activity pulsed along the streets and avenues like arteries, supplying the vital energy to keep alive the never sleeping, never slowing city. The streets and buildings were thronged with people, some visiting tourists, but most going about their daily business. Daniel Carlisle was a man on business. He was a successful shipping agent and for dealing with everyday import or export business he had plush offices in his warehouse complex in Lower Manhattan, only a stone's throw from The World Trade Centre. But today was going to be different. Today his business was of a more delicate nature, and he'd made a point of meeting his potential business associate on neutral ground and well out in the open. As the Yellow Cab drove him to the rendezvous, the sun mirrored on the steel shafts and glass faces of the multitude of skyscrapers, creating the image of being on a planet with a hundred suns. But Daniel's thoughts were more terrestrial. It was an occasion not so different to many that had occurred in the past, but none were ever the same; it was dangerous, and he had to be prepared for any eventuality. There was to be a meeting and a discussion on his ability to carry out a contract for importing or exporting certain sensitive goods. Sensitive because of embargo, or sensitive because of secrecy. Whichever, he knew he could succeed where many others would fail. His contacts were world wide, most of which he had built up and come to know a long time in the past. He paid off the cab, took a cheroot from his shirt pocket, lit it and began to walk. A jazz band was playing somewhere in the distance and the air was filled with chatter of walkers and the laughter of a group of young girls playing basket-ball.

Everywhere there were people, nowhere private, yet it was ideal for a clandestine meeting.

Up ahead, towards the boating lake, and standing beneath the sprawling branches of an ancient beech tree, he spotted his quarry. He knew Pyotre Vlatsov from old and trusted him as much as a parachute with no canopy. If he ever needed support in a tight corner he knew Vlatsov would let him drop rather than risk any possibility of being caught up in the strings of an unsavoury deal. This was to be such a deal. Vlatsov never hired him to ship anything that was not either barred from export or illegal in some respect. Daniel didn't mind what it was or where it had to be shipped, he could move it. The only thing he would not move was drugs. He'd once been caught up in that unsavoury business and he didn't like it or the people in it. He'd not intended to do anything illegal at the time, but he put his first foot on the ladder of business enterprise by smuggling heroin. It happened literally by accident.

Daniel was born in the East End of London in 1945. At the end of 1969, after having left the British Army and having travelled over much of the world, he was involved in a car accident. The car belonged to his friend Pierre Beaumont, a Frenchman he met during his travels through Europe, and together they were working and dealing to make enough money to carry on travelling. It was during a trip to Turkey that the accident occurred, a near fatal trip for his friend Pierre, but luckily, Daniel escaped with only a mild concussion and a broken arm. The car, though badly damaged was not a total wreck, and was awaiting the time when the two men could raise enough money to have it shipped back to France in order that the insurance company could initiate repairs. It was then that Daniel met Hassan Abdullah in Istanbul. As if by magic he appeared at the seedy garage where the damaged car was being stored. He agreed to ship the Renault, and because they were flat broke, he even paid Daniel's and Pierre's fare back to France. Neither Daniel nor Pierre were inclined to reject the offer.

Pierre was still in hospital in Istanbul when Daniel went to the wharf in Marseilles to meet the ship that carried their car. Not surprisingly, when it arrived at the French port on *La Belle St. Marie*, Abdullah was also there waiting for it. He turned to see who was approaching, and when he saw it was Daniel, he threw him a grin, a broad beam that showed all the gaps between his large white teeth as they sparkled against the dark tanned face and mop of black hair. "Hello," he said. "It won't be long now before you get your car back."

Daniel had had plenty of time to consider the arrangements. He knew there must be some condition, but was willing to do what he could to repay Hassan. "So what's the catch? What do you want in return?" he asked bluntly.

"There is no catch. I paid for you to get back to France. I shipped the car, and as soon as the car is unloaded off the ship and cleared by customs, I will take what is mine and go."

"What are you talking about?"

"You'll see," the Turk assured him and turned his dark brown eyes away to watch the unloading of the ship. Daniel did the same. The car came off the ship on a yellow low loader behind an ancient Series One Landrover. It was a good hour and a half more before it came into sight through the customs barrier. Hassan Abdullah stood and waited patiently until the vehicle had drawn past. Then, "Come," he shouted and jumped into an old blue Mini. The passenger door swung open for Daniel to get in as Hassan gunned the engine, and he sped off in the same direction as the Landrover before Daniel had pulled in his legs. When he looked up, the Landrover was nowhere to be seen. But Hassan knew exactly where he was going, and after several minutes' driving, he swung the car into a small asbestos clad warehouse, parked the Mini facing the doors, and then, taking Daniel by the arm, ushered him into a small workshop in the furthest corner of the building.

The driver and the Landrover had disappeared leaving the Renault behind. After making sure nobody was approaching, Hassan began stripping out the car's seats. Casually, he explained what he'd been doing and how it wasn't by chance that he happened to turn up at the garage in Istanbul. The car seats had been stuffed full of heroin. It was a regular method of bypassing the customs officers. They rarely checked wrecked cars for contraband. He paid Daniel 4,000 francs to give to Pierre for the car; twice what it had been worth before the crash, and told him he should replace the seats before his friend put in the claim to the insurance company. "You can pick up the car any time you like," he said and left with Daniel close on his heels.

Hassan Abdullah excited him. He wanted to know more about the smuggling business. In 1970, lured by the prospect of earning easy money, Daniel got involved with the smuggling fraternity. The Anatolian provinces of Turkey was where he began. The Anatolians used all of the poppy except the gum, which they sold either to the Turkish government or to smugglers. Hassan Abdullah, whose family had been growing poppies for a thousand years, was one of the smugglers, and he had a factory in Istanbul that rendered down opium gum to heroin by a simple chemical process which reduced it to a tenth of its original weight. Daniel was paid to drive a TIR truck; that is a Transports Internationaux Routiers, sealed by heavily bribed customs officials in the country of origin. They were never opened at the borders and he shipped the contraband to Marseilles where the overworked customs men hardly ever came upon the real big caches. It wasn't long, only a matter of months, before he got to know the Bulgarian government officials who were all in on the smuggling game. They had their own import and export agency.

Eventually, however, Daniel realised just how much he disliked being connected with the smuggling of hard drugs. Even worse, he began to realise that hard drugs provided much of the income of the mafia. Ever since he was a boy he'd sworn never to be involved with the kind of people who had been responsible for the death of his father. Suddenly, and without giving the Turk any reason, he declined to be involved with drug smuggling any more. He'd had enough. He'd earned enough money to move on.

Two years later, he set up his own small import and export business. But his dislike of the mafia cost him dearly.

He had dealt with Pyotre Vlatsov several times since then. He didn't like the Bulgarian but he always paid exceptionally well and gave Daniel a free hand to manage contracts as he liked. Pyotre knew never to ask for Daniel's services if he required drugs moving. But he had enough contacts in the mafia for that. The New York Godfathers were regular customers of Pyotre and dealt with him regularly. Daniel had a deep seated hatred of gangsters and protection racketeers who used violence and intimidation to establish themselves in the position of respectable business people, when in fact they were just out and out thugs and murderers. It wasn't without a struggle that he'd avoided being taken over by the New York Families but rather than pay protection money, he paid twice as much on installing and manning a security company within his own freight company. By smuggling what he called 'legitimate contraband' he financed that security. Without the use of violence or intimidation, Daniel would put a price on shipping anything from microfilm to munitions, anywhere in the world. If the port of collection or the destiny of the goods was not on regular shipping route, Daniel would arrange for charters. His philosophy was quite clean cut. Security should start at source. If a product was top secret then it should be guarded where it was made, not panicked over when it had leaked out. Everybody was playing the same game. It was a game that every government participated in. Agents would acquire a new piece of equipment, stick it in a diplomatic bag or crate, and without any risk of being caught, stopped or punished, they would pass it over the borders to their own scientists to copy. The Russians with their G.R.U. agents never missed a trade fair or exhibition where new devices were on sale to anybody with a legitimate business use for it at that side of the Iron Curtain. There, they would pay substantial sums to dealers for just one of a particular device, giving him five or six times its resale value, and as much again for the detailed plans and specifications. It was the same game that Daniel played, only he didn't have a diplomat's immunity, and he worked for companies or individuals more often than governments. He had to use his skill to ship contraband. Where a diplomat had nothing to lose, he had.

The stakes were much higher and so were his charges. If arms were manufactured for export to other countries, then he could get them to a country that was under an embargo. There were companies all over the free world that made gigantic profits from manufacturing arms and ammunition, chemicals and drugs. All had industrial spies, and all had stolen secrets from somebody else at sometime in their past. What he did was help distribute the commodities more evenly either way. He had taken microchips every which way from companies in Japan to Britain, from the United States to Romania, even from Britain to the U.S.

The part that he enjoyed most was knowing that most of the companies that had used his services at one time or another, were competitors and most thought he worked just for them. Apart from Pyotre that is. But then he knew Vlatsov always had more than just profit in mind when he shipped something. Pyotre Vlatsov was a political animal.

As Daniel approached, Pyotre threw him a casual glance and carried on chatting to the man by his side. Both wore white short sleeved shirts and light cotton trousers and looked as if they'd been to the same outfitters. 'No imagination,' Daniel thought as he saw them wearing the same shade of stockings in the same make of sandals. They could have been twins, only that Pyotre, at fifty five, and with a pot belly, was five feet four inches tall, with dark hair and a lined face worthy of a North Sea fisherman, and his bodyguard, at thirty seven, was a foot taller, had receding golden hair, and had a body that was honed to the fine edge of fitness that was dreamed of but never expected to be reached by the most dedicated athlete. Daniel kept his face straight. No one held out a hand to shake. He just fell in beside them as they moved away.

In Central Park they could talk freely. Although he never managed to find any, Daniel was always afraid that the F.B.I. had listening devices in his car and in his warehouse. Pyotre too regarded closed spaces as being extremely dangerous, and even now, out in the open and for anyone to see, he had his bodyguard frisk Daniel to make sure he had no recording or transmitting equipment strapped to his body. The action got a couple of odd looks, and a young boy went past muttering 'Pigs!,' but apart from that, nobody seemed to take the slightest notice.

"We cannot be too careful these days," Pyotre said to Daniel with a broad half apologetic grin."

"Whoever it is you're afraid of, they haven't asked me to work for them yet," smiled Daniel knowing full well that Pyotre didn't believe a word. "Though who knows, if the price is right..." He lifted his arms and shrugged his shoulders in a gesture of willingness to deal with anybody.

"You are a true mercenary, Mr. Carlisle," Pyotre stated bluntly. "I too will deal with anybody. Necessity transcends ideology, but I don't work purely for financial gain. You would sell your best friend down the river if the price was right."

“Perhaps I'll have to one day," laughed Daniel. He knew that Pyotre would do exactly that for political motives. "Things are getting a bit tight around here."

"We'll we see if we can't help your cash flow then." Pyotre stopped walking. The crowd was thinning slightly. Two men and a woman jogged past and stopped just ahead of them. The Bulgarian waited till they had set off again and were well clear before he began to talk again. He took a hold of Daniel's arm and lightly turned him around to face him. "First of all I will ask you if you can do the job, then I will tell you how much I am prepared to pay."

"I can do the job," Daniel said confidently. "You just tell me what the job is and *I'll* tell you how much you are prepared to pay," he added with a smile. It was a familiar ritual.

Pyotre knew he wasn't joking. On the other hand he knew Daniel Carlisle very well from past deals, and was confident that if anybody could do the job, he could. He had never failed him yet. "It is an importing job," he stated.

"Into the States?" Daniel said with a look of surprise.

"From the United States," Pyotre corrected, "to,..." He paused. "To India."

"India! What the hell are you up to in that hot stuffy place?" asked Daniel.

Pyotre ignored the question, and went on as if Daniel had not spoken. "We want a packing case delivered to New Delhi. You will state when you will arrive with it, and I will arrange for you to deliver the shipment to the recipient."

"And where is the shipment now, how big is it, and who is going to deliver it to me?"

"All questions that will be answered in due course," replied the Bulgarian. "However, the main question to be sorted out is your price."

"Can't say unless you tell me how big, and where from. It depends if I have to get it out of Fort Knox."

The Bulgarian scowled, not at Daniel, but at the floor. "It will be less than two hundred kilos. Just precisely how heavy, I cannot say," he said to his foot. "As far as place is concerned, it will be delivered to you anywhere you wish in the United States."

"And how long do I have from collecting it to deliver it?"

Vlatsov studied for a moment. "Not more than three weeks," he said as if he was still thinking about the question. "Yes, three weeks maximum," he concluded after a pause.

"I see," said Daniel. "You want it out fairly quickly then." He took his turn to study for a moment. "Well, I would have to have transport arranged for it as soon as it is delivered to me. That means being on standby unless you can say exactly when it will be ready. Not a lot of time to play with if I only have three weeks. It'll take nearly that long to ship it." He stared hard at the

Bulgarian. “Is it capable of being flown in a non-pressurized cargo hold?"

"I will find out and let you know about that."

"I presume it wouldn't be wise to x-ray the crate."

"I doubt whether x-rays would affect it, but we wouldn't want to take the chance of someone discovering what it is from one, would we?"

"Quite," Daniel conceded. "Haven't you any idea when it will be ready?" he asked once again.

"I don't know that yet. A week or so, perhaps less. I cannot be sure until we are certain we have acquired and tested it."

"I see," said Daniel. "That leads me to think it will be stolen, and you want it out of the country as soon as it falls into your hands."

"I am not prepared to go into any further detail, except to say that the container will be sealed, and it will remain so for the entirety of its journey."

"One million," said Daniel, outright.

"Dollars?"

"Pounds sterling. Convert it to Swiss francs and then put it in my usual account."

"Half will be paid immediately, the other half on completion of the contract," the Bulgarian said without a flicker of surprise on his face.

"Sorry Pyotre old boy; all up front this time. You've dealt with me long enough to know I'll come through on the deal."

"And you know us well enough to know that we always pay you what we owe," retorted Pyotre.

"Well this time I'm changing the rules. The job will be done...” I have a feeling I may have to watch my back with this one, he restrained himself from saying, and wondered why he had even thought it. He regained the track of his conversation. "I'll have to plan everything and hold it open until you say go. Could be pretty expensive that, especially as I may have to use one of my own boats."

Pyotre turned and walked on along the side of the Lake. Daniel walked beside him. A glance behind assured him he was still being closely dogged by the Bulgarian's watchdog. "Very well," Pyotre said finally. "It will be in your account by tomorrow morning."

7.00 a.m. 3rd August.

At his apartment on Fifty First Street, Daniel read the headlines in the New York Times. *"Search for missing research scientist," was the leader. He read on. "In response to increasing speculation about road blocks and car searches by the military in the states of Nevada and Oregon, the U.S. Assistant Secretary of Defense has made a statement that his department is concerned for the safety, of research scientist Edward Taylor, who failed to arrive at his mother's home in Medford yesterday. He was on leave for two days from the Scientific Weapons Research Center in Utah. A state-wide search is being made because it is feared that he may have been kidnapped. The Secretary of Defense also told reporters that they fear he has been kidnapped by mistake since Taylor was only involved in minor research at the centre. On being asked if a ransom note had been received, the Secretary refused to comment."*

"Huh," remarked Daniel. "Big fuss over a minor employee. Shouldn't even have made it onto the missing person's list yet, let alone the desk of the Secretary of State for Defense!" He finished his breakfast, went into the library and took down an atlas. "Right," he muttered to himself, "This is it or I'm the Czar of Russia." He picked up the telephone and dialed a number.

"Hello Andre, Daniel Carlisle here. Can you have your hold ready for my freight? I think it is on its way."

Daniel arrived early and spent an irritable morning at the warehouse, chewing his way through half a dozen unlit Havana cigars that had been lying about on his desk. The secretary in his office had strict instructions to make sure he was paged if there were any phone calls for him. By noon he'd had enough. There had been plenty of phone calls but none about his consignment from the East Coast. Routine business was boring to him and it was well managed by his staff. He had delegated his work so often to reliable employees that he no longer felt to be an integral part of the multi million dollar freight shipping business. The real excitement still came from dealing in contraband, as it had done in the first years of his journey up the ladder of free enterprise. He sent a Telex to his ship the *Silver Ambassador*, which was due to dock in Rio de Janeiro, and then prepared to leave.

"Transfer any calls for me to Malterswood," he instructed on his way out. "I'll be there for the next couple of days."

2.00 p.m. 3rd August.

The Spitfire closed in on a white painted concrete landing pad in the middle of an expanse of lush green lawns surrounded by yuccas and palms. Edward could see the water sprinklers distributing the life's blood to the sun-drenched landscape, a picture of pathways and lawns amidst acres of flowering hibiscus and bougainvillea, scented jasmine and the gardenias. It looked cool and refreshing like anyone would imagine paradise to be. As the wind off the rotors rebounded from the concrete pad, the breeze carried the scented air in through the open cockpit window, and over the acrid smell of stale sweat-soaked clothes it smelt like paradise.

Chris Metcalf settled his machine down expertly and Edward unfastened his seat belt and swung the door open. His face held a two-day grey stubble that aged him even more as it accentuated the deep lines in his face, yet for the first time in years he felt younger. The air was fresh and cool coming in from the distant bay, in contrast to the stifling hot dry air from the arid desert that had been his home for too long. He felt free. He felt like bursting out into uncontrollable laughter as he stepped to the ground, but he regulated his emotion to a broad grin that split his face from ear to ear, revealing a remarkably well kept jaw full of teeth. He ducked his head automatically as the rotors swished overhead; a strange reflex that many passengers of helicopters have, despite the fact that the rotors had a nine foot ground clearance at the tips. His dusty sweat stained cotton suit flapped wildly against his body bringing back a little of the circulation to his tired limbs. It felt good.

"Welcome to my private retreat," said Marvin Belk as he shook hands with Edward. Marvin had silver grey hair that surrounded a bald patch on the crown of his head, making him look almost holy. His six foot trim figure and bronze sun tan helped him deny the sixty-one years he had been on earth. He wore light shorts and a short sleeved rainbow coloured shirt. He gave a wave of acknowledgement to Chris who grinned, waved back and then took off again. Edward watched him disappear over the tops of the trees and wondered what his next job would be. “Do you like it?" Marvin asked as he pointed behind him to his sprawling multi split level villa set into the hillside.

Edward gazed around in wonder. "Can't believe it," he gasped, as he looked towards the mountains and then back across San Francisco Bay. The clear cloudless sky reflected in the warm sea. Only the distant silver breakers broke the golden line of the beach from the infinite expanse of water. "I never thought I would even see the light of day again once I loaded that cargo into my Jeep. If they'd caught me red handed they'd have locked me away forever, or worse. I never thought it was possible." He shook his head.

Marvin chuckled. "I think you must have had some faith in me or you wouldn't have gone along with it."

"Well, once you'd persuaded me how easy it would be then I began to doubt myself and my own ability to do it. I'm not a devious man by nature, and I'm certainly not used to nerve shattering excitement."

"Nothing devious about it," Marvin said, patting him on the back and walking up the steps towards the villa. Edward fell in by his side. "It was pure logic. Not unlike your own really. I have an analytical mind like yours, only we put them to different uses. As with any problem, it is entirely a matter of applying the known data to the hypothesis to come up with an acceptable answer."

"Wouldn't do for us all to be working on the same problem then," laughed Edward. "There'd be so many different answers nobody would know which one was right!"

Marvin laughed. "It pays to specialise in your chosen field. It's made you a rich man."

"And you by the looks of it." He strolled up the steps to the villa, and then turned to face his host. "I still feel as if I'm going to wake up and find myself back in those cold mountains. I really did think they'd track us down. They got so close, so damned close, but they missed us."

"Don't worry, it's no dream. This is real." He pointed around at his home. "It all went according to plan Edward, every eventuality was planned for," replied Marvin proudly. "Remember, you gave me all the information I needed to arrange for decoys."

"And those men, they looked like real undertakers you know," Edward praised.

"They were," answered Marvin. "Undertakers are a very useful commodity in our business. I have contacts with a Sicilian who owns, among other businesses, a funeral parlour. He finds it invaluable for getting rid of bodies! I've heard of him putting as many as three bodies in one coffin," he laughed. Edward stood with his mouth open. "Once they're cremated who's any the wiser?" He laughed again, only louder. "That's what happened to Orgreave and Barking," he stated in a matter of fact tone.

"Who?" Edward had never heard of them.

"The men in the tail car, your chaperons," Marvin said, waving his hands indifferently. Death was an everyday commodity to him. He dealt with it every living day in one form or another, either by direct order of execution, or indirectly as a consequence of the application of his plans.

Edward gave a shiver. "I hope you realise I'm still worth keeping alive," he said bluntly. After all, he'd delivered the goods. He felt a slight tremor in his right leg.

"The secret data you have in your head is worth yet another fortune to a friend of mine," Marvin chuckled as he approached a large paneled door at the centre of a flagstone verandah. He put his hand on Edward's shoulder reassuringly and led him inside. "After all, if we were going to bump you off, there would have been no reason to go to the trouble of bringing you here, would there?" He didn't wait for an answer. "Your money is already in the account we have set up for you. You'll be able to live like a king when you are through with this game," he said, closing the door behind him. "But in the meantime, you have to lie low for a month or two."

"Here?"

"Why not? Ample room for you to disappear for days if you want to without bumping into anybody," he said slapping him on the back.

"Oh," Edward said with a tone of disappointment. He laughed nervously and his leg still trembled. He was still a prisoner of his own making, richer now, but captive all the same. It looked as lonely a place as the one he'd just left, and his host was even more fearsome.

"First of all we have to let you get cleaned up," Marvin said. "Then we'll eat."

"Wouldn't mind a drink of fresh cold water first," Edward replied. He'd had two days of being flown from one place to another without the faintest idea where he was or where the pilot was taking him. "Just orders," Chris had said and left it at that. A few hours here, a few hours flying, and then a few more hours baking or freezing in the helicopter somewhere else. He hadn't been allowed to go into villages or towns, being restricted to the immediate vicinity of the Spitfire, and that was parked well away from any place that might tempt Edward away. There had been scanty dried up sandwiches to eat, cockpit-warm water after the flasks of coffee had gone cold, nowhere to bathe and not much comfort for sleeping.

"Sure," Marvin grinned. "Forgive me. I wasn't thinking." He went to a small table grasped a portable telephone, and stabbed a number. "Janine, bring us in a couple of iced lemonades will you." He saw by Edward's face that he would be well pleased with that. He was smiling. The thought of lemonade was making the saliva glands under his tongue squirt uncontrollably. And there was more, there was somebody else in this vast place. It had seemed so empty with the two of them standing next to the heli-pad, surrounded by the sprawling villa and its lush green envelope. "Have a seat," Marvin waved in the direction of a long mahogany table and matching spade-backed chairs.

Edward did as he was bid. It gave him chance to see the room and appraise the paintings that adorned the walls. "Like them?" asked Marvin proudly when he saw him admiring them.

"Beautiful," replied Edward, not wanting to seem too indifferent. He'd had little time in his life for beautiful things. He'd only ever taken a passing interest in the beauties captured in creative works of art. But now he was thinking he might have time to indulge in the leisurely activity of admiring things for their physical attractions. Paintings, antiques, and... 'Jesus,' Edward thought as Janine entered the room with a silver and gold tray. On it were two tall tumblers and a glass crystal jug of clear liquid with fresh cubes of ice rattling and bobbing about on the surface. *That* was beautiful. But despite the attraction of the lemonade, it was dulled by something even more awe inspiring. Not withstanding his parched dust filled throat, he would have gladly traded the iced lemonade for even a smile from the beautiful creature that bore it. She floated into the room like a breeze of fresh air, wafting over to the table and hovering in front of him. He could smell the fragrance of her perfume, as his eyes drank in the tall slender body draped in a long clinging blue silk dress. The colour matched her dark blue eyes the same as the sun drenched sea matches a clear cloudless sky, and it enhanced the fair complexion that lay beneath her light sun tan. Her dark brown hair rolled down onto her bared shoulders like waves breaking gently over polished marble, and a deliberate and well positioned split in the silken robe ran up to her hip. Now *that* was beautiful! No painting or sculpture could create the same pure chemical reaction in anybody who had an eye for real beauty. His tired and supine body had, with one glance at that Venus, been charged with the vital electricity that was essential to keep the soul alive, and the will to go on living.

As Janine placed the tray on the table in front of Edward he felt awkward. She glanced at him, a pleasing glance, but not with distaste at his dirty bewhiskered face. God how he wished he'd got cleaned up first! He felt dirty. He *was* dirty. He smelt like the empty hold of an old trawler and she smelt like the sweet scented jasmine outside. "Thank you," he said as he turned his eyes away. He felt ashamed of himself, his sudden urge for life abated. He wanted to crawl away and die.

"This is Janine, Edward," Marvin said in his friendly tone as he stood and assessed the situation from beneath a Rembrandt.

Edward smiled nervously into the face of the paragon that was dutifully pouring out a tumbler of refreshment. She was only a couple of feet away from him, her high cheek bones and firm chin exuding confidence. "Hi," he said with no thirst for drink left in his fatigue-racked body. He picked up the glass and sipped the cold sweet liquid.

"Hello," she said softly, and then it came, like a bombshell. She looked him in the eye and smiled. Edward felt dizzy. He felt his head go light as his vision blurred. A hand grabbed a hold of his shoulder and leaned him forward onto the table. There was the sound of voices in the background, coming louder and then fading back into oblivion. The anxiety was gone and everything seemed so peaceful. No elation, no pain, just peace.

CHAPTER 3.

5th August.

Daniel sat at home at Malterswood Lodge, a large villa on Long Island. It was late evening two and a half days since he'd read the article in the New York Times. The captain of the ship that was to transport the cargo would be getting impatient. Another day and he would leave without Daniel's shipment. Daniel was busy working out ways of keeping everybody ready for the time of action, when the telephone rang. He picked up the receiver.

"Carlisle?" a steady voice asked on the other end of the line.

"Yes," replied Daniel.

"Your shipment is ready for collection." The phone clicked as the person at the other end rang off, and Daniel hung up. He dialed a number, said, "Go," and then hung up.

"Right," he said and put on his coat. He stuck a cheroot between his teeth, went into the connecting garage, pressed a button, and the doors opened. He got in his car and drove to the docks. It was an hour and a half's drive even at that late hour, but he felt no compunction to rush after all his waiting. After all, he'd already been paid, and he knew now he had time, for the ship couldn't sail without the tide, and that wasn't due for another four hours. He pushed in the car cigarette lighter and then held it to his cigar. It would be good thinking time.

He glanced in his mirror. Nothing behind. He'd had a feeling, nothing definite, but just a twinge in the back of his neck that warned him there might be somebody tailing him. He'd had the feeling for the last week whenever he went outside. Normally he had his bodyguard with him, not a big man with a neck like a tree trunk and muscles like granite, but a thin tall man by the name of Carl Donovan. Daniel had always maintained the idea that big bodyguards were more likely to attract trouble than small and harmless looking ones.

Carl looked harmless. He looked like a good meal would build him up to double his size. But nobody who knew him ever underestimated him. Daniel had become aware of the thin man's talents after he'd applied and been accepted for the job as one of his security staff. He wasn't employed as a bodyguard until a few months later, when he disabled two heavy-duty thugs who'd been appointed to the task of breaking every bone in Daniel's body. During the quasi-darkness of an early winter evening, as Daniel and Carl were walking to the warehouse from the World Trade Centre, they were approaching the junction of Beach Street and St. John's when two men, with clubs, got out of their limousine and closed in on them. A third man cruised the car alongside. He wore a stupid grin on his face. Somehow, (Daniel didn't quite see it), Carl scythed them down like ten-pins, and as the third pulled up, and struggled, with a heavy pick-axe handle in his hand, to get his large frame out of the car, Daniel neatly jammed his head in the door. Ironically, Daniel had to lift their limp bodies back into the car for Carl.

Things had heated up a lot more in the last couple of years. There had been more and more pressure put on him by the different mafia groups in the city. He'd stood his ground, but it had cost him, and cost him dear. He picked up the hand-phone and pressed the buttons. Carl's voice came over clear. "Carl," he said simply.

"I'm two blocks away," Daniel said. "Is it there?"

"Two men and a crate, Mickey and I have their hardware."

"Okay. Open up." The tyres crunched on gravel as he swung his Lincoln into the loading bay of his warehouse. He sounded his horn and Carl closed the doors behind him. In his headlight beams he could see what looked like a steel bound crate on the floor at the back of a Ford transit. The lights went on and two men, dressed in expensive suits, stepped out of the shadow of two large wooden packing cases.

"Took your time getting it from Oregon," Daniel said chattily. "Fly in did you?"

His sarcasm cut no ice. Neither answered, knowing that it was their business to get it to the dock, but not to say how they did it. One thing he noticed and that was they didn't seem at all surprised that he knew where they'd brought it from.

*****

Captain Andre Kercheval leaned on the ship's rail and stared down at the reflected lights on the surface of the water. It was a still airless night. He would be glad to get back out to sea where the air was clean and the wind blew fresh. He saw the docks for what they were, dirty, oily, foul-smelling places. Where other sailors relaxed on shore, he became more tense. Only when the ship was well out to sea could he feel at one with the world, in his isolation from everything and everybody. He hadn't always been like that. He'd been a student of divinity thirty years or more ago, driven with the passion to convert the sinners, the heathens and the non-believers into the ways of God. He studied at Toulon, mastering more than eight languages, and thereafter, travelled over much of Europe preaching at universities and colleges. He loved mankind, he wanted to help them. But his devotion to his fellow men was not reciprocated and finally, after a humiliating event at Oxford, when his speech, "Gentiles of the world unite with me and pray to God for your salvation," was laughed out of the city as his words were printed in the local papers. His mastery of English was almost fluent. He couldn't understand how they could mis-quote him, a man of God, as using a word like '*genitals*.' He found solace in the bottle, and finally, after deciding mankind wasn't worth saving, went to sea and ended up working for a French shipping company. His ship, *La Belle St. Marie*, had carried contraband for Daniel many times since Hassan Abdullah had introduced them in Marseilles. Although Daniel had many ships' captains on his payroll, it was opportune that Andre was due to dock in New York, for few captains would have instigated repairs on the ship's generators in order to delay departure to coincide with a consignment from a smuggler. Willing as he was however, Andre was due to sail in thirty six hours with or without a delivery from Daniel.

He was glad when Daniel arrived on board with his inimitable smile for he knew then that he was $20,000.00 richer. He, like Daniel, was a mercenary, and he too had a bank account in Switzerland. He knew he would never spend all his money, but it made him feel good to know how it had been earned. He was glad, too, because he liked dealing with Daniel. Daniel was an out and out professional. Everything planned ahead, paperwork all done, everything paid up front. He liked his style and he liked his methods. It was easy getting contraband, especially in insignificant and reasonably sized containers, onboard ship an hour or two before leaving port with a few heavy bribes here and there. It was even easier off-loading it as a legitimate consignment of machine tools, or tractor parts at the other end, when the necessary documents and bills of lading were in order and matched the ship's manifest. As captain of the ship he was not responsible for the cargo being what it was documented as being, so he took no risk of being involved by the customs officials should they open the crates. Daniel had his own local export control procedure where goods were cleared in his own warehouse, and then, under a simplified system for freight less than 1000 kilograms, were declared after shipping. He always found that to declare a dutiable item in a crate rarely ended in inspection at the port of destiny, and the goods were passed through after the payment of tax, whereas non-dutiable goods were inspected more frequently.

14th August.

Edward awoke between soft clean sheets. The sun, low on the horizon, dappled the shadows of the leaves across the wide white bedspread, and a faint cool breeze drifted in from the open window. He glanced around. It had been a nightmare; the whole thing from planning to leave the Research Centre, to the animal fear of being caught. Or had the Research Centre been a dream as well? He wasn't there now, that's for sure. He'd never had a huge spacious bedroom with a cool breeze and a view overlooking palm trees and a large stretch of water. That wasn't something that the government laid on in the middle of a lifeless desert. They provided a small apartment in a block of more apartments, with a window that had to be perpetually blinded from the constant glare and the consuming heat of the sun. It was air-conditioned no fresh breeze, no view, and no privacy. Each place had its own lounge, bedroom, bathroom and study. It was furnished with Government Issue furniture to designs chosen by someone high in government who probably was also responsible for the decor of fall-out bunkers. The few personal belongings that Edward had, had been abandoned in his flight to the outside world, an ornament from his mother, a caricature of himself done by an artist friend of his when he was at Boston, sex books, textbooks, a few girlie magazines, and a few more books. He wouldn't miss them much, especially the books. He could happily never pick up another book as long as he lived. Anything he wanted he could buy now, and that included a new Jeep to replace the one he'd abandoned.

As he sat up, his arm felt stiff. He turned his head. His neck felt stiff as well, but he managed to see a stainless steel stand with a bag of clear liquid hanging on it. "A saline drip," he whispered to himself as his eyes followed the connecting tube to his forearm. His arm was strapped to a board to prevent his bending his elbow where the needle was inserted. He felt fresh and clean. Then he remembered the lemonade. His body wasn't yearning for it any more, neither was it yearning for sleep. He'd fainted from the exhaustion of fatigue and fear. It had all been too much of a relief, first reaching safety, then seeing a lovely cold drink, and then, then he remembered it, the smile from an angel when he'd expected a look of revulsion. He sighed, leaned his head back against the pillow and dozed. He could feel the breeze on his hands and against his arms. He lifted his face towards it to feel it against his cheek. His eyes suddenly opened wide. There was no air flowing past his cheek. That, like his right arm seemed stiff and immobile. He lifted his free arm, touched the side of his face and then groaned.

There had been no dream. Bandages weren't part of any dream. They were part of the plan, the long laid scheme of events that were to follow his organised disappearance from the Research Centre.

"You awake," a voice said from the doorway.

He looked across and saw Janine. She was just as beautiful as he had seen her before, only this time she was wearing a light white cotton dress that fell just below her knee, and a blue necklet to match her eyes. Now there were no tricks of the mind brought about by tiredness and salt deficiency. She *was* beautiful. "Just," he mumbled a reply and found he couldn't smile.

"You'll be all right now," she said with a gracious smile. I think you'll be surprised when we take off the bandages.

"When?" he asked, finding it hard to move his lips.

"Seven more days."

"Seven more! How many have I been out?"

"Oh only four."

"Only!" He found it hard to talk and tried to pull himself up onto the pillows so that he could see her better. "What happened?" he asked as her warm hands gave his arm some leverage.

"You fainted." She smiled at him, her face not twelve inches from his. He knew it had been her smile that had tipped the balance in his struggle to combat exhaustion. If he was going to die, that smile was the acme of his life, the time to go out on top. He'd felt like dying of shame.

"Who cleaned me up?"

"The doctors and nurses."

"I see. What made them operate before I came round?"

"The surgeon and his team were already here to do the operation. There seemed no point in delaying. Your state of unconsciousness was only temporary, so they got on with the job and left."

"What about you?"

"How do you mean?"

"Well how do you fit in to all this? Are you Marvin's wife?"

Janine laughed. "Oh dear," she chuckled. "No, I'm not his wife," she said after gaining her composure and looking towards the open window. Edward was going to ask who she was then, but she spoke before he could maneuvre his lips. "Now you just lie back and take it easy. I expect that you could use a good meal so I'll fix you something not too chewy. Okay? We can't do with upsetting the stitches." She fluffed up his pillows, her firm breasts brushing against the bandages on his face, and turned to leave.

"I like French fries," he suggested as she went out through the doorway.

She turned and smiled again. "We'll see," she said before disappearing.

Janine was gone a full half hour before she returned, and when she did, she carried the same gold and silver tray that Edward had seen before, only this time, instead of cold lemonade, it held a bowl of steaming soup and a tureen.

"What's on the plate?" Edward asked her as she placed it on a small table at his side.

"Soup first," she ordered and put her hands on his shoulders to help him sit up from the position he'd managed to slump into. Her hands felt soft against his shoulders and he felt like taking a hold of them. But he didn't.

"Will I be able to get up when I've eaten?" he asked instead.

"It shouldn't be impossible. We'll have to disconnect your tubes though."

Edward looked at the saline drip. It shouldn't be too difficult to do that.

Janine fed him his soup, holding the dish up to his mouth so that he had less distance to spoon it. With his mouth bandaged he made ridiculous slurping noises as he sucked the liquid off the spoon. He was pleased it made her giggle.

"Did you make it?" asked Edward after she'd emptied the bowl.

"All right I hope?"

"Delicious."

"Right then." She put down the dish picked up the tureen and opened the lid. "Will that do?" she asked with a grin.

"French fries!" Edward exclaimed, and then winced as the bandages broke the momentum of his jaw. "How did you guess?"

"Oh, you know what they say," she smiled. "The way to a man's heart is through his stomach." She fed him one French fry at a time until he had cleared the plate.

"Couldn't eat another thing," said Edward as she took away the tray. "How about undoing this contraption now?"

"I'll be back in a minute," she stated, and went out with the breeze. Edward felt better now. Better than he'd felt for months, or was it years? He couldn't ever remember having felt so relaxed. Janine came back in a few moments later with an elderly grey haired woman wearing a white work coat. This is Nurse Ball, she announced. The nurse smiled at him and placed a bowl and some surgical appliances on the bed beside him. "We'll do the drip first," she said.

"First?"

"You'll see," she replied, letting a smile escape from the corner of her lips.

Janine turned to go out of the room. "Can't you stay?" he asked with a chuckle. "I'm scared of nurses."

"Only if you want me to," replied Janine.

The nurse skillfully separated Edward from the needle and the tube, and placed them and the bandage that had held them to his arm to one side. "Right, now for the catheter," she said.

"Oh shit!" murmured Edward. Janine casually and tactfully strolled out of the room.

During the next few days Edward saw Marvin Belk only once. "How are you?" he asked as Edward strolled along the patio.

"I feel like the invisible man," he replied. "Take the bandages off and I'll disappear."

"Exactly," Marvin remarked. "That's exactly what will happen. Edward Taylor came here, but he won't be seen again."

"Oh?"

"You won't be Edward Taylor any more. Wait and see. Your face will be that of a younger man." He shrugged his shoulders. "You are what, forty five?"

"Yes."

"But you looked much older."

"Considerably so I've been told."

"Well you'll look younger, perhaps around the forties mark."

"But that's impossible."

"How old did you feel when you were in that hell hole in the desert?"

"About as old as I looked."

"And how old do you feel now?"

Edward laughed. "Twenty years younger," he said. Marvin just smiled.

The last three days in bandages was the worst after that. His curiosity was almost unbearable. Every day Janine had to persuade him to be patient. "You can't afford to spoil it now," she would say and slap his hand as he fingered the bandages. Edward did it to tease her. The more he did it the less likely she was to leave him on his own. He'd had a lifetime of being on his own. Now he wanted only to be alone with this woman, someone he'd never seen before he came to the villa, but someone from whom he never wanted to be separated. She spent most of her time with or about him. It was as if she was meant to be part of his life. She asked him about the work he had done and the way he'd lived and breathed for science. He explained it the best he could and the more he explained the less he found he could justify what he'd been doing for the last twenty years.

"In retrospect I don't think I was ever happy," he stated. "The trouble is I thought I was."

"Do you think you can live happily without the mental challenges that you craved for when you were younger?"

Edward thought about that for a long time before answering. "I think I could find something to stimulate my mind, set up a business of some kind or do something that will satisfy my brain while the rest of me can enjoy itself."

Janine gave a little chuckle. "Yes, I've heard of your vacations to Portland."

"Oh." Edward seemed unhappy that she knew about his trips to the brothels. "I didn't know you knew," he said in almost a whisper. "You see..." Janine didn't let him finish.

"Well that's all in the past now," she said and walked on. Edward followed. He so longed to tell her that he was a changed man but that would make no difference. He knew she knew what a squalid little man he'd been. He knew she couldn't feel anything but pity for him, and he didn't want pity from her. She sat beneath a large rhododendron on a plank-seat bench.

"Will you be here as long as I'm here?" he asked her as he sat beside her.

She took his hand and squeezed it. It was their first real intended contact. He kept a firm hold on it, afraid that she might pull away, but she didn't. "I'll be here, she said."

"Tell me about yourself," Edward said. "I've told you about me, now you tell me about you."

She frowned. "Nothing to tell," she stated rather too quickly.

"But what are you doing here?"

"Well suffice it to say, like you, I am just another of Marvin's business associates." She paused a moment and then went on. "That should make you feel better."

"I'm not sure what you mean."

"Well Marvin is not a particularly nice person. Oh I know he has the looks *and* the money, but basically he's a gangster. So we both have something in common whatever our pasts may be." She looked straight at him. "What I mean is that we'd better make the most of our stay here, because you can rest assured he hasn't finished with us yet."

It left Edward wondering. who she was? Why was she there? He knew why he was there, and as much hinged on what he still had for sale as what he'd already sold or Marvin would have saved the trouble of giving him a face lift. He must need her pretty badly as well for something.

"Are you lovers?" Edward asked.

"She sighed. "I've told you before, there's nothing like that." She didn't seem angry at his asking. "Come on lets go make some dinner," she said and led him by the hand up the terraces to the house.

"Your bandages can come off tomorrow," she said as they sipped at some white wine."

"I can't wait."

"You'll have to get used to looking different," she stated in a matter-of-fact way."

"I don't mind looking forty again," Edward laughed.

"You don't seem to understand," she told him. "You'll be younger, but you'll not look like you did when you were in the prime of life."

"I don't think I ever went through that phase," he joked. "Straight from adolescence to geriatric I think."

"You still don't realise, do you? You'll not look like yourself. The whole idea of the operation was to make you look different so that nobody will ever recognize you even from a photograph."

"I hadn't thought of it like that. Ever since Marvin told me I would look younger than my age I've been unable to think about anything else, except..."

"Except what?"

"Oh well, I'll just be glad to get these things off now and see just what a mess they've made of me."

Edward could hardly sleep that night. He needed to know if he was going to look like he'd been feeling. He'd felt like a million dollars. The only time he didn't feel like that was when he wanted

Janine to look at him and like him as much as he liked her. Then he felt like a penny against a gold sovereign.

*****

"Hold steady," Nurse Ball said as she unwound the bandages.

Edward sat on the edge of his bed impatiently. He fidgeted like a child who had been promised a trip to a pantomime. “Can't I have a mirror?"

"There'll be plenty of time for all that. Now you just be patient a few more minutes."

His face tingled as the last swathe peeled off. Nurse Ball carefully prodded and poked at the white wrinkled flesh, and teased out a couple of un-dissolved stitches. "You heal well," she said.

"Now can I see?"

"I'd give it a couple of hours in the fresh air first," she advised. "You know how your finger goes if it's bandaged for any length of time. Give the blood time to bring a little colour to the epidermis."

"I'll watch him," Janine said as she sat and watched.

"It will of course be quite a while before the marks disappear all together," the nurse explained. “But if you can look at your face and imagine the lines not there then you’ll have a good idea what you’ll eventually look like.” She packed up her things and left Edward sitting facing Janine.

“Well?” he asked. “Tell me.”

Janine studied the face for what seemed like an eternity to Edward. “Well,” she said finally, “you’re even better looking than I thought you were before they did the operation.”

“Stop messing about will you,” he said half angrily, half flattered. “What’s it like?”

She stood up and came over to face him, studied his features again and then kissed him on the forehead. "You'll do," she said and gave him one of her special smiles. "You'll do just fine."

Even through the pale skin of his cheeks she could see him begin to blush. He smiled up at her, stood up and kissed her lightly on her cheek.

"Thanks Janine," he whispered. "Thanks for being here, and thanks for being so kind."

She took a firm grip on both his hands and pulled him to her. Her breath was hot and he felt drawn to kiss her on her moist lips. "You are the most beautiful woman I've ever seen in my whole life," he whispered as their lips joined. His heart slammed against the inside of his chest as her mouth responded touch for touch. The tips of their tongues met and tasted each other, and then chanced an intimate lick. He could hear her breathing faster, controlling it, as her warm luring fragrance filled his nostrils. Their hands parted and she wrapped her arms around his neck. His hands slid up her back and pulled her soft body against him, pressing her full firm breasts tight between them as they kissed and kissed again. "God I've wanted to hold you for so long!" he breathed heavily.

She held her head back from his and looked into his eyes, and as she did, so her lower abdomen pressed against his rigid body and the force was equalized. They'd both held back the forces of nature and now they were going to let them go, to take over and control them. But she let her hands and body work with controlled experience, drawing reactions from her every action, tempting, teasing, letting him gain a little ground at a time and then holding him back, reeling him in on her line again and again and each time loosing him in a different way upon her flesh, regulating her body and restraining his from lunging uncontrollably, until she finally drew him into her, and with a frantic cry, she felt the full power of his thrusting loins as both their bodies bore down hard on each other in the final frenzied throws of painful ecstasy.

*****

The sound of chattering bluebirds outside the open window brought Edward back from the sleep of the fulfilled. Seeing that he lay alone on the bed, he sat up and let his head clear. Janine had gone, no doubt to make him the steak she'd promised when he'd had his bandages removed. He moved his jaw in a cudding motion. Yes he could chew freely now.

It was peaceful there, so peaceful that it was an effort to go for a shower. He dragged himself up from the bed and stepped into the bathroom, casually glancing in the large wall length mirror. His eyes widened as the sight that confronted him startled him. Someone was looking back at him, a younger man than he of around forty, with a pallid complexion which uncovered several fine purple lines on his face. “My God!" he gasped and stepped closer. "My God!" he repeated and touched the skin on his cheek. He felt his fingers against his own flesh and watched as the reflection touched the corresponding cheek. He prodded it a little and then, slowly, as the realisation struck him, his mouth spread into a smile and then a grin. His lungs fought to restrain him but failed as he burst into a fit of laughter. He laughed until tears fell down his face. He laughed harder and louder.

*****

Marvin Belk was at the dinner table with Janine when Edward joined them. "Well, what do you think?" he asked.

"Janine said that you'd been taking your time getting used to it."

"I keep saying this is me, but I'd have never thought it was possible." He shook his head. "And what's more, I feel younger as well!"

"Rightly so," Marvin stated. "You've had your share of wearing yourself to a frazzle for other people. Now it's your turn to draw. You must remember though, that even your mother won't recognize you."

"I hadn't thought of that."

"You do realise that they will be watching her house don't you?"

Edward sighed. "Yes, I realise."

"And you do realise that we've not changed your prints. They can always pick you up on those if you give yourself away."

"Yes," Edward submitted.

"Well, he'll be here for a couple more months yet, won't he?" asked Janine.

"Sure he will," answered Marvin with a broad grin. "I just don't want him skidaddling down to Portland and throwing all our good work away."

"He won't," Janine said positively. "He's going to stay here with me." She threw him her smile. So she'd told Marvin. Or at least she'd made it clear that she was going to be with Edward.

"Good girl," Marvin said and took a drink of black coffee.

So he didn't mind either. Things were working out all right. All right that is, until he'd given him all he wanted to know. Then what? Edward smiled. "All I need to do when I leave here is find a quiet relaxing place to live, somewhere I can enjoy life and take it easy."

"No rush," Marvin said. "It'll be a while before we can finalise our agreement so you'll have plenty of time to look through the real-estate columns."

"How long?"

"Well, as Janine as said, you ought to stay a couple of months at least. Get a suntan, fill yourself out a bit, and give the dust time to settle. They're still looking for you, you know."

"How long is Janine staying?"

"As long as you want her to of course." He wasn't a bit bothered.

Janine suppressed a smile and got up from the table to serve Edward his steak.

16th August.

Daniel waited to pick up the crate at Lisbon where *La Belle St. Marie* docked to discharge part of its cargo before sailing on to Marseilles. After the expected formalities, the crate was picked up on the quay side and transported to another cargo ship, *Fortune.*

Using the same documentation, he had the freight loaded and sailing within three days to Cape Town, its next port of destination. He watched the ship sail. It would take a week to reach that port, and by that time, his own boat *The Silver Ambassador*, would have set off from Rio de Janeiro and reached there in time to collect the case for the last leg of its sea journey.

He booked out of *The Sheraton* and caught the next flight to Paris, arriving at the *Le Corbusier* later in the evening. It was an extravagant post war building of functional design, erected in the cantilever style, with the harmonic mathematics of the famous French architect.

"Bon soir," he said to the desk clerk as he signed the register. "Vous avez une chambre retenu pour moi, sil vous plait?"

"Yes sir, we're expecting you," the clerk answered in English after seeing Daniel's signature in the book. "Room 409." He took down a key and held it out. "Enjoy your stay sir."

Daniel took the key. "Thank you," he said and went to the lift. He pressed the button and waited. The doors opened and he stepped in, turned around to face the doors, and noticed, just as they were about to close, a young fair haired woman about in her mid twenties, running towards them. He pressed the button to reopen the doors and she stepped in.

"Merci," she said as Daniel pressed the button for the fourth floor.

"You're welcome," replied Daniel.

"Ah, you're English," the woman said with an American accent.

"If New York's in England I am," he replied with a broad grin."

"You don't have much of an American accent."

"I've been there for the last fourteen years. I was English."

She smiled at him pleasantly.

"Am I too late for a meal at this place?" he asked her, knowing full well the answer.

"Not if you eat a la carte. The restaurant is open till midnight."

"Thank goodness, I couldn't have faced walking around outside looking for somewhere to eat."

The doors of the lift opened. "Good night," he said to her as he stepped out. He looked along the corridor at the numbers on the doors and set off in search of 409. He soon came to the right door and unlocked it at the same time as he glanced back down the corridor. He wasn't sure if out of the corner of his eye he hadn't seen someone's head poking around the corner, but there was nobody there now. He looked around his room, saw the normal sort of thing, threw his case on the bed and looked out of the window. "Good view of the Champs-Elysees," he commented aloud as he turned back to the centre of the room and undressed for a cool shower. It felt good after the last few days. He was going to make the best of his short stay in Paris, he always did.

He felt refreshed as he sat at the table in the busy restaurant. The waitress that had shown him to his table came with a wine list and he picked Chablis. "I'll have the wine while I'm waiting," he said after choosing a simple Carpe Matelote.

It was while he was sipping his wine that he saw the blond woman for the second time that evening. He watched as she talked and chatted with a well dressed dark haired man at a corner table, hardly throwing a single smile, but shaking and nodding her head as if discussing something of grave importance. Between her slender fingers was a long black cigarette, which she put to her lips and drew on hard at every break in the conversation until she finally stubbed the butt in the ashtray. They talked as long as Daniel was there and beyond. Only once did she glance in Daniel's direction, giving him the same brief smile that she had passed to him in the lift. He smiled back and turned his attention to the waitress. She spoke good English and she seemed to have the time to stop and talk to him more as the restaurant cleared. As he left his seat she came over and smiled.

"Hope you enjoyed your meal," she said politely.

He gave her a tip and replied.

"Very much thank you. Do you want to have a drink with me when you finish?"

"Oh, that will not be for another half an hour," she said and shrugged her shoulders, her apron, lifting slightly against her as she did so, unable to disguise the soft warm contours of her figure.

"What's your name?"

"Michele," she answered with a controlled smile.

"I'm Daniel. Meet you in the lounge bar then," he said and left.

She was already at the bar when he came down from his room half an hour later. The barman was laughing with her at some little joke as she turned and, still chuckling, said, "Hello."

"Hi," he replied. "What will it be?"

"Martini," she replied. "That'll do for a start."

And a start it was. They spent a very pleasant evening talking about themselves, building up a good friendly relationship in between more drinks, the warmth and magnetism between them growing stronger as the night progressed, until finally the evening reached a climax in room 409.

*****

During the next morning Daniel allotted his time to visiting the *Musee d'Art Moderne*. Then he had a light meal at the *Café St - Moritz* on his way to visit a massage parlour. He liked a good massage. In New York he'd made regular visits to *La Parisienne Massage Parlour*, until life started to get complicated with bodyguards and people trying to force him out of business and into the East River. He still managed to get there occasionally under protests from his chief of security, but he liked the way the masseuses worked with their hands. They had a way of going about their work that no man could have. Not for Daniel at least.

In Paris he would have completely different treatment at *Henri's*. He would go there whenever he visited the city, and come out feeling like a tenderised steak. But it made him feel good. He knew that Henri and his staff of two men and three girls were all as queer as a three pound note, but he found them much the same as some hairdressers he knew. He'd go in for a job doing and come out with it well done, no hassle, no come on, just a damned good haircut, or in Henri's case, a body full of jellified, pulverized muscle. But there was another reason for having his body pummeled by Henri when he was in Paris. He always insisted on Henri doing the work because Henri was a contact. He in turn had contacts all over Paris who helped and dealt with Daniel on many a smuggling trip. Henri was a confidant through which a great deal of business had been arranged in the past.

"Jacques has some work for you," he would say as he chopped at Daniel's back with the sides of his hands; "Gilbert has got that equipment for you from the factory," digging his thumbs deep under Daniel's shoulder blades; "Marietta wants you to contact her in Toulouse," kneading him like a lump of dough. All good business for Daniel. Henri always had a good fee for his service. The massage parlour could have been just a good front if he hadn't enjoyed his work so much.

Daniel returned to the hotel and spent the rest of his time making telephone calls from his room. Business didn't end just because he was in the middle of one job. It was his life's blood, making deals, arranging meetings to obtain or collect items required by another customer. He prided himself on being able to get anything for anybody; at a price. France was a wealth of business opportunities of that kind, as was most of Europe. Only two months ago he had obtained some of the world's leading technology from a firm in England for a man in San Francisco. A good deal that, though he had his suspicions about the man he had been dealing with. But Marvin Belk had paid cash on the nail.

Few days went by when Daniel didn't transact some business somewhere. It was in him to do it. That's why he had so many contacts. That's why he was so successful at what he did.

It was later than he thought when he finally put down the phone and had a shower. He went down for his evening meal at roughly the same time as he had the previous night. He had a couple of drinks first to strip his mind of the heavy clothes of business, although his subconscious always retained the threads to work to weave on, and then he looked in the restaurant for an empty table.

It wasn't as busy as it had been the previous night and there were several cleared tables with newly laid, snow-white tablecloths over them. Daniel went to the nearest one and pulled out a chair to sit down. Then he noticed the blond woman again. She sat at the same table as she had been at the day before, studying the menu and drawing on another black cigarette. He looked at the shoulder length wavy hair, as she tossed her head and threw the bouncing tresses to one side. As she did so her eyes caught Daniel staring at her. He smiled awkwardly and she looked down momentarily and then glanced back and returned the smile. She gave a little wave. Daniel wasn't sure if it was just a wave or a beckoning for him to join her. He decided on the latter and walked over to the table.

"May I join you?" he asked.

"Please," she answered and pointed her hand to the opposite chair. "I was just about to order." She took a final draw of the cigarette, crushed the half smoked remains into the ash tray and wafted the aromatic smoke away from the table. "Here," she said and handed him the menu.

"What are you having?"

"The Alouettes Sans Tetes with sautéed potatoes."

"I'll have the same. Shall I order some wine?"

She smiled and nodded. "I'm Anita, Anita Holt," she announced.

"And this is Daniel," a voice came from behind. Michele was waiting for the order. Her lips were tightly closed as Anita ordered the meals.

"Can we have a bottle of Moet et Chandon?" Daniel asked softly. She seemed upset.

"Of course," she said in her gentlest voice. She gave him a singular smile and left with a flurry of her thin cotton dress.

"You haven't got company tonight?" asked Daniel?"

"You mean the fella I was with last night?" She grinned. "That was my brother. He was in Paris for a meeting. He runs a computer consultancy business. He travels all over the world. Paris yesterday, London today I believe.

"You don't work with him then?"

"Hell no; I don't know the first thing about those things. I'm a journalist."

"That sounds more interesting to me as well, I must admit." They both laughed.

"Your drinks," said Michele. She brushed Daniel's shoulder with her soft undercarriage as she leaned forward and poured some of the champagne into a glass.

Daniel sipped it. "That's great," He said and nodded for her to leave the bottle.

"I'll pour it for you," she said willingly, and carefully filled the glasses, purposefully standing close to his arm and carelessly brushing her hip against him. He needed no reminding how soft her body was. "I'll bring you your food shortly," she said to Daniel as if Anita wasn't there, and then she glided out through the door.

"Do you think she'll bring mine as well?" Anita said with a chuckle.

"She's all right," Daniel said with a smile. "We had a few drinks together last night, that's all that's bugging her."

"Oh I see," Anita said understandingly.

"You were saying, about your job."

"Was I? Oh, well it's a job. I get about a bit and meet lots of interesting people."

"What are you writing about at the moment?" Daniel asked as he sipped his champagne.

"Just a few articles. Mainly about organised crime."

Daniel somehow got some liquid down the wrong hole and coughed. "Sorry about that," he said as he recovered. "Drinking it too fast."

"Do you know anything about organised crime?"

"I thought most crimes were organised to some extent."

"No, you know what I mean. The big time."

"I know they exist, that's about all."

"Oh, I see."

"Sorry I won't be much help to you I suppose."

"It doesn't matter. It wasn't my intention to give you a grilling."

Daniel smiled at her sympathetically.

"Here we are Daniel," said Michele as she brought two plates of stuffed beef rolls and placed them in front of them. She still worked from Daniel's shoulder, serving the potatoes and a puree of fresh French beans.

"Thank you," said Anita sharply. Michele didn't acknowledge. She walked away busily. "I wonder if she's poisoned mine," Anita grinned as she started to eat. Daniel felt a bit awkward, but as the evening progressed he and Anita built up a rapport. She was quietly spoken and her slate grey eyes flashed unspoken messages as she deliberately used innuendo. It was more pronounced whenever Michele was at the table. "Does your room have a good view at night," she asked Daniel, as Michele cleared away the plates. "I find my bed most uncomfortable," she stated coolly as Daniel ordered her a Drambuie. Daniel had got the message. He hoped poor Michele wasn't going to take it too hard.

"Is there anything else I can give you?" Michele asked Daniel. She bounced back once too often. As she leaned over the table for the empty wine glasses, Anita knocked her Drambuie hard against the young girl's dress. The thin white cotton stuck to Michele's skin, eagerly displaying her soft inner thigh in a golden carnal patch.

"Oh, I'm dreadfully sorry," said Anita, forcing a look of concern. "Perhaps you'd better go and change into something more respectable. The other waitress will see to us."

Michele left the table with nothing less than a look of determination on her face. She had a brief word with another waitress and disappeared.

With Michele banished from the play Anita was no longer the cool restrained woman that she had portrayed when her younger adversary had been around. As they sat and chatted well into the evening, her manner became sultry, her movements suggestive. She'd successfully banished the enemy, now she was to have the prize, and she meant him to know it. Every movement, each touch of the hand displayed her intentions. She wasn't going to let anybody come between her and her goal now.

Daniel realised that Michele must have completed her shift and knocked off for she didn't return. It was a relief really. The nineteen year old tigress could soon get fixed up again, and nothing was everlasting with Daniel.

They finished off another couple of drinks before linking arms and walking silently to the lift. As the doors closed them in he leaned past her and pressed the button for the fourth floor, squeezing her body tightly against the side of the lift. Her firm matured breasts teased into his chest as they heaved beneath her satin blouse. His rigid body pressed against her soft form as she held her head back so that he might kiss her neck. It was but a brief kiss before the doors opened and released them on their way to room 409. Their hips rubbed together as he held his arm around her. He took out his key, unlocked the door and let her go on in front of him.

"Go on in," he said, and bumped into her as he locked the door. She'd frozen in her tracks. Daniel looked past her and across the room, his face registering his look of total disbelief. In front of them, lying serenely on his bed beneath a single, thin white unwrinkled sheet was Michele, her shapely youthful form protruding through it shamelessly. Daniel felt awkward again. He didn't know what to say. He didn't know what to do. He looked at each in turn, his eyes pleading for one of them to admit defeat. Both looked more determined than ever they had downstairs. Then suddenly the two females looked at each other, Michele smiled and Anita thawed.

With a casual shrug of her shoulders, Anita walked over to the bed. Daniel stood like a marble statue in the doorway, afraid to move lest he made matters any worse. He was expecting hair to fly at any moment. But instead of initiating a cat fight, Anita unbuttoned her dress slowly and let it fall to the floor, then, she sat on the side of the bed and carelessly unfastened and unrolled each stocking slowly down legs of polished bronze. She stood up, turned her back to him and snapped off her bra then wriggled out of her suspender belt and her knickers and lifted the sheet. Daniel felt himself harden as he watched her soft nubile bottom and what nestled beneath it, settle onto the mattress.

She looked straight into Daniel's eyes. "Well," she said. "Aren't you coming?"

"Er, yes," he croaked, and cleared his throat as he tried to casually walk towards them. It was difficult to do anything casually with two naked women lying beneath a revealingly thin sheet in front of him, and his trousers straining against every thread that held them together. He began to struggle with his tie. He could feel himself sinking in a mire as the knot stuck.

Here darling," Anita said and knelt up in the bed. She pulled his body against hers and skillfully undid his tie. Then she went to work on his shirt, pulling it out of the top of his trousers and peeling it back off him.

"My word," chimed in a French accent as Michele, who had knelt up beside Anita, busily unfastened his belt. She put the tips of her fingers behind it. "Plenty for all you see," she commented to her accomplice, circling and manipulating with her fingers whilst Anita unleashed Daniel's body upon them.

When Daniel awoke, he was alone. The neat white sheet was now a thin twisted swathe draped carelessly across the top of his abdomen. He'd slept an unconscious sleep but insufficient for his body. His loins were tight, his body still rampant as he sat on the side of the bed cradling his head. He glanced at his watch. 9.35. Too late for breakfast. It didn't matter, he wasn't hungry. Thirsty but not hungry. As the words wandered through his mind he heard a key turn in the lock. He covered his lower parts by dragging the rope of sheet across his legs, so that the cleaning lady would not embarrassed.

There was no cleaning lady. It was Michele. She brought in a tray with a large pot of coffee and three cups. "Just what I needed," Daniel smiled.

"You will you greedy boy," she said in a mischievous voice. She placed it down on the table.

Why the three cups?" asked Daniel.

"Well you aren't starting without me," came a voice from the bathroom.

*****

The longer Edward stayed at the villa, the more a feeling of foreboding shadowed him. Life there had been good to him since he stepped out of the helicopter. He'd had peace and quiet, he'd been given the youth he'd so carelessly mislaid, and he had a new identity so that no-one would ever find him. But that was the catch. Only a handful of people knew who he was and they knew where he was as well, and that was the worst part. They were the last people he wanted any thing to do with. Then there was Janine. Edward was a logical man. His brain had been his strong point at one time. But Janine didn't fit. She wasn't a prisoner, but then neither was he. He'd been a prisoner and escaped, and now he was free. Or was he? Marvin Belk still needed him, so he would tempt him with more money. And then what? What when he'd outlived his usefulness. Marvin wasn't the sort of person to leave you to talk; he'd said as much himself. Was his end to be in a communal coffin or something equally as bizarre? "God," he said to himself as he leaned on the low wall that surrounded the patio. It was a beautiful morning. Janine had risen early from the bed they had shared for the past three nights. She had gone alone into the gardens while Edward dozed out the last dregs of sleep. He'd awakened with the shrill chatter of the birds, but he had a headache when he finally lifted his head from the pillow. He rarely had headaches. Only when he had a mental problem that was resisting all his efforts to work out did he get such cranial pain. He'd thrown a satin robe over his shoulders and secured it around his waist as he went through the open French windows. "God," he repeated. "What have I got myself into?"

"You talking to yourself?" asked Janine. She had come up from the orchard without his seeing her. "That's the first sign of madness you know," she stated sarcastically.

"Oh, thought I was alone," he said apologetically.

"That makes it all right then," she giggled. "It is only a sign of insanity if you do it when you're in a crowd."

Edward laughed. She'd made him laugh a lot, more than he'd ever laughed in his whole life. His laughter turned to seriousness as he watched an armed guard on the distant roadway disappear from view behind a clump of azaleas. "Am I a prisoner here?" he asked her outright.

Her face too, turned grave. "I don't know Edward," she said softly. "I really don't know."

"But you live here. Can't you say what's happening?"

"Live here?" Her glance was inquisitive.

"You don't fit in here either, do you? It's a huge place, hardly anybody about, guards on the entrances. It's as if you and I were both prisoners."

"In a way, yes."

"And what a coincidence. It's as if you and I were supposed to meet."

"Supposed to become lovers you mean?"

"Well, if you want me to say it, yes, it's as if..." He stopped himself from saying it.

"As if I were supposed to make you want to stay, is that what you want to say?"

Edward watched her face as she said it. He'd half expected anger, half expected a denial. Her face was calm, her manner resigned. “I'm sorry, I didn't mean that. You're the best thing that's ever happened to me. I don't know what I was thinking of."

"Perhaps you were thinking that it's been too much of a coincidence. Too much like a fairy story."

"It is like a fairy story though. The trouble is, I am afraid. I'm afraid it's just a dream. I'm afraid it won't last."

“I don't think it's meant to."

"What?"

"It isn't meant to, Edward."

"I see." He frowned as his mind began to churn over. "No, I don't see. I should, I know I should. I can feel it." He looked at Janine, his eyes pleading with her.

"Do you want it to last darling?" she asked.

"Yes I do."

Janine frowned this time. Her face became hard, her eyes wide as she took a breath to speak. "Then we'll have to be very careful my love."

"But I thought Marvin didn't mind. I thought he approved of us..." He paused.

"Of course he approved of us being lovers," Janine said, her voice shaking. Her eyes began to fill with tears. "He approved of it because he set it up."

Edward couldn't believe she'd meant what she'd said. "Yes, but he didn't know we would, did he?" He didn't want to believe it. "He couldn't have known, not for sure."

"It was about as sure a bet as the earth goes around the sun," Janine said, turning away to prevent his seeing her face streaked with tears."

Edward couldn't move. He wanted to take her in his arms and squeeze her, and tell her that everything was all right. He loved her. Nothing else mattered. "He paid you didn't he?"

"Yes," Janine's voice was almost lost as she fought hard to control the sobs that were welling up inside her.

"He paid you to be nice to me and you played the game."

"Yes," she whispered.

Edward ached inside. There was a rage down there that he'd never experienced before. He'd never been able to get really cross with anybody in his whole life. Not his wife, not his teachers, not even Felspars. But now he *was* angry. His finger nails dug deep into the palms of his hand as he tried to control the alien feeling. "And you played it like a real pro." His voice was low and shook uncontrollably. "You *are* a pro!" he shouted. "A bloody prostitute, a fucking high class whore." His voice echoed against the walls of the villa.

"Yes," she choked.

"You bitch!" He turned to go back inside but then turned back again. "I suppose you were to screw me to stop me wanting to go out looking for some arse, while they, in their own way, screwed everything out of me that they wanted." His eyes were wide with rage. "Suck me dry and then bury me I bet." He ran up the steps and disappeared inside the villa.

Janine bit her lip and suppressed the urge to call after him as she watched him go.

*****

Daniel wasn't himself. His aching body was in need of a full service. His mind was on the phone call that he'd had from Henri. He was glad Anita and Michele had sated themselves. He needed the rest. If only Henri had rung an hour earlier he might have left the two women slightly less fulfilled but he wouldn't have been as sore. The phone rang just as they fell exhausted beside him.

"Telephone," he said as he scrambled breathless out of bed with a sigh of relief. Saved by the bell. Who knows for sure when they'd have given up. They'd got responses from him that he didn't think he had left.

"Henri! So good to hear from you. What is it?"

"I must talk to you urgently," he said. "Can you come right away?"

"Of course, of course! I'll be there within the hour." Thank goodness he rang!

Daniel showered, dressed and left the two women in his bed. "Sorry girls," he said as disappointedly as he could. "Business you know." He shrugged his shoulders and strolled casually out of the room. As the door clicked behind him he blew hard, his cheeks puffing out like a squirrel with a face-full of nuts. "Thank God for Henri!" he said aloud and tried to keep his body straight as he walked to the lift.

"Hah, Daniel mon cher!" Henri greeted him.

"Less of the '*my*' if you don't mind."

Henri chuckled. "You know you're always welcome to have one of the girls," he stated. I offer every possible alternative. That is why I have my name above the door so people will know they have a choice."

"Non merci beaucoup," Daniel rejected the offer.

"Marie has a very good pair of hands you know. I'm very surprised you've never tried her."

"What is all this Henri? I need her hands at this moment in time as much as I need mumps."

"Mumps?"

"You know," Daniel said pointing to his throat and gesturing a swollen neck. "Mumps."

"Ah, you mean les oreillons," laughed Henri cupping his crotch in his large hands. Les mumps eh?"

"That's right. Mumps." Daniel shook his head in dismay. There was no hope for Henri. He was past redemption.

"Never mind, perhaps another time then?"

"Yes, another time Henri. Now what about a damned good massage and you can tell me what you wanted to talk to me about."

"Come," he said. He led the way to his massage room. Daniel went into the cubicle and undressed, wrapping the towel that hung there around his waist.

Henri was ready with the embrocation. He shook the bottle as Daniel eased himself onto the bench. Straight away Henri's hands began to pummel and beat some feeling back into his body. "You're not in good shape Daniel. If you need your body it will let you down. You should exercise more often."

"You know you have a gift," Daniel stated, his voice vibrating as he was jabbed and basted by skillful hands. He could feel his body begin to relax.

"You're being followed," Henri said in a matter of fact way.

"Relax, you're tensing up."

"Who?"

"Hah, that I don't know. But I had a man in here. Asked for a massage, but then he started asking me questions."

"What sort of questions."

"Like if I knew you, did I give you any other service apart from the massage."

"What did you tell him?"

"I told him that since I would not discuss his business with anyone else so I would not discuss other people's business in that manner."

"What did he say to that?"

"He said he just wondered because he thought he had recognised you as an old friend of his."

"I see."

"You were expecting something like this, no?"

"No."

"Huh, then you take care my friend. He was a hard man."

"Hard?"

"He needed a massage like as you say you need the mumps. His body was all muscle and as supple as a tiger's. He was a man used to using his strength, you mark my words."

A shiver ran up Daniel's spine.

"Was he an American?"

"No, he sounded not so American. He spoke in French all the time. Fluent French."

"Let me know if you hear anything else, won't you? I'll be in Paris for another five days." He let Henri finish his work, paid him double, and left. He decided he would eat at the same cafe that he'd stopped at the day before. He needed time to think and he didn't want to bump into either of the two women he'd left at the hotel. It was a busy little cafe, busy and popular. He recognised several faces there that he'd seen in the cafe the day before. Some of them glanced at him, some of them didn't. None looked interested in him, but then they wouldn't.

When he got back to the hotel he went straight to his room. There was a blue envelope left on the bed. He picked it up and caught a whiff of perfume as he opened it. "Sorry I can't stay and enjoy your company any longer," it said in a neat woman's handwriting. "Had to follow up a story. Au revoir, Anita."

Well, that solved one problem. He couldn't stand many more nights like last night. From now on he was a one woman man, even if they were only one night stands.

*****

"How do you mean he won't speak to you woman. What the hell have you done?"

"He's locked himself in his room. He won't answer when I call."

"Then you'd better get him to answer. That's what I'm paying you for. A damned high class bitch like you and you can't keep him interested in the one thing he lives and breathes for. I could have brought his old brothel here lock stock and barrel for what I'm paying you!" Marvin Belk was used to things going his way, the way he planned. He hadn't calculated on Edward wanting to change from a brothel creeper to a loved man. He'd expected him to screw her, not fall in love with the woman. Why had people to change the habits of a lifetime just when he'd counted on them staying the same? And to top it all, the damned woman was feeling sorry for the son of a bitch. "Holy Jesus!" he swore after her as she ran up the passageway to Edward's bedroom.

"Edward," she shouted, as she rapped on the door. "Edward you must let me in. You must listen."

"Go to hell."

"If you don't answer me he'll send me away."

"Go to hell I said."

"At least let's talk in a civilized manner and not through a thick door," she pleaded.

"Civilized! You call what you do civilized?"

"You didn't complain," she said angrily. "You couldn't wait to get your hands all over me."

"Bitch!"

"Your mind was hanging out of your mouth!" she shouted as loud as she could.

"You fucking bitch," Edward cursed as he went to the door. No piece of wood was going to stop him saying what he was about to say to her face. He unlocked the door and flung it back against the hinges. "You..." He hadn't time to finish. "Humph!" He gasped as a something heavy hit him square in the solar plexus. He fell backwards and crumpled to the floor, his chest heaving for some air, any air. It was hard to find.

Janine stepped into the room, threw the iron boot hook to one side and slammed the door closed. "Oh darling, I'm sorry!"

Edward mouthed an unintelligible word or two, a ruckle escaping from the back of his throat.

"Forgive me darling, I had to get in to speak to you."

"Bitch!" he managed to exhale in a coarse grating whisper.

"I know. But neither of us knew we were going to fall in love."

"Damn stupid bitch!" He'd caught some air somewhere.

"I love you for God's sake! Damn it, doesn't that count for anything?"

"Damn near killed me. Stupid bitch." He was managing to breathe again now.

"I had to tell you. You have to believe me. I didn't know it would happen any more than you did."

"No need to have hit me so damned hard!" He was still on his hands and knees.

She put her hands on his shoulders. "I love you Edward. I never thought it could happen to me, but it has."

"Then don't do that again, d'ya hear?"

"Yes my darling."

He pushed himself into a kneeling position and put an arm around her shoulder while the other hand rubbed beneath his rib cage. I feel sixty again. Does that alter anything?" he stated flatly as she steadied him to his feet."

"Not if we can get out of here alive she said in an almost inaudible whisper."

"Heh?"

"Not if we can get...."

"Yes I heard you first time. My hearing is A-one." He started to smile. "The rest of me is jiggered, but I can hear all right."

Janine laughed; a small tear in the bottom of each eye. "Oh Edward!" she shook her head. "You're so damned funny!"

Edward moved his arm from her shoulder to her waist and rested his head against her temple. "Hell that was painful!" He took a few more deep breaths.

Janine swiveled around to face him and kissed him on his nose. "We will have to plan," she said quietly. "Marvin Belk doesn't leave people that can tell tales. You are in danger. When he's got what you can give him then he will kill you. I know, believe me."

"And what about you?"

"I'm dispensable the same, as soon as I'm no further use to him."

She looked into Edward's eyes. "And that isn't why I have made up with you."

"Why not? I'd probably do that."

"Well I'm scared, I must admit," she said as she snuggled into him. "What can we do?"

"Let him think we've put aside our differences in the cause of sex."

"You have a way with words, you know that?"

"I'm better at sums actually." They smiled at each other and kissed briefly. Then Edward pulled away.

"What's the matter?"

"From now on you play the whore and I'll play the lecherous old dog."

"Shouldn't be hard for either of us to carry that one off!"

"No, and I can't wait to play my part."

"Well I'm not playing till tonight," said Janine. She opened the door and walked out. "As far as he's going to see, it is purely business from now on so you can behave yourself."

*****

Daniel spent three long nights with Michele. It was as if the orgy of the night before hadn't happened. She never spoke of it, and when Daniel asked her if she'd minded she put her fingers to his lips, smiled and said, "Shh." He never broached the subject again.

The days were less relaxed. He had a feeling that he was being watched all the time. He never saw any particular person watching him or casually waiting on a corner. But then he knew that the man Henri had mentioned was a professional. He would merge into the background like the cryptic adaptation of a moth, just one of a passing crowd, nothing outstanding, just a phantom never to be seen.

On the third day he caught a flight to Toulouse to see a woman there who worked near an electronic components factory. She'd obtained for him a piece of electronic equipment the size of a box of matches. An American manufacturer of aircraft components had asked him to obtain it and he could, at a price. Marietta's services were not cheap. The article would be commonplace within a year, being copied by anyone wishing to do so, and modified to prevent breach of patent, but they needed it now if they were going to compete successfully. In a business connected with electronics, advancement of technology is so rapid that months are important. Today's product is obsolete by the time it comes onto the open market. It has already been superseded by something better on the drawing board.

He caught the early morning flight as a matter of habit. He'd brought many things to France and bypassed the customs by catching a flight to Orly Airport. Then, with his hand luggage by his side, he'd sleep over in the airport lounge without going through the customs barrier. In the morning, he would catch the first internal connecting flight to Toulouse, a commuter's flight, packed with busy businessmen. He'd never seen a customs man there as they all filed off the plane to waiting cars. Even baggage that had been carried in the cargo hold, rolled off the conveyor unsupervised, a matter of yards from the exit to the car park.

Marietta smiled as he approached. "You'd pass for a commuter," she said as he kissed her on the cheek. All he carried with him was a briefcase.

"Well, so I am," he stated. They got into her red Porche and they sped away to her large house in the Chemin de Croix Benite, set in the rural landscape to the south. She drew up the driveway and stopped the engine.

"Is this where you live now" he asked.

"Yes, do you like it?"

"A good move from where you lived before."

"Yes, I think so." The door was unlocked. She turned the handle and walked straight in. It was as beautiful on the inside as it was on the outside. It was decorated sparsely with antique furniture, the curtains were red velvet and there was a scattering of ornaments. Daniel's eyes fell on one ornament in particular. It was a bronze and ivory figure of a lady horseback being helped off by a gentleman. "You like it, I see."

"How on earth… A Poertzel!"

"You gave me expensive tastes. I've never seen a collection like yours, ever."

"Not for sale, I suppose?"

"Sorry, mon cher."

"I'd offer you a good price."

"Money is no good unless you spend it. I buy what I can afford, but I never buy anything for myself unless I really want it. I spend the money as I make it and I enjoy the things I have bought."

"With something set aside for a rainy day I suppose."

"Bank accounts are for those people who live for tomorrow. I live for today. What happens tomorrow doesn't matter."

"But you plan ahead?"

"Well I made the bed if that's what you mean."

CHAPTER 4.

24th August.

Daniel spent the whole day with Marietta. It was like old times. They'd had much in common five years ago when they first met. She was new to the business of industrial espionage, but at the age of twenty one and having been shabbily treated by the son of a leading politician, she decided to make her own life, her own way in the world. She had the looks, with long rolling copper red hair, larger than life brown eyes set into a face with high cheek bones, a well proportioned chin and teeth like pearls, a face that could only have been dreamed of in an artist's mind. Her five foot five inch frame carried all the right amount of flesh in all the right places.

Her father, a widower for five years, was quite wealthy, and when he died he left her a small fortune in stocks and bonds, naming his close friend's son, a lawyer, as executor. That son, one Marc K. Duvant, had ambitions of becoming a politician like his father. But first of all he wanted to become wealthy enough to live in the style to which his father was only just becoming accustomed. He wanted money. Then, along came sweet innocent little Marietta, ripe for the taking in more ways than one. He wooed her and screwed her and then systematically embezzled all her money. He told her that the investments he'd made were falling, and moved the capital around so much that it became impossible to see how he could fail to lose it all. And he did lose it all, or that's what he told Marietta. In fact he had doubled the amount of the original stocks and bonds in his own name. With an inept apology and a more truthful statement that he was unworthy of her, he turned her out of the penthouse apartment that he had bought with her money, said goodbye and closed the door in her face.

Marietta was thunderstruck. She not only hadn't known he had lost all her money, she had been turned out in the street with just over 3000 francs and the clothes on her back, an hour after making love to him. It was enough to make a decent girl turn to crime. And she did: but not straight away. She was a clever girl, and, at twenty, she was well able to look after herself. She soon found herself a small apartment and got a job as a secretary in a firm of accountants. There was nothing special about that, until one day, eight months later, she had to deal with some correspondence from a client company, an electronics component factory. The name of the company, *Elements Electonique Superieur*, meant nothing to her. It was the name of the directors that caught her eye, Jean J. Duvant, and Marc K. Duvant. It was the company owned by the politician father of the one man she loathed more than any other in the whole world, and he was a director now himself. So, the firm she worked for handled their accounts! That was a start. From the accounts she was able to find out every customer's name and every supplier's name. Then she found out what they were buying and selling. It was surprising that the small insignificant company of a year ago, *Elements Electonique Superieur*, had been liquidated and renamed, and was now expanding with injections of private capital into a leading company in the field of electronics, micro-circuitry, and research.

Marietta spent most her spare time cultivating a friendship with Etienne, a research worker at the factory. Through him she discovered exactly what components were being made and what research was taking place. The rest of her spare time she spent on discovering who the major competitors of the company were. It wasn't an unpleasant task, for Etienne was a pleasantly attractive married man of twenty seven, with three children and no intention of leaving his wife. It was a casual affair that suited both of them. He had a mistress that was un-possessive and he gave her what he thought she wanted. At the same time she *did* give him what he wanted and took what she really required, though he never realised that she had ulterior motives until she started to blackmail him.

After obtaining the first detailed diagrams and technical data by stealth, the competitor company that had offered to buy the information sent a man to help her in her new found career. That was the first time she met Daniel Carlisle. His principal had asked him to get an actual component to go with the plans, and that was impossible as far as Marietta was concerned. But then, nothing is impossible. Not with the money Daniel was paying for it. She had got the equipment and more within two days of first meeting him. It was a shame that poor Etienne was such a devoted husband.

From that time on Daniel and Marietta had a firm business association and a pleasurable personal relationship. It suited their life style and whenever he had business in the South of France he made little effort to prevent himself from calling her even if there was no business involved between them. Two years later, when Marietta was busy dealing with a client in California, she summoned the help of her friend in New York. Over a period of three weeks they stayed at three of the houses that Daniel had throughout the States, sharing their lives and sharing their interests. They became very close, and it hit them both hard when they had to resume their professions thousands of miles apart. Daniel had thought of asking her to marry him, but she was casual about the affair and he knew she didn't love him, so he saved himself the embarrassment of spoiling the relationship they had already built up, and resisted the temptation to ask her.

After that they saw each other two or three times a year and always enjoyed it like new found lovers.

This day was no different. Marietta had cooked him a meal for when he arrived. He never dined immediately before flying, and having caught the early morning flight he had not eaten since the previous evening. They laughed and flirted and drank German wine. "You don't mind German wine, do you?" she would always ask. "I have French if you prefer."

"I'll forgive you your little foible," Daniel grinned, knowing full well that she had picked the habit up off him whilst she was in the States. Daniel rarely drank any other type of wine over there.

“We're going out later," she instructed. "There is a dealer who has set up a meeting with me this afternoon and I'd like you to meet him."

"What kind of dealer?"

"You'll see," she laughed and took his hand. "Come, I'll show you my house now.”

Daniel found the tour revealing. She had good taste. Good taste in houses, good taste in furniture, and good taste in antiques. The last room was the bedroom, but at the last minute she guided him away from it. "You'll see that tonight," she said and led him back down stairs. "Something to look forward to."

"I look forward to everything you have to show me Marietta," Daniel replied. "You're like a breath of fresh air in what is becoming a rather sordid world. You know that don't you?"

She laughed and kissed him fully on the mouth. "I enjoy your company too, mon amour."

Daniel frowned. The wine had been good, too good perhaps. He always said what he felt when he'd had a little too much. "Pity we couldn't get our act together in one place," he said. There, he'd done it again.

"Where?"

"Anywhere." He took hold of her and hugged her. "Here, if you like."

"You know that is impossible. You know you must run your business from New York Daniel."

"Well I damned sure wouldn't ask you to live over there," he said sharply.

"Oh, I see."

"No, damn it, you don't see."

"Come," Marietta said suddenly. "We are forgetting that we only have the day together. Let's not spoil it." She walked towards the door. It is time we were going. It is an hour's drive."

The Porche squealed around the narrow winding roads that led away from Toulouse. She sounded her horn on every bend as all French drivers seem to do whichever way they are going. Daniel kept a firm grip on the dashboard. Suddenly she braked hard and swerved into a narrow driveway. "I'm glad you know where you're going," he chided.

"We are here now." she pulled up in front of an old farm house. "In here," she said and knocked on the door. A few seconds later an elderly man, most unlike any farmer Daniel had ever seen, swung the door back.

"Ah, Marietta! How good to see you again," he said.

"Daniel, this is Monsieur Diacre," she introduced.

"Pleased to meet you Mr. Carlisle," the man said and proffered his hand. Daniel shook it. "Come in young man." He turned inside and they both followed. "Marietta has told me a great deal about you."

"Oh," Daniel replied with reservation.

"Oh indeed." He led through into a well kept living room. "Please, take a seat." The two callers did as they were bid. "Can I get you a Pernod?"

"Not for me thanks," replied Marietta.

"Ah, but you wouldn't let an old man drink alone, would you?" he said to Daniel.

"A Pernod would be fine," he answered.

"This is my little country retreat. I don't often get the chance to come down here these days," he said as he poured some water into two tumblers.

"Really?"

"Now, have you told him about it?" he asked Marietta.

"No, I am leaving everything to you."

"Yes well. My work takes me all over Europe. You see, I deal in high class antique porcelain. I have a contact in the United States who buys everything I get."

"Good," Daniel nodded and encouraged him to go on.

"Well he has asked me to ship him something that is banned from export and Marietta said you might be able to, how can I put it, lubricate the wheels of free trade."

"Very well put, I'm sure." The Pernod on top of good German wine made Daniel rather jolly.

"Can you help me?"

"At a price," replied Daniel. "It depends what it is."

Monsieur Diacre looked at Marietta.

"Go on," she prompted. He went to a cupboard and took out a rolled canvas. He unwound it on the table in front of them.

"Hell!" exclaimed Daniel. "You didn't buy that did you?"

"It is worth a lot of money to the man who wants it for his private collection."

"It's worth ten years as well."

"He's got plenty of money. He told me to offer you one hundred thousand pounds."

"I'll think about it."

"There is just one other thing,"

"Oh?"

"Well if you'll come through, I'll show you in the next room."

Daniel and Marietta stood up and followed him through a connecting door. "So this is where you bought your antiques, is it?" he asked her.

"Oh, all these are genuinely bought," Monsieur Diacre broke in. "There are bills of sale for them and everything. The painting is the only thing I have ever knowingly handled illegally."

"Really!" Daniel gazed at the cabinet of bronze and ivory figures in front of him. "A Lorenzl, a Chiparus, two Preiss, a Philippe and a Laurent," he summed them up. "A nice little collection."

"You certainly know your hobby, Mr. Carlisle."

"Looks like you know your trade as well," Daniel commented.

"Marietta told me about your obsession. They are all yours as well as the money if you can do the job."

"I'll let you know within two weeks. Marietta will know where to find you I presume."

"I'll be here in two weeks." They drank off their glasses and Daniel took hold of Marietta's arm.

"Thanks for the drink," he said politely. "We may be able to do a deal Monsieur Diacre."

Marietta seemed more subdued on the journey home. "You aren't sure are you?"

"No," Daniel said firmly. "I'm not."

"What is it?"

"Something seems wrong, that's all. How long have you known him?"

"A year or so. We got talking at an auction. I don't know him all that well really."

"How long has he had the farmhouse?"

"I don't know. I only found out he had it when I bought some porcelain off him three months ago."

"You bought the Poertzel off him?"

"Yes, but that was only one month ago."

"And that's when you discussed the painting?"

"No, a few days later."

"When did you mention I was a collector of those figures?"

"When I saw the Poertzel. No," she corrected herself, "rather, when he delivered it. That's when he mentioned the painting."

"Did you tell him you wanted the figure before he got it for you?"

"No, he had it there when I collected a piece of Meissen."

"Did you see the other figures?"

"No, none of them. What is wrong, Daniel?"

"He must have some good contacts to get all those together in just a few weeks, a porcelain man at that. It would have taken me a year of going around all the top salerooms in Europe to get that collection." He looked at Marietta. She glanced quickly at him and then back at the road.

"You don't trust him do you?"

"Not yet I don't, no."

"I'm sorry; it might have been a mistake."

"Let's not think about that for now," Daniel said and put his arm around her and squeezed hard. "I'll sort it out."

She smiled. "I know."

That evening, in bed, Daniel lay awake with his hands behind his head. Marietta leaned her elbow on his chest. "You're thinking about Diacre, aren't you?"

Daniel nodded.

"What exactly are you thinking?" she said, frowning.

"I'm thinking I have an idea." He lifted her chin with the tips of his fingers. "If I make a phone call or two can I stay a few more days?"

"You know you can stay as long as you wish," she said as her face lit up.

"No, I don't think that will be possible," he replied.

"Only a joke mon amour."

He stroked her face and smiled.

*****

Daniel had been able to make contact with the *Silver Ambassador* by Telex before he left New York. His instructions had been brief and precise. The captain already knew he had to pick up the cargo at Cape Town and proceed to Bombay. Daniel gave him instructions what to do when he arrived. He had one message to broadcast and then had to wait until he was contacted. The message had been received and understood.

2nd September.

Shyam Khan headed out to the Arabian Sea. He had bargained well to hire the launch so cheaply. As he sat at the stern watching other boats and launches coming to and going from Gateway of India as they rounded the tip of the peninsular, he smiled at the thought of returning home under such different circumstances to those under which he left. As an eight year old child he had moved to America with his father who had been offered work in his profession as a doctor with a weekly wage more than he could earn in a year in India. But when Shyam was thirteen years old his father was killed in a road accident. It had left him, as the eldest boy of three, to go out into the world and make a wage to keep his mother and his brothers. He'd never had the chance to follow in his father's footsteps. Bombay is a place apart from the rest of India with a polyglot population of every different Indian sect living and trading in harmony. The sight of the women in their brightly coloured chiffon and silk saris and cholis reminded him of his mother. She still wore the same style of Indian clothes she had worn in Bombay so many years ago. She'd lived to a ripe old age and owed much to Shyam, who was now in his fifties, for having been able to make his own way in the strange American world. But it hadn't been so strange to him. Wheeling and dealing is part of Bombay culture as much as maritime trade. He'd been steeped in it for eight years. It was an ideal training background for survival in New York.

The launch chugged steadily out to sea leaving the ancient bristling urban seaport, with its modern high rise buildings, vanishing over the horizon into the evening dusk. Shyam held up a small radio receiver and pointed the aerial out across the ocean plane. As he moved it in a sweeping motion a red light flashed on and then off, and then on again as he adjusted the direction. A small ship is hard to find in a large ocean in darkness without a guiding radio beam. Now it would be easy. He ordered the skipper to pull alongside the *Silver Ambassador*. He did so with ease in the becalmed waters. Two ropes were thrown down to tie her and a ladder uncoiled and fell onto the deck. Everything was ready. It took less than three minutes to hoist Daniel's crate to the launch, secure it under canvas, and cast off. No ships in sight, no aircraft. Just two ships that passed in the night.

5th September.

Daniel met Shyam in a busy Delhi car park. Shyam had driven from Bombay with the crate in the back of an old Ford Transit van. He telephoned Daniel at the hotel and he arrived in a taxi twenty minutes later. Daniel glanced in the back as he sat in beside his friend. "Had any problems?"

Shyam laughed. "Only a small puncture near Indore," he replied.

"Have you arranged everything?"

"Everything is ready."

"Right," Daniel said. "You stay with it until tomorrow morning. Then I'll pick it up."

Shyam handed him the ignition key as he got out of the Transit. Daniel put it in his pocket and walked over to the waiting taxi. "The *Oberoi Intercontinental*," he instructed the driver as he got in the back. The car sped away.

It was a magnificent hotel. He had only stayed there once before, years ago, but had always thought he would take the opportunity to stay there again when it arose. Now it had, and he made the most of it. He made a couple of local calls from his luxurious suite and then spent the rest of the day by the swimming pool. In the early evening he went for a ride in a taxi, located an address, and returned without calling. He was up and had breakfast early the following morning. It was the hottest place he'd been that year, and after taking a cold shower, he dressed in a thin cotton shirt and slacks to combat the heat. It was right what the Indians said about the English, he thought, 'Only mad dogs and Englishmen go out in the mid-day sun.' The Indians had more sense. They took it easy during the hottest part of the day and stayed in the shade. Even in the morning it was searing. But Daniel seemed fully relaxed as he left the hotel and took a taxi back to the car park. The Transit was still there, the steel-bound crate inside. He paid off the taxi, took out his key, opened the van and started the engine.

"At least he got one that starts all right," Daniel grinned. Shyam tended to be a bit lax on things like that, but he was one man he could trust to be loyal and carry out a plan to the best of his ability. And in India he was a bonus! He parked outside a hotel, went inside, and asked to borrow the telephone. He dialed a local number, chatted for five or more minutes, and then hung up and stepped outside. He leaned on the side of the Transit in the full glare of the sun and lit a cheap Burma Cheroot. He took his time smoking it, then, after tossing away the butt, looked at his watch got back in the van and drove north east. The route he took bypassed the centre of the city by leading him along the Upper Ridge Road. He'd had plenty of time to memorize the road map whilst lounging at the hotel and had no difficulty in reaching an empty looking house on Arya Samaj Road, the one he had visited the previous evening. It fitted the description that the voice on the other end of the telephone line had given him the previous day, but it still looked deserted.

He parked around the back, got out and walked up to the door. Before his hand could rap it more than twice, the door swung back wide, and in front of him, closing the gap that had been filled by the door, stood a giant of a man. The Indian was dressed in western style clothes and had a huge jaw that sagged open as he grinned a greeting to his caller. The skin around his bloodshot eyes crinkled as he spoke in near perfect English. "Come in Mr. Carlisle."

He stood back from the door, letting Daniel walk into a well lit interior ahead of him. It was a big house, one that must have belonged to a high ranking English official in the days of colonialism. But now, with the passing of time and the absence of servants and cheap labour, it had become a lifeless structure with none of the polish and veneer that had once adorned it. The great entrance hall resembled a cave more than a vestibule, the magnificent colours paled and grey, the doors dry and unpolished.

The Indian closed the outside door and opened one into a large room that must have been a library, for its walls were filled with empty, ornately carved shelves. It stood empty except for a large table and a trio of cane chairs. Daniel glanced around. A lifeless room, with a large shuttered window facing out to the front of the building. He had seen the shutter the night before. The whole house had an empty ring to it as the Indian spoke.

"Lal," he said without raising his voice. A connecting door opened and two more Indians entered, one small and hairy like a chimpanzee, and one equally as big as the leader, possibly bigger, a gorilla, with a shaved head. They also donned western clothes. Both stepped into the room as lightly as ballet dancers, displaying their fitness and agility unashamedly, and both held small sub-machineguns. Daniel recognised them instantly. Ingrams, Model 10. He'd moved a few of those in his time.

"I apologise for the inconvenience, but we have to be very careful," said his host. "My two men will search you," he said directly in a matter of fact tone. No 'please,' or 'I'm sorry but,' but just as if he had said, 'My men will take your coat.'

Without another word the smaller of the two guards frisked Daniel.

"He's clean," he concluded.

"Ah, now we can trust you a little more," laughed his host. "Bring in the crate," he ordered the guards.

Daniel tossed the van keys to the chimp and they both placed their guns on the table and marched out leaving their leader standing between Daniel and their weapons. A couple of minutes later they returned, one at each end of the crate. The big man held his end out in one hand as if it were a tea cup, the smaller man struggled to heave his end of it up as they placed it onto the table. Their leader checked it carefully. The pre-arranged seals were unbroken.

"Please take a seat," he gestured. Daniel didn't argue. Two of them at least looked as though they could pull his arms and legs off like a rag puppet, not withstanding the Ingrams. At eleven and a half inch long, with stock retracted, Ingrams are a deadly gun at close quarters, that can empty its thirty six round magazine in less than three seconds on fully automatic. He sat in the cane chair next to the window.

The smaller man produced a pair of cutters from his pocket and proceeded to release the metal straps. The giant guard took out a large clasp knife, eased the wood lid from the body of the crate to give him a finger hold and then ripped it off as easily as Daniel would have opened a box of chocolates. Daniel couldn't see inside the crate from his sitting position, and under the circumstances he didn't feel at all tempted to stand up and take a look. He crossed his legs, folded his arms and sat patiently as their leader moved forward to see what was in his Pandora's Box. His bloodshot eyes lit up as they fell upon the contents, gleaming like two rubies in his parchment covered face. It obviously held his objects of desire. Or did it?

"Haggh!" he bellowed. Daniel resisted the temptation to jump up and make a run for it. A bellow like that meant something was wrong in his part of the world, and then only with a caged lion with its testicles caught in the gate. He watched the leader's face for more tell-tale signs, but oddly, he was still grinning. An evil grin Daniel thought. "Haaah." It was more prolonged now.

What the hell was wrong with him? He sounded more satisfied this time, like a gorilla that had just suffered the pain of a long awaited orgasm. The other two men just gazed into the box, mesmerized by the contents. Then, in an expression of total satisfaction, the leader sighed as if relieved it was all over. "Hah, Drim Balhi has it." He clasped his hands at either side of the box and nodded his head, making his huge jaw oscillate. "I'm the only person to possess CHEF outside of the United States, I," he said, pointing to his barrel chest and bursting into an uncontrollable fit of raucous laughter. Daniel gave a sigh of relief. It was what he'd expected it to be. Thank God!

Drim Balhi went out of the room chuckling to himself. He neither looked at his men nor at Daniel. He closed the door behind him and picked up the hand-piece of an ancient black telephone. He dialed a long number and almost immediately someone answered.

"Yes?" the disembodied voice said curtly.

"I have it."

"Is he there?"

"I have him also."

"You know what to do." It wasn't a question. "I'll see to it right away." He heard the line go dead and hung up.

Daniel watched the two guards as they resealed the crate. He was beginning to feel that they were talking about him. He'd never picked up much of the Indian language and it wouldn't have helped much for they spoke one of the many regional dialects of the south. Most inconsiderate and rude he thought. Drim Balhi came back into the room looking as cool and unconcerned as he had when he'd left. Obviously nothing had gone on beyond the door to alter his demeanour.

The two guards turned to face him and he gave them an almost indistinguishable nod. To Daniel the nod seemed harmless enough. It was the way the huge jaw sagged that convinced him things were not going to go as smoothly as he'd have liked.

"Stand," said the big shaven headed leader. Daniel understood that. Drim Balhi spoke good English. He did as he was ordered, supporting himself on the back of the cane chair.

"Right gentlemen," Daniel announced. "If you're all happy, I'll leave now."

Drim Balhi shook his head. "No, I'm afraid not."

"Nothing wrong with the merchandise is there?" asked Daniel.

"Nothing."

"And you've informed Vlatsov?"

"Who?" Drim Balhi grinned.

"I see," Daniel said quietly. Drim Balhi sensed Daniel had more courage than he'd first thought. He'd expected outright panic when he faced the little Englishman with a fait accompli, but instead, Daniel just leaned back against the bare window sill and sighed. He looked towards the door expectantly. No way out there. "You have no intention of letting me leave, have you?"

He didn't wait for an answer. The small guard was moving towards the table to pick up his Ingram. Daniel knew that would be the end of his contract. It had all been very neatly done. Before the guard could grasp the sub-machinegun, Daniel picked up the cane chair, and with all his strength put into a backward swing, smashed it through the shutters behind him. He knew it would take a trained man less than a second to aim the gun and push off the safety lock at the same time. He swung the chair forward towards the three men to throw them off balance. The gorilla fielded it like a professional footballer tossing it lightly to one side, and rushed forward to catch Daniel in the same manner, in his huge hand, as Daniel turned and threw himself headlong out of the window. A hand with a grip of a boa constrictor grabbed his ankle making him swing in an arc against the outside sill and dangle, head down, on the sun-scorched grass outside. Effortlessly the arm attached to the hand hoisted him up and inwards. The fall had dazed him and it was more by a panic reflex than design that his free foot smashed under the big man's nose. If he could get out of the house he knew he'd be safe, and he kicked again landing his heel in a soulless eye. The grip eased a little but he was almost back inside. With every ounce of strength left in his body he kicked again but lower this time. He heard a pained grunt as his foot landed square on the Indian's testicles, and Daniel felt himself falling backwards again, the heat of the mid-day sun beating down on his face. He was dazed again.

The voices of shouting and laughing in Hindi, or some dialect like it, had no meaning to Daniel as hands grabbed him and helped him to his feet. Gradually his vision cleared and he found himself facing the gorilla that had so nearly dragged him back through the window to a certain death. He was leaning out and gesturing to the six armed policemen as if he couldn't understand how it had happened. Of course he'd done his best to save Daniel from his fall, Daniel could imagine him explaining.

"Are you all right sir?" asked one of those that had helped him to his feet, in broken English.

"Quite," Daniel replied and walked shakily to the road. "Could you help me to my vehicle?"

Two police officers escorted him around the back of the building and saw him seated safely in the driver's seat. "Thank you," he said and drove away. The six policemen jumped in a Landrover and followed. Daniel could still hear them laughing.

As the distance between the mad Indians in the house and himself got greater, so he regained his composure, and he let a faint smile trickle across his lips. He drove the Transit to the same car park from which he had picked it up.

"You certainly took your time!" Daniel shouted as a police officer walked towards him.

"Just about right I thought," said Shyam as he slapped Daniel on the shoulder.

"You were supposed to bloodywell knock on the door." He was still shouting.

"Daniel boy," Shyam laughed. "You don't think I would have come all the way over from New York and dressed up in fancy dress with my cousins, if I wasn't going to make sure that I got the other half of what you owe me, do you?"

"I sometimes wonder why I bother with you Shyam, I really do."

"Perhaps it's because when it comes down to your real friends you have very good taste."

"Pillock!"

*****

Daniel wished he could have stayed another week touring the ancient city from the sumptuous suite in the *Oberoi,* but it wasn't to be. He knew he'd been betrayed. It wasn't the first time someone had tried to stop him carrying on his business, but this had been someone he'd dealt with before. If Vlatsov wanted him out of the way then there was more reason for it than just growing tired of their business relationship. It would be a necessary part of his plan. He never did anything that wasn't planned down to the last tiny detail, and Daniel's demise was to have been one of those details. He knew he was still in mortal danger. The sooner he got onto his own territory the safer he would feel.

The departure lounge at Palam was a busy bustling throng of Orientals. Daniel was alert and scanned every face that looked towards him. "Have a safe journey," Shyam told Daniel as they shook hands at the doors.

Take care old friend," he replied. "See you back in New York." He paused for a moment. "Thanks," he added.

"What are old friends for?" Shyam gestured.

"I'll do the same for you and your brothers someday."

Shyam laughed. "You have helped us, remember? And besides, I'd dress up as a dancing girl for the money you have paid us. I am just glad you knew what you were doing."

"Calculated chance, Shyam. I'm only glad that one of your cousins is a genuine policeman."

"He wasn't so sure it would work."

"They wouldn't risk a showdown with the police if they have more important plans in mind. They'll bide their time and try and get me later."

Daniel boarded the flight to Paris. He knew he should get straight back to New York and the safety of Malterswood. But there were plans to be made and things to organise. He couldn't do them where he was. The perfidious behaviour of his client had seen to that, and despite his tight security, he would be looking over his shoulder all the time in New York. A week in France was the next best thing. He still had unfinished business to take care of in Toulouse. It meant spending a few more days with Marietta. It was an easy choice to make.

CHAPTER 5

6th September

It was plain to Marvin Belk that Janine was carrying out her perfunctory duties satisfactorily. She kept herself apart from Edward during the day, only going to his bedroom in the evening. Whenever he checked, he found Janine back in her own room in the morning. She was obviously doing her job, no more no less, now that Edward had realised that she had been bought solely to stop his mind from wandering off the task that lay ahead. He, too, was beginning to realise the worth of having his own paid room service rather than having to make frequent trips to the local brothel. It made good sense not to be seen out and about until his face had healed and he had got his new identity set up.

Marvin smiled at the success of his own foresight. A small hiccup here and there but he had sorted it out. "Good morning Edward," he said jovially. "I see you have sorted out your emotional problems."

"I've been in the desert too damned long, that's the trouble."

"Yes," Marvin said with a chuckle, "these mirages can be real deceptive until you get up close."

"I eventually managed to see what I was looking at," Edward said and sat at the table. A servant appeared from nowhere and placed a huge bowl in front of him.

"Got to keep them in their place. Women are all right if they are kept in bed where they belong."

The servant, a man in his late twenties Edward guessed, unless he was suffering from his own geriatric looks syndrome, placed a choice of cereals in front of him on the table.

"When do we get down to the business of my new identity," Edward asked as he filled his bowl with corn flakes.

"Plenty of timefor that Edward my boy. Plenty of time; no rush. You only had your operation a month ago."

"My face has healed fine. Hardly a mark shows."

"That's true. You heal well," Marvin nodded.

"When do I have to fulfill the rest of my bargain then?" He poured on some iced milk. He would have to keep his cool at all times.

"I've got a man coming to see you tomorrow."

Edward hadn't expected such an early meeting. He thought for a moment. "Is he foreign?" he asked.

"Yes. Does that bother you?"

"Not in the least. What nationality is he?"

"Bulgarian."

Hell! The Bulgarian Peoples' Army: the puppet assassins of the KGB. His face remained unchanged. "I see," he commented calmly after swallowing a mouthful of half-chewed food. "So it's going to the Soviet Block."

Marvin nodded. He had to tell him sometime.

"You do realise that they will want me to go with them?"

"Possibly, but it would only be for a short time, I'm sure." He didn't even sound convinced himself. Edward had guessed all the answers days ago. He just wanted Marvin to spell it out. There was still some talking to do, some creases to iron out. "I don't mind that so much," he said.

Marvin smiled. "Good."

"Only I'll need two things."

"Oh what?"

"I want Janine to go with me. I know what she is, but I would like to have her as long as I can. I need to keep my emotions balanced when I'm using my mind."

"It's no good having a lap dog and having to go visit it in the kennel, eh?" Marvin bantered "That's easily arranged."

Edward doubted that it would have been that easy. Marvin would have been unlikely to be able to make her keep on with her duties unless he had some control over her. She had already realised what sort of a hole she had got herself into, and was unlikely to enter into such an agreement again. That would mean being a prisoner by acquiescence.

"And what is the other thing?"

I want to go to the bank and transfer the money you say you have put aside for me out of it." He looked directly into Marvin's eyes. Cold eyes he thought. Their shade of blue made them look like chips of glacier ice. "It's my insurance, my pension, if you like, that I know I have when it's all over. Something to fall back on."

Marvin grinned. It was the sort of grin that bathing beauties put on when they are in a competition, a buoyant mask of mirth covering what only they and God know lay beneath. It didn't give anything away.

"If I am leaving," Edward continued, "then I'll require the balance at the same time. I don't want to have to come back to collect it later."

Marvin still grinned. He must have known that Edward wasn't stupid enough to come back and ask for it.

"I'll also require all the money withdrawn to be in cash."

"Well that's more difficult," Marvin said, standing up from the table. "You see, my customers won't pay unless they get what they want."

"Bit of a catch twenty two really." Edward remarked. "They don't trust you, you don't trust me and I don't trust them." He was careful to say that he didn't trust Marvin either.

"But that's the point. It's all about trusting one another," Marvin replied.

"They can afford to be trusting if they have the goods. Once they have me then you'll never know for sure what I tell them. And to tell the truth, I have no intention of turning up to tell you."

"Ah, you don't trust me either."

"It isn't that, so much as when I disappear I don't want *anybody* to know where I am. I need the temporary ID that you can fix me up with, but I sure as hell won't keep it once I get my hands on my wages."

Marvin laughed. This time it seemed like genuine amusement. "Edward, I am beginning to like you. We'll have to see what we can do."

"I can make the deal a lot easier."

"How?"

"To enable you to get your money out of them, I will outline everything I can give them in detail. If they agree I am worth it then they can pay you and you can pay me. Then they can take me somewhere nice and sunny and I'll spill my heart out."

*****

Edward was surprised when he saw the Bulgarian. He was nothing like he had expected. To look at them, he and the three men with him might have passed for American citizens. But only two would have passed on the test of fluency; Vlatsov and his interpreter. The others, a huge man, obviously a bodyguard, and a frail man who reminded him of his former self, obviously an expert in research sciences, only spoke broken English. It was necessary to have an expert there, for only an expert could distinguish fact from fantasy in much of the outline he had prepared. It was obvious he was on hand to check Edward's story. So they must have already planned to put their money up front.

No one introduced Vlatsov by name as they all gathered at a table in the centre of a study-cum-library at the back of the villa, but Edward knew who the one was that was doing the dealing. Marvin spoke to none of the others. He chaired at the head of the table. Edward sat on the right next to the thin scientist, Vlatsov sat opposite with the big guy. He made a mental note as to how the two big men opposite him wore practically the same clothes. Good job they aren't women meeting at a dinner party, he thought.

"Well gentlemen," Marvin began, He spoke to Edward first. "I've outlined your proposals and they've agreed to assess your value at this meeting."

"I am not worth a penny. It's what I know that is valuable," he corrected.

"Quite," Marvin placated but Edward had made his point. He was dispensable once they had got what they wanted. It suddenly crossed Edward's mind that Marvin hadn't agreed to his plan. It had already been his intention to carry out the exchange in this manner. He might have saved a little money had Edward not stuck out for his share in his hand, but basically, his plastic surgery had been expedited for two reasons. First, his new face was to inspire him with confidence that Marvin was doing all he could to keep his end of the bargain stuck seven and a half months ago in Portland. Secondly it served the purpose of getting Edward out of the country. That is why the meeting had been put off until he was about ready to leave. He couldn't logically explain his new face as being in any way intended to set him up in a new way of life with a permanent and new identity. That was far too risky for them. He should have seen through it all long ago.

Vlatsov opened the negotiations. "Mr. Taylor," he said plainly and with little inflexion in his voice. It sounded like he was reading out a statement. "The position is quite clear. We are here to make a purchase. The price we are to pay has already been agreed, with one condition. You have to be able to outline what you will tell us once you have been paid."

"Where is the detail expected to be produced?"

"We will escort you to a place where suitable facilities can be set up for you to complete your side of the bargain."

"You aren't answering the question. You are stating the obvious."

"It will be outside this country."

"And what facilities have you set aside for my safe return?"

Vlatsov stayed cool. The scientist shuffled some sheets of paper in front of him. Marvin might just have been showing a slight touch of anxiety, but Edward wasn't sure.

"Provided you have a place to go to, you will be taken there. We will do all we can to make your trip as pleasant as possible and we will endeavour to leave you with such identification you require." He sounded almost convincing. Marvin's facial muscles relaxed.

"Then I'll tell you a little about the work I was involved in." Edward handed out two sheets of paper; one to the interpreter and one to Vlatsov. "Here's a list I have prepared for you to study at your leisure. You will know, of course that in 1969 the then President of the united Stated, President Nixon, abandoned production of all chemical and biological weapons."

There was no outward response by his audience. "Well that's true," he continued, "but he did not abandon research. Research into new gasses, research into new viruses, and research into antidotes and protective clothing." There was still no response. The interpreter babbled away in the background. The scientist just kept nodding that he understood.

"I can give you no information regarding biological research. I am a chemist basically. I can give you some information regarding chemical weapons but it is not likely to be up to date, and you are likely to have been in receipt of more up to date information from your agents on the university campuses.

"So what can I tell you? Well I can tell you the exact refining data on the product I brought out with me. You will no doubt have had it analyzed, but if you are unlucky it could take you two years to discover how the chemical bonds are produced."

The scientist was writing in his notebook with a pencil.

"I can tell you about two new psychedelics."

The scientist scribbled some more.

"I can also tell you who I was working with and what part they played in the developments that I was working on and I can tell you what part I played in theirs. I can produce formulae and procedures for producing all the items listed on that piece of paper. I am prepared to write out just one for you here so that you can decide on my truthfulness. Any one that you pick except the one for which you have the product." He knew that the U.S.S.R. had data on two if the listed items already.

The scientist listened to the interpreter as he read out the list. He nodded, circled one item and passed it over to Edward. Edward ignored it.

"I can also tell you what research is scheduled for the future and which universities are likely to be involved in it or to be supplying research staff." He pulled the piece of paper forward and looked at what had been circled. Bingo! The scientist had circled one that he knew he could verify. Edward picked up his own pencil and began writing on his own sheet of paper. It took him fifteen minutes for him to finish, during which he filled four full sheets. No one spoke as they watched him, transfixed by the speed at which he worked, never pausing for thought nor lifting his eyes off the paper. He wrote vigorously like a student in an examination, emitting a continuous flow of writing and mathematical formulae. When he had finished, he pushed it over to the scientist, stood up and walked out of the room. "Let me know your decision as soon as you can," he said and closed the door behind him.

*****

"Well, good news Edward," Marvin said as he walked into the orchard. "They've bought it."

Edward looked up from the lie-low. He preferred the orchard to the side of a swimming pool for sunning his body when he wasn't picking apples to eat or plants to brighten up his room. Besides, Janine would be by the pool. Marvin noticed that they rarely spoke to each other even when they met in the house. She no longer fussed over him. She left that to the servants. Well everyone to their own jobs, he thought. Keeps things on a proper employer/employee relationship. "Good," Edward said, turning over to give his back a burning.

"They want you to move out tomorrow. Do you still want to take the woman with you?"

"Yes, I suppose so," Edward replied lethargically, to the grass.

"I can pay her off if you like."

"Knock it off what you owe me if you like."

"No need for that," said Marvin. "She has served her purpose."

"The Bulgarians will continue to pay her if they think it will keep me sweet. They'll have to keep my mind on my work."

"You're a changed man, Edward. You've toughened up a lot in these last few days."

"It's a pity I didn't have some backbone a few years ago then," he replied, knowing that he wouldn't have let himself get into such a tight hole to start with.

"We're going to drive into town this afternoon. Which bank had you in mind to go to?"

"Any. But there's just one thing."

"What?"

"I want my cash and I want it so that I can put it in a safety deposit box. I want it in large notes drawn from your own bank and I want it in an air-flight bag."

"It's all arranged, I keep telling you."

"A driver's license will do for identity, provided you give your name for a reference. You know the sort of thing: you've known me for years and I am staying with you and all that."

"You don't want to tell them we're married or anything, do you?" Marvin still had a sense of humour even when he was dealing with an irksome little shit.

"What's the matter? Don't you like somebody else doing the thinking?" Edward goaded.

"Now you just see here," Marvin said as he tipped Edward off the lie-low. His patience was wearing a little thin. It wasn't so much a show of anger as a show of strength. "You'll get nothing if you aren't careful. I've given you a long line up to now so be careful I don't start hauling it in. he waived his finger as Edward rolled against a tree. Over the past few weeks with easy living, his body had filled out to the normal shape of a man. It cushioned him nicely.

"Hardly necessary to emphasize which end of the dung fork I've got, Marvin," Edward said with a grin. "The Bolshies want me more than ever now. They won't like it if I get hurt. There's something on that list that they don't know about. Something worth ten times what you have been paid."

"Oh yeah? Well you don't know how much I've made out of this deal indirectly so don't over-rate yourself."

"So do I get that reference or not?"

"Sure. Anything for a quiets life." Marvin shrugged. He held out his hand and pulled Edward to his feet. "What name do you want on the license?"

Edward thought for a moment. "Matthew T. Roland. T for Thomas." Yes that sounded just fine. Matthew was his middle name and Janine had suggested the surname. Then she had insisted on adding the T for Thomas to make it complete.

*****

Edward didn't go up to the villa for his mid-day meal. Instead he went to his room. He stayed away from Marvin, away from the Bulgarian and away from Janine, but he was ready to go when the time came.

A large red Mercedes rolled up through the open gates and stopped below the steps. The driver stopped there and waited for everyone to assemble. It was the bodyguard's job to act as chauffeur. Edward sat in the back with Vlatsov at one side and Janine at the other. Marvin took the front passenger seat.

It was three o'clock when they got to the front of The Western States Bank. The bodyguard stayed in the car with Janine. Edward, Marvin and Vlatsov went inside. A man standing in an office doorway stepped back and let Marvin go into the room before closing the door behind him. The others stood and waited. A couple of minutes later Marvin emerged with a Pan-Am flight bag. He handed it to Edward. "Now what," he asked.

"I'd like to take it to another bank." He put his hand inside the bag and felt at the money. It felt good. He slipped a note off a wad and screwed it into the palm of his hand before withdrawing his fist and zipping up the bag.

"Jesus," Marvin exclaimed. "Right, come on." They all filed back out. "Which?"

"That one," Edward said and pointed to the bank next door. He carried on walking and went through the front door and walked straight up to the desk.

"Yes sir?" the clerk asked politely.

"Can I leave this in a safety deposit box? I am going away for a few months and I have put all my valuables together to be stored in a safe place."

"Have you an account here?"

"No, but I would like to open one with this." He opened his hand, unfolded a crumpled one thousand dollar bill and placed it on the counter.

"You'll have to fill in some details first, sir."

Edward handed him his driver's license and introduced Marvin as his referee. "He lives locally."

"Fine," the clerk said amiably and handed Edward the application form.

Edward thought of his assumed name, Matthew T. Roland. He scribbled as many answers to the questions as he could and pushed the form forward across the counter.

"Won't be a moment, sir," the clerk said and turned away.

Edward held his breath.

"Right sir. If you'd like to come this way our security man will take you to the vault." A man looking more like a customer than a security guard, dressed in casual slacks and a loose-fitting open necked shirt opened a door towards a pair of steel gates. The guard unlocked them, they both stepped inside the vault and he locked the gates behind them. He produced a key and unlocked one box in a wall of boxes, slid it out and carried it to a small cubicle. He placed it on a low shelf, opened the lid and stepped away.

"There you are sir," he said. "When you have placed what you want to keep safe then close the lid and I'll do the rest."

Edward unzipped the bag and tipped in the cash. He flicked through a few wads just to feel what it was like to be rich, and then peeled off ten one thousand dollar bills. He put them in his back pocket and placed the bag in the container on top of the money. He closed the lid and nodded for the security man to come over. He watched as the guard lifted up the box and placed it in its slot in the wall. He handed Edward the key.

"Thank you," Edward said and followed the man back out of the vault. "What if I lose the key?" he asked.

"You'd have to prove your identity. You will have to match the signature with or without a key. Have you made a note of the number?"

"7948."

"Good. But it is always best if you don't misplace the key," the guard said with a pleasant smile. "Have a nice holiday."

"I will," Edward replied and turned to leave. Marvin stood up from a seat by the door and they went outside together. The host looked like it was a relief that it was all over.

Marvin said a few words to Vlatsov through the back window of the car and walked away. He'd done his part and been paid. Taylor was the Bulgarians' pigeon now.

Edward got back in on the back seat next to Janine and slammed the door as the motor cruised away. "Where to now?" he asked.

"We have tickets for the next flight to Paris. From there we will fly to Sofia."

"I suppose you have all my necessary documents."

"Yes."

"Not mine," Janine said coldly. "I wasn't told we were going abroad."

"We have papers and a passport for you also."

"I'm not going to Europe unless I use my own passport. I intend travelling in my own name."

"Have you got a passport?"

"At my apartment. We can call in for it on the way to the airport."

"Then we had better stop and collect it," Vlatsov stated impatiently.

Janine directed the way and they soon arrived outside a tall apartment block. "Victor will accompany you," Vlatsov stated as he got out of the car. Janine stood up with her elbow out for the bodyguard to take hold, and smiled. Hesitatingly, he placed his hand on her arm and they walked together up to her front door and went inside.

"Pity you feel like you need to be bothered with her," Vlatsov stated bluntly. You can have as many women as you like where we are going."

"Nobody told me that," Edward said, showing interest.

"It would save us a lot of problems if you changed your mind about her."

Edward knew it would. "Would she be all right? I mean you wouldn't..."

"We aren't interested in her. She has been told nothing by us. Have you told her anything?"

"No," Edward lied convincingly. But he knew that they knew she had seen Edward have the plastic surgery. He knew that they would take no chances. "Then she can go as and when she pleases."

They waited another five minutes. Vlatsov began to drum his fingers impatiently. Five more minutes passed. He was about to speak when he saw the bodyguard running towards the Mercedes. There was a dialogue in what was probably colloquial Bulgarian and Vlatsov banged his fist against the dashboard. He thought for a moment and then relaxed back into his seat. "Well," he said to Edward as he forced a smile. "It seems like you will have to have a new girl."

From their reactions Edward could tell that they hadn't intended letting Janine just walk away whenever she pleased. She and Edward had planned it. The only way she could escape being silenced was to pretend she needed to go to her apartment. There was already an escape route from the ladies room in case a client became dangerous. It was an occupational hazard. She had long gone before Victor realised that she had done a runner.

Edward knew that they would send somebody to find her and silence her; she wouldn't have much time to make her escape even with the money he had passed to her. But it was the only chance she was going to get. One down and one to go. He knew that they wouldn't let him out of their sight now. If he had to go the toilet then Vlatsov would go and sit on his lap!

"When we get to the airport," Vlatsov explained, "we shall be travelling on diplomatic passports. There will be no searches, no questions. All they will do is check your credentials and then let us pass. You need not do or say anything, understand?"

"Yes," Edward said. "Just as well really. I never could speak your language."

He was going to co-operate. Good!

"Every effort will be made to make your stay comfortable." He was trying hard to make things run as smoothly as possible. It struck Edward that Vlatsov was not as used to moving people as to having them killed. It must be very prestigious to have obtained a top research scientist with precise information about things that the Politburo had not heard of. They would be well pleased with him, but he couldn't fathom why Vlatsov had insisted on his bringing what he did from the Research Centre. They would have been soon able to match it and more once they got him to reveal the formulae. He knew that once he had been wrung dry of all he knew he would be for an early grave anyway, especially when they found out that he knew nothing about some of the things he had listed on his piece of paper. The end wouldn't be pleasant. But the deception had been necessary to keep everybody happy. Vlatsov was happy to pay Marvin, Marvin was happy to pay Janine and to put up with his demands for cash, and most important, it meant that he was out of Marvin's reach.

A shiver went down his backbone as the car cruised silently towards the airport.

The airport was very busy and Victor was left in charge of keeping Edward under guard while Victor made several calls. More than likely he was setting up some kind of search for Janine, another call to perhaps bring more men in to guard Edward. He wasn't sure but he didn't have much time if he was going to give them the slip. When Vlatsov did eventually return, Edward asked if he could possibly have a tea while they waited for their flight.

"Why not?" Vlatsov said joyfully. Something had definitely cheered him up. They went to the cafeteria and sat at a table while Victor brought some cups of coffee and a plate stacked with ring doughnuts, suggestively penetrated by sticks of chocolate flake. Edward hadn't realised how hungry he was. His mouth watered at the sight of food. "Help yourself," he said as Victor put down the plate.

"No thanks, I'm not really hungry," Edward said. "A cup of tea will be just fine."

Victor shrugged his heavy shoulders and began to demolish the pile. Edward watched and stirred his tea slowly and then he placed the cup to his lips. He sipped the hot liquid. Everybody seemed relaxed. He watched a pretty young waitress serving at the busy counter and the hustle bustle trains of people pass steadily by. God, don't let this be the last sight I have of earth, I've waited so long for freedom.

The plate was empty in front of him now all except a few chocolate crumbs. He licked his finger and absent-mindedly prodded at them, letting them stick before dabbing them on the tip of his tongue. They tasted like food in heaven should taste. He glanced at the two Bulgarians casually and at the same time, and quite un-noticed, he slipped a minute pellet under his tongue.

"You should have helped yourself," he could hear Vlatsov commenting. "Do you want Victor to get you anything?"

He shook his head, not daring to speak. God, let it be just right. He saw them looking at him strangely. Then came the pain; a dull ache in his chest as his heart began to falter. Everything was spinning. He couldn't breathe. He stood up and fell over the table sending cups and plates shattering to the floor, and then, with a last glance at the Bulgarian as they struggled to release his collar, all life left his eyes.

Vlatsov knelt over him and felt Edward's jugular. "What in God's name has happened to him?" he shouted as the whole place sucked in a crowd of onlookers. Victor moved them all back. He's dead," Victor announced.

"What's the matter?" the voice of a man sounded as he pushed his way through the crowd.

"He's had a heart attack," Vlatsov stated as he stood up. The man moved forward and felt Edward's throat. "Dead," he confirmed. "Do you two know him?"

Vlatsov shook his head grimly. His face had turned as white as Edward's. "No," he said. "We don't know him."

The man thumped Edward's chest a couple of times and opened his mouth so that he could administer artificial respiration. Somebody call an ambulance," he shouted as he positioned Edward's head backwards to clear the way to his trachea. He looked up and the two men had gone from the table.

"One's on its way," came a voice from the doorway.

The stranger lifted Edward's tongue to stop it falling back against his throat and removed a speck of food from under it before breathing carbon dioxide into Edward's lungs in an attempt to trigger a breathing reflex. He continued between CPR and mouth to mouth resuscitation until two men came with a stretcher. "Heart attack," he said to the paramedics. They placed an oxygen mask on Edward's face. Administered morphia to relive the heart muscle spasm and carried him out on a stretcher to a waiting ambulance.

"He's coming round," Edward heard the voice of a woman in the hazy background. His eyes were open but he could only see a misty outline of what should have been the sharp features of a Japanese nurse. Her face was angular, her skin like Jersey cream and her eyes would have melted granite but all Edward could see was the shadow of her short black hair and a halo where her face should be. She mopped his brow.

Edward moved his fingers and toes. No paralysis. He'd survived. His calculations had been right; only just right but right enough. His days alone in his room had paid off; his collecting a selection of plants from the vast gardens that surrounded the villa, his compounding them and making an extract from them. It was a common drug, one that he had discovered by accident a long time ago at the Research Centre and which affected him the same way. By an allergic reaction it had dropped his blood pressure, starved his brain and his heart muscles of oxygen and had almost killed him then. His colleagues had thought him dead until, lying on the floor of the laboratory for half an hour with a white coat over his face, pending his removal to the medical centre, for an autopsy, his blood pressure gradually raised again. A pulse was detected soon after he stirred and he was up and about as if nothing had happened two and a half hours later.

It had taken all his knowledge and skill to make the tiny poisonous pellet that would emit the substance into his bloodstream via the sensitive blood vessels beneath his tongue. It had been an act of sheer genius to calculate the flow from the pellet and an act of god that Janine had been able to get her friend to arrive at the airport and follow Edward to the cafeteria to remove the pellet in time to prevent carrying on the process of killing Edward. She had described Vlatsov and Victor in great detail.

The cataleptic state induced by the poison had passed now. He took a deep breath. Please God don't let me have awakened in Sophia.

"You'll be all right now," the face said in a West Coast accent. "Just you rest and take it easy,"

Had he any choice, he wondered. "Where am I?"

"Mount Bright Nursing Home."

She'd done it. Janine had got him away! No hospital, no newspaper reports, just as she had said she could. She had some influential connections whatever her trade. He wondered if they had been customers or just friends. Not that any of that mattered.

His sight began to clear, "Hi," smiled the nurse. "I'm Leony."

"Hi," Edward whispered, his throat parched. "How long have I been out?"

"From the time of the attack, about four hours Mr. Taylor."

Four hours. That long? Well at least he was all right now. Janine would be on her way to New York by now. She had a friend in Grey Oaks, a place to stay until he could meet her there. He could collect his key, wait a few weeks and then, together, they could fly over to San Francisco. Collect the money and go anywhere they liked.

"Can you get me my clothes?" Edward sat up. His heart thumped erratically, his head throbbed. His vision was blurred again.

"You must rest. You are lucky to be alive."

"I'll be all right now," he replied as he held himself steady by bracing his hands against the mattress. The nurse left the room quickly. A man in a white coat came in and placed a hypodermic needle to his arm. Edward felt a faint prick as it entered the muscle and two strong arms helped him lie back against the pillow.

"That's better," the man said.

Edwards's heart slowed down as he relaxed and let the sedative take its course. His mind wandered, thinking about the Research Centre, then about Janine, and then the nurse. What was her name? Oh yes, a pretty name, Leony, that's right. She had a nice velvet voice as well. What was it she had said? About four hours, Mr. Taylor. A beautiful voice. About four hours Mr. Taylor. Mr. Taylor!

He tried to sit up. He couldn't. The sedative was already taking effect. He had to get up. He had to tell them. He could hear himself shouting but no sound came from his throat. A he fell deeper and deeper into sleep his voice rang in his ears. "My name is Roland, Matthew T. Ro…l…a…n…d."

CHAPTER 6

2.30p.m. 9th September.

It was a relief to see the welcome smile of Marietta as she leaned against her car. She held out her hand and Daniel took it in his. He pulled her forward and gave her a long kiss.

"My, you have missed me!" she said in her strong accent after catching her breath. "It has been less than a week."

"Yes I've missed you," he said and walked around to the passenger door of the Porche. It had been five days. Three in Delhi and two back in Paris. He'd booked into *The Napoleon*, not the most modern of hotels, but a place with a charm and pulchritude that set it apart from many others. He still had the feeling that he was being watched, a feeling that had not left him since his previous stay in Paris, but he felt safer by not appearing in the same hotel and the same places. He wanted to keep a low profile the best he could, but deep down he knew that there would be no release from the relentless pursuit of his enemies. Sooner or later Pyotre Vlatsov's men would find him; enemy number one. In New York, the mafia would be waiting to take his business over; enemy number two. But the third enemy was harder to come to terms with; fear. There was a dark and malignant threat linked with being followed by unseen eyes, a sinister omen of things to come, neither advancing nor retreating, just lingering there in the background ready to strike. It brought with it an uncertainty that gnawed away at his confidence. He could take steps to avoid enemies one and two but he couldn't fight what he couldn't see.

He arrived at the hotel in the early evening, had a meal in the hotel restaurant and spent the rest of his time alone in his room. He didn't emerge again until 9.00 the following morning. He had a good breakfast and then went to see Henri.

"Have you heard anything for me?" he asked as Henri worked on his trapezius.

"My friend Jules has been looking into these matters for you," he replied. "He told me that Monsieur Diacre has not been active in the antiques business for a long time. He sold his shop in Reims and bought a large mansion outside Versailles two years ago. Jules has not been able to trace any business that Diacre has transacted since, but he is still looking into the man's affairs. He has told me that he has a friend in the Tax Department who may be able to help." He dug his thumbs into Daniel's deltoids.

"How long before we get anything positive from him?"

"Is that not positive enough?"

"Up to now all he's found out is what Diacre hasn't been doing. I want to know what he has been doing, especially over this past year."

"You are not an easy man to please, Daniel."

"There is something wrong about that man and I want to know what it is. And I want to know just who is behind him, understand?"

"Of course, mon cher, but it cannot be easy or he would have found out by now. Jules is a very clever man, believe me."

"Okay, that'll do for now." He swung his legs off the bench and went to the sauna. "You know where I'll be after tomorrow, don't you?" he said to Henri as he dressed, then he left *Henri's* and walked slowly back to the hotel.

The streets were as busy and crowded as normal. Still, he felt he was being followed. He walked down a shaded side alley and stood in the black shadow of a doorway. Whoever it was behind him would have to follow him down there and Daniel would see him. He waited five minutes and nobody came past. He looked at the chain of pedestrians as they filed past in the sunlight of the maim street. Nothing. "Phew," he said with relief. He was getting too old for this kind of business. He was becoming obsessed.

He gave himself another five or six minutes before rejoining the crowd. He felt better now. He decided that he wasn't going to worry about it anymore.

"Well hello there," came a voice off to his left. Daniel turned his head. It took him a moment to pick out the body that went with the voice.

"Oh, hello. You're back in Paris again, are you?" He said it in an off-handed manner.

"Well don't sound too pleased about it, will you."

"No, I didn't mean it like that."

Anita grinned at him. "I know," she said as she linked arms with him. Are you staying *at Le Corbusier*?"

"No, I thought I'd have a change."

"Get away from Michele, heh?" she jibed.

"In a way." Daniel tried to sound convincing. "What a coincidence though, bumping into you."

"Oh, on my way to book in at the hotel. Which one are you staying at?"

"*The Napoleon*." He had to tell her. "I'm leaving tomorrow or the day after, though."

"So am I. Back to the States for me." She walked along with him as if they were old friends. "What is it like at *The Napoleon*?" she asked to break the silence.

"Oh, you'd like it," he said and then wished he had held his tongue.

"Good."

That was it. She accompanied him to the hotel and booked a single room. Daniel noticed that she had no luggage, but didn't mention it. She would probably have it sent round from *Le Corbusier* later. She joined him for a light lunch and then he made his excuses to leave. "Well I must go. Got to see a man about a dog."

"A what?"

"Just an expression," Daniel explained. Will you be at dinner tonight?"

"Do ducks quack?"

Daniel smiled and left her sitting at the dinner table and went out. He had hoped to spend some time in his room but he knew that he would not have been alone if he had told Anita. She was persistent. He awarded her full marks on that score. The rest of the afternoon he divided between touring the antiques shops and later calling in on Jacques Reynaud. Jacques had asked Daniel to ship some freight for him a week ago. Daniel had said that he would see what he could do but now he wanted to let him down lightly. He didn't want any more work at the moment. It was six-thirty when Daniel arrived back in his room. He took a long hot shower, changed into some clean clothes and met Anita in the restaurant at seven-thirty. He was surprised just how well they got on. It was as if he'd known her for years instead a single night of lascivious gratification. After a good meal and a bottle and a half of *Chateauneuf du Pape*, Daniel felt himself relaxing more than he had done in the last four days. It felt good to tell her about his business in New York. She even asked if he'd had an encounter with the mafia. She seemed astonished at the lengths he had gone to, to keep himself apart from the drug smuggling and the protection racketeering underworld.

"It's commendable," she said. "Many other people might easily have given into them."

"Well I have a good reason to hate anybody who uses threats to get what they want. It's the mafia that was responsible for the death of my father."

After that it seemed like they were even closer. She also hated the mafia because they had been responsible for the death of her younger brother. "They caught him up in their drug dealing and when he wanted out they overdosed him." She explained. "The coroner's verdict was death by misadventure. Some adventure! His last trip." Her face was taut with anger.

"Yes, they have it off to a fine art," said Daniel, holding her hand tightly. "No bruises; no sign of a struggle, just a corpse and an empty syringe. There are hundreds of people that have gone that way, actors, pop singers, businessmen, you name it and they have touched everybody's lives. And why have they been killed? Because they won't toe the line."

Daniel found himself telling her more and more about his life as they discovered that they had much in common, besides an inextinguishable libido. That was to be abated later.

The next morning, Daniel left her sleeping in his bed and went out to *Henri's* once more. He had been awakened early by the telephone. Henry sounded agitated. "You must come and see me at once," he shouted down the telephone.

"Can't it wait?" he asked, not wanting to disturb Anita. She was just beginning to stir.

"Only if you aren't afraid to die."

That worked. Daniel was there in half an hour.

"Come through, mon cher," Henri beckoned. He led Daniel to a back room. "I'm afraid," he said, "that you have got mixed up in something bigger and more dangerous than you think."

"What exactly are you talking about?"

"Jules, he was dragged out of The Sienne last night. See." He handed Daniel the latest edition of *Le Monde*. Daniel read a small piece on the front page about a man who had been found floating down the river, a man, the article said, whose death was described as suspicious.

"Looks like he was digging a little too hard," Daniel said with a frown.

"He rang me last night. It can't have been much before that happened."

"With what?"

Henri passed him a piece of paper on which he had scribbled some notes. "That," he said and let Daniel read it. Daniel put the paper in his pocket, his face drained with blood. "Christ!"

"Where does that leave us?" asked Henri.

"God knows," Daniel sighed. He left the massage parlour and went back to the hotel as fast as he could. As he walked away, another of Henri's customers pushed past him and went into the lobby. Daniel was in too much of a hurry to notice anything about him only that he was a well-built man who looked to be at the peak of his fitness. Obviously a customer for the masseuses, he thought.

He was wrong. The man went in and asked for Henri personally.

"What can I do for you?" Henri asked nervously.

"I want one of your massages," he said. "Like the last time."

"You had better get ready then," Henri said and went to get his preparations. When he went through to the massage parlour the man was already lying face down on the bench. Henri rubbed some embrocation onto his hands and set to work.

The man was quiet and Henri did his job dutifully. There were no awkward questions, none of the inquisition that had taken place the time before. Henri didn't speak either. The massage was as good as any he had given before. "Right," Henri said lightly and tapped the man on his shoulder. You're done."

The man swung his body off the table and faced Henri. He didn't look at all harmful. In fact he gave Henri a gentle smile of appreciation as he rolled his head around on his shoulders. "You certainly know how to treat your man," the stranger said.

"I have a good touch," Henri said with a glint in his eye.

"What sort of touch would that be?" the man asked as he placed his hand against Henri's abdomen.

"The massage is only half the service." Henri smiled as the man's hand rubbed further down his body. Henri rubbed the man's chest affectionately with the palm of his hand. The man released Henri's belt and slid his hand inside his trousers. "What have you told that man?" the stranger asked still smiling.

Henri froze. "What man?"

The man's hand closed on him. "Your friend who left as I came in," he said in a firm voice.

"He's no friend of mine," Henri said as he tried to pull away. The man's hand tightened on his genitals.

"You aren't answering me," the man said and tightened his fist even more.

Henri winced as the pain ran up into his torso. "I…I don't know what you are talking about," he gasped.

"Then we are wasting our time here are we?"

"Yes," Henri whispered.

"Jules told me everything before he died," he said in a low to tone.

The pain shot through Henri's body from the roots of his hair to the souls of his feet as his flesh was wrenched forward, ripping it from him like it didn't belong. It made a muffled sound like a joint being dislocated. He sank to his knees with paralysis as the pain wracked his body. He hardly felt the pain when the blow to his temple struck like a hammer. It seemed small and fleeting by comparison.

*****

Anita was in the lounge when Daniel reached the hotel. He went in and sat opposite and looked at her across the coffee table. "Hello darling. You look as if you've been rushing."

"I've got to leave this afternoon," he said with an apology in his voice

"Back to New York?"

"Not straight away. I'll be there on Thursday if you want to look me up."

"A bit sudden all this, isn't it"

"Business I'm afraid. Never know when something urgent is going to turn up."

"You'd better let me have your number then."

Daniel wrote his ex-directory number at Malterswood on a serviette and passed it to her as he stood up to leave. "I'm sorry," he said and turned to go.

Anita got up and followed him to his room. After ringing the airport for the times of flights to Toulouse, he said, "I'm catching the twelve o'clock flight. She helped him pack and there was just time for a quick kiss before he went down for his taxi. "Have to go," he said, giving her a tight hug. He picked up his case. "See you soon," he said as he got into the taxi.

Daniel sat quietly as Marietta drove them to her home. She hadn't been in when he rang from Orly Airport but her answer-phone had taken the message Even the recording of her voice had been warm and welcoming to his ears. "What's the matter, mon cheri?" she asked.

"I'll tell you when we get to your place," he said and said no more. Marietta knew not to push him. He would tell all once he had sorted it out in his own mind. It wasn't long before she was pouring him a whisky.

"Here, drink that." She handed him a glass and went through to the kitchen. "Are you hungry?" she asked. Daniel knocked back the drink. It warmed his throat and eased his mind. "Just a bite for me." He had no appetite for big meals, but he knew she had made him a meal. It smelt wonderful. She watched him as he picked at his food with a fork, the enlarged pupils of her dark brown eyes showing real and deep concern. He looked shaken.

Daniel looked up and saw her melting eyes. He took his hand in his pocket and pulled out a folded piece of paper and handed it to her.. Marietta took it, unfolded it and laid it on the table in front of her. "Who is Alex Horton?" she asked.

"The man who has been trailing me since I came to Europe. Henri told me that the person he had got this information off had been murdered. He had got a phone call last night. Jules had discovered that Diacre's shop had been a dead letter drop for agents of the C.I.A. before he retired.

"The C.I.A. in France?"

"It doesn't sound too incredible to me. France and America have a patchy relationship at the best of times and especially when there is a conflict of interests."

"Such as?"

"Like selling arms and aircraft to non-aligned countries."

"So Diacre is an American agent?"

"Seems like he was before he retired to a life of relative luxury. The question is, is he still an agent and what is it they have got him setting me up for?"

"Work it out. They must want to catch you with a stolen French Masterpiece."

"I worked that one out already."

"They want to put you away."

"Nope, it isn't as easy as that. They could arrest me any time they want. They probably have enough on me."

"Then why haven't they?"

"Because I have given both the F.B.I. and the C.I.A. odd tip offs about the mafia and their activities. Up till now they have felt it worthwhile to leave me alone."

"Then what's changed all of a sudden?"

"I can only think that The French Secret Intelligence Service is behind it. They must want to catch me in France with something French."

"No, I don't believe so," Marietta contradicted. "The French wouldn't go to all the trouble of bringing in the C.I.A. to arrest you. They just wouldn't do that. There's got to be a better reason."

"Then the C.I.A. must want to catch me in the States."

"And?"

"I don't know. Threaten to extradite me to France perhaps to face a charge of theft."

"And why would they do that?"

"To scare the shit out of me, why else?"

"That means they would be wanting you to do something in exchange."

"And I have an idea what."

Before Marietta could ask him what, the telephone rang. She got up from the table and answered the call. Daniel could hear her voice in the distance and then she put down the receiver on the cradle.

"What's the matter?" Daniel asked when he saw her biting her lip.

"Henri is dead."

"What? When?"

"This morning. Someone saw you leaving just before his body was found."

"Christ almighty! The man in the doorway. That must be the one that Henri told me about before."

"Do think it was that Horton man?"

"C.I.A. No I don't think so. They would..." he paused. "Whoever killed Henri killed Jules as well." He stood up from the table. "Why, for God's sake!"

Marietta din't answer. She knew that he was asking himself. He paced the floor with his hand on his forehead,. "Right," he said. "Then we'll bloody well find out. Have you got a number for Diacre?"

"On the pad by the telephone," Marietta said and pointed to the table in the corner of the hallway.

"Ring him and see if he still wants to meet."

"But he'll probably not be there. We said two weeks to him."

"Oh I have a feeling he'll be there all right."

Marietta dialed the number and let it ring. She was about to put the phone down when Diacre answered it. "Hello," he said.

"Hello. This is Marietta," she explained. "I have Mr. Carlisle here to speak to you." She handed Daniel the receiver.

"Hello. Do you still require that job doing?" he asked outright.

"Er, yes, of course."

"We'll be over for it within the hour. Make out a receipted bill of sale for the bronzes to Marietta Pepin."

"They are yours only when the job is done."

"Then forget it." Daniel rang off.

"Did you mean that?"

"Yes, it's a pity about the figures but I can always work on you to sell me your Poertzel."

"There's no way you will get your hands on that one," she grinned. "Unless..."

The telephone rang. She picked up the receiver. "Hello."

"Monsieur Diacre here. The bill of sale will be ready for you when you arrive. You may take them with you."

"Right, I'll tell him." She hung up. Daniel had heard. He had put his head next to Marietta's ear.

"Okay. Let's go." He went to his case, got out a few bits and pieces and followed Marietta to he car. They arrived at the remote farmhouse forty minutes later.

Diacre opened the door as they walked up to it. "Come on in," he invited.

Daniel followed him into the room where they had been seated before. The bronzes were all packed in separate boxes. Diacre had left the lids open for inspection. Daniel looked at them and then told Marietta to load them into her Porche. He held out his hand and Diacre handed him a signed receipt, Daniel checked it and pushed it into one of the boxes. "Meanwhile, we'll get on with our other business in the other room," he said.

Diacre led the way through and Daniel closed the door behind them. He waited for Diacre to take out the rolled-up painting. "You were lucky to catch me here," he stated as he reached into a cupboard.

"Bullshit," Daniel replied in an even tone. Diacre looked surprised but didn't reply. "You wouldn't go off and leave this little lot unguarded," Daniel grinned.

"Very true Mr. Carlisle. You are very astute."

"More than you think"

Diacre lifted his eyebrows interrogatively. Daniel put his hands in his pockets and asked Diacre to unroll the painting and rest his hands on the oil canvass.

"Certainly, but why?"

"You heard. I want your prints on it if I get caught."

"That is absurd. I didn't bargain for this." He pulled away from the table.

"Either you do it or you take it yourself. Either way you have passed title to the ornaments. Diacre knew he was in a corner, but he knew that his prints could easily be removed later. He placed his hands on the face of the painting and pressed down.

"There. Are you satisfied now?" He said with a brave smile.

"Not yet." Daniel pulled out a pair of surgical gloves and pulled them onto his hands. He rolled up the canvass and snapped a couple of elastic bands around it. "Now all I need to complete the contract is the name and address to where it is to be delivered.

Diacre smiled. Small beads of sweat that had been gathering on his forehead evaporated as his tension subsided. He opened a drawer and took out a ball-point pen and a sheet of writing paper. He wrote a number on it. "You will ring that number when you get the painting to New York. He will tell you where to deliver it."

"Right, and now the money."

Diacre's face went sullen. "You are to be paid on delivery. I made that clear before."

"Then you had better give me another bill of sale for the canvass."

"I can't do that."

"Then I shall ring the police and tell them that you have just tried to sell it to me." He went over to Diacre's telephone.

"What do you want?" Diacre asked with a resigned shrug of the shoulders.

"A bill of sale with your dealer's stamp on it." Diacre looked shaken now. "What's the matter? If I am not betrayed then there is nothing to worry about. I can get it over there. You should not worry."

He went over to his bureau and took out the receipt book and a rubber stamp. He wrote: Sold to Mr. Carlisle for 50,000 francs a painting by an unknown artist. "I could see no signature on it."

"Forgot your glasses, heh?" Daniel smiled. "Your finger prints should tie them together nicely."

Diacre didn't seem at all concerned. There was still a card or two up the old Frenchman's sleeve. Daniel folded the receipt and put it in his inside pocket. Then he pulled out a piece of Christmas wrapping paper and rolled it around the painting before removing his gloves. He went through to where Marietta was waiting patiently. "Everything okay?" she asked.

"Everything unless Monsieur Diacre wished to tell me why the C.I.A wants to set me up."

Diacre stiffened. He didn't speak, knowing that there was more to come. "Well, do you?"

"I don't understand what you are saying." Diacre said almost sincerely.

"What have you been watching me for?"

"You talk in riddles Mr. Carlisle."

"What about Alex?"

"Who?"

"Alex Horton. He's an old acquaintance of mine."

"Is he? Well I never heard of him."

Daniel took Marietta's arm and led her to the door. "Here is an offer for you," Daniel said, turning back to Diacre. "I will make a deal with you if you come clean. Tell Alex Horton that."

"I don't know what you are talking about, Monsieur."

"Tell him that the people that told me I was being set up are now dead if he doesn't already know it. Tell him that they know about his poking his nose into French business."

"I can't tell anybody anything. I simply don't know what you are talking about."

"Tell him," said Daniel and slammed the door behind him.

"You really think that we are in that deep?" Marietta asked as she gunned the Porche out onto the road.

"I don't really know. I'm only guessing. But whatever happens now, they have a choice of messing up an operation that they have somehow got me involved in or taking the blindfold off so that I can see where I am going. One thing I do know is that I don't intend being their bloody patsy."

"What about the picture?"

Daniel grinned. "I'll tell you later."

"You wouldn't steal it would you?"

"I don't look that soft in the head, do I?"

He put his arm around her shoulders. "You will remember to sign those bronzes over to me, won't you?"

"I don't look that soft in the head do I?"

They both exploded into fits of laughter.

*****

An hour and a half later they pulled up in front of Marietta's house. As they got out of the Porche a police car drew into the driveway behind them. "What the hell?" Marietta exclaimed.

"Take it easy. We are about to find out something."

"Monsieur Carlisle?" a plain clothed Surete officer asked as he produced his identification.

"Yes," Daniel answered.

"And Mademoiselle Pepin, Marietta Pepin?"

"Oui."

"I'm Inspector Vasselle and I have a warrant to search your car and your house for stolen property." He waved a piece of paper at them.

"Just what exactly are you looking for?"

"Stolen works of art," he replied confidently.

"Go ahead," she said.

He waved four uniformed men out of his car. The search was done in an experienced and professional manner, first the car and then he and his men went into the house.

The inspector walked over to a table and picked up a Poertzel and looked at it admiringly.

I have a receipt for it," Marietta stated. And it is recorded on my insurance policy as an item of particular value. I would be obliged if you would handle it carefully."

"Quite," the Inspector said and placed it carefully back on the side table.

The team regrouped in the hallway half an hour later. The inspector had a brief word with them and then turned to Marietta. "I don't think there is any point in going any further." He signaled for his men to leave and they filed back to their car. "I apologize to you both," he said politely and turned to walk back to his car.

"Wait," Daniel called after him. "Tell me what you are looking for and I might be able to help." Marietta cringed.

"That is most unlikely, Monsieur."

"Then try me."

The inspector turned and walked back to him. "You know very well what we are looking for, Mr. Carlisle. Don't treat my like you treat those other idiots."

"It's those other idiots I want to know about."

"I'm not at liberty to disclose any information to you about an ongoing enquiry." He touched the tip of his hat. "Good day Monsieur, Mademoiselle". He got into his car and it drove off into the distance.

"Well, you were right not to trust Diacre."

"Just cautious. Diacre was too cool about it for my liking."

"So he's in with the police?"

"No, I think someone else is pulling their strings but I have a feeling that the Inspector doesn't like it much either. Did you notice how careful they were to leave everything as they found it? It's as if they didn't expect to find anything, He knew he was being set up. If they had really thought that we had what they were looking for then they would have torn the place to pieces. That's the usual; procedure to intimidate villains, but the Inspector knew when he searched the car that he wasn't going to find anything. He was just doing as he was told as painlessly as he could. I'm sure of it."

*****

"What are you thinking about?" Marietta asked as they lay beneath the silk sheets.

"It just isn't working out. Whichever way I look at it there seems no logical answer. There's got to be some connection."

"Between Diacre and the police?"

"Between Diacre, Alex Horton, The death of the two men in Paris and at least one of the French intelligence Services. But I can't see the link."

"And you. Don't forget that you are in that list."

"And me," Daniel said as he closed his eyes and tried to doze. "And me." He lay there against the pillow with his hands behind his head and a deep sigh that was cut short when he stopped and sucked in a sharp breath.

"Are you all right, mon cheri?" Marietta asked.

"I am now," he said and sat up. "My love, we are going to have to talk." He slid out of bed and put on his dressing gown. Marietta followed him downstairs. Daniel put a pan of milk on the stove. "It's you, darling," he stated.

"It's me what?"

"It's you they're after."

"Rubbish."

"When Diacre contacted you did he specifically ask for me to do the job?"

"No, I don't think so, but he knew about you because we had discussed your hobby."

"Oh," Daniel said and scratched behind his ear. "Well anyway, I still think it is you first and then me. Jean Duvant is a prominent politician, isn't he?" He took off the boiling milk and scalded some hot chocolate.

"Yes he's a minister now."

"And his company does research for major arms and aircraft manufacturers, doesn't it?"

"Yes."

"And those companies have more than a little influence with the French government don't they?"

"Too right they do."

"And they know that their technology has been disappearing from under their noses."

"Probably."

"Well you are getting too complicated. They have traced the leaks to you and have linked me in with you." He poured the hot chocolate into two mugs.

"That explains setting you up with an art theft does it?"

"It explains that Marc Duvant would rather we be put away for art theft rather that anything connected to his father's company. It's a diversion."

"From what?"

"Well for a start, they don't want it known that Diacre is or was a C.I.A. agent. If Jules could find that out then so could the French D.S.T. He must have known that his anonymity would still remain whatever. It has got to be the D.S.T or the S.D.E.C. They are the only ones that can bend the Surete with political pressure." Daniel scratched his chin "But why stop me revealing that Diacre is an American agent?"

"How about double agent?" Marietta said not too seriously.

"That's it! Marietta, I love you."

"Does that mean you would like to make love?"

"It mean, silly, that you are still in danger."

"I knew that when you first kissed me."

"I'm serious."

"So am I."

9th September 11.pm

It was dark outside the window. The moon passed behind a grey cloud leaving the only light in Edward's room squeezing beneath the door. It was a yellow light, silent and persistent until a shadow passed across it from one side to the other and then back again a few moments later. The footsteps were soundless on a thick woollen carpet but he knew there was someone out there.

He lay on his bed and let his mind clear, thinking back to what had been happening to him. There was nothing wrong with his memory, at least. He remembered too well the flight from The Research Centre, the terrible ordeal of being flown sightless in a helicopter, the stench of stale sweat on his clothes when he arrived at Marvin Belk's villa. Marvin Belk. He would remember him as long as he lived. The man who had sold him to the Bulgarians. He tried to assess his position now. What had gone wrong with his carefully laid plan to escape; the calculations he had made, the poisonous pill he had compounded and Janine all came into his mind now as clear as if it were happening all over again. Janine had escaped, the poison had worked, and she'd got help to him in time to save his life. So what went wrong? The hospital staff should have got his name from his driving license but they had used his real name, the name he had undergone plastic surgery to escape from. It could only mean one thing. The Bulgarians had not left him for dead.

His head throbbed as he sat up. No straps! The Bulgarians were slipping. He took several deep breaths to help steady his blood pressure. He could feel the strength he had built up in his body over the past weeks returning to his limbs.

The shadow passed before the door again, only this time it remained there, blocking out the meager light. A hand fell on the door handle. Light burst into the room as the door opened wide. A nurse peered into the room at the sleeping patient and then went out again as silently as she had entered.

Edward sat up again, threw back the sheets and stood by the bed. He glanced around the room but nothing was clear until the full moon appeared from behind a thick cumulus cloud and shone into the room like a kindly face to reassure him that he was not alone. Now he could see. There was a small table against the far wall and a locker behind the door. He would need his clothes to escape. The hospital gown was neither use nor ornament; it could bee seen for miles as he fled his captors. His captors! Oh God! What if they'd already got him on a plane and got him out of the country? He'd never escape. What had the nurse said? Four hours since your collapse. He must still be in California.

He went to the locker and pulled on the two handles. He twisted them and the doors opened with a faint scraping sound. He didn't stop to see if it had been loud enough to arouse anybody, but felt inside. Empty! "Shit," he swore almost letting it emerge as a shout but restraining it to a whisper at the very last moment. Now what? His mind raced over the possibilities. He went over to the window and looked out. The moon was still clear of cloud cover and lit up the grounds of the nursing home adequately for him to see the driveway leading to a haze of lights in the distance; the glow of the street lights.

He fumbled with the catches on the window and eventually released them. The window wasn't as willing to be moved. He pushed hard against the frame until the muscles in his arms ached. He took a deep breath and pushed again. It was fastened somehow. He just couldn't budge it. Well no choice now He went over to the door and placed his ear against it; nothing; no sound to tell him what lay outside. He wiped the palm of his hand on the gown and reached for the door handle. It hovered momentarily before clasping tightly around it and then he turned it slowly as far as it would go. His breathing was faster now as his heart hammered against his chest. He took another two deep breaths before easing it away from the jamb.

He blinked his eyes as the light from the adjoining room streamed in through the crack. His eyes followed the walls past a desk to a cabinet in the corner. There was not a soul in sight. He opened the door a little more and peered into what was an ante-room with a thick red carpet, some filing cabinets, a desk and a chair. There was a kit-kat portrait on the opposite wall but of nobody he recognised and another polished wood-paneled door off to the side.

Edward wondered why his leg had not yet begun to shake. It was just the right conditions to trigger off his affliction; outright fear. But there was not a twinge. He walked swiftly to the next door and was about to turn the handle when he saw it start to turn from the other side of the door. But his thoughts were not on how convenient it was for somebody to turn the handle for him. His body froze and his mind boiled with panic.

A young nurse came into the ante room carrying a mug of coffee; the same nurse he had seen before, the oriental with a Californian accent, the one who had known his name. He stood behind the door as she walked in and turned to close it behind her. Her eyes widened when she saw Edward facing her. He placed his hand on hers and finished pushing the door to.

"Mr. Taylor," she gasped.

"Who?" Edward asked innocently.

She looked at him with a puzzled frown. "You do know who you are, don't you?" she asked as she walked over to the desk and placed the coffee on a small, floral table mat which she teased from beneath a pile of papers. "Coffee helps keep me awake," she said and turned to face him.

"Who told you my name?"

"It's on the admission sheet. We always write a patient's name down on that first. It saves complications when people pretend to be someone else. One glance at the sheet and we can see."

"You get people pretending to be somebody else, do you?" Edward asked with an air of total disbelief.

"Had Thomas Jefferson in here last month," she giggled, "But it's easy to remember someone's name after we've done one shift, though it can be awkward when you come on duty and a new patient truly believes he or she is someone else. We have to use their correct name all the time so that they break the association with the character they have formed in their minds."

"So who told you my name in the first place?"

"Oh, I don't know that." She sipped her coffee. "Well, Edward, you'd best be off to bed then. Not much you can do about your clothes until the morning."

"I haven't finished yet," Edward said angrily. "I want to know who brought me here, who told you who I was, and what sort of asylum is this that leaves a single pretty nurse in charge of a new patient."

"It's not an asylum, Mr. Taylor," she said officiously. "We only help people who have suffered from some mental trauma when they are on their way to full recovery. We don't treat raving mad men." She paused. "Or women if it comes to that."

"What's to stop me walking out of here right now?" Edward asked.

"Nothing apart from catching your death from freezing cold and being arrested for wandering about showing your backside."

"I'll take that risk," he said and went to the door. He swung it back expecting to see a row of men in white coats as it opened into a larger corridor. There was nobody there apart from another nurse pushing a small trolley to another room. He looked back and young Nurse Leony was still watching him.

"What the hell's going on?" he demanded. If the Bulgarians hadn't got him then who had brought him here? Who told them his name? The only identification he had on him was his driving license. Somebody must have told them. Janine! Of course. It was all becoming crystal clear. He should have seen it coming. That '*Oh Edward I love you*' crap. He'd fallen right into it. Got him away safe and then she goes after the money while he's tied up with explanations as to just why he absconded with top secret materials, how he just happened to have had major plastic surgery and how he was on chatting terms with the mafia and the Bulgarian agents. It was clear now, oh so clear. I gave her the key to the safety deposit box, she tells the police who I am, they arrest me for espionage or worse, and she takes all the money. Well, she'll be lucky. There's no way she could pass herself off as Matthew T. Roland even on a good day, and even with the driving license she'd need my signature and an accomplice who could forge it. The bitch! It hasn't stopped her trying though.

"We are detaining you until we are certain that you are who we believe you are," came an unexpected voice from his left. Unseen by Edward, Leony had pressed a small button on the front of her desk. A door had opened and in the space it had occupied stood a thick-set man with black bushy eyebrows above a pale, lined face. Edward thought the lines reminded him of someone he'd known in the past. The man looked about as old as he had done as well.

"Who are you?"

The man produced a badge from his pocket and held it in front of Edward's face. "F.B.I. Chief Antonasi."

"And who is it that you believe I am?"

"Edward Matthew Taylor, former research worker and scientist at The United States Research Centre at..."

"You can cut all that shit. You aren't charging me."

"Not yet."

"Meaning that you are going to?"

"When we've had your finger prints verified, yes."

Edward just stood there in silence. The nurse and Antonasi just stood there waiting for a response. When it came, it wasn't what they expected. Edward knew he was in a corner, he knew he should be afraid, but something inside his brain was blanketing out his fear. Something at the back of his mind was reassuring him. It was the words of Antonasi that brought them to his conscious mind. *Former research worker.* Suddenly he gave out a chuckle. He was in the right place for it to be described more as an insane cackle before it swept up inside him and burst out filling the corridors with echoes of laughter. They stared at him in disbelief but said nothing until he had lapsed to a more sane level. He squeezed his side to relieve the pressure in his diaphragm.

"What's so funny, Mr. Taylor?" asked Antonasi.

"You said former research worker." Edward said bringing his laughter finally under control. He chuckled again and pressed his side as he went back into the ante room. He went through to his bed, shutting the door behind him. They could still hear him cackling through the closed door. Eventually after a half hour or so, the whole place fell silent as Edward fell into a deep sleep. They knew the window was unbreakable and unopenable. They would deal with the poor little mad scientist in the morning.

10th September

Edward awoke to the sound of voices in the next room. He sat up just in time to see the door open and two men walk in. They stood at either side of it. The third man was Antonasi. He closed the door behind him and threw a bundle of clothes on the bed. "Get dressed, Taylor," he ordered.

Edward didn't need telling twice. He got dressed quickly. The sooner they got him out of there the better. "Where are you taking me?"

"To our head quarters; not far."

"Are you charging me?"

"When we get there, the charges will be read out to you."

"Any clue as to what they might be?"

"You know damned well what they will be you stupid little arsehole."

"Aren't you going to question me first?"

"Sure."

"Well you will let me ring my attorney, won't you?"

"Shut up you little fart," Antonasi shouted. "You'll get what we want to give you."

"What, no constitutional rights?"

"Come on," Antonasi said, taking hold of Edward's arm before he had fastened his belt. The three of them bundled him out of the building and into a waiting car. No one spoke during the journey into the city. It was like riding alone. Edward's body was relaxed and slouched comfortably on the back seat of the Buick, but his mind was doing press-ups. He loved using his head. At one time it had been all that he ever lived for but it had been just so overbearing to have his mind straight-jacketed for so long. He had enjoyed making the poison back at Belk's villa. It had been an application of sciences he hadn't used for years. Now he could exercise his mind in another direction. He looked out of the window as the outside world flashed by, unseen by his eyes. His focus was inwards.

"Right, out," Antonasi ordered. Edward hadn't even felt the car stop. He climbed out and they led him through the front doors of the building, to a room. It was bare except for a steel-legged table and three similarly built chairs.

"Sit down," he was ordered by one of the guards. He did as he was told. Antonasi left them standing over him. It was fifteen minutes later that the F.B.I. chief returned clean shaven and looking a little fresher.

"Right," he said and flicked his head to one side. The two guards disappeared. Probably gone for their breakfasts, Edward thought.

That's a good idea. "How about some breakfast?" he asked.

"When you've answered our questions."

"Haven't eaten for… How long was I out?"

"We picked you up the day before yesterday."

"I haven't eaten since that morning."

"You'll do well to get this over with then."

"Breakfast and I want a lawyer."

"Are you trying to rile me because it's working?" He hovered over Edward threateningly.

"What next; electrodes on the testicles? Or just old fashioned police brutality?"

Antonasi leaned away. "I don't operate like that. All I want is an informal chat about your position. No witnesses, No statement; just a little cosy chat."

"If it's a cosy chat you want I know just the girl." He thought of that bitch Janine. She knew the meaning of a cosy alright.

"You're a smart little arsehole, aren't you?"

"Chief," Edward said sympathetically, "I understand your position more clearly than you think. Basically it boils down to this: If I don't confess to anything then there is nothing you can do. All you are doing is hoping that I am dumb enough to make a confession. Well, I'm not feeling particularly sinful today, thank you."

Antonasi looked up at a small button on the ceiling and sighed. "Switch that damned thing off and get him some breakfast. And be quick about it." He got up off his seat. I'll try again when you have had some food inside you." He left and a guard came in and stood by the door, Edward tried to chat to him cordially but he told him to keep his goddamned mouth shut. He thought it best to remain quiet after that. Fifteen minutes later, Edward was served with a large breakfast from the canteen. It felt good but it was beginning to wear off by the time Antonasi returned with another man two hour or more later.

"This is Jack Hart. He's a C.I.A. official. He's here to outline just how serious your position is."

"I know how serious it is thank you. Did you bring my attorney?"

The two men spoke to each other and then Jack Hart spoke. "In simple language, Mr. Taylor, we are going to charge you with the grand larceny of top secret experimental materials; with espionage on behalf of a foreign power; undermining the security of the United States and perverting the course of justice."

"Gosh. I thought it was going to be something serious."

"What we need is cooperation, Edward," Antonasi said soothingly.

"Edward is it now? I was a fart this morning and an arsehole this afternoon, would you believe," he said to Hart with a look of surprise on his face.

"What have you got to say for yourself?" growled Hart.

"Er, how about *Not Guilty*," Edward retorted. Hart winced.

"You can't deny that you stole certain materials from the Research Centre, can you," he said forcefully.

"Can't I?" Edward ran his fingers through his hair. "What materials would that be? Whose stock figures have you been looking at? Where are those materials now? Have you any proof that I took them?"

"Sure you took them," Antonasi smiled patronizingly. "They went missing when you made your run from The Research Centre."

"Made a run? Edward scowled. "I was on leave, remember? You said it yourself, a former research worker. I was entitled to drive away in my Jeep."

"Loaded with Research Centre property."

"Who on earth told you that story? I had nothing but my usual hand luggage, the guards will testify to that."

"In the spare gas tanks and the spare tank," Hart put forward.

"You found my Jeep then?" Edward asked with a purposely formed guilty look.

"Too damned right we did," Hart grinned. Now they were getting somewhere.

"I see, so you found some missing merchandise in the gas cans then?"

Hart flushed red with anger, his grin turning into a sneer. "You know damned well we didn't."

"Do I? Then where did you find it?"

"We're asking the questions," Antonasi broke in.

"Then I'll have my lawyer now." Edward sat back in his seat.

"What happened to them?" Hart asked, ignoring Edward's request once again.

"To what?"

"The gas tanks of course," Antonasi said, trying to soothe the situation.

"The gas tanks!" Edward exclaimed. "What *has* happened to them?"

"We're asking you that."

"You mean they've been stolen? Well they'll take anything these days!"

Hart shuffled on his seat.

"Why don't you give us your version of what happened?" Antonasi asked.

"It appears to me that you want me to confess to something I didn't do."

"Just tell us what happened."

"When?"

Hart was clenching his fist. "You said that you didn't take anything from The Research Centre, is that right?" he asked as calmly as his voice would allow.

"I didn't take anything."

"Then who did? Answer me that will you."

"Probably…" Edward watched the anticipation on their faces. "Probably never went missing in the first place. Sounds like the usual security cock-up we got around there."

"Usual?"

"Yes. They spent so much time looking down the lavatory basins that they forgot how much shit there was there in the first place. The security in that place is basically ineffective. Nobody trusts anybody. You have guards searching more guards. They spend so much time expecting something to go missing that when they got a hiccup in the system they really believed it had happened. The stuff that is supposedly gone missing was probably never there in the first place, or was recycled. It could have been a simple stock-taking error, a mis-keying into a terminal, or anything like that. It is unlikely that such an error could be detected months after it occurred. Such discrepancies are usually put down to natural wastage. That's common with chemical used in experiments. In a reactive substance they can lose half the mass in gas form, explosives will lose all but a small fraction of the solids when ignited."

Hart produced a piece of paper with a formula on it. "Were you responsible for that?"

"I developed it with a colleague, yes."

"And who would be responsible for keeping a tally on stocks?"

"In the experimental stages, me."

"So if you had less stock than recorded on the computer how would you explain that?

"As I say, human error or testing losses."

Hart stood up and paced the room. "What about the pass?"

"What about it?"

"It had been altered."

"Not that I know of."

"It was issued at…" He checked another scrap of paper. "At 18.00 hours, yet you did not leave until 22.30. It was impossible to get out unless it had been altered to the same time as you actually left. There is only a margin if fifteen minutes either way."

"Ah! Another example of security madness," Edward exclaimed, pointing to the ceiling.

"What do you mean by that?"

"Unnecessary waste of time and money. It never did work, though I must admit, nobody actually knew it. But I was already late and I had a long night of driving ahead of me so I just ran a magnet over the card and erased the time and the check code. The computer was never programmed to reject a blank card going out. It only checked for that on cards coming in to stop just anybody wandering in without authorized access. I knew they would give me a bulling over it when I got back but they wouldn't have done anything. I was too valuable to them, and anyway I'd have just pointed out another fault in their security system."

"So what are you saying Mr. Taylor?"

"What am I saying?" he said as a prompt to a further question.

"Are you saying that you never stole anything?"

"I never stole anything, correct," It was mine anyway, he thought.

"So why did you disappear in a helicopter and change your identity?"

"You mean my face?"

Hart nodded.

"I was kidnapped and I awoke with bandages on my face. I was told I had been in an accident and it would be a few weeks before I could take off the dressings. So I lounged around in what I thought was a hospital and then voila! Off came the bandages and out appeared the new me. I not only looked younger, it made me feel younger."

"You weren't in an accident, were you?"

"Probably not. I don't know. I was drugged. It turned out that the new face was simply to smuggle me out as a diplomat."

"What kind of diplomat?"

"A foreign one of course. They were going to take me to Sofia. I tricked them though by making them think I was dead."

The two interrogators looked at each other and shrugged their shoulders. Antonasi stood up. "We'll send you in some food," he said as Hart stood up to join him at the door.

"What about a lawyer now?"

"We'll see," Antonasi said as they went out.

Edward thought he had done well. It seemed as plain as day when he thought about the answers he should give them. He wasn't one of the research workers anymore. They didn't deserve him. He was his own man now.

Another guard came in with a canteen meal and went out to leave him to eat alone. He remained there well into the afternoon, nobody coming to speak to him, not even to collect the tray. It gave him time to think. He wondered if he had succeeded in stopping them hounding him. His answers made no case for them, he was sure. But why was he being left alone? What was going on that he didn't know about? That was the worst part; not knowing. There had been no lawyer. Perhaps it was a mistake to give his answers before he had a witness of his own to say what they talked about. But he hadn't been cautioned. The MIRANDA warning was a constitutional right. And there was nothing on any recording that could be doctored to make it look like he had confessed. Nothing that had passed as yet would stand up in court with a good defense attorney.

Antonasi startled him by opening the door while he was in deep thought. "You can come through now."

He stood up and followed Antonasi through an open plan work area. Nobody bothered looking up. They entered a room with a large desk, proper office furniture and several filing cabinets. It was Antonasi's office. Jack Hart was waiting for them. Antonasi waved Edward toward an empty chair.

"What money do you have?" Hart asked him.

"Didn't I have any on me when you found me?" They wouldn't have. He had passed the money and the key to Janine. All he had was the driving license. "Of course I didn't have any. They were about to get me onto a plane."

"With this," Hart waved the driving license at him. How was he going to explain that? "How do you explain that?" he mimed Edward's thoughts prophetically.

"What?" Edward asked as he leaned forward for a closer look. It gave him time to think. If he didn't get the license back then he would have a hell of a time trying to collect his money from the safety deposit box. He leaned back casually. "The Bulgarians gave it to me. It was a deal I made with them in an attempt to get away."

"What sort of deal?"

"You must realise that they took me against my will. They'd altered me so nobody would recognize me as Edward Taylor. They were hoping to ship me out, suck me dry of everything I knew and I knew that then they would kill me."

"They couldn't have forced you to work with them."

"They have their ways as you well know. If they can't induce it with drugs or torture they could use blackmail."

Hart's eyebrows rose with interest.

"I have a mother over here. How safe can I keep her if I am behind the Iron Curtain?"

"Tell me about the deal you made?"

"In order to convince them that I was willing to help them I asked for a forged driver's license. They are good at that sort of thing like you," he taunted. "They got it for me in a matter of hours."

"Go on."

"Well the only reason that I could want that license is if I was going to return to the USA. Of course, I knew that they weren't likely to let me do that, but they weren't going to tell me, were they? But they wanted me to believe them."

"Anything to keep you happy?"

"Quite. That in turn gave me free time to make my poisonous pill, the one I used to escape."

"Poison, yes," said Hart. "And how would you have come by that?"

"Made it from the plants on the property where I was being kept prisoner. It was a desperate measure but it worked."

"He sure spins a good yarn," Hart sniggered.

"It's no yarn. I induced an allergic reaction with a substance I knew would put me on a state of catalepsy, and it worked."

"Desperate indeed," said Antonasi. "I doubt if I'd have trusted my luck for somebody to find the pill under my tongue and then give me C.P.R. It looks more like an attempted suicide to me.

"Attempted suicide?"

"D.O.A they said to me at first."

Luck? What the hell was he talking about? It was all planned. Janine rang to tell them. She must have. Edward broke into a cold sweat. "I came out of it all right didn't I?"

"Once again, why did you try to kill yourself? Had you already divulged your secrets?" Hart asked again, firmly.

"I'm telling you, it was calculated to a thousandth of a milligram." I can show you the calculations necessary to cause catalepsy but not death."

"I've asked a leading toxicologist. He says it is near impossible to work it out safely; not unless you are counting on help before you sink irreversibly from living death to just plain death."

"Well I was counting on getting help. That's why I picked a crowded place to do it,"

"You weren't expecting a friend to help you then?"

"Such as?"

"You tell me," said Hart with a sly grin.

It unnerved Edward now. He wasn't sure just what the facts were. He had no intention of telling them even if he did. I'll catch up with that two-timing whore myself, he thought. The problem was, who had tipped this lot off as to who he really was and were they involved in resuscitating him?

"Someone who you had met perhaps?"

Edward shrugged. "Nobody."

Hart tamped his pen on the desk. "Tell me where you were kept prisoner."

"No idea. The Bulgarians blindfolded me and stuck me behind a car seat when they drove me to the airport," he lied.

"Huh." Hart rubbed his hands together in the front of his face as he thought about the situation. He stood up and spoke to Antonasi. "Well, I have no further questions, have you?"

"No," Antonasi replied." You can go. You are free," he said to Edward.

"Can I have my driving license?"

"A forgery? What do you think we are?"

"I know what you are. You do just as you please when it suits you. New identity for defectors, cushy place to live, plenty of money."

"But you hardly fall into that category."

"I need to have some means of identity if they aren't going to find out that I wasn't really dead. If they know that I am still alive then they will get to me through my mother. Then it will all start again."

"But they know the name on it. They got it for you."

"I don't think that they would be looking. Only if I reappear as my old self am I likely to get into the news. You know, *Kidnapped scientist returns safely.* That's what the newspapers were told, wasn't it, that I'd been kidnapped and that I wasn't important. Well I wish to remain unimportant. I've had enough excitement for a lifetime."

Hart looked at Antonasi and shrugged his shoulders.. "We will have to keep him under surveillance, anyway." He paused. "We will let you have it later."

"What about money?" I can hardly get a job as a top scientist."

"We can get some for you provided you agree to stay at a safe house. There is still a lot of work to be done connected to this case and you are only a small part of it. I don't believe a word you have told us, Taylor, but if we can salvage something out of this then we'll all be happier."

"Will I be able to go out?"

"Under escort."

"Have I any choice?"

"No."

Things were no better. In fact they looked worse. No freedom, no identification to enable him to go and collect his money, no woman even. It would be months before he could get anywhere near one. It made his mind wander to Janine. He'd loved more than his own life but she had betrayed him. She'd left him to die a certain death. She must have done. But who had told Hart and Antonasi who he was? Something didn't fit right, but he didn't dare ask.

The safe house was staffed with armed, plain clothed police officers; all men. Nothing seemed to come of the Bulgarians. They had long gone and it wouldn't have made a great deal of difference if the CIA had found them since they were travelling on diplomatic passports, and had diplomatic immunity. They couldn't be arrested even if they stood in front of The White House and flashed themselves.

It was early Tuesday morning when Edward arrived at the safe house. Antonasi knew that he had lied, but without concrete evidence there was unlikely to be any trial. He also knew that although Edward was unlikely to be any more use as a scientist in the United States they couldn't let him fall into the hands of the Soviet agents. "I've got a deal we can make with you," he said as Edward was looking around his new prison.

"Oh yes?"

"We need somebody to do a job for us. It isn't a big job but we need an outsider all the same. Somebody nobody knows as an agent,"

"Go on."

"It will mean a little more plastic surgery; not a lot, and a change in the colour of your hair. We could pay you well while you were doing the job and give you a lump sum afterwards with identity papers and everything. It would be necessary in order to make sure that the Bulgarians or the Soviets did not know you had survived."

"What about the identity I wanted before?"

"Too risky."

"Wouldn't hurt to have a spare driver's license."

"What the hell's so important about that one?"

"Indulge me a bit. I rather like the idea of playing at being an agent. I've spent my whole life being a reclusive old fart. You actually said it. Well it's absolutely true. But by planning my escape from the Bulgarians I have seen a new self, one that can cope with adversity at its worst. I used to have a nervous twitch when I was afraid. I haven't had it since I became Matthew T. Roland."

"I once thought you were a very bright guy. I wonder if all this it hasn't all been a little too much for you."

CHAPTER 8

11th September

"Where the hell have you been?" Dianne Barker demanded.

"I've been a bit tied up in Europe," Daniel replied as he came in through the doorway of his offices.

"I was beginning to wonder if I still had a job. I'm supposed to be head of your security and I didn't have the faintest idea where you were. God man! Four weeks and not a single word. That's taking it a bit too far. For all we knew you could have been in a concrete jacket in the Hudson."

Dianne Barker at thirty two had been Daniel's Head of Security for two years. She was five feet eight with short cut brunette hair and dark grey eyes. Her body was mature and slim and her face showed a determination that was emphasized by her angular jaw. Her job was to make sure that all possible steps were taken to keep Daniel alive. She had a big task. Much of the time Daniel would disappear on his smuggling jaunts without a bodyguard, not return on schedule and expect his employees to understand. Dianne had to vet all visitors to his mansion on Long Island, something that Daniel objected to vigorously at times and she had to keep a twenty four hour surveillance on the place to help prevent any attempts on Daniel's life. Whenever Daniel was away from Malterswood he should have had at least one bodyguard to accompany him to his warehouse, which had the same stringent security. It was more vulnerable than the house and Dianne controlled the security of both. She had her own living quarters at the mansion and her own suite of offices with her own staff at the warehouse. She had taken over the position after the death of her father. He, too, had been employed by Daniel, not as an employee but as an independent security consultant and contractor. The fact that he had more than one customer was his undoing. Spreading himself too thin, he was unable to protect himself as well. The mafia wanted him out of the way and he became an easy target. It was just another unsolved murder in The Big Apple.

Daniel knew then that his life was in more danger that ever. He had crossed the Gambinos, The Colombos and the Lucceses once too often. He was to be sought out and made an example of. It was Dianne who stepped in and prevented that from happening, but the security came at a cost. She formed her own security firm within Daniel's company. In return, he provided her with living accommodation the size of a penthouse and offices to match his. She had voting shares in Daniel's company and took a vice president's salary. She never slept with him.

"I'm sorry Dianne. I would have called if I could," he said to calm her down.

"Bullshit."

"No, I mean it this time. I've been in a spot of bother," he said, trying to throw her a conciliatory smile. She parried it.

"Tell me something new," she grated. Daniel could tell she was still angry.

"No I mean big trouble." He went over to the paneled wall and pressed a button. A drinks bar appeared from nowhere and he poured himself a scotch. "You want one?" he placated.

"Holy Jesus, I give up. You are incorrigible, do you know that?

"I would if I knew what it meant," Daniel said with a shrug of his shoulders.

"You'll get blown away one day and when St. Peter opens the gate and asks you how it happened, you'll say 'The same as old man Barker.' Only you won't have been too busy looking out for danger to somebody else, you won't even have been watching out for yourself. You have to tell him that you went out for a screw and you got caught with your end up."

"You're mad at me, I can tell." He handed her a glass half full of neat whisky. "Here, Dianne. Knock that back and I'll explain everything."

"Unless it has a bearing on your safety I don't want to know about your shady deals."

"How the hell do you think I have held out so long if it wasn't for my shady deals?" Daniel asked indignantly.

"You do it because you like it. You've put people into this business so that you can indulge yourself with your little games. Well it's going to stop, do you hear. It's going to stop or I'm going to leave and let you sort out your own funeral arrangements."

"All right, I'm going to stop. Does that make you feel any better?"

"I would if I thought you meant it. Do you realise how many sleepless nights I have had wondering if I was out of a job?" She swilled the whiskey around her glass and then downed it in one.

"Another?" Daniel asked, holding out his hand for the glass.

"I'll get it myself," she answered and went over to the bar.

"It's good to hear your voice again, Dianne. It really is."

"You slimy sod. If you can't win an argument then you flatter people round to your way of thinking. You'd talk yourself out of a hangman's noose."

"That's what I am trying to tell you. I have been busy doing just that." Dianne sat down on a big sofa and he sat down beside her. "While I was in France," he continued, "a couple of guys I knew got killed."

"That doesn't surprise me at all."

"Somebody over there was trying to frame me, first for theft and then for murder. Henri and one of his informers got whacked."

"Henri? He's dead?"

Daniel nodded, got up and went over to the bullet-proof window. For a whole minute he gazed out towards Jones Beach., He sighed. "I really don't know how much longer I can hold out. It's all getting a bit too much."

"Why don't you get out?"

"Out? Yes that's what I was thinking of doing, getting out."

"I mean out of New York. You could set up somewhere that isn't riddled with Mafioso. I know I'm talking myself out of a job, but I really do believe it is the only way to keep you alive."

"You think it's as bad as that now do you?"

"Yes I do. If a president isn't safe in this country then I can't guarantee your safety, not any more; not if they give it their best shot."

"Well, I think you are right. But it isn't just the mafia now."

"Who the hell else have you riled?" Dianne was raising her voice again.

"Oh, a few butchers, bakers and a few intelligence agencies."

"I might have guessed you couldn't do anything by halves."

"Still want your job?"

"Have I any choice?"

"Nope."

Dianne stood up and looked out of the window beside him. "You've had a few calls lately."

"You managed to sort them out?"

"I put most of them through the office. Legitimate stuff."

"That's what they are paid for."

"It's the personal calls I didn't know what to do with."

"Personal calls?" Daniel looked alarmed. "What personal calls?"

"From a woman."

"Who, damn it?"

"A Miss Holt."

"Who the hell is she?"

"She had your personal number. I thought you'd know."

"Never heard of her. Sent her packing, did you?"

"No, I didn't know if you knew her or not."

"So what's the position?"

"She'll ring again. She's been ringing every evening over these last few days."

"Huh. When did she ring last?"

"This evening just before you turned up."

*****

Daniel spent the evening talking to Dianne. She was very attractive, but to Daniel she was a business partner, a shareholder, a person whose emotions had to be cool and calculating. She had been the only thing between him and death on many occasions over the past two years. He needed her there for that good reason and not something frivolous like sex. That was something he seemed to get whether he wanted it or not from other women.

It was the following evening that Daniel answered the telephone and the voice on the other end of the line said. "Hello, is that Daniel?"

"Yes," he said as he lounged on the couch.

"Anita Holt here."

"Oh, hello. How are you?"

"Fine thanks I've had a hell if a job getting hold of you."

"Have you?"

"You said you were going back to The States straight away."

"Did I? Oh well, business and all that."

"I left the same day that you said you were going to Toulouse."

Same day I went to… Oh that Anita Holt!

"So I rang you. Some woman answered the phone. Thought it was your wife or something at first until she said she worked for you. Housekeeper is she?"

"Er, sort of. She looks after me in a way."

"Can't wait to meet her. Sounds a jolly old bird." Daniel grinned. He bet Dianna didn't know she'd missed a few decades and advanced to fifty.

"Meet her?"

"You invited me to get in touch when I came to Manhattan, remember? Well I'm here."

"Oh, of course. Forgive me. I have had a lot on my mind lately. Would you like to come over one evening?"

"I'm free tomorrow."

"Great, I'll send a man in a car to pick you up. Where are you staying?"

"Oh, you aren't coming for me yourself?"

"Not been over well lately. Doctors say I have to stay at home for a few more days, till I get my strength back," he lied. I'll need all my strength if she's coming over, he thought.

"What you need is a bit of good company. Tell your chauffeur to pick me up at *The Alfredo* on Central Park South. Do you know it?"

Chauffeur? What does she think I am? "Sure, I have an apartment near there."

"Good. Say six o'clock. Is that all right?"

"He'll be in a light grey Lincoln."

"I'll see you then, Good night."

"Good night." Daniel grinned. Just wait till I tell Dianne what she said. On second thoughts, better not.

The following night, he sent Mickey Spiller to collect her. He had no inclination to venture out from the safety of his mansion. When Anita appeared through the connecting doors to the garage, he realised what he had been missing in the outside world. She looked different. She was attractive, but now she'd had the works. He guessed that she had spent the whole day getting ready for her visit. It made him feel guilty of only spending half an hour in the shower and five minutes having a wet shave. "Hello," he said and embraced her like an old friend.

She gave him a warm moist kiss fully on the lips. "Hi, I've missed you."

"Well, you're here now. Come on through." He led her the way to his lounge, a large sprawling room with plenty of space between a flotsam of comfortable furniture. He was glad to have company. The problems of the last week had brought him to a near state of depression. He'd had to make choices and sacrifices he thought he would never have to make. He'd come back to New York to pack up and get out, but as yet he had done nothing about it. It would take month, during which he was always going to be a target, hunted by one of his enemies. It depressed him but Anita had lifted that cloud a little.

"What sort of place do you have?" he asked Anita as he handed her a glass of wine.

"Me? Oh I live out of a suitcase. My work takes me all over the world. I've never had a chance to get a place of my own."

"What exactly is your work?"

"I've told you. I'm a freelance reporter. I do different articles while I gather information about the mafia."

"Are you in New York for long?"

"Until my sources dry up."

"You haven't come to interrogate me have you?"

She laughed. "Oh, you are silly Danny. Work is the last thing on my mind tonight."

"Are you hungry?" He asked as he walked through to another room. There stood a large mahogany table with two place settings and silver candelabra casting long shadows over a parquet floor.

"I sure am."

"Hope you can't tell herring roe from caviar."

"I wondered what the candles were for. Have you cooked the meal yourself?"

"No, I rely on my cook for that sort of thing."

"Oh you have a cook as well? What is her name?"

"Howard fits all sorts of descriptions including general dogs-body but I don't think he has ever been described as a *she*."

It was quite a lot later that evening when Daniel asked her if she wasn't putting her life at risk by researching the mafia.

Anita lifted her head off the pillow. "What are you saying, that I should stop my work and find something else to write about?"

"It would be a lot safer."

"And not a lot of use to anybody."

"Well living in a hotel makes you a sitting duck."

"I have no choice; I'm not loaded like you"?

The problem was solved in the short term while she stayed at Malterswood Lodge for the following week.

17th September

"You know, you're turning into a recluse," Anita told Daniel whilst eating another of Howard's meals. I have been out every single day and I haven't been able to tempt you to take me out even once."

"Well, you know how it is. I can do most of my work from here." He'd been out to the warehouse a couple of times, escorted by Mickey and Carl. He didn't want to explain to Anita just how dangerous it was for him to leave his premises without his bodyguards. He had told her about the mafia, but not about the Bulgarians, who seemed to be lurking somewhere, hidden in the shadowy dealings of his company. "There was a bomb defused in the warehouse," he explained to quell her objections.

"A bomb? Who would do that?"

"Who do you think? It's a campaign of intimidation that's gone on for years."

"So what have you done about it?"

"Increased securiy. That's all I could do. It's a good job we check absolutely everything or we would have lost the warehouse umpteen times."

"You've got insurance, haven't you?"

"Sure I do but that's not the point. I won't let them squeeze me out."

"You would be better getting out while you have something to sell."

"I have most of the stock and I am not selling it."

"You have most of it? Then who has the rest?"

"Dianne."

"Oh I see the whole picture now."

"The whole picture?"

"I just don't like the idea that they might kill you to get what they want. If they kill you then the mafia can walk in and take over your stock anyway."

"That wouldn't happen. My stocks would be offered to the vice-president of the company first. She would have first option to buy them."

"She? You mean Dianne?"

"Not many other people would be interested unless they wanted to face the problems we have."

"Have you made a will? Your stocks would automatically go to your next of kin if you haven't."

"As I said, Dianne would still have the first option to buy them. It's in the Company Articles."

"Haven't you got any next of kin then?"

"I have a mother and a brother over in England. I don't even know if they are still alive." He thought about them. He had never got on with his mother. He was never as close to her as he had been with his father. And he hadn't seen his younger Brother, Benjamin, since he left fourteen years ago. He had been to England several times on business and had never made time to visit.

"Your family would still get everything else if you haven't made a will," Anita still persisted. "You might consider that Dianne has a good reason for letting you get killed."

Daniel turned round. "You have no idea about my partner," he said angrily.

*****

"Best advice I've had in a long time, Daniel stated to melt the ice that had driven a wedge in their relationship. He'd been to see his attorney, Bertram Cayley and he had taken him though all the ins and outs of intestacy and making a will. "I went to see my lawyer today."

"So you saw sense after all," Anita said and hugged him tightly.

"The stocks weren't any problem though," said Daniel. "Cayley confirmed Dianne's right to buy the stock at a nominal price should I die. It was already in the contract when she first came into the business. He confirmed that the pre-emption clause was and still is in the articles."

"What does that mean?"

"It means so long as she wants to buy them she can."

"Even if she hasn't got the money?"

"She probably has got the money, but as vice-president of the company she could theoretically borrow the money off the firm and pay it off out of profits without touching a single dollar note."

"Does Dianne know this?"

"Of course."

"I see," Anita said, scowling.

Now Daniel scowled. "You see what?"

"I just thought you would have left your company to your brother."

"Dianne is entitled to it. She has held it together with me for the past two years."

Anita looked tense.

"What's the matter?"

"Darling," she said, clasping her hands together and placing them between her knees, "I don't know how to put this without being hurtful, but I don't want to see anything happen to you."

"That isn't hurtful."

"No, but what I have to say next might be. I just think that it would be safer for you not to be a benefit to anybody. That way, nobody will want to kill you. If you sold your stock to the mafia they wouldn't want you dead and if you didn't have that silly clause in whatever document it is then Dianne might not be careless…"

Daniel sat upright. "Dianne isn't like that."

"That might be so, but it isn't in her interest to keep you alive."

Daniel pulled himself away from her.

"I knew you'd feel like that! I just knew it." She turned to him with tears in her eyes. "But I had to say it Danny. I want to see you get out before anything happens to you."

"Nothing is going to happen to me."

"It's already happening. Look at you. You live like a hermit; you only go out with your bodyguards. That isn't living. You are half dead already." She got up and ran out of the doorway, slamming the door behind her and headed into the bedroom.

Daniel started to go after her but then stopped. There were lots of things to sort out but at this moment running after Anita wasn't one of them.

An hour later, Dianne knocked on the door and walked in. It struck Daniel as strange because she usually waited for him to reply before walking in, "You know she's leaving, don't you?"

"What?"

"Anita is packing her bags. She's asked if one of the men can run her into New York."

Daniel stood up and looked at his reflection in the darkened glass of the window.

"Shall I get her some transport?"

"No." Daniel was emphatic.

"You aren't thinking of taking her in yourself are you?"

"I'll go and talk to her," Daniel said solemnly.

"Dianne stepped in front of him and barred his way. "She's got you eating out of her hand, Daniel. What the hell's wrong with you? You've never let a woman influence you like that before."

"Do you realise what they will do to her if they get their hands on her?"

"Do you care that much, Daniel? She's a whore and you knew it when she first rang you to come here. She's a good-time girl that is onto a good thing."

"Oh, for God's sake, Dianne, give it a rest. You never have approved of the way I run my personal life."

"You don't owe her anything, Daniel; nothing." She grabbed at his arm as he moved to go past her.

Daniel got hold of her hand and plied it away. "Dianne," he shouted. "Give me credit for having a bit of sense, will you? If they get hold of her then they will have a hostage. Where does that leave me?"

"Let them have her," Dianne said coldly. "If they wanted her that badly they would have got her already. She's been into the city on her own every day before she turned up here and every day since."

"Daniel took hold of both her hands. "Look, I'm going to persuade her to stay, all right?"

"That's what she wants. You've gone soft in the head."

"Trust me Dianne. I know what I'm doing."

"Well if she stays then I'm going. Would you mind leaving go of me?"

"Bloody hell fire. That's all I need!" He let go of her and turned back towards the window, throwing his arms up in the air in despair.

"Well, what is it to be?"

"It's going to be neither," he shouted. "Do you hear?" He took several deep breaths and turned back to face her. "Dianne," he said firmly. "Please don't let me down now. You know that I've made plans and I don't want anything to happen that will spoil everything."

"It wouldn't spoil anything at all if she left as far as I'm concerned."

"Then that means only one thing."

"What?"

"Get me my things together. I'm the one who is going away."

"What the hell for? You can't go away now."

Daniel's resolve was unabated. He took hold of Dianne's arm and led her into the office. "Wait here," he said. "I have something to explain to you, but first I have to see Anita." He turned and left Dianne watching after him, her brow creased with concern. Daniel went up stairs to find Anita. She was sitting at the dressing table, facing the mirror with her coat already on.

"Anita," he said, "I do realise how you feel, believe me." He put his hands on her shoulders. "I don't want you to leave."

She leaned her head against his hand. "She doesn't like me you know," she said to their reflection in the mirror.

"Oh, that isn't true," Daniel said, injecting as much sincerity into his voice as he could. "She remains impassive to my private life, but she has a job to do."

"I'm just afraid she has a motive for getting you out of the company. The mafia might not be trying as hard as you think to get you."

"I trust her Anita, I always have done. Nothing is likely to make me change my mind."

"It would still be better if I leave," Anita insisted.

Daniel knelt next to her. "I'm going away for a few days. Can't you stay until I get back?"

"When are you going?"

"Straight away. I'll be travelling around quite a bit so I'll contact you when I get back, probably Monday or Tuesday. I'll give you a ring to meet me at the warehouse and we'll go out together, just you and me."

"Well that was sudden."

Daniel grinned. "I'll be back in five minutes to see that you have unpacked."

She smiled into the mirror and peeled off her coat.

Dianne stood tapping her foot and leaning against Daniel's desk. "Well, you've got round to me at last have you?"

"You know I always leave the best till last." He closed the door behind him.

"I suppose that means that I can't leave you to stew in your own juice then?"

"I prefer it if we stew together." He took out a pen and paper from the desk drawer and scribbled something down.. "I'll ring you at the warehouse every day that I'm away, I promise."

"Oh yeah? Where have I heard that before?"

"I want you to see Cayley while I'm away. He has some papers you need to sign." He handed her the paper. "And if either of these people ring me, you tell them I'll ring them back as soon as I come in. "I want nobody to know where I am. I'll be back in a couple of days. I'll ring you at the warehouse with the ETA before I set off back."

"What about her?" She threw her head in the direction of the door.

"She stays till I get back. I want to speak to her at Malterswood the evening before I return. You will see to it that she gets the phone call won't you?"

Dianne shrugged. "If I have to," she said in a toneless voice.

CHAPTER 9

19th September

Jack Hart had plans for Edward, plans that didn't include him disappearing again until he wanted him to. He realised that Edward was nobody's fool Edward was looking out for himself and that was characteristic that made fitting people into an already set plan difficult. If they can think for themselves then they can alter a plan at the very last minute, a plan that has taken a long time to set up and co-ordinate with different people, a plan that has to succeed in order for another plan that relies on it to be developed. Nothing was ever finite with him. As soon as one plot ended so it led to another in a continuum of devious schemes.

He went along with Edward and let him have his driving license but he had no intention of giving him a vehicle. Appeasing Edward was his only motive for being nice to him.

"What about the new identity you said I was to have?"

"No time for that now. It will take too long. We'll just have to concentrate on your hair. Give it a colour more in line with your age."

"I thought grey was rather becoming."

"Yeah, becoming old." Hart grinned at his own humour "The whole idea is for you to pass as somebody else, not yourself." He left with a smile on his face. Taylor was going along with his plan nicely. He told his men to give Edward a free rein during the coming week. He had a job to do and he was going to do it with finesse, and in order to do that he had to keep the scientist happy. Although he never played chess, had he done so then he would have been a grand master if going by his manipulation of human pawns was anything to go by. He had an uncanny degree of foresight and calculation which had gained him his senior position in the C.I.A.

"Give him plenty of space," he instructed his men as Edward was getting ready for a trio out. "But keep an eye on him and watch where he goes. I want to know every move he makes."

"Okay boss Chester Barnham said. "We'll keep an eye on him, don't you worry."

"Where are we going?" Chester asked Edward as he put his coat on and followed him out to the car.

"Into town. Got a bit of shopping to do."

"How long do you intend taking?" asked David Townson, the other minder.

"As long as it takes for me to have my fill of it," he replied. "In fact I have twenty years of window shopping to catch up on. If you can reckon a week for every year I've been shut up in the desert then you'll have some idea as to just how much living I have to catch up on."

"Well I sure hope that you can wait until your assignment is over because we don't have that long to pamper you."

"Sure," Edward grinned, "I can wait so long as I can have a taste of things to come. We all have to have something to look forward to, haven't we?"

"You're right there Buddy," Chester said sympathetically.

They parked the car in a car park in the centre of town. "We'll meet you back here at four-thirty," Chester stated as they got out and watched Edward walk away.

"Suits me fine," Edward said, knowing full well that they were going to follow him. Hart didn't trust him any more the he trusted Hart. As he walked down towards the crowded streets and headed towards the bank, he thought it more than likely that Hart still wanted to get him indicted for crimes against the State. He knew for sure that he would expect him to skip off once they had given him some spending money so he wandered about, going in and out of a few shops, buying a pair of *Reactolite* sunglasses and an ice cream. He looked around several times but never saw Chester or David once.

He went into a bookshop and bought six books novels which he wasn't going to read, and at a shop a little further along the street he bought a sports bag to carry them in. Gradually, he worked his way towards the bank and looked round again. Still no sign of his minders. They would see him go into the bank. That might make them show themselves, he thought.

"Where the hell is he going?" Townson muttered to himself as he watched Edward heading up the steps into the bank. "Did you see that?" he spoke into his hand held communicator.

"What's happening?" came Chester's voice. "I've lost him."

"He's gone into the bank."

"Don't say he's going to open an account," Chester laughed.

"There's no saying what the crazy old fool has in mind."

"Get up close. Don't want to lose him when he comes out."

"That's affirmative."

Edward walked up to the clerk at the desk. It wasn't the one he'd seen before, but he was confident he could get to the deposit box. "Can I help you sir?" he asked.

"I wish to go to my safety deposit box," Edward said politely but in a businesslike manner.

"Yes sir. You have your key?"

"No, but I was told I could go to it if I told you the number and signed a form. Here's my driving license." He handed it to the clerk.

What number id it, sir?"

"7948," Edward said automatically.

"Could you wait a minute?" the clerk asked politely and walked over to a glass-fronted office at the rear of the cahier's section.

Edward watched him knock on the door, and a bald-headed man with thick-lensed glasses called for the clerk to enter. They talked for a minute or so and then the clerk returned. "Could you sign the form sir?" and pushed a piece of paper towards Edward.

"Sure," said Edward and signed it in his normal handwriting. He pushed it back to the clerk.

"Won't be a moment sir." He went back to the bald headed man and talked some more. The manager shrugged and the clerk returned. "A security man will be with you shortly," he said. "Would you mind taking a seat over there?" He pointed to a seat by the door leading to the vaults. Edward did as he was told, sat down and crossed his legs.

A few minutes later, a guard came up to him. "Would you come this way, sir?"

Edward stood up and followed the same procedure as he had gone through when he had gone down to the vaults previously. Each door he went through was locked securely behind him. The guard took out a key, unlocked box 7948 and placed it in the booth.

Edward could feel his heart beating faster as he stepped forward and lifted the lid. He sucked in a sharp breath as he looked inside. The box was empty. Not even the bag remained. He clenched his fist but restrained himself from hammering it on the counter. Restraining the urge to scream out aloud, he drummed it on the rim of the box until his anger subsided. A million dollars gone. The bastard. I'll kill her, he vowed.

"Are you all right sir?" the guard asked as he saw Edward pass through bright pink to puce and back to crimson. The arteries stood out on Edward's neck and forehead. All a sign of a seizure where he came from. He stepped forward to catch the falling body.

"Quite," Edward snapped and slammed the lid closed on the box.

"Are you finished sir?"

"Some people would like to think so," Edward said sharply.

"I don't understand," the guard said apologetically. "Have you finished?"

"For now," Edward said and stepped away from the booth.

The guard returned the box to its slot while Edward wiped the perspiration off his forehead with his handkerchief. He followed the guard back to the lobby.

The cool breeze outside was refreshing but still felt hot. He hadn't expected this. It had to be Janine. She had the key and she had the notes with the samples of his handwriting. But how the hell did she get identification? His mind churned over as he walked back to the multi-level car park. He didn't even know her last name. God what a fool I've been, he thought. I trusted her with everything I'd got and for what? He shook his head at sheer disbelief at his own gullibility. No alternative now but to do the job for Hart and get his pay off. Then, at least, he could go somewhere and live in peace and quiet. Damn it though, A million dollars would have helped that peace and quiet enormously in a posh New York apartment. It would have been great to have an apartment in New York. He was only a few hundred yards from the car park now, his mind thinking about the apartment. New York. Why New York? Why not in Washington or Dallas? What made him think of New York? Then it hit him. She said she would meet him at an apartment in New York. Grey Oaks. That was it. It could have been a false address because she never intended meeting him there because she hadn't intended him to still be alive. She had left him to die at the airport and told the police who he really was. She might just have been telling the truth about the apartment.

The men were standing at the car as if they had never moved. The tall frame of Chester leaned against the car smoking a cigarette while the shorter, stubbier David, with his moustache that made him look like a modern-day Zapata, lounged with his feet out of the open rear door. "You finished for the day?" Chester asked amiably.

"Not used to all this walking about," Edward said, wiping the sweat off his face. "I haven't done half what I wanted to do."

"I suppose that means that you want to do the same tomorrow?" Dave asked sarcastically.

"Right," Edward laughed and they all got back in the car and drove back to the safe house.

Edward slept fitfully that night. His mind kept flitting from one thing to another, trying to make sense of everything that had happened. Janine had tricked him into thinking she loved him. She had made it appear that she had been in danger as well. She had helped him plan his escape and even suggested his fictional name that he could use to save his money at the bank. How had she stolen the money? Then his mind switched to Hart. What the hell did Hart want with a burned-out scientist? The C.I.A. had enough agents to pretend to be somebody else without recruiting an absolute amateur who had to be followed about until the right time came for him to carry out the job, whatever it was. The whole thing smelled of a set up.

He came out of his semi-conscious state with a jerk that saved him from plunging into a chasm of sleep. He was sweating, despite the chilled air. "That's it," he said aloud as he sat up in bed. "Matthew T. Roland, that's it."

He looked at his watch. 04.30. He jumped to his feet and dressed quickly. His hunch had to be right. He had no other choice but to follow it through. He was dressed and standing in his stockinged feet by the time he had worked out what he was going to do. The two minders were down stairs sleeping in the front room so he decided to try the back door first. The front door faced the bottom of the staircase so, carrying his shoes, he tiptoed along the passage to the back. Nobody could have heard him as he moved like a shadow. Not even the floorboards creaked as he felt his way past the front room door. A miracle, he thought. He knew that the back door only had a drop latch on it besides a strong bolt. Provided the door opened quietly, he would be able to escape. He put his shoes on the floor, stood up, and turned the latch with a click. He held his breath and listened for the sound of stirring bodies. Nothing. Slowly, he turned the bolt and slid it down. It made a grating noise which sounded like a house side falling down in the deathly silence of the back passage. Still no sign of the two men. His heart thumped in his ears as he opened the door. It took a whole minute before the gap was wide enough to squeeze out into the cold night air. Leaving the door ajar he slipped on his shoes and walked away to the main highway as fast as he could. There was no going back now. Never.

It was ten miles to the outskirts of town, a two and a half hour walk. He looked at his watch 04.45. By 07.10 he had hailed a taxi and was on his way to the airport. He was making good time. He paid off the cab, booked a ticket on the 08.30 flight to New York and had half an hour to get something to eat. He had thirty dollars left for his taxi fare to Grey Oaks when he reached the other end of his journey. It would be enough. He had no intention of going back to Hart, nor had he any intention of leaving Grey Oaks if Janine was there. Not without his million dollars, anyway.

Edward knew it was a calculated risk. The address might not even exist, but at least he was two and a half thousand miles away from the people he was afraid of. He bought a hamburger with his last dollar as he walked along Hoover. There had to be a Bourneville House somewhere along there. He stopped and asked a passer-by but he hadn't heard of the place. He asked a few more, but they couldn't help him either. He was beginning to wonder if there was anybody in New York who actually lived there. Every one of the people he asked was a stranger to the city. He was just about to conclude that he had made a bad guess about the apartment when there it was., straight in front of him, Bourneville House, an apartment block that looked like an Arndale Centre. The steps to the entrance were wide and elaborate. A top class place he thought. Just the place for a millionaire. Ashe entered the lobby a security man scowled and said, "Good Day." He sat with a computer terminal, a telephone and half a dozen closed circuit television screens, and managed an uninviting smile as Edward spoke.

"Roland," he said and realised that he must look like a tramp. He hadn't shaved since yesterday morning. He stood sideways to avoid the searching stare of the guard.

"Yes sir, quite. What can I do for you?"

What can he do for me? Hell fire, that name was supposed to mean something to him. Edward had counted on the occupant of the apartment having that name. It had been a logical conclusion. "Do for me?" Edward asked as his brain raced for the right thing to say.

"Forgotten your key again have you?" he said with a grin.

"Er, yes," Edward said, wondering just what the guard was talking about. He was supposed to say something like, 'Yes sir, who shall I say is calling?' What sort of open house was this offering keys to scruffy strangers?

"If you wait a moment, I'll let you in."

"Certainly." Let me in! He smiled and waited until the guard had checked his monitors and then followed him obediently to the third floor. The guard stepped out of the elevator, walked over to a door, unlocked it and stepped to one side.

"There you are, sir," he said and walked back to the elevator. Edward watched as the elevator doors closed and the light flashed to indicate the guard was on his way down. He shrugged his shoulders and walked into the room. As he walked through to the inner door he leaned his head forward to see if there was anybody there. Nobody in sight! What a guard! He checked all the rooms and soon established that he was alone. He was impressed. The whole place was expensively decorated and very roomy. He walked over to the drinks cabinet and swung open the door. "Bourbon?" he asked himself. "Don't mind if I do. Help yourself. Don't worry, I will."

He poured a drink and splashed some water into it, took a long swig of the hot liquid, breathed out the fumes and then he went about exploring every corner of the apartment. He found a wall safe behind a picture in the front room. It had combination lock. Sometimes he wished he had studied something other than chemistry. A degree in safe cracking wouldn't have gone amiss at this moment. He knew what would be in there if the guard hadn't let some stranger in to crack it already. He twiddled the dial and took another slug of his drink. He let the picture slide back over the safe door and carried on his search via the drinks cabinet. There was nothing in the bedroom apart from a king-size bed with blue silk sheets, and a small dressing table. He went through the drawers, careful not to ruffle up any of the contents until his hand slid against something solid. He pulled it out and unwrapped it from the muslin cloth that held it tight. A Smith and Wesson .36 calibre revolver. Quickly he checked the cylinder. Six live rounds. He felt around in the drawer a bit more, but found no more live rounds of ammunition, so he slid the revolver into his pocked and carried on searching. He found nothing else of interest except, from checking the clothes in the wardrobe, there were sure signs of a man and woman living together. Janine was definitely the woman. He recognised the dresses, including the one she wore when they made their supposed escape from Marvin and the foreigner. He wondered just how much the escape had been an act and how much had been fear of being killed. He wondered if Marvin Belk was involved with her at this end. After all, he knew whose face he was giving Edward, it had to belong to the man who was now living with Janine; he must have done. He shivered. Marvin was the most terrifying man he had ever met even unarmed.

"Right place, anyway," he said as he went through the bathroom. He stripped off his clothes, had a stinging hot shower and a wet shave with a *Bic* that was lying on the bathroom vanity unit. He felt better as he put on his shirt. "What the hell," he said aloud. He flung off the shirt, went back into the bedroom and took out a silk shirt from one of the drawers. He felt rich now. He had never worn silk in his life, and as for silk sheets, he only wished that he had had them when he was sleeping with Janine, but that was no longer to be. He went through to the bathroom and finished dressing, threw his jacket over his shoulder and went into the kitchen.

He realised that he hadn't eaten anything since the hamburger. And that was hours ago. He made himself a cheese and pickle sandwich and a strong cup of coffee then sat back in an easy chair and dined. The rest of the afternoon he spent lounging in the chair and listening to a record of Bach's Brandenburg Concertos until he eventually fell asleep.

It was much later in the evening when he was awakened by the sound of the door being unlocked. The record player had switched itself off and the room was silent. He picked up his jacket and placed it over the chair arm. He lifted what remained of a glass of Bourbon in one hand and moved his other hand close to the pocket that held the revolver. He could hear voices and laughter as someone opened the inner door.

Edward hadn't anticipated the sheer look of terror on Janine's face when she saw him sitting facing her. Her face drained of blood and her gleaming smile turned into a hideous mask. Her lips quivered without forming a word. Edward grinned triumphantly for a brief moment and then his face also froze. It wasn't fear of the man who stood behind her. He knew the face well. He had been seeing in the mirror ever since his bandages came off. He had realised that he must have been made to look similar to the man who the guard thought was the tenant of the apartment, but the likeness was uncanny. He was the first to speak. "Well, this explains everything."

"Everything?" the man asked. He was still lost for words.

"Everything," Edward repeated. "First the name; Matthew T. Roland. That must be your name no doubt?"

"Yes."

"And the bank of course. With a fair copy of my handwriting, a key plus identification you had no trouble collecting the money for me."

"For you?"

"I had thought that the security guard was a little lax, but with your face, his mistake was completely understandable."

Janine forced herself to speak. "I didn't plan on you getting caught," she said.

"Caught? Who told you I had been caught?"

"Well I presumed…" She began to shake.

"You presumed that you had left me to die and that you had succeeded in getting rid of me for good when you told the police who I really was and where they could find my dying body."

"No, it wasn't like that. I was afraid to tell anybody."

"More afraid than you are now?"

Edward watched as the man went into the bedroom and returned a moment later with his face even more sullen than when he went in. "Looking for this?" Edward asked, and lifted the revolver from his coat.

"What are you going to do?" asked Janine in a trembling voice.

"I want to know first of all how you got the doctors to give me that face." He pointed at Matthew. "It's not perfect but with whiskers it sure fooled the guard downstairs."

"They asked Marvin what they wanted you to look like and I was the only person with a photograph on me. They said it is always more rewarding if they rebuild a face they want to create."

"They obviously are well practiced at it."

"What else do you want to know?" asked Matthew.

"The combination to the wall safe."

"I see, but the money isn't there."

"No you don't see. *I* see."

"How do you mean?" asked Janine.

"I see that you robbed me and you betrayed me. He drank off the remains of his Bourbon. "I also see Matthew leaving here."

They looked at him quizzically. Neither spoke. "I see you putting on my clothes and walking out of here to get my money."

"I'll do that," Matthew said a little too eagerly. I also see you being seen to be the last person to leave this apartment alive."

"How do you mean?" Janine sobbed.

"I mean, if there is any argument about who shot you, it will be evident that Matthew here will be the only person to have motive and opportunity, since I don't exist."

"Damn it man. I don't intend getting framed for murder."

"And I don't intend being murdered," Janine put in quickly. "You'd better open the safe for him."

Matthew sighed and went to the picture on the wall. He lifted it off its hook, stood on a chair and turned the dial of the wall safe until the door lock clicked off.

"That will do," Edward said before he could pull the door wide open. "I'll do the rest." He went over and pulled the safe door wide open. A deep metal cylinder went into the wall. He put his hand in and pulled out a cloth bag. It isn't all here, is it?" he said as he opened the bag.

"Only half of it," Matthew stated. "The rest is in a deposit box at the airport."

"The key." Edward demanded and held out his hand.

Matthew put his fingers inside his shirt pocket and pulled out a key. He tossed it to Edward who caught it and put it in his own shirt pocket. He got up and paced the room, the revolver still firmly in his grip. "What are you going to do with us?" Janine asked as Edward gazed sideways out of the window to gain inspiration. He watched the traffic and the pedestrians for a minute or so and then he burst out laughing.

"What am I going to do with you?" he said and then burst out laughing again. "I'll tell you what I am going to do," he said bringing his laughter under control. "I'm going to do nothing."

"What do you mean?" Matthew asked.

"Just what I said. Here," he said and took off his jacket. "Take that and these," he said and stripped off his trousers. "Put these on and the shirt that's in the bathroom. It's on the floor."

Matthew didn't argue. Edward had motive enough to kill them both. All they could do was tell that he had gone a little insane. There was no telling what he might do next. He went to the bathroom and emerged wearing Edward's clothes. "Do you want these?" he asked and threw over his own trousers.

"Very good of you, I'm sure, but I intend leaving my pants off for a while. In the meantime, you can go."

"What are you up to?" Matthew asked, warily.

"Would you rather I shoot you?"

"I'm going," he said and went out rather more quickly than he came in.

"What about me?" asked Janine.

"It all depends on how much you want to share my money darling," he replied smiling.

"Matthew will come back to kill the both of us. He'll neither let you leave here with the money nor let you collect the rest from the airport. He's not soft like you. He'd have killed you if he had the chance."

"Come over here," Edward said as he peered out of the window, Janine went over and stood beside him. "See, That's Matthew just coming out."

"Yes, I see."

"And I'll bet you all the money in this bag that the men in that car over there get out and follow him."

"Who are they?"

"I'll alter my bet," he shouted excitedly, "I'll bet they grab a hold of his arms and escort him to the car," he said as they bustled Matthew into the Buick. "The tall one is called Chester and the other is David." He grinned. "They are friends of Edward Taylor."

"What, your friends?"

"I said they were friends of Edward Taylor. I am Matthew T. Roland, remember?"

21st September.

"We picked him up outside an apartment in Westchester," Chester explained to Jack Hart, back in the New York office. We tailed him there to find out what he was doing but decided to be safe rather than risk him really getting away."

"What the hell was he doing there?"

"Seems like he already had some accommodation set up in an apartment block. He had no trouble getting in or out of the building, and the guard said that the pad was in his name."

"Possibly that's why he wanted the license. The crafty little devil."

"It shows that he was going to do a runner if he could."

"That's not important now," Hart said. "We already knew what he was. But we'd have had a devil of a job proving it. The fact that we have proof now is of no real use. We have a plan to carry out. Once that has been completed it will all be purely academic."

"He's flipped sir."

"Flipped?"

"Gone completely around the bend. Swears blind that he is the real Matthew T. Roland."

"Sure he is. Anything so long as we can hang on to him long enough to carry out our job for us."

It might not be easy. He refuses to accept that we even had a deal."

"Wasn't much of a deal for him, anyway," Hart chuckled. "We most likely would have had to force him to do it anyway."

"Is it going to be possible?"

"Anything is possible, Chester, anything."

"One other thing, sir."

"Yeah?"

"He was with some hooker."

"So what?"

"So she was some high class whore. Not his usual class of ass."

"Who was she?"

"By the time we'd got her name out of him, she'd flown the nest. The name is Janine Westcott."

"Get a couple of men onto tracing her."

"Already done sir. They should pick her up in no time."

"And get that crazy man's hair fixed. No telling when we'll be needing him."

"Yes Sir. What if he won't cooperate?"

"Tell him that the sooner he gets the job over with the sooner he can get back to his high class whore. Failing that, threaten to shoot his cock off. Anything. We've planned for him to do his bit and there is no time to find anybody else."

"Hell, if he only knew!" Chester laughed. "He might go for that option." He carried on laughing until Hart broke in.

"I don't see anything funny about it. We have a job to do and all we are doing is getting him to help us."

"Yes sir," Chester said, wiping a tear from the corner of his eye. "Well he came to the right place, anyway."

CHAPTER 10

20th September

Mark Stevens stepped into Benjamin Carlisle's office. "There's a man out here. Says he wants only to speak to you," he stated.

"Who is he?"

"Didn't give any name. Said he knew you before you had a garage."

"Okay. Tell him I'll be out in a minute."

The young sales assistant went out leaving Benjamin tidying some papers into a file. "Another prospect," Benjamin whispered to himself. He went to a mirror in the back of his office and straightened his tie. He was particular about showing people he was successful. Being well groomed and wearing expensive suits was part of his image, besides driving the latest model of a car in his garage.

He looked in the mirror and thought how he had changed in the last three years. He hadn't put on a lot of weight, nor were any of his golden curls falling out but they were beginning to debase themselves to silver around h is temples, and his marine blue eyes looked tired as if he had lost a couple of nights' sleep. Still, he consoled himself that he didn't look any older than any other men of thirty seven years and turned away with a snort.

He walked across the showroom floor towards Mark who pointed to a red Mercedes 450SL. Benjamin went over and peered inside. The person in it didn't get out, but turned to face him. "Good God!" Benjamin exclaimed.

"No need to stand on ceremony. 'Daniel' will do." He grinned.

"Well, the prodigal's returned. Dam it Danny, it's good to see you after all this time. Where the hell have you been?"

"All over the place, actually."

"Well what brings you here then? Can't be the sunshine." He said, pointing to the rain clouds outside the showroom window.

“I’m looking for a house in England. Got my eyes on one in Surrey. Thought you might want to come and view it with me.” He patted the dashboard of the car the way some men patted their wives’ backsides. “I’ve been meaning to get one of these. How about a run over to Surrey?”

“Benjamin looked at his brother for a long moment before saying, “Great, when?”

“I was thinking about now,” Daniel said with a smile.

“Now? Well I suppose I can. I can leave things in Mark’s capable hands. He’s a first class salesman.” He turned to go back to his office, and Daniel got out of the car and followed him. “So where have you been if you haven’t been in England?”

“Got a shipping business in New York. But I am thinking of retiring and settling down.”

“You’re not married then?”

“Nope,” Daniel said, grinning. “But I have every intention of being very soon. What about you? Did you ever get over your shyness with women?”

“I wasn’t that bad,” Benjamin objected. “Just needed time to find the right person, that’s all.”

“So you’re married then?”

“Was. She died three years ago. The big C.”

“Sorry to hear that Ben. It makes me feel like I ought to have kept in touch. Never got the chance to meet her,” he said with sadness in his voice.

“You would have liked her. Never knew where to get in touch with you. Not even when Ma died last year.”

“I’m sorry, Ben, I should have kept in touch.”

“God dammit Danny, we didn’t even know if you were still alive.”

“I know that now, but life has just flashed by.”

“There’s such a thing as a telephone you know. Well you’re here now, so come on, you can tell me about yourself and what you’ve been up to. It’s been too many years…”

"Fourteen I reckon," Daniel said with a faint trace of a Brooklyn accent.

"I really thought you were dead."

"I'll live forever," Daniel said with a forced laugh.

Benjamin leaned on the edge if his leather-topped desk and pointed to a leather Chesterfield armchair. As Daniel sat down, the light accentuated the lines on his face making him look more his age. He was only two years older than Benjamin but looked two years his junior. He, too, had fair hair but it was a darker shade and displayed a marked tendency to grow straight rather than turn into curls. It was closer cut giving him a more executive appearance. Apart from that they bore a remarkable resemblance to each other; same height, same blue eyes, same prominent chin with a cleft in it. There was no mistaking them as anything other than brothers.

"So what have you been doing these past fourteen years?" asked Benjamin.

"Everything you can imagine," said Daniel as he looked around the plush office. "Doing alright for yourself, I can see," he said, shuffling in the leather armchair, getting the feeling of it.

"Not too bad now," Benjamin responded with a smile. He eased himself up on his hands and sat on the desk. "Bit of a struggle at first, though, I must admit." He leaned forward. "You aren't in any kind of trouble, are you Danny?"

"Trouble? Hell no. I've been everywhere and done about everything. Now I want to sit back and forget about most of it."

"Just what is it that you do now?"

"I'm a dealer, not unlike you really, only I deal internationally. Import and export, you know."

"In what?"

"In anything and everything. I buy and sell anything I can make a profit on, mainly foreign stuff. I'm what is called a shipping agent and I forward freight for people from my own warehouse."

"I might have known you'd be wheeling and dealing," Benjamin said and waited for Daniel to continue.

"It's a long story Ben and I don't want to bore you."

"Then the sooner you get on with it the sooner we can go and have a look at that house of yours."

"Not got it yet. Just got an appointment to view."

"Well?"

"It's Georgian and…"

"Not the bloody house, man. I can see that later."

"It's quite boring really. I made a few contacts as I travelled around the world and I ship things to them and from them. Eventually things worked out so well that I opened a warehouse in New York. That's where my legitimate business address is now."

"Legitimate?" Benjamin queried. "You mean you have an illegitimate business as well?"

"No," Daniel faltered. "It's just that at first I… I just worked from other people's warehouses. It's as simple as that."

"So why the house in England? Are you moving over here?"

"I hope to. In a couple of week's time actually."

"Why come back to England after all this time?"

"Oh, suffice it to say that I want out." He grinned at his brother. "Well do I get a spin in the Merc?"

Ben stood up, went over to the door and shouted out, "Mark, get the Merc out will you?" He turned back to Daniel. "Can't say I'm not impressed though, Danny. You were always a go ahead type. I am more the stuck in the mud type really."

"I know you always liked getting stuck into a good scrap." Daniel laughed. "I thought you might end up being beaten to death or something."

"Gave that up after I got shot."

"Yes, a bit of a bad do that," Daniel conceded. "The army was all right except for people trying to kill us. Seem to be doing all right now, despite the hole in your back."

"Oh, I never feel it now. It's as if it never happened."

"Damned near thing at the time, though. We didn't think you were going to pull through at the beginning,"

"You never told me that, Danny."

"Never told you a lot of things, Ben boy, like I knew what went on when you first got the garage,"

"Well I might tell you about my business if you promise to behave yourself now that you are back in the country."

Daniel laughed. "Are you coming to see this house then?"

Mark had parked the red Mercedes outside the front of the showroom window. Daniel was in the driver's seat before Benjamin had got out of the door. "I'll drive," he called and looked for the ignition keys.

Mark handed them to Benjamin and shrugged.

"Here," Daniel said as he tossed them to his brother before walking to the passenger side of the car and getting in.

Daniel gunned the engine and sped off towards the ring-road. "Do you always drive your cars like this?" Benjamin asked, holding onto the dashboard as the car rounded a corner.

"Worried about your car, Ben?"

"Just worried."

"Then you've no need to be. I'll pay for it," said Daniel as he slowed to the speed limit. "Just getting the cobwebs out of the engine."

Benjamin just smiled. His brother hadn't changed much in the years he'd been out of his life. He still knew his brother well enough to know that he would use somebody else's car rather than have to buy one himself. But Benjamin was glad to share it with his long-lost sibling. It was like old times again, joy-tiding in an old Morris convertible when they were on leave, the wind blowing in their faces, singing, not a care in the world. Bugger the car, he thought. He couldn't remember a day he'd enjoyed so much in years; at least not since he had lost his wife Karen.

They drove out into the country and along a maze of intersecting side-roads until Daniel finally pulled into a tar-macadamed drive. He'd seemed to know where he was going at first but Benjamin realised that he must have got lost. "Hand me the brochure," he said. "I'll look to see where you are supposed to be going."

"We're here," Daniel said with a grin.

"I didn't see any 'For Sale' sign," Benjamin stated, but then he wouldn't if they had parked in some tycoon's driveway.

"Well this is it, I'm sure," Daniel said as he placed the brochure in Benjamin's hand. It had a glossy colour picture of the house on the front of it. As they approached from around a bend masked by a row of mature beech trees the double-fronted mansion came into view. It was the right house on the brochure, a huge building in its own grounds on the outskirts of Godalming. There was a huge mature yew tree off to the left of mature lawns that ran right around the Georgian mansion. Benjamin would enjoy looking around it if nothing else. Daniel had never considered price; that was certain; probably never even asked. Daniel wasn't averse to going to look at something just for something to do but Benjamin didn't mind. He was enjoying himself. It would be therapeutic.

"When you said a house, I thought you meant a house," he exclaimed as they walked up to front door.

Daniel just laughed and knocked on the front door with the big ornate knocker. After a few seconds, the door opened and a man stood before them holding a clip-board. "Good afternoon," he said pushing a pair of gold-rimmed spectacles up onto the bridge of his nose. "Mr. Carlisle, isn't it? I'm John Prior of *Weedle, Bent and Prior.*"

"Hello," said Daniel. "Is this all of it?" he asked in a demure voice, and glanced away back towards the driveway.

"Two and a half acres in all, Mr. Carlisle," Prior replied, "just as it says in the brochure."

"Seems smaller than in the pictures," Daniel said bluntly. "I was looking for something a bit bigger, really."

Mr. Prior waited for Daniel to carry on.

"Still, better have a look around before doing anything else."

They spent what was left of the afternoon walking around the house and gardens while Mr. Prior waited patiently in the kitchen doing what he said was 'paperwork' on the huge central worktop.

Finally, after an hour and a half, Daniel asked if Benjamin would sit in the car as if he were ready to leave. "I could stay here all day," Benjamin complained and went to sit in the Mercedes.

"Well it doesn't seem exactly what it says in the brochure," Daniel said to Mr. Prior as he waved the booklet at the estate agent.

Mr. Prior frowned. "We've tried our best to portray it as it is. However, it always comes down to the potential buyer viewing the property." He could see Benjamin waiting to go in the car outside. "I could ring the executors and see if there's any leeway on the price, if you like."

"Better had. It might save me having to look at a couple of other properties before I return to The States." He went and walked through the downstairs rooms again.

"Mr. Carlisle," Prior called. "We have a sales package ready for taking the property to auction later this month if it isn't sold. There's a contract in it. If you would sign it and pay the deposit subject, of course to your searches turning out alright, then we can take it off the market and let you have it at the price you have suggested. The package contains a title search done by us. You can of course get your own searches done but I am sure they will coincide."

"That sounds good to me." Daniel took out his cheque book. "The contract and the conveyance must be in the same name," he said and handed Mr. Prior a piece of paper. I am paying the deposit as the agent. The name on the conveyance must be that one."

"That's quite all right. The name on the contract doesn't need to be the same, so long as you know that you will be obliged to pay the balance if the other person does not."

Daniel nodded. He picked up his folder of papers and said his goodbyes. Benjamin was waiting patiently in the car. "You decided to buy it then?"

"You bet. Best place I've seen. It's a steal."

"That sounds like the Daniel of old," Benjamin said as Daniel drove away. "You must have some money then."

They drove back to the city, had a meal at Daniel's favourite Chinese restaurant and went for a drink at *Mike's Cocktail Bar* just around the corner from Benjamin's flat in Kensington Palace Gardens. He had taken to popping into the cocktail bar occasionally in the evening. Since Karen's death he had done very little socializing but quite a bit more drinking. In the main, the clientele at *Mike's* were a generation younger than Benjamin and although there was always a bevy of 'available' young women, he had never felt inclined to look at anybody as a new partner since Karen's death. He led the way down into the bar. Mike looked up from pouring a *Cardinale* and winked, "Hi Ben, I'll be with you in a minute," he beamed.

Three girls at the bar put their heads together and chatted sotto voce. One lifted her head. "Hi Ben," she said cheerily. "Who's your friend?"

"Oh, hello er…" Benjamin faltered. He knew her by sight but couldn't put a name to the face. "My brother Daniel," he said, trying not to be distracted by the young lady's tight dress.

"Usual, is it?" Mike asked.

"Two please," Benjamin replied.

"Never knew you had a brother," another of the girls piped up in a shrill voice. Benjamin looked at her, but like the first, he couldn't put a name to the face. Then he looked at the third face and recognised the girl. He knew her name. She'd been to his apartment one night when he had had one too many cocktails and had lost his inhibitions.

"Daniel," he said, "meet Susan."

"Pleased to meet you, Daniel," all three girls cheeped in unison.

"No wonder he comes for drinks here," Daniel said to the three girls. They all gigged.

"Just on our way to the disco at *Barney's*," the first girl said. "Do you fancy coming?"

"Might do later," Daniel said with a definite glint in his eye.

"Two *Freddies* coming up," said Mike as he placed two full glasses on the bar.

"Hope you can make it," said Susan..

"We'll try," said Benjamin, watching them waft out of the cellar like three feathers on a breeze. "We'd be the only geriatrics there," he said to Daniel after they had disappeared.

Daniel laughed. "You'll never change, will you Ben?"

The evening passed quickly as they talked while the cocktails gradually went to their heads and practically every other part of their bodies after several drinks. "Let's get another one before we go," Daniel said as he stood up, none too steadily, to go over to the bar.

"Yes sir?" Mike said.

"Another couple of Freddie Fucputtersh, Fuddutters… Fup… Oh jush give ush two Walbangersh."

"With Tequila" Mike asked with a broad grin.

"Thash right," Daniel giggled.

"Your last one is it?"

"I shuppose it'll haf to be. Got to get up early thish morning.

Mike handed him the drinks and Daniel swayed through the smoke-laden atmosphere. Benjamin looked at Daniel. He didn't look like he had a worry in the world, but he knew that his brother was nobody's fool. Gradually, they made their way back to Benjamin's apartment, singing all the way except for the moment when they tripped over the step and stumbled through the doorway. Then Daniel became somber as drunks often do, "That Vlatsov hash a lot to answer for, Ben my boy," he said solemnly.

Benjamin picked himself up. "Wash him that put that step there wash it? I wondered… hic… what silly clot did that."

"Mark my words Ben, he's mad, utterly mad, him and hish Sheff."

"Oh his chef helped him did he?"

Daniel staggered into the room and leaned on a small table. "Nice little occasional table, that," he commented. "I ship an occasional table," he said and giggled. "Only occasionally, mind." He chuckled again. "Not to Vlatsov, though."

"Who?" Benjamin asked.

"Vlatsov. Poitre Vlatsov."

"Am I shupposed to know him? He hasn't bought a car off me has he?"

"I doubt it unless you happen to know anything about… Oh well, it doesn't matter."

*****

They were up and awake within five hours.of falling into their beds. Daniel was none the worse for his night out. "You not got a house then?" he asked Benjamin who was sipping black coffee at the breakfast bar in an attempt to stop the hammering inside his skull.

"Never used it since I lost Karen."

"Loved her a lot, didn't you?"

"What time is your flight?" Benjamin asked to change the subject.

"Twelve o'clock. You know, you ought to get out a bit more. Do you good. Life goes on you know." Daniel chewed on some toast. Benjamin couldn't face anything.

"I felt so helpless, Danny. She was fit and full of fun one day and the next she was told she would be dead inside three months. I was so useless. All I could do was watch her dying and make sure she took her pain-killers to make it as peaceful as possible for her. Damn it all, all I could do was fill her so full of pills that she hardly remembered me some days."

Daniel put his hand on his brother's arm. "I wish I'd known her. She must have been something really special."

Benjamin rubbed his eye. "She was Danny. To me she was."

"Can I borrow your car for a couple of hours?" Daniel asked. As he stood up and moved away from the table. "Got to sort out old Mr. Prior."

"Sure. You can come to the garage after and I'll run you to the airport."

Daniel got himself ready and was soon away. He left Benjamin staggering about with a cup of black coffee, got in the car and went first to a firm of solicitors. A Mr. Deschamps greeted him. "Hello Mr. Carlisle. You bought the property I presume?"

"Yes."

"We can speed things up as I explained yesterday morning with what we call a special search."

"That suits me. What I want is for the searches to be done as soon as possible and then you ring this number. She will be here to sign the conveyance and take possession. You have the balance, so there are no hold-ups, okay?"

"Very well Mr. Carlisle. Leave it with me." Deschamps got out of his seat and showed Daniel out.

Daniel's next stop was *Weedle, Bent and Prior.* It took him less than fifteen minutes to sort out the particulars of the purchase and to be on his way again. He arrived at Benjamin's office at 11.02. "Have I time to make a call to New York?" he asked his brother who was already waiting for him.

"You'll have to be quick if you want to catch your flight."

"I should get through okay." He dialed his number and Carl picked up almost straight away. "Hi, Daniel here Carl. Can't waste a lot of time explaining, but will you let Dianne know I'll see her at the warehouse before she leaves."

"Okay, is that all?"

"No, can you put me through to my lounge?" Daniel heard a click and a ringing tone.

"Hello," came Anita's voice.

"Daniel here, sweetheart. I'll be late back tonight. Do you still want that date?"

"Try stopping me," she laughed.

"Well I'll meet you at the warehouse at nine o'clock tonight. Get Mickey or Carl to see you safely into the building and up to my office."

"Nine o'clock. It's a date."

They both hung up.

"Right," said Benjamin.

"Hold on. Just one more call to make," Daniel said and began to dial another New York number. A gruff voice answered. "I'll be arriving between eight and nine." He waited.

"Okay," the voice replied and they both hung up.

*****

Benjamin said goodbye to a Daniel at the airport. "You get all your loose ends tied up and get back here as soon as you can." He gripped Daniel's hand.

"I should be back here in no time, by the end of the month at the latest. He put his hand in his inside pocket and pulled out an envelope. "But if I'm not here, then here's a cheque for the Merc. Deliver it to the house in three week's time. It will make a pleasant wedding present for my new Missis. Try and make her at home. She isn't at all familiar with England."

"You bet Danny. It's the least I can do for you." As their eyes met they realised that they had lost none of the fondness they had for each other as children growing up in the East End of London, and as comrades in the army. Benjamin would have asked why they weren't moving over together, but the flight had been called and Daniel had to rush to catch up with the other passengers. Obviously winding up a freight business had some complications.

*****

"Thank goodness you made it all right," Dianne said as she greeted Daniel in his office above the warehouse.

"Bit of a rush, I must admit."

"Here's a list of the people that are expecting a call from you." She handed him a sheet of paper. "And I signed those contracts," she added with a smile.

"Okay." He placed the list on the desk in front of him.

"Aren't you going to tell me who all these people are?"

"Business. You know," Daniel said evasively.

"Still shady dealing Daniel? I thought at least you might have given that up."

"I am; just as soon as everything is wound up here."

"Daniel," she said looking him straight in the eye. "You're full of shit. You deserve everything that's coming to you."

Daniel finished dialing the first number on the list and smiled. "You can be quite nasty Dianne, do you know that?"

"I'll be in my office if you need me. What time are you leaving?"

"Oh, get Mickey to drive you back. Carl will drive me home." The call connected. "Hello, Daniel here."

"Are you ready to go ahead now?"

"Yes, we're ready if plans haven't been changed."

"See you in the car park then. Nine fifteen," the voice said and rung off. Daniel looked at his watch. 20.52. Anita should be here soon. He looked out of the window. Her Cavalier was parked out front in the warehouse yard where he had told her to leave it for when he returned. Carl would be bringing her in the Lincoln and they would wait till darkness fell and they would drive off for their long-awaited night out. Dianne wouldn't know they had gone without a bodyguard until it was too late to do anything about it.

He made another call, this time to Paris. The line was engaged. No matter, everyone knew their part of the plan. He would try again later. He dialed the last number on the list. No answer. Good, he was on his way.

There was a tap on the door. He turned around and saw Anita. She gave him a little wave as he pressed the remote lock release button to let her in. She was early. It was only 20.58. He decided not to re-dial the Paris number and hung up the phone. "Hello darling!" he said as he walked across the office to greet her.

"Oh, darling," she panted as she threw herself into his arms. Her lips were as warm and wild as he had ever known them. "God, I've missed you!" she said and gave him another long kiss.

"Looking forward to our little night out, are you?"

"Are security still around," she asked and broke away.

"I haven't seen them leave yet. I'll take a look in the office next door."

Anita smiled. "Don't be long, darling," she beseeched. "Make sure they've gone and I'll stay here."

Daniel went to the door and was walking out of it when she spoke again. "Oh Daniel darling," she pleaded. He turned and saw her large eyes entreating him to come back over to him.

"Yes sweetheart?"

"Darling I forgot…" she said as she rummaged through her handbag. She took out the keys of the Cavalier and tossed them to him. "Could you be an angel and pop out and get me my spare cigarettes from the car glove compartment. I've run out and if we are going to be waiting for them to leave…" She gave him one of her gentlest smiles, the sort that melted a man's resolve. She knew Daniel couldn't say no to her when she let all her charm flow out.

"Sure," he said, tossing the keys in the air and catching them. A broad grin cracked his face. She had him just where she wanted him and they both knew it, she thought.

Daniel went next door to the office of his Chief of Security. There was no one there. He hadn't seen the Lincoln drive away, but then he hadn't been watching out of the window. He checked his watch and took his time going down to the basement. He had to see somebody in the company car park beneath the warehouse at 21.15. He had six minutes to go.

Anita watched for Daniel going outside and across the yard to the Cavalier. He was taking his time, but then, there was no rush. She had all the time in the world. She went to the desk where she had left her purse and picked it up. She opened it and took out a packed of her special imported cigarettes and slid one out. They were black, long and sensual, made by *Benson and Hedges* in England. Daniel knew not to offer her one of the company cigarettes that lay in wooden boxes in various parts of the huge office. He knew she smoked nothing but her own imported brand. She placed the packet back in her bag, got out a lighter and lit up. She kept the lighter in her left hand and drew hard on the cigarette. Two slender fingers held it away from her face as she blew out the smoke. It billowed against the glass as she looked out of the window again. Still no sign of Daniel. She folded her arms and waited, and then, as she took another draw of the aromatic smoke, she saw Daniel. As he walked casually across the yard she was ready to give him a wave, the kind that lovers give each other, when he turned around. But he didn't turn. He strolled up to the car, unlocked it, and pulled open the door. He took something out of his pocket and then leaned over the seat towards the glove compartment. As he undid the catch, a charge of explosives under the seat detonated and ripped it through his body, tearing his chest cavity apart and spreading it against the roof. In a mass of pulverized jelly as the force of the explosion carried on upwards taking the roof and his remains high into the still evening air. Anita turned away, walked over to the desk, stubbed out her cigarette in the ash tray, picked up her bag and went out of the office door. The shockwave of the explosion had shaken the whole building, shattering windows and pitted the walls with debris.

Dianne appeared from nowhere, closely followed by Mickey. They ran down the staircase and out through the front doors into the yard. There was nothing to be done. Very little remained of the body and there would be less as the car continued to burn. What wasn't burning in the car lay around in little pieces, ragged flesh, some still quivering, but most stilled by death.

Dianne covered her face as Mickey turned her away. Anita came running towards them. "My God!" she screamed hysterically. "They've killed him. They've killed him," she screamed again and sobbed uncontrollably into her hands.

Dianne walked over to her. "Tell me," she shouted. "Who was it?"

"Daniel," Anita sobbed. "My Daniel."

Dianne gave out a screech and grabbed Anita's hair. "You fucking bastard whore," she shouted and pulled her to the ground. "He was never yours you bitch."

"Come on," Mickey said and dragged her away. "There's nothing we can do now."

"I'll kill that bitch," Dianne screamed. "I'll kill her, so help me!"

PART II

CHAPTER 11

27th September

The sun fought hard to get through the clouds that late September afternoon. A mist had fallen during the night and had remained all day, coating the grass with silver droplets. The branches of the beech and sycamore trees bowed over the road and their cascades of leaves dripped large blobs of water onto his windscreen as he passed beneath them.

As he drew into the park, he glanced at his watch. It was 16.20. It had been a long slow journey and he had only another ten minutes in which to catch the 16.20 flight that would get him to New York airport by 21.00 that evening. He had booked in advance the day before when he received the telegram.

"Damn," he swore to himself. "Damn the traffic. He jumped out of the Lotus, locked the door as it slammed shut and ran towards the terminal. "Damn, he swore again and turned on his heel. He had forgotten his hand-luggage. Everything he needed for his trip was in his bag including his passport and visa. By the time he reached the desk, he realised that he had missed the flight. "What time is the next flight to New York?" he asked.

"At 11.00 tomorrow morning," the clerk replied.

"Damn, that will be too late."

The young girl smiled apologetically. "There's always Concord," she said. "There's room on the 19.00 flight to New York and since you are booked on *British Airways* you could transfer your tickets. It arrives at 05.50 New York time."

"How much," Benjamin asked bluntly.

"Two hundred and ninety one pounds on top of the normal first class fare which you have already paid," she said after a brief calculation.

"Hell fire! Never knew brothers could be so expensive," he muttered under his breath. "A whole day wasted at the American Embassy to get a visa and now this. Okay," he said, lifting his eyes to hers "Might as well get there now that I've made all the effort."

"You'll get there three hours earlier," she said and gave him a ticket. "But you have two and a half hours to wait at this end as well."

Benjamin nodded and went into the departure lounge. "Two and a half hours." He sighed and slumped onto an empty couch. He was tired and leaned back in his seat with a resigned grunt, letting his mind ramble over the time when he and Daniel had been as close as any brothers. He thought about their childhood, a contented childhood for him but not so for Daniel. He had never been happy to live in near-poverty. Benjamin felt a kind of numbness inside. He put his hand in the side pocket of his jacket and pulled out a piece of paper. It was the telegram.

"DANIEL DIED YESTERDAY EVENING. FUNERAL AT CHICKFIELD CHURCH, LONG ISLAND, N.Y. AT 2 PM. ON28TH. BENJAMIN CARLISLE BENEFICIARY AND EXECUTOR OF WILL. TO BE READ 4.30 PM. WILL MEET YOU AT N.Y.AIRPORT AT NINE PM THURSDAY. WEAR ROSE TO BE RECOGNIZES. J.B.WEBBER."

How can he be dead, he asked himself. He must have died the same day that he had seen him off at Heathrow. The telegram had given no indication of the circumstances. It was signed, but who the hell was Weber? What did he look like? It was only a week ago that he had seen Daniel for the first time in fourteen years and then, to Benjamin, his brother had seemed indestructible. "I'll outlive the Devil," he had said and laughed. And laugh he did. Daniel never did seem to worry about anything, even under the greatest stress or faced with the gravest danger. Benjamin thought how close they had been.

Daniel was the eldest of the two sons of Denise and John Carlisle by two years and three months. They were brought up to be tough strong boys by their elderly father who ran a small and not too profitable greengrocer's business in the East End of London, a small shop over which they all lived. They got up early in the mornings to help him unload the vegetables from the wholesaler's pickup and stack them before the shop opened at

8.00 am sharp. On fine days they would argue who was going to stack the bags of potatoes in the back store and who was to arrange the display out at the front of the shop. Neither of them liked arranging vegetables in still-life poses.

"It's so that the customers can see the quality of our wares," father would remind them.

"They ought to know by now that you have never sold a bad potato or cabbage in your life," Daniel grumbled on being assigned to the task.

"That isn't the point son. Customers like to pick what they like for themselves. They don't like being told what to have because that makes them uncertain, and people don't like uncertainty, see?"

"But they must be certain. You only sell good stuff."

"Well take it from me, nobody likes being told to have a particular cauliflower, or a particular bunch of daffodils," he said picking up a broom to sweep up the fallen leaves from the pavement. You will find that when people are told what they have to have then generally they will find some fault with it, whereas if they are permitted to pick for themselves they go away happy in the belief they couldn't have done any better."

"Ma tells us even what kind of shoes we have to wear."

"Yes, but when you leave home, you won't let anyone tell what you can and can't do." He reached into his pocket, pulled out a pipe, put it between his teeth unlit, and walked into the shop. Daniel had told Benjamin that it was that moment he decided he would never get tied down with a business and a family that would force him to work so hard that he would have no time to make a real fortune. He was sixteen now and looking at his life ahead, he couldn't envisage spending his adult years toiling from dawn till dusk only to get up and do the exact same thing the next day and the day after that.

Shortly afterwards Daniel had asked his father who that man was who called each month, a well dressed man with a scar over his right eyebrow. "The insurance man," his father replied, Just the insurance man." Daniel didn't believe him. He had met the insurance man, a friendly soul who had time to stand and gossip. But this man with the scar didn't look friendly and never stopped to chat. He would call and leave his father shaking with rage. Three weeks later he saw the burly man shaking his fist at father and it concerned him that his father had lied to him. He had never known his father to tell a lie but he had done and Daniel knew it. He went over to the connecting door and stood quietly listening to the raised voices. "It isn't possible on what we make here," he heard his father protesting.

"You'd better find it," the man shouted and stormed out.

A week later the shop burned down in the middle of the night. Mrs. Carlisle managed to get out to safety with her two sons, but their father's remains were found the next day in the ashes. The police said that they thought that he must have fallen and banged his head. They said his pipe started the fire. Daniel knew otherwise and told Benjamin about the protection racket and how it was run by people like the man with whom Daniel had heard their father arguing. "All dad wanted was to run his little shop in peace and quiet," Daniel told his younger brother. They both felt so helpless, but there was nothing they could do to either bring their father back or vindicate his death. But one thing they did do that day was vow never to let anyone do to them what had been done to their father.

Two months later, Daniel came home and announced that he had joined the army. Unable to find a job that suited him and tempted by the offer to see the world,. He had taken his chance to get out of poverty and signed up for five years.

Two years later Benjamin did the same, but after being wounded in Northern Ireland, he was medically discharged after only two years of his commission. He started and finished several enterprises ranging from renting a market stall to buying and selling antiques. He eventually settled to buying and running a small garage on the outskirts of the City.

Meanwhile, Daniel finished his stint in the army and got work in the warehouses at the docks. Finally in 1970 he visited his mother and disappeared from their lives saying that he had many more places to go and people to see than the army had offered him.

From that day Benjamin had neither heard from Daniel, nor seen his brother for fourteen years until, out of the blue he had called at the garage. Benjamin recalled the early days of starting his business. It hadn't been easy.

"Hello, a guy called Emerson said as he stepped through the Judas gate in the sliding door. He was a man in his mid fifties with snow white hair and a face that bore many scars of a tough life in the East End. His piercing blue eyes took a few seconds to adjust to the dark interior of the workshop. Before he spotted Benjamin, back came a reply.

"How do you do," Benjamin greeted in his deep quiet voice. "Can I be of any assistance?"

Emerson regarded Benjamin for a long moment. He was adept at summing up people's characters in just a few seconds. His conclusions about them rarely turned out to be wrong. "Yes, I live out on the Bexely road, half a mile past the cross-roads. I used to bring my car to this garage for servicing before it closed down a year ago.

Benjamin nodded; the garage had been unoccupied for quite some time before he had taken it over a month ago. "My car needs a few things doing to it I haven't done much driving lately so you've opened just in time to keep my custom if you want it."

"Well yes, I appreciate any new business. It's taking quite some time to build up trade again. The previous owner seems to have let things run down a bit."

"Oh," the well dressed visitor said. "I don't want to put you off, but old Bill Watson packed up for money reasons. He had the place for five years and at first everything seemed to go well, but after a few months he became dejected and complained that he couldn't make ends meet. He was near retiring anyway, but I was surprised that he didn't sell it as a going concern."

"Just as well he didn't or I wouldn't have been able to afford it," said Benjamin. "But I can't see why I can't make the place pay. I've sold a couple of cars already. The service side seems a bit slow but I hope to get business from the people who buy cars from me."

"Yes," Emerson said in an understanding manner.. "Well I hope things work out well for you. What about this car, then, you'll do it for me?"

"Tomorrow morning all right?" asked Benjamin. "I'm just packing up for the day now."

"Fine, I'll drop it off at nine." He turned and stepped back into the sunlight. Emerson lifted his portly frame into the Rover and clicked the door shut. "Right, tomorrow, first thing," he said through the open side window as he drove off the forecourt. A late tea tonight, Benjamin thought to himself. He hadn't seen the Jaguar turn up and park outside. He was hungry and wanted to finish for the day. Stepping back into the workshop, he went through to the office and picked up his keys. He had already taken off his overalls and washed before Emerson arrived. He turned to go when he heard the door chime telling him that the Judas door was once again open. As he looked across the showroom he saw a thick-set man with dark hair and a moustache walking towards him. The stranger wore an expensive-looking suit, no tie and a curious gaze.

"Can I help you?" Benjamin asked as a second man, equally as big as the first, stepped inside. He was younger looking and seemed unconcerned as he glanced about the place until his eyes fell upon a notice that informed all those who wished to know, who was the proprietor of the establishment.

Moustache leveled his gaze on Benjamin. "You the new owner, then?"

"Yes," replied Benjamin softly.

"We sell insurance," the man said and just stood and stared.

It crossed Benjamin's mind that the two men in his office didn't look like insurance salesmen, and they certainly didn't have much 'patter.' In the back of his mind he recognised them from somewhere, but on second thoughts he decided he couldn't possibly know them. "Well, I'm sorry gentlemen, but you're too late. I have all the cover I need. I have had the place insured since the day I took it over. Perhaps if you leave your card I might be able to pass on your details."

Moustache just smiled and stared as if Benjamin hadn't spoken. "He doesn't understand, Geoff, came a voice from over his shoulder. The other man, tall with blonde hair glided up beside Moustache.

"No you don't understand," Moustache echoed. What 'patter' they did have seemed well rehearsed.

"What don't I understand?" asked Benjamin as if to cue them for their next line. He thought about the old hello-hello-hello jokes in the theatre, but he was already beginning to realise that this was no pantomime.

"You don't understand, what we mean by insurance," chirped Blondy, "We cover you against the things that ordinary insurance companies don't."

"Such as?"

"Such as interference by other people who might want you out of business," said Moustache.

"Oh, you mean protection," Benjamin said without any sign of surprise. "I was wondering how long it would take you to get round to visiting."

"We call every week," said Blondy. "We can't emphasize how important it is to pay the premiums regularly." He squinted at Benjamin. "Tomorrow is our first collection-day. We will call about the same time. Our rates are not too unreasonable; we know you have to build up your business."

"How much?" Benjamin asked.

"Say one hundred a week to start with. We can increase the premiums when there is more to insure." With that, and without waiting for a response, they both turned on their heels and went out the same way they had entered. They said something to each other, got into the Jaguar and sped off the forecourt. Benjamin went back into his office and sat on the desk. For a full ten minutes he contemplated the alternatives. He remembered all too well what had happened to his father. He remembered the vow he had taken. I can't involve Daniel, he thought as he stood up and paced the floor. Ten minutes later he turned, picked up his keys and left.

It was rather chilly as he parked on a yellow line outside *Ling Wo's Restaurant.* "Is it the usual Meester Carile?" the pretty Chinese waitress asked, breaking him out of his daze.

"Oh, er yes," he responded and walked over to the farthest corner. He sat and ate his meal, trying not to think about the preceding hour but something kept tweaking in the back of his mind. He finished his food, leaned back in his chair and began to doze.

"You really tired tonight Meester Carile? You can pay tomorrow of you rike."

"What?" Benjamin said, waking with a start.

"You say you can't afford, Meester Carile."

"Oh no, I was only dreaming. Of course I can pay you for my meal," he reassured gently. "I've had a very long day…" his voice tailed off as he saw old Mr. Ling Wo talking to a customer. He remembered him saying that once to two men; the same two men. That's where I've seen them before! "They have their claws into the old Chinaman!" he exclaimed rather too loudly.

"What, Meester Carile?" asked the waitress.

"What? Oh, er, dreaming again," he said with pleasant smile.

The next day was a busy one for Benjamin. Mr. Emerson dropped his car off promptly at nine, there was the usual entourage of business throughout the day and at six o'clock, Emerson arrived, driven by his wife in a Cortina. "Hello," he said to Benjamin.

"Hello Mr. Emerson. Not much wrong with the Rover, I did track the wheels, though. The tyres looked to be wearing a little unevenly."

"Call me Doc, everyone else who knows me does. How about settling my bill?"

They walked through to the office, Benjamin shedding his overalls on the way. "Going home early tonight?" Doc asked as Benjamin wrote out the cheque.

Benjamin nodded. "Yes, got an errand to do before it gets too late."

As he drove away Doc caught a glimpse of the same Jaguar that he had seen the evening before, only this time it was parked two hundred yards down the road. He looked in his rear mirror and saw the car pulling away.

Benjamin was waiting when the Jaguar spun into the forecourt. He wanted to get the business over and done with. Moustache and his younger partner climbed out of the car, leaving the third man in the driving seat. He noticed how the two men walked side by side and he thought how funny it would be if they tried to walk through the doorway together. A second glance told him that his humour was misplaced. The look on their faces was serious to the point of menace. He sat down at his desk, leaned back in the seat as casually as he could, opened a drawer and pushed a wad of notes forward.

"Good to see that you are being realistic," said Blondy, letting his stone face crack into a grin. He flicked through the wad. "It's all there," he stated and they turned to go. "Same time next week," he said as they went out through the door.

Benjamin watched them leave. When their car had pulled away, he locked up, jumped into his old Morris. The Jaguar was well on its way but it wasn't speeding. He had no difficulty keeping up with them from a distance as they called at one destination after another. Always the same two got out while the driver waited in the car. At ten pm all the men got out and went into *The Flying Horse.* It was eleven when they emerged laughing and talking. Benjamin followed them again. This time, Blondy drove. He dropped the driver off at a nightclub and he and Moustache finally drove into the grounds of a large mansion. When Benjamin was sure that that was their final destination, he drove back to his flat.

It took six weeks and five more payments for Benjamin to find out all he could about the men who had demanded the money from him. The driver, one Michael Stall worked for the nightclub owner, Max Hastings. Hastings was surrounded by a stable of thugs; Benjamin had counted and identified at least sixteen. The two men who came regularly to collect money from him were Donovan and Sloan, who Benjamin had known up till then as Moustache and Blondy, They didn't live as close to the club as the others and Benjamin thought that was handy for Hastings keeping any connection with protection recket at a distance.

The following week, Donovan and Sloan called for their next payment only to find a note pinned to the door of the garage saying:

GONE OUT ON URGENT BUSINESS PLEASE CALL BACK AFTER ELEVEN.

At eleven pm sharp, the Jaguar cruised into the forecourt. A light was on inside the garage but not in the office. "He's back," murmured Sloan. "Just as well for him."

"He'd better not have us calling back here at this time again," cursed Donovan as he led the way into the workshop, "Where the hell is he?" he cursed. "I have a good mind to break a few of his fingers to teach him a lesson."

"No need for that," came Benjamin's voice from behind the door.

They turned around but could only see the driver standing in the doorway. He jerked forward as a hand pushed him through the doorway. "What the hell do you think you are up to?" Donovan growled as Benjamin stepped forward. He had a colt automatic pistol leveled at the driver's head.

"I want all my money back," Benjamin replied calmly. "Six hundred to date, I believe."

"In the car in a case," said Sloan. "We collect three times that in the night," he bragged,

"You are a bloody fool," Donovan cursed. "Your business won't exist after this."

A look of regret came over Benjamin's face. "No, I'm afraid I know that only too well."

Max Hastings, a six foot, heavy-skulled man with a sloping forehead that disappeared into a pointed hairline of shortly cut grey hair couldn't work out where the three men had gone. It was three days now since they went on their Thursday round. He checked with the pubs and the shops. They had all paid as usual as had the man at the garage, but the men and their car had disappeared after their habitual call at *The Flying Horse.*

That Sunday late evening he received a telephone call. "Max, Harry here. Bad news I'm afraid, the warehouse has burned down. Taken everything with it."

Hastings slammed the phone down. The warehouse didn't just house the stores of stolen booze, it was also the place that housed most of his money stored in a twenty foot, locked, shipping container. By the time he got there the Fire Brigade had already brought the fire under control and cut open the container that was seeping smoke. Apart from some charred notes, the rest of the contents were reduced to a sludgy black ash. As he looked up at the roof of the steel 'safe' he could see a hole had been cut in the roof. It wasn't hard to imagine how an accelerant had been piped on onto the stack of money. Three bodies were found nearby. It would take forensics to identify them.

Hastings wasn't sure which mob it was that was trying to edge him out, but a turf war began where several of his men and quite a few from other gangs were killed. Still he had no answer to who was responsible until one night, he had a phone call. "Yes," he snapped.

"Pity about the fire. Your three men were stupid. I told them not to collect in my area."

"What area?"

"The one they cover on a Thursday. That's my patch and always will be. Leave it alone and there will be no more fires." The phone clicked as the receiver at the other end was replaced on its cradle. Benjamin knew that it wouldn't be as simple as that. Within weeks, Hastings had men once again collecting from the same area including Benjamin's garage. Benjamin meekly paid up, but two weeks later the 'collectors' disappeared and Hasting's son was kidnapped. His car was hijacked and he was found dead at the wheel. Eventually Hastings left that area alone. That didn't stop other people from trying to Muscle in but when the same thing happened, each time, the gangsters eventually withdrew to the area where they knew that they had control.

The threat never went away completely, but Benjamin knew that by meekly paying up, he was never identified at the avenging angel. He'd had no choice. It was a war after all.

*****

Since then, Benjamin had prospered. He had opened new premise in The City, and got new franchises on cars at the luxury end of the market. He thought about the way he had met Karen and the nine glorious years he had spent with the woman he loved. He hadn't realised that Doc had a daughter until he turned up one day in the autumn of 1971. Doc drove up into the forecourt.

"Hello Doc," Benjamin said as he walked towards him. "What can I do for you today?"

"Looking for a good second had car; not too big," replied Doc.

"You've not decided to get rid of that thirsty brute at last have you?"

Doc smiled. "No the Rover's okay for now. I'm looking for a car for my daughter." He nodded back to his car. "She's just finished her degree at Leeds University and now she insists that she has a car so that she can shop around for a job."

"What sort of job is she looking for?"

"You'd be best asking her that yourself. She doesn't seem to have a clue. Three years taking a degree in economics and nowhere has there been any teaching on how to get a job."

"Benjamin grinned. "It's easy getting a job, but not at all easy finding the right one to start with. The trouble with a degree is that it gives the potential employers the idea that the subject you have taken is the only thing that you know anything about."

"You're right," came the voice of Doc's daughter from behind Benjamin's shoulder. "If you've specialized in it for three years, they can't understand why you don't want to carry on with it for the rest of your life."

"What did you want to do it for in the first place?" taunted Doc.

Benjamin turned to face the subject of the conversation. He was surprised; more than surprised, he was speechless. The daughter of the man he had known and befriended over the past four years was stunningly attractive. Her large blue eyes cast a spell over him that would never be withdrawn. At first he hadn't realised that he was bewitched. To Benjamin she was just a beautiful young lady with flowing natural blonde hair and a mature rounded figure. That wasn't easy to conceal even under her heavy overcoat.

"University is a way of life. I went there to learn about living an independent life, not to become an expert on Keynes."

"Huh. And after telling me that you went there to get away from your mother and me you want me to buy you a car."

"Yes please," she said, pulling herself close into Doc's arm and smiling up at him. It was easy to see how she could get anything she wanted from her devoted parents. At that moment Benjamin would have given her any car in the garage if she had so much as brushed past his arm. A feeling inside him had been stirred with a devastating effect on his insides. He had had girl friends before, even been in love with them, but not to such effect that butterflies and bats fluttered with free abandon inside his abdomen.

"Well what have you got?" asked Doc. "I'd better know the worst."

"Have you?" Benjamin squeaked and cleared his throat. He took a deep breath. "Do you like Escorts?"

She smiled at him; the first of many that he was to remember. "I'd love one," she said mischievously. "Where are you taking me?"

Benjamin just stared at her, He regained his composure. "Er… I… What about a test drive for a start?" He looked towards a red Escort GL. "It's only done eight thousand miles," he said regaining a modicum of detachment from his customer.

Doc looked at the price as he took it off the windscreen, "A thousand pounds!" he exclaimed. "Cant you direct her to something more in line with my pocket?"

"How does eight fifty sound to you Doc?" he asked, determined to sell Doc the best used car he had. He had always had a policy of dealing fairly and keeping customers happy, but this was one customer that he intended to keep at any price.

"Well..."

"Unless you'd like to buy her a new MGB?"

"Oh this looks just fine," Doc replied as quickly as he could and got into the Escort.

"I'll drive," said his daughter as she held out her hand for the keys. Benjamin placed them in the centre of her palm. The tips of his fingers brushed against her skin. The bats flapped about manically. "I'm Karen by the way," she said.

"Benjamin, pleased to meet you." Their eyes locked, they shook hands and he could hardly pull his hand or his gaze away from her. They got into the car and she drove, Benjamin knew not where. He had no eye for place or direction. All he knew was that he had never enjoyed being driven by anyone else before but when the car came to a stop outside the garage fifty minutes later it was hours too soon.

From then on it had happened as if in a fairy story. Doc had bought her the car, Benjamin had escorted Karen to the theatre the following evening, and they saw each other every night after that, became lovers after two weeks and finally got married in the march of 1972.

Benjamin smiled when he recalled what Doc had said at the wedding. "Trust you to sell me a car for her and *then* marry her."

"Always had an eye for a good deal," Benjamin replied. It had been a good deal. Benjamin couldn't have found any other woman that could have held a candle to his wife. Nine years they had been together during which she had worked with him to build up his car business to one of the most successful in the City. They had a large detached house within easy commuting distance of the business, a holiday cottage in the countryside and they had each other. More than anything, they had each other.

A tear welled up in the corner of his eye as he thought about the sheer waste of life and energy that her body had had, all drained away from her in a matter of weeks. First of all the uncertainty, then knowing that she was going to die, and finally seeing her wither like a plant starved of water and sunlight; seeing her pass through the barrier where neither life nor death was the reality to a point where all hope of a miracle was lost, just before she gave up her brave struggle to stay with the man she loved so much and still loved beyond the end.

*****

Benjamin blew his nose with a sound that reverberated around the International Departure Lounge. He glanced around self-consciously but nobody had seemed to notice. He rarely gave himself the time to feel self pity and realised that he was sinking into the depression that had overtaken him time and time again over the past three years. Determined to fight it he dragged his mind to Daniel. It had little effect. He, too, had gone. He'd appeared from nowhere after God knows how many years and promptly exited for good this time, again without so much as a note to say what was happening or that he was ill.

Benjamin gave a start when he heard the announcement of his flight. Two and a half hours had flown.

CHAPTER 12

Benjamin closed his eyes as Concord cruised over the endless expanse of blue sea. The stewardess tapped him lightly on the shoulder. "We're here," she said softly. He opened his eyes and the plane was taxiing off the runway.

"Here? In New York? What time is it?" he asked as the first passengers were beginning to stand ready to alight.

"Six o'clock New York time," said the stewardess.

"Thank you," he said and adjusted the figures on his watch. He unfastened his safety belt, picked up his hand luggage and disembarked.

"Three hours to wait," he said to himself and then realised that he hadn't brought a rose in order to be easily noticed. "Weber can have me paged if he wants to find me," he muttered and went to book in at the hotel. After leaving a message at the airport reception for if anyone enquired about him, he went to the *International.* Once there, he began to relax. He finished off a couple of sandwiches and a cup of coffee, settled back in his chair with a brandy and read a copy of *The New York Times.*

*****

A small, stockily-built man with dark hair and wearing a heavy overcoat and a trilby hat had approached the airport at 8.35. He drove into the car park in a Monza, stepped out lightly for a man of his stature and walked towards the terminal. Within five minutes of his arriving in the airport lobby an announcement over the tannoy took him to the booking desk. "Phone call for you Mr. Weber in booth four, the girl said, pointing to the line of booths.

It was 8.45 when Benjamin arrived at the terminal where the 747 flight that he should have caught was due. He sauntered over to a seat and positioned himself so that he could see if there looked to be anybody seeking him. It wasn't an easy job. There must have been a hundred people hanging around waiting for someone. The flight arrived on time and Benjamin watched the passengers disembark and disappear as he waited to see if there was anyone left after everyone had gone their way.

At 9.02 a woman wearing a red woolen scarf draped casually over her shoulders, and a brightly coloured yellow and red raincoat, pushed her way through the crowd, frantically scanning the faces of the people in it. She made an enquiry at the desk and then went over to the entrance through which the incoming passengers were emerging. Benjamin sat and watched her as he waited for the man called Weber to page him. The crown never seemed to get any thinner. The woman with the red scarf was wearing a large pair of glasses that made her look rather like an owl, he thought. She still continued to look around apprehensively. Then Benjamin spotted another person looking around as if trying to find somebody. He was a small silver-haired man of about forty, in a dark overcoat and wearing a trilby hat. He stood about fifty feet away and about thirty feet from the woman who was beginning to make her way from the entrance through which the disembarking passengers had arrived. She shot a glance at him as she went by, stopped, turned around and said, "Can you come with me please?"

Benjamin stared at her. She was a five feet eight brunette with dark grey eyes and a near-English accent. "You are Ben, aren't you?" she asked.

Benjamin stood up. "Er... y... yes," he stuttered.

"Quickly," she said and walked away.

Benjamin followed close on her heels. "Who are you?" he asked as they approached the exit doors.

"Weber," she said and carried on walking.

Benjamin looked around and noticed three other men in overcoats walking over to the one he thought had been Weber. As he pushed at the door, he noticed that one of the men took something out of his inside pocket but at that moment one of the other men walked in front of them and blocked his vision.

"Quickly, Mr. Carlisle," the brunette said as she turned and saw Benjamin looking backwards. Benjamin ran to catch her up and she walked even faster.

"Where are you going?" he asked when he eventually caught up to her amidst the parked cars. He was beginning to get angry at her domineering manner.

"Somewhere safe," she said and got into a big grey Lincoln. She took off her glasses, unlocked the passenger door and waved for him to get in. He did as he was commanded and she accelerated away before he'd even slammed the door.

"I didn't expect Weber to be a woman," he said apologetically. "I'm sorry for not wearing a rose. Forgot to get one."

"Rose? Of course," she said when she realised what he was talking about. "Good job you didn't."

"How do you mean?"

"They were waiting for you."

"That's what I expected."

"Not the people you expected, though. I realised you hadn't caught the scheduled flight. It saved your life. You'd be dead already if you had."

"What on earth are you talking about?" Benjamin asked indignantly.

"I have no doubt that those men in the airport lounge were waiting for you. They'll have found out you were on the scheduled 747 flight and were waiting for you to emerge with those passengers."

"What the hell are you talking about?"

"I'm not Weber."

Benjamin gave a start. "Then who the bloody hell are you?" he demanded angrily "And just where are you taking me?"

I used that name because I was in a hurry and I knew it would be the only one you would take any notice of."

"I had noticed you were in a hurry to get home," Benjamin snapped She didn't respond.

"My real name is Dianne Barker."

Benjamin took a deep breath. "Then who is Weber?"

Weber is probably dead. I'm Daniel's security chief. No one is supposed to know Weber that's why I hired him myself. But he's been substituted and the man taking his place was to escort you out of the terminal."

"Like you did?" Benjamin said sarcastically.

"Yes, like I did, only they would have taken you away and buried you."

"Oh yes? Well just who are *they* and how come you are here to meet me if nobody knows that Weber is dead?"

"Because we have a security system that works. I was watching for him meeting you off the plane as his back-up."

"A security system? Back-up? What the hell is going on?"

"I guessed they would try to pick you up. Hiring an outsider seems like a good idea for throwing them off your track but it didn't work. Somehow they must have known who was supposed to meet you because he disappeared and was substituted. Somehow they got hold of his name. I watched him all the time until he went to answer a phone call. That's when the other guy turned up in his place."

"The one in the trilby, I suppose?"

Dianne didn't answer. "It was a stroke of luck that you came in on Concord."

"Was it? Bloody expensive."

"I only found out at the last minute before the 747 was due in. I knew they wouldn't have had time to check the passenger list off Concord so I was looking for someone who was waiting. There were so many people hanging about that I was beginning to lose any hope of finding you before they did. When three other guys made enquiries at the desk and then began to walk towards the entrance, I knew I had to do something pretty quick. Luckily, you do resemble Daniel or I wouldn't have risked even talking to you. There could have been more of them about and if you had been one of them then I'd have joined Weber by now."

"So, explain to me why anyone would want me out of this world?"

For the same reason they got rid of your brother."

"Got rid? You mean he was murdered?"

"I'm sorry we didn't explain it too carefully in the telegram. The trouble is, we're up against something pretty big."

"Something?"

"I'm not sure. The mafia more than likely. But I think the C.I.A. are involved somewhere along the line. Just whose side they are on I wouldn't like to guess. Probably their own. I know that Daniel got into a deal that stirred up a hornet's nest and got him killed into the bargain."

"But why kill me?"

"He was with you over in England a couple of weeks back, wasn't he?"

"Yes."

"You and he arranged to buy a house over there."

"Right."

"He wanted out," said Dianne, taking her left hand off the steering wheel and making a gesture to the effect that Daniel's actions spoke for themselves only, to Benjamin, his actions hadn't said a thing. The whole episode was turning from a riddle into a whole mish-mash of seemingly unrelated statements and events. "But there is no was out now," Dianne continued, "and anyone who was seen to be connected with him can only be suspected of knowing what he knew."

"Which is?"

"I don't know."

Benjamin grinned and let out a resigned sigh of frustration. "Well that's helpful. So why all this buggering about getting me over here in the first place? I can manage very well without getting topped three thousand miles away from home. God, it would have been cheaper to fly his body over to England if you wanted me to go to his funeral."

"Because of the will."

"Will? What about the will?"

"You are in Daniel's will. You are a beneficiary, a major beneficiary."

"I'm quite well off enough, thank you, without coming over here to inherit his bit, especially if my coffin is an integral part of the deal"

"Some people would think that thirty odd million is worth taking the risk for."

"Eh?"

"You heard right; thirty million."

"Bloody hell. He never mentioned anything like that."

"Obviously he didn't know he was going to die or he would have done," Dianne said with a cutting edge in her voice.

"I take it that I'm not staying at the hotel then?" Benjamin stated to ease the atmosphere.

"The only safe place is Daniel's. We'll be there in twenty minutes."

Half an hour later, Dianne drew the Lincoln into a driveway. She pressed a button on the dashboard and a pair of heavy wrought iron gates opened before them. They passed through an avenue of poplars to reach an impressive three storey house. She pressed another button on the dashboard and a garage door opened for her to drive straight in. The door closed behind them and she turned off the engine. Benjamin sat there for a moment and contemplated how easy it had been to lead him to this place, how nobody knew where he was, and how the hell he could get out if things started to turn nasty.

Dianne got out of the car and bent her head down to look back in at Benjamin. "You coming?" she said.

Benjamin got out, closed the car door and followed her through another door connecting the garage to the main building. "Whose place is this?" he asked, looking around what seemed to be a large vestibule.

"Daniel's," Dianne replied. She opened a door into a big square office. Two men who were sitting at desks watching closed circuit televisions turned to face them. "Mickey, Carl, this is Benjamin Carlisle," she introduced.

"Pleased to meet you," Mickey responded. Benjamin thought he looked like an athlete, a tall man about six feet tall and with short dark brown hair and dark grey eyes. He wore a shoulder holster.

"Hello sir," Carl followed. He was taller and thinner than his colleague, had dark hair and dark brown eyes that looked almost black.

"Hello," Benjamin said, not sure what else to say.

"I'm leaving you in their hands for tonight," Dianne explained. "They'll show you to your room and get you up in time for the funeral. Don't want you to be late. Jet lag can make you oversleep if you aren't used to it." She turned to leave.

"My things are still at the hotel," Benjamin said, wondering if the whole thing wasn't some kind of horrific dream. He would probably wake up in the hotel dining room having nodded off again.

"Your passport. Have you got that on you?" she asked.

"Yes." Benjamin took it out of his inside pocket. She took it and glanced through it before handing it back to him.

"Never thought to check you out," she grinned. Benjamin noticed that she could be quite attractive when she wasn't being so officious. "We'll go and recover the rest of your stuff. Was there much?"

"Just a hold-all. I didn't intend taking a vacation."

"Carl will get you something of Daniel's to wear tonight. I suggest you get something to eat and then get a good night's sleep. You'll need it." She left the room and closed the door.

"I've already eaten," Benjamin said to Carl. "If you would take me to my room I wouldn't mind taking her advice."

"Right, Mr. Carlisle. That suits me. The cook is away on holiday anyway. If you'd follow me."

Benjamin slept fitfully. There were too many questions churning over in his mind, not least of all being what the hell was he doing there in the first place? Daniel had turned up in London out of the blue after fourteen years and then had promptly returned to New York and been murdered. Paying his last respects to his brother wasn't turning out to be a quiet funeral with a modest wake and a swift return back to Benjamin's own life and business. On top of that, Daniel's murderers were looking to kill his brother. What the bloody hell had he got himself into? He turned over in bed a tenth time and eventually dozed off to sleep.

He was awakened by a knock on the door. By the time he'd responded and opened his eyes, Carl had entered the room and placed a tray with coffee on it on the bedside table. "Thought you'd need a morning call," he said with an expressionless face.

Benjamin looked at his watch. It was 11.30 am. "I see what you mean," he said and pushed himself up into a sitting position.

"Mickey is making you some food for about twelve."

"Right oh," Benjamin nodded. "Did Daniel always get this sort of service?"

"Not from me he didn't." Benjamin thought he saw a smile try to escape from the thin man's lips.

"So what did you do for him?"

"Bodyguard," Carl replied as he closed the door behind him.

Benjamin shook his head. No wonder Daniel's dead, he thought. I wouldn't want to hide behind that thin streak of bacon. When he went to the dining area he was surprised to be greeted with a full English breakfast. It was the first decent breakfast he had had since Karen had died. Since her demise he felt no enjoyment in catering for himself. His usual breakfast was either some toast or buttered crumpets washed down with a couple of mugs of tea that he made at the same time to save returning to the kettle. "I could get used to this life of leisure," he said to Mickey as he poured Benjamin more coffee.

"He lived well. Dianne and Howard the cook did most of the running about after him. We are just standing in to try and make your stay as comfortable as possible, though…" He paused.

"Though what?"

Mickey seemed to struggle to find the right words. "Well you don't seem to be what we expected."

"And that was what exactly?"

"You… Well you don't seem to be the kind of person to take over Daniel's business."

"Take over? Who said I was taking over?"

"I'm sorry. I thought…"

Benjamin's eyes narrowed as they locked on Mickey's. "Let's get one thing straight," he said waving his toast sternly. "I am here for Daniel's funeral, that's all. That's all I came over for, and I'll be catching the evening flight back home. That will be all. What Daniel did for a living doesn't at all appeal to me and sounds even less so when I discover that not only has he been murdered but I am due to receive the same treatment from the same people who did it to him."

"I'm sorry sir. I had been led to believe that you were intending to take over."

"Well you've been well and truly misled, that's all I can say." Benjamin slammed his toast into a dish of marmalade, stood up and went over to the window. He plunged his hands deep into his pockets and looked out overland towards the sea which formed a clear dark blue line between Jones' Beach and the clear light blue sky.

Mickey hardly said a word after that. He dutifully ushered Benjamin to Chickfield Church, arriving promptly at 2.00 pm.

As he looked around at the people in the church Benjamin tried to decide what each person there had to do with his brother. He noticed Mickey chatting to Dianne over in a far corner. Dianne was facing towards Benjamin and as she nodded at something that was being said her eyes fell in line with his. They stopped talking and joined the assembly.

The service was short and the coffin was carried out to the graveyard He noticed that it had not been left open for members of the congregation to pay their last respects.

"Hello," came a familiar voice behind him. He turned to face Dianne.

"Hello. I saw you in the church. I thought you were avoiding me."

"Funerals aren't my scene," she said quietly. Her face looked sadder than he'd seen it. It was pale in the daylight, the palour of a nightclub dancer, a nocturne, someone who worked only in the darkness of nights or under artificial lighting.

"Was it you that Daniel was going to marry?" Benjamin asked.

Dianne shook her head. "No," she said with a pleasant smile. I just worked for him. He met somebody called Anita Holt. She came along a few months ago and swept Daniel off his feet."

"Where is she now?"

"She won't be here," Dianne said, pursing her lips.

"Why not? Isn't it her scene either?"

"Hardly," Dianne grated and linked arms with him. "Come," she said after the coffin had been lowered into the ground, "We'd better leave." Benjamin let her lead him to her car. He noticed that Mickey had remained in sight of him since he reached the church. Now he opened the back door for Benjamin and Dianne and got into the driver's seat. An hour later they were in the substantial offices of *Bertram Cayley*, Attorney at law. Already there had appeared a number of people on the row of chairs facing his desk.

"Please be seated," he said after Dianne had introduced Benjamin. He indicated the three chairs in the front row. "This shouldn't take long." He sat behind a large kneehole desk and pressed the intercom button. "Miss Lawson?"

"Yes sir?"

"Please make sure we are not disturbed."

"Yes sir."

"Good, now we can get down to business, "He took a key from his waistcoat pocket unlocked the drawer of the desk and took out a blue folder. "This is all that concerns us at the moment," he said and laid it open in front of him.

"First of all there's a letter for Mr. Benjamin Carlisle, Daniel's brother. It is sealed and given to me on instructions that, in the event of Daniel Carlisle's untimely death, it should be handed to Benjamin Carlisle to be opened and read by him only." He picked up a brown envelope and handed it to Benjamin. "You can take it into the spare office if you wish to read it privately," he suggested.

Benjamin had already stood up and picked up the paperknife off the lawyer's desk. "No, it will be all right here," he said and pulled out a sheet of typed paper. He unfolded it and read it several times, refolded it, put it back in its envelope and went back to his seat. "Right, that's that," he said with a poker face. "You can carry on now."

The other people in the room had been watching him closely He wondered if his curiosity would have been the same had he been in their place.

The attorney continued. "Yes, well then, the next thing is to read the will. This won't take very long." He took up the document and began to read it. "*This is the last will and testament of me, Daniel Carlisle, of Malterswood Lodge, Long Island, New York. I hereby revoke any previous wills and dispositions theretofore made by me and declare this to be my last will.*"

Cayley broke off for a few seconds. "He names as executors, myself and Mr. Benjamin Carlisle."

He cleared his throat. "*I Hereby bequeath my house and land named above as Malterswood Lodge on Long Island to…*" He paused and looked up. "*Miss Dianne Barker,*" he said, not looking at her but over her shoulder at a blonde haired, trim figured woman of about twenty seven. Benjamin looked around towards the back of the room. Anita Holt stood in the farthest corner away from the lawyer. He studied the face and guessed that it belonged to the bereaved fiancée.. She looked neither sad nor elated. Her relaxed jaw and calm manner showed no emotion whatsoever. He looked back at the lawyer as he resumed his text.

"I *bequeath the rest of my estate after all due taxes are paid, comprising of all that property real and personal to which I have title to...*" Cayley looked up again, this time at Benjamin. "*To my brother Benjamin Carlisle.* The will is dated the 21st September 1984. He had me draw it up only four days before his death."

"Is that it?" came a light voice from the back of the room.

"That's it Miss Holt," the lawyer stated sharply. Ladies and gentlemen you may leave now. I would, however, like to have a further discussion with Miss Barker and Mr. Benjamin Carlisle, thank you."

Dianne whispered for Mickey to wait in reception. The room emptied leaving Benjamin and Dianne still seated and Anita Holt standing her ground at the back. Cayley waved Anita out of the room with a gesture of dismissal as he gathered up the folder and papers. She bustled out noisily and when he was assured of privacy he lifted his head and examined the two beneficiaries with his penetrating eyes. "No doubt that came as a shock to some of them," he stated with a smile.

"Came as a shock to me," Dianne said. "I thought Anita Holt would get it."

"No doubt he had his reasons," Benjamin stated.

"Quite so, Mr. Carlisle." He took up another paper from the folder. "Here I have a list of all the property to which the will refers. The real property other than Malterswood comprises of a couple of houses and a couple of apartments in various places throughout the United States. All the deeds will be transferred into your name as will those of Malterswood will be transferred to Miss Barker."

"That sounds all right," Benjamin said with a shrug of his shoulders.

"The personal goods and chattels will, of course remain in those properties until you decide what to do with them."

"Right." Benjamin slapped his hands on his knees as he was about to stand up.

"Then there's the company," Cayley announced, waving him to remain seated. That comprises the holding company by the name of Carlisle importers and Forwarding Agents and half a dozen subsidiaries. All his unsold stock goes over to you Mr. Carlisle."

"Unsold?"

"May I point out that Daniel intended to retire from his business and offer his stock at a nominal valuation to his vice-president after he made the will."

"Me," said Dianne.

"So I have a few shares then?"

"Quite so," said Cayley. "Then there are his private bank accounts," he went on without a pause. "There were two Swiss bank accounts, but he transferred them to his future wife before he died."

"You mean Anita?" Dianne said sharply. "She did all right after all."

"I mean nothing of the sort," said Cayley and carried on. "A New York account in The Bank of America which has just under one million dollars in it…"

"Phew," whispered Benjamin.

"Finally," Cayley continued, "there are two small ocean-going ships both owned by Mr. Carlisle and leased to the company. The total estate will be around thirty million dollars after I have sorted taxes."

"I see," said Benjamin, slightly dazed.

One word of advice before you go," said the lawyer. "Daniel was murdered. The police are no further forward in finding out who killed him. Your motives cannot be questioned because I was the only person to know what was in the will. But they will want to speak to you. Lieutenant Mathias was present when I read the will. He'll no doubt be waiting to have a word with you outside."

"As yet, nobody has told me how he died," said Benjamin.

"Car bomb," Dianne said almost inaudibly.

"So who identified the body?" Benjamin enquired.

"Anita Holt," Dianne stated sourly.

"Difficult job by all accounts," Cayley stated with an inflexion of sorrow in his voice. But how she could make out what he was, let alone who he was, was a mystery to me."

"She saw it happen," Dianne explained.

"It was that bad?" Benjamin asked.

"It wasn't good, Mr. Carlisle; not good at all."

"If that's all, I would like a word with Mr. Cayley in private," Dianne said softly.

Daniel stood up and shook hands with the lawyer. "Thank you Mr. Cayley. You have my home address?"

"Yes, Mr. Carlisle. I'll be in touch in due course."

On his way out, Benjamin was joined by Mickey. "Old Mathias is waiting to speak to you," he said as a thick-set man in his late thirties came up to them.

Benjamin turned to go back into Cayley's office, pushing past Dianne who, looking a little ruffled was on her way out. "There's something I forgot to ask, Mr. Cayley," he said as the door closed behind him.

A few moments later he emerged and joined the police officer. "I'm Lieutenant Mathias," the detective said, holding up his badge. "Can I have a word with you, Mr. Carlisle?"

"Yes, if you like."

"There's an office in here," he said opening a door and leading the way into a small filing room and closing the door behind him. I'd like to know what your brother said in the letter."

"All it said was that he'd made me the beneficiary of his will because he couldn't trust anybody any more. He also wanted me to keep all his shares in his companies."

"May I see the letter?"

"I'm afraid not. You see I asked Mr. Cayley to shred it."

"And why did you do that?"

"Because it was supposed to be private."

Mathias rushed out of the filing room and onto Cayley's office without knocking, Finding that office empty he walked through to the adjoining office. "Can I help you?" asked Cayley. He had just finished shredding some papers.

"By the way Lieutenant, you won't mind my leaving for London later tonight, will you?" He was in the right place to get this situation sorted out if there was going to be any aggravation from the police officer.

"Mr. Cayley has already pointed out that you had no prior knowledge of what was in the will. I see no reason for insisting that you do anything. You may come and go as you please." He gave Benjamin an acid glance. "If your brother told you anything that might explain his sudden death, you'll let me know, won't you?"

"I'd have thought the beneficiaries under his previous will would have been more likely suspects."

"We're looking into that Mr. Carlisle, believe you me, and it appears that he had no previous will."

"Then I can throw no further light on the matter, Lieutenant."

"Mr. Carlisle," Mathias warned, as Benjamin was about to leave, "this is no game, especially for amateurs." He stared hard. "In fact, Mr. Carlisle, it is not a game at all. It's deadly serious. Your brother found that out."

Benjamin wondered if he had done the right thing as he joined the others. Something didn't fit. Daniel came to see him three days after making him the major beneficiary in his one and only will. Cayley had indicated that Anita Holt had not been his intended wife. So what had happened to the rest of his money?

"He won't have liked you destroying that letter," Dianne said as she drove away. The letter! That hadn't cleared anything up either.

"What time does the bank close?" asked Benjamin.

"Which bank?"

"The Great Western."

"Five o'clock. Why?"

"Would you take me there please? There's something I have to collect before I go to back to England."

"We pass it on the way. We'll be there in just a couple of minutes."

Dianne fell silent. A few moments later she pulled into a parking lot. "It's over there," she pointed. "I'll go with you."

Mickey got out and opened the door for Benjamin whilst Dianne got out at her side. Leaving Mickey with the car, they walked into a large multi-storey building and went to the foyer of the bank. Benjamin produced the letter that he had been given by the lawyer and handed it over to the clerk with his passport.

"Just a moment, please," the clerk said as he went through to his manager's office. He returned with a portly, balding man. "Have you got the key," the manager asked.

Benjamin tipped up the envelope that had held the letter. A strongbox key fell into the palm of the man's hand. "Here," he said.

"Come this way please," he said and handed the key back to Benjamin. He led him through a door and down a flight of steps and through another door. Up ahead a guard stood by the door of the vault. He let them through and closed the door behind them. A strongbox was brought out and laid on a shelf in a booth. Benjamin opened it with his key. There were three envelopes, two fat ones and a thin one. He took out the thin one first and took out a hand-written letter.

"Dear Ben, If you are reading this then I am already dead. If you listen to the tape in the envelope it will explain why I have been killed. It is for this reason that I warn you to be prepared to have your life put in danger by the same men that I opposed. They will kill anybody who gets in their way. And I mean ANYBODY. Take care. Danny"

Benjamin put the letter back in its envelope and placed in the bottom of the box. Then he opened the second envelope. That contained a single cassette tape. He placed it in his overcoat pocket. The third envelope contained a wad of fifty pound notes. And a wad of one hundred dollar bills along with another hand-written note. *"Just some spare cash to see you through until the estate is settled."* He put that note and the cash in the inside pockets of his jacket, closed the lid of the box, turned the key and left.

He joined Dianne in the foyer and they walked out to her car. Suddenly she snatched at Benjamin's arm and flung him to the ground with what seemed like comparative ease. As he fought in vain to keep his balance, Daniel's words rang though his mind. *"Don't trust anybody".* A moment later he crashed to his knees on the pavement by the side of the parked car. A fraction of a second later he heard the sound of a high velocity bullet passing over the hood only inches above his head. A loud crack echoed off the tall buildings. He turned to see where Dianne had gone but saw nobody. "Bloody shit!" he swore at the car's front wheel. "What the hell have I got myself into?"

He dived to the cover of the next car. When nothing happened he chanced looking through the side windows and caught sight of Dianne making her way towards the Lincoln where they had left Mickey. He was nowhere to be seen. "Now what?" he said aloud to the car door. Somebody was taking potshots at him and he didn't even have a lump of stone to throw back. He decided to keep moving and jumped up and ran towards the cover of another car. In a split second a man stood out from behind a concrete pillar to get a clear shot at Benjamin. Benjamin realised that he had laid himself open to the assassin as the man leveled his rifle. A resounding crack echoed off the surrounding high-rise buildings and before the rifleman could squeeze the trigger again he was thrown backwards through a plate glass window by the force of a bullet smashing through his breastbone. The noise of the Colt Trooper .375 Magnum was still ringing in Benjamin's ears as a man stepped out of a nearby doorway and walked over to the would-be assassin. It was Lieutenant Mathias.

"You're a man of action, I see," said Mathias.

"I learned to keep moving when you don't know where the sniper is, if that's what you mean," Benjamin retorted.

"You know about snipers then?"

"Northern Ireland," Benjamin said and brushed the dust off his knees. He walked over to the Lincoln where Dianne was standing. "Where's Mickey?" he asked.

"They got him," she said and pointed to the car. A single drop of blood trickled down his face from a neat hole in his head. Benjamin walked over to the dead sniper.

"Who is trying to kill me, Lieutenant?" he asked looking down at the blood-soaked body of the gunman.

"He's a hit-man by the name of Ludwig Kalten. We've had him under surveillance since he came into the country. Interpol has never been able to pin anything on him, but his reputation precedes him. Whoever wants you dead was prepared to pay for the best."

"Did he kill my brother?"

"He might have, but he hasn't been known to be connected to car bombings. I suggest you invest in some high class security if you are remaining over here. This man wasn't cheap. There are a dozen men already in The States that would have done his job at half the price."

"So why the import?"

"Because whatever Daniel discovered, was big," Dianne said. "Internationally big."

"And no doubt you still don't know what he's been up to Miss Barker?" said the Lieutenant "Something, perhaps to do with his spare-time business?"

"What's that?" Benjamin asked naively.

"Exporting illegal arms, Mr. Carlisle. Your brother was a crook. He used his legitimate business for moving contraband. God knows how. His premises were searched umpteen times by Customs but they came up with nothing, yet in between his legitimate cargos, he somehow smuggled his own contraband."

"I just don't believe it. Daniel a smuggler? No way," Benjamin said as earnestly as he could.

"Believe what you like, Mr. Carlisle. The facts speak for themselves. He got himself mixed up in international terrorism and didn't live to regret it."

"That doesn't make sense. If he was working for them then they would have wanted him alive."

"Not if he found out what they were up to and didn't like it. Whatever it was, it was worth losing him as an asset to protect the secret. Somewhere there's a deep and secret politically motivated plot. These guys are not just fanatics."

"And you don't know what it was he was involved in?"

"We were hoping that you would tell us."

Benjamin shrugged. "I told you, I have no idea. You wouldn't believe this but I have just got my business in England running smoothly enough that I can start to take it easy and now I look like getting myself shot before I can enjoy it. It's bloody sickening."

Mathias grinned. "Then do your best to help me find out what it is that you are supposed to know and I might be able to keep you alive a bit longer. I can't be standing behind you every time somebody takes a pot shot at you."

"I didn't know you were."

"That's what saved you. He would have had you with that second shot."

Benjamin nodded. "Yes, I am grateful for that. I'll let you know if I find out anything." He went over to the car and then remembered that there was a body in it. "You couldn't give us a lift home by any chance?"

"The New York Police Department is well known for its taxi service," Mathias said sarcastically. "People call us whenever they can't get a cab."

Benjamin knew he had gained all the help he was going to get from Mathias. He was just about to tell Dianne that he was going to call a cab when Mathias went over to his car and spoke into his radio receiver. He turned to Benjamin. "If it will prevent you getting killed over here then it's worth it. A car is on its way."

*****

"How did you know I was going to be shot at?" Benjamin asked Dianne when they arrived at Malterswood.

"Because I know that someone is out to kill you," she replied. "You don't seem to have let it sink in yet. When Mickey was nowhere to be seen I began to look around. I still hadn't seen that Ludwig fella but if I'd been wrong the worst you would have got would have been a couple of bruises. As it was, I cut things a little too fine."

"Well not so fine in the future mind. I never have liked having a parting in my hair."

"That sounds as if you might not be returning home tonight." She smiled as she led him through a door into the library. It was the first real smile she had given him. Until then she had been rather poker-faced and businesslike, a career woman with no apparent social agenda, above all a proper bossy boots. "What will you have to drink?" She went over to a paneled wall and made some obscure movement which resulted in the panels sliding apart and a drinks bar smoothly motoring out. She poured herself a vodka and added a tiny splash of lime.

"Whisky, please, on the rocks," Benjamin answered. He paced up the middle of the room. "Well," he said after a long silence during which Dianne handed him his drink. "I'm not sure what I'm going to do. But thanks for getting me out of the way of that bullet anyway." He looked her straight in the eye. "You know, Daniel said to trust nobody but I think you're the one person I can trust around here." The corners of his eyes crinkled as he sent her a soft smile. He sat down on a large sofa.

Dianne's eyes smiled back at him. "When did he say that?" she asked as she sat beside him.

Benjamin began to realise just how shapely this woman was without her scarf and coat. "A letter he left for me at the bank. It said for me to trust nobody."

Dianne remained silent for a long minute. Benjamin watched her eyes as she sipped her drink and stared sightlessly ahead. Suddenly she threw both hands in the air. "He realised it," she proclaimed. "And that's when he made his will." She looked at Benjamin with sad eyes. "The trouble is, he realised it too late."

"Realised what?" Benjamin asked, perplexion written all over his face.

"He must have realised that Anita Holt was not what she was pretending to be. I thought he was too love-struck to see it but he saw though her. I know it now. But it was too late to stop her from killing him," she grated.

"But did he or didn't he leave her his Swiss bank accounts?"

"No. I wondered what Cayley meant when he said he didn't mean Anita Holt. I waited and asked him about it."

"And what did he say?"

"He said he didn't know. Apparently Daniel had intended to keep his betrothed anonymous to protect her from what happened and is still happening."

"Well I have a feeling that unless she's a very good actress, Daniel left his money to somebody else," Benjamin agreed, drinking down his whisky in one.

Dianne looked at Benjamin with her soft-eyed look again. "You underestimate that woman, Ben. Honest to God she's the coldest calculating bitch I ever laid eyes on."

Benjamin smiled. "You know, I think I detect a small hint of jealousy." Dianne blushed but before she could respond, Benjamin carried on. "You know, having met you and having seen that woman at the lawyer's office, I can't see why on earth he didn't marry you. You're ten times the woman she is."

Dianne's pale cheeks reddened again. "We were just working partners, not sleeping partners. It would have been impossible for me to live in my apartment here and work for him while his train of suitors passed through, if I'd got emotionally involved."

"But you loved him?" Benjamin asked.

"In a way I did, yes. He gave me more than a husband would have. He gave me my own business within his company, he gave me a partnership and he offered to sell me the rest of his stock at a nominal figure when he sold out."

"And he gave you hell as well."

"No, I gave him hell." She chucked and shook her head. "I suppose that's why we never hit it off."

"Well, I think we can both agree that whoever he was going to marry it wasn't Anita Holt."

"He certainly led me a merry dance and that's for sure. I think he must have suspected she had some ulterior motive with her sickening '*Oh Daniel*' shit."

"You think that she thought she was going to be the one?"

"Yes, I do, but I think she killed him expecting that he had left her his money. But she had another reason to kill him, I am sure."

"Such as?"

"Such as she was planted on him by somebody else. She certainly worked hard to get in here. He didn't even remember her when she rang up, and yet the next day she moved in."

"Sounds like Daniel, that."

"It sounds most *unlike* him," Dianne corrected. "His behaviour was not that of the Daniel I had come to know. He turned hundreds of women away in his time, and some whose names he could remember."

"So why did he let her come and stay then?"

"Because it must have suited his plans to play along with her for some reason; but don't ask me what that reason was." She shook her head.

"Where did he get blown up?"

"In the warehouse yard. That's another thing that doesn't fit. He went out to the parked car by himself; no bodyguard, and with no reason to go out to a car that wasn't his. It was her car so nobody would have expected them to go anywhere in that heap of junk. So why was it booby-trapped?"

"How do you mean?"

"I mean he always got driven about by his bodyguards. The car he got blown up in was Holt's car. She had driven it there. She told us later that they were going to have a night out, but he wouldn't have gone in her car. She must have got him to go to the car for something. It must have already been set to explode when she arrived in it because nobody went near it after she arrived, the CCTV confirmed that."

"And didn't the police pick up on that?"

Dianne shrugged. "They reckon that it was remotely detonated. The bomb could have been put in it any time."

Benjamin stood up and poured two more drinks. He looked at Dianne. He found her face appealing. It had been a long time since he had looked onto a woman's eyes and seen that spark of something that we all recognize when it is there; a spark of attraction or of intersecting auras. The trouble was, he didn't know what to do about it. He was catching a plane back to England soon and despite his whole body telling the opposite, he had no intention of staying in the trigger happy Big Apple any longer than was absolutely necessary.

"I'll get a bite of food ready." Dianne said, standing up and heading towards what Benjamin expected would be a kitchen. "It's been a long day."

"Even longer for me," Benjamin replied.

"How do you mean?"

"I've got a plane to catch in a couple of hours."

Dianne gave a start. At least, Benjamin thought it was a start. For the first time she actually seemed disconcerted. "Oh, then you've decided?"

"Well the longer I stay the more chance there is of somebody taking a pot shot at me, that puts you in unnecessary danger as well." He watched Dianne's reaction. "Not that I don't like a good scrap now and then, but I do like to know who my opponent is."

"You're quite safe here," Dianne insisted, taking his glass and replenishing it.

Benjamin sighed. "Well I don't relish travelling all night." He looked at those eyes again. They still transmitted the same message, perhaps a little warmer if anything.

"Well then," Dianne said and smiled again. "I'll make you something to eat and then you can decide what you want to do."

"Right," Benjamin said meekly. It had been a long day; too long. And he was just beginning to relax for the first time. While Dianne was in the kitchen, Benjamin thought about what she had said. Anita Holt was responsible for Daniel's death, but how could she be so sure? She seemed to have a sense about these things. She sensed danger outside the bank as well. He rubbed his forehead and leaned back in the comfortable settee. "So Daniel didn't trust Anita Holt, you think?" he called out to Dianne.

"He probably guessed that she had something to do with the mafia," Dianne shouted back, "Unless she had something to do with that smuggling business."

"What smuggling business?"

"He had definitely got mixed up in smuggling something, a valuable commodity or something."

"You really think that?"

"Mathias knew about it. Daniel made a big part of his fortune on the wrong side of the law and I knew that for a fact; not many people knew it, but I did."

"But the will? How come he made it so near to being killed?"

"Holt mentioned it to him. He told me that when we discussed the sale of his stock. We had a good laugh about it."

"Laugh?"

"Yes, when he offered me the stock at a nominal price I asked if it was to prevent me killing him."

"What did he say?"

"He told me the names of the companies that were likely to be interested in buying the stocks off me should I be interested in selling them."

"And are you?"

"Oh yes. No point in putting up with the hard work and aggravation any longer. I'm as tired as he was about the whole thing."

"But you didn't decide to sell them together for a good price?"

"He was in a hurry. He didn't explain why but I suspect he wanted a clean break so that he could go away and get married. It would have taken months any other way."

"Is that the real reason though?"

"I'm not sure. I'll have to work on that."

"Think of a theory and fit the facts to it, is that it?"

"I didn't hear that," Dianne chuckled.

Benjamin smiled to himself, got up and walked over to the open kitchen door. "How is it I get the feeling that you aren't telling me everything. Just what do you know that I don't?"

She shot him a mischievous grin. "That's for me to know and for you to find out," she taunted.

"Hmm," Benjamin said with a sigh of resignation. "We are talking about the same thing aren't we?"

She grinned again. "Are we?"

*****

Benjamin finished off his glass of Robert Mondavi Pinot Noir. It had been a pleasant meal. His mind hadn't left the problem that had engulfed his life but he managed more easily to talk to his hostess about New York, its people, the docks, Long Island, the house they were in without once actually bringing Daniel in as the subject of their conversation. He was very aware of being alone with an attractive brunette, and somehow he had begun to think less about his predicament outside the safety of the walls of Malterswood Lodge, and more about the situation inside. Finally, his mind had circled around to the other people in that large house. "Where's Carl," he asked.

"He's sorting out the guard duty for the men; it's his job."

Benjamin got up from the table and walked over to the settee and flopped down in one corner. "You know, with a good meal inside me I don't feel half as scared of being shot at. I wonder if that's why the condemned are supposed to eat a hearty meal."

"Sounds quite illogical to me," said Dianne with another gracious smile. Daniel smiled back as she came and sat within his aura. As she sat, looking straight forward, he could feel her magnetism. He looked at the side of her face and her neck and felt awkward. Benjamin had been with other women since Karen's death but he had never been a womanizer. He had never really needed them. His soul was still with Karen but he knew, from the way he was feeling, that he wanted Dianne. He wanted to put his face near to hers and smell her. He found himself leaning towards her ever so slightly. Her head tilted towards him as his lips touched the pale and delicate skin on her neck. He felt light headed and his heart was drumming in his chest. She emitted a small but unmistakable sigh and emitted a sound with its own timbre, a soft deep growl, a deep and unique chord from deep in his throat. He felt she was about to melt into his arms when, suddenly, the telephone on he occasional table began to ring. "Shit," Dianne swore.

"Just what I was thinking," Benjamin said as he leaned away and she picked up the receiver.

"Hello." She gave a deep sigh. "Oh." She pursed her lips tightly. "When?" She leaned back in her seat "Okay. Will do," she said and leaned forward to hang up the phone. She gave out another big sigh and stood up. "I've got to go. Something has come up at the docks." She looked deeply into Benjamin's eyes and shrugged. "Sorry. Will you be all right?"

"As right as I'll ever be."

"Do you still want to catch that plane? You still have time if you want me to drop you off."

"No, it's been too long a day already. Better leave something to do tomorrow." He stood up to face her.

She gave him an awkward look. “I’ll be back in two or three hours. Dial six on the internal phone if you need anything, otherwise, Carl’s men will work their shifts without disturbing you.”

“I can come with you if you want.”

“Nope. One of the men will go with me.” She picked up the receiver and dialed six. “Carl, have we got the Lincoln back?”

“Just picked it up ten minutes ago.”

“Meet me in the carport straight away will you?” She hung up.

Daniel didn’t want to argue. He felt safer in that house than anywhere, despite not being able to see any of the guards. Right, see you later then, he was going to say but, “I’m coming along,” was what came out. “I might as well. There’s nothing else for me to do,” he found his lips saying.

“Hope it doesn’t take all night,” Dianne said as she went through the hallway to collect her coat. Benjamin watched as she disappeared into the connecting garage. Carl came out of a door on the left and followed her. Benjamin did the same and looked at his Timex. It was seven-fifty.

Dianne sat quietly in the back of the Lincoln and Benjamin got in beside her. Carl did the driving. “You realise that you could be in danger?” Dianne asked him as they cruised towards Manhattan.

“No more than you are. Are you going to tell me where we are going?”

“To the warehouse. There’s been a break in warning.”

”Shouldn’t the police know about it?”

“It was they that told us about it.”

“Oh,” Benjamin was quiet for a good while after that and the he asked, “Does this kind of thing happen very often?”

“No, we usually succeed at keeping people out.”

Benjamin couldn’t help feeling there was more to it than that. He was going to ask her if she knew who had rung her when Carl jammed on the brakes. Benjamin and Dianne both caught a glimpse of a row of oil drums across the road just before they ended up on the floor behind the front seats. "What the hell?" Dianne cursed as Carl struggled to get the car into reverse. Headlight beams broke through the black night and lit up the interior of the car. Dianne had just got herself into a sitting position when the spinning tyres bit hard into the road and threw the car backwards. Dianne lost her balance and ended up leaning on Benjamin.

"It's an ambush," Carl shouted as he slammed on the hand-brake and skillfully spun the car around to face the way they had come. It was already in a forward gear as the nose leveled with the road. The car accelerated away without losing any of its momentum. Dianne pulled herself up onto her seat, letting Benjamin climb back into his.

"They'll be behind us as well," Dianne stated just as the headlights picked up two cars parked in the middle of the road up ahead.

"They'll cut the car in half if they have automatics," said Benjamin as they looked down on the barrier.

"It's bullet proof," said Dianne."

"Don't you think they'll know that?" he replied. Straight away, Carl slammed on the brakes and spun the car once again. They could smell the burning rubber as they steadied themselves against the seat.

"He's right," Carl agreed.

"Have we any guns?" Benjamin asked with a silent prayer.

"I have my Colt," he said lifting his .38 automatic into the air with his left hand. "There's an M3A1 behind your seat. The spare magazines are in the side-cupboard."

"I've already got it," barked Dianne. "Stop where you think we can make a stand."

Carl swerved the car off the road into a cluster of rocks and trees.

"What about me?" asked Benjamin. "I need a gun."

"Can you use this?" Dianne asked sarcastically and waved the sub-machine gun at him.

"Too bloody right I can," he shouted and snatched it from her as he pushed three spare magazines in his belt. She scowled and took out a small revolver from her pocket. She was about to speak, but Benjamin had already thrown open the door and dived out. He was already rolling away into the darkness. Suddenly all his combat training came back to the surface as if he had never left the army. He loved fighting. If he hadn't been discharged on medical grounds he would have never left. The car slid to a halt a few yards further on. Already the headlights of the pursuing cars bore down on it, lighting up Carl and Dianne as they ran for cover. Only a second or so later the first of the cars screeched to a halt beside Benjamin. The hunters had seen their quarry flee from the Lincoln twenty yards ahead. Now Benjamin knew they couldn't have seen him. He'd been thrown down behind the front seat when the car first stopped and he'd got out before the headlights of the cars behind them had come in line with the car. His adrenalin flowed freely now, giving his body the strength and agility he thought he had lost years ago.

Within seconds all four cars had stopped in a straight line and each seemed spew out at least six men. They crouched down behind the open car doors, peering into the darkness, waiting for the tell-tale flash of gunfire to locate their prey.

"God help us if that idiot has killed himself rolling out of the blasted car," Dianne growled.

"Might just be behind them," Carl reassured her. Don't fire and give our positions away until they move forward into the open."

"Hell, have you seen how many there are!" she groaned. "If he isn't helping us we haven't enough damned bullets between us!"

Carl just kept his head down. "Then make sure they get close enough to get one with every shot!" he half laughed.

Nobody saw Benjamin has he crawled forward and lifted his body into a squatting position. The hunters were all lined up like turkeys. As yet they were unaware that they were now the hunted. He knelt on one knee and leveled the machine gun at the front of the line. A man was shouting orders for them to spread out and circle around. Just as they began to rise, with sub-machine guns in their hands, Benjamin opened fire. Short bursts. He'd lost none of his skill. He just hoped that the magazines had been checked and reloaded regularly. What he didn't need now was a spring fouling up. Short bursts. The first mowed down the men at the rear of the first two cars as they straightened up and began to run. Short bursts. As he counted, that volley caught the rest of the men at his side as they swung around to face the white flashes of light that spat out .45 calibre rounds into their already crumbling bodies. He heard hand-gun fire as he leapt to his feet and sprang forward onto the concrete road, diving and then rolling to break his fall. He knew that the hunters had similar weapons to him, so the handgun fire was to draw the fire of the men he hadn't seen at the other side of the cars, who would have otherwise turned their guns on Benjamin. He rolled again in the darkness as a sub-machinegun rattled bullets at the spot where he had been crouching. Yet again he rolled as he heard the handgun fire of his two friends. Still they were drawing the enemy fire. More machine guns rattled but this time in the direction of Dianne and Carl. Benjamin just hoped that they were well concealed.

Another roll and he was on the grass verge. He saw two men running off to the side. "Easy," he said between clenched teeth. "Amateurs!" he shouted as he mowed them down. More bullets thumped into the grass as he rolled back into the road behind the cover of the cars. Another clip. Thirty seconds. He'd slowed down in his old age. He fired another burst underneath the cars at two more men who had decided they would be safer inside a car. He hit one in the legs but at the same time a stray bullet hit the tank. The explosion took him as much by surprise as it did the attackers. Some of them fell away with the blast; others ran off screaming with their clothes on fire. They rolled on the grass to put out the flames, but in vain. The men left at the front opened fire as the flames lit up Benjamin's position in the middle of the road. He was already coiling his muscles to spring when the men turned to fire on him and the bullets raked the ground inches behind him as he catapulted himself away. Now they were firing blindly through the thick dense smoke. Benjamin was so close to the burning car that he felt the hairs on his hand shrivel up and the skin on his face smart. He had no other cover now.

Suddenly the firing stopped. They were changing their clips. Now was his only chance .He jumped up and walked out from behind the flames. To the hunters whose guns were pointing down, he looked as if he was emerging from the flames; a soulless spirit with eyes that burned fiercer than the fire. They couldn't escape from this menace. It had seemed like such an easy mission. Make a phone call; say that the caller was the NYPD; block the road; and when they tried to break through the barrier, a single anti-tank rocket would sort out the armoured plated car and the occupants inside it.

It hadn't worked at all well. Only half a dozen left out of the twenty five that had left on the mission. Who the hell had sent them into this? They hadn't been told that Carlisle had recruited his own army. It was about to wipe them off the face of the earth. As they raised their guns they began to fall forward as the arc of bullets hit them in the lower half of their abdomens. Only two remained when Benjamin's magazine ran out. They already had their guns raised in the pathetic hope of warding off this evil. Suddenly, realizing that Benjamin was out of ammo, their spirits soared. They gleamed in triumph. They had him at last and at least they were going to go home tonight. There was nowhere for Benjamin to roll now with the fire on one side and a well fire-lit road to the other. One man, some kind of leader growled, "He's mine." He clenched his teeth and squeezed the trigger. Benjamin stood his ground, carefully replacing his last clip. He knew the end was coming. It had been a hell of a good fight though! A hell of a good fight! Jesus, how he's missed it!

Nothing happened for a moment and then Benjamin realised that the man's weapon had jammed. The second man was already leveling his gun ready to fire when a hand came up from behind and hit him on the back of the neck. As his knees buckled the leader turned and got a blow to his throat. He went down beside the unconscious man, landing on his hands and knees. His tongue hung out grotesquely. He choked and gasped as he slumped over on his side, his eyes catching sight of Carl's face as he lost control of his body and his sphincter relaxed as the last life drained out of him.

Benjamin finished replacing his clip and looked around for any other assailants. "Thanks," he said to Carl. "I reckon that puts me in my place."

"How do you mean?" asked Carl.

"You are easily underestimated," he replied and grinned broadly.

"*He's* easily underestimated," said Dianne from behind Carl. "We thought you were a London shopkeeper!"

"Garage, really."

"We only let you come along because we didn't want to hurt your feelings. When that lot turned up I thought you'd just get in the way." She put her hands in her pockets and looked at the dead and dying.

"Who are they?" Benjamin asked.

"Mafia most likely or hoods hired to do the job for them. We'll soon know when Mathias gets here."

Within ten minutes the place was buzzing with the sirens of police cars and ambulances. It was another hour before Lieutenant Mathias appeared on the scene. By that time the whole area had been floodlit and chalk lines were being drawn around the nine deceased mobsters. Flash bulbs were going off and detectives and patrolmen were busy taking statements.

We have taken statements off these three," a patrolman said to Mathias.

"How many all together?"

"We've counted twenty five, sir. We aren't sure if there is anybody in the burnt out car."

Mathias gave out a deep sigh. "Can I rely on you showing up at the Police station in the morning to give me the full story?"

"We'll be there," Dianne confirmed.

"Have you got your passport with you?" he asked Benjamin. Benjamin took it out of his pocket and handed it over. "Good, well make it ten-thirty; all right?" He got in his car and drove away. He looked as if he hadn't had a very good day.

It was 23.30 when they arrived back at Malterswood. There was no way Benjamin could leave now without his passport. Dianne let him to go ahead into the house while she had a word with Carl. He was tired and would have to be up early in the morning. He went to the staircase and had his foot on the bottom step when the door behind him opened. "Pour me a drink will you? A large one," Dianne called to him as she discarded her coat in a business-like manner. She looked as tired and haggard as Benjamin felt. Diving out of a car onto concrete hadn't exactly loosened him up. She pushed back her tousled hair with her hand and stood and looked at him.

"What?" he said, smiling as he looked back at her. She looked wild and untamed yet he had come near to seeing a soft and gentle side to her a few hours earlier. Somehow his stare seemed to bring domestication to the wild feline that had just walked in. "Vodka, isn't it? With a splash of lime?"

"Right." Her voice had softened "Not too big a splash mind."

He poured her drink and turned to hand it to her. She was standing at his shoulder. He turned away as she sipped at it, and he poured himself a drink. Turning back to her, he raised his glass, "Good health," he said.

"And the same to you," she said, smiling.

"Bit of an exciting evening. We ought to do it again sometime."

"Well it did contain a little pinch of action, I suppose."

"Usual sort of thing around here, is it?"

"Getting that way since you came, anyway." She grinned and held her glass forward for a refill.

"Knocking them back a bit, aren't you?"

"I've no intention of going out again tonight whatever happens."

Benjamin handed her another drink and she knocked it back again. "I'd like a really big one now," she instructed, smiling.

Benjamin drank his own drink and turned to refill the glasses. "I'll try my best," he said and drained the Vodka bottle.

Dianne was beginning to relax. She had obviously felt the stress of what had happened, but the alcohol was slowly sorting that out. "I wouldn't have minded you taking over the company. You'd have been able to handle it. Nobody would have forced you out."

"I know nothing about shipping." He knew Daniel was not the fighter that he was. He would run away rather than stand and fight, if he could, whereas Benjamin would always stand his ground and fight on whatever terms were offered.

"I'd have taken you through it step by step."

"You mean you would have held my hand while I grew up enough to handle it."

She took a hold of his hand. It felt hard against the soft skin of her palm. She squeezed his fingers. "Oh, I think you are grown up enough to handle it," she whispered.

*****

Benjamin lay awake early. Dianne's head rested on his shoulder as he ran his fingers gently through her hair. "What time is it?" she asked as she took a deep breath and came to full consciousness.

"Six-thirty," Benjamin replied. "We'll have to be getting up soon to go and see Mathias. Goodness knows when I'm going to get back to London now."

"It should be straight forward. He knows what happened; the scene speaks for itself."

"Too many dead bodies for my liking," Benjamin sighed. "He's going to kick up a fuss, I can feel it."

"I bet we're out by lunchtime," Dianne said with a gleam in her eye."

"I still think you know something that I don't."

"You'll have to hang around a bit longer then and find out."

"I must see to my own business as well," Benjamin said, trying to avoid the mischievous look she was giving him.

"When will you be coming back then?" Dianne asked as she rubbed her hand gently across his abdomen.

"I'm not sure. I will have to come back over to sort out Daniel's affairs even if Mathias doesn't want to lock me up." He kissed her on the cheek. "Perhaps I'll be able to stay a little longer. The trouble is, the Crazy Gang is still trying to stem my growth."

"Can't do that," she said as she felt his body respond to her caresses. They kissed and then the clinch broke. "What's the matter?" she asked.

"I… I just thought that with the shooting and all you had possibly had a little too much to drink last night."

"You think that's why I got you into bed, do you?"

"Wasn't sure," he said. "Perhaps."

"I'm not so sure how to take that."

He looked into her dark grey eyes. They reflected warmth and affection. "No, I'm being silly. I don't think what happened out there had anything to do with it."

"All that shooting stuff should blow over soon," she said prophetically. She certainly knew something that Benjamin didn't. "I'm sure you'll be safe in a while."

"I hope so. God I do hope so." Benjamin said as she slid on top of him.

*****

They were early arriving at Lieutenant Mathias's office. It was ten-thirty and he was already there waiting, sipping at a plastic beaker of hot chocolate as he skipped from one officer to another, supervising their statements of what happened the previous evening. "Ah," he said as Dianne led the way in. "Come on through and sit in my office. Gene," he called to a police officer who had just come in. "Get a couple of extra chairs for me will you?" The officer did as he was requested and all three of them. Dianne, Carl and Benjamin sat in a row in front of his desk and waited until he burst into his office with a handful of typed reports. "Now then," he said and spread them out on his desk on top of a pile of other paperwork. "Lets see what we can make of all this." He had a self-satisfied smirk on his face.

"Has somebody typed up our statements?" asked Dianne.

"Sure, but we'll get round to them soon enough. He looked over the reports again and leaned forward with his elbows on the desk. "Right, let's start at the beginning by telling me why you were all out together."

Dianne took a tape out of her pocket. "This is a report of all calls in and out of Malterswood yesterday. Not proof, I know, but it does answer your question."

Mathias slipped it into a cassette player and listened. The tape replayed the call that she had received that evening. "I see, he said. Only one of you mentioned this in your statements." It had been Benjamin. He had been as cool as before the shooting started.

"I didn't think about it at the time," Dianne confessed, "and Carl wasn't there when the call came through."

"I see. And have you brought the documents relating to one M3A1 sub-machine-gun?"

Dianne handed over a green leather wallet. He inspected the permit and sniffed. He knew she was covered; he had already checked the records. He also knew that she was a first class security agent. The trouble was, that in the last two days since Benjamin had arrived she had fired more shots and been involved in more killing than in the whole time she had worked with Daniel. He knew Daniel only believed in passive resistance, but this brother of his was turning out to be a completely new kettle of fish. He handed the permit back. "Now, Mr. Carlisle, what do you think we should do about you?"

"How do you mean?"

"You aren't authorized to use a gun in this country."

"Neither was that mod authorized to ambush and kill us all… Unless that telephone call was made from this office."

"I think that remark is likely to make matters worse, Mr. Carlisle."

"Either you have laws about self defense in this country or you don't." Benjamin stated bluntly. "Either you look at the position of the cars that were chasing us and the numbers of automatic weapons that the passengers had and the rounds fired by them, or you turn a blind eye to the truth. I thought you realised what had happened."

"Not a man of few words, I can see."

"Well then, is this an informal meeting or do we need lawyers?"

"Don't go getting on the defensive so much," Mathias placated. "If it wasn't an informal meeting then you'd all be in separate rooms. I know exactly what happened. What worries me is that you might decide you want to stay a little longer in our fair city. I couldn't stand another day like yesterday."

"I'll leave as soon as you say it's all right for me to do so. I'll even agree to give evidence if you like."

"I'll try my best not to hold you to that agreement."

"I might have to return when my brother's estate is sorted out."

"Then I would hope that I am given plenty of warning. At this moment in time, you can read your statements and sign them." He passed several sheets of paper to each of them. Each read through them, signed their copies at the bottom of each sheet as requested by Mathias, and handed the papers back. That concluded the meeting.

"Can I have my passport?" asked Benjamin.

"I'll have a man meet you at the airport with it. I'd like to be sure you are leaving the country. I need a good night's sleep. What flight will you be catching?"

"I think there's one about four o'clock," Benjamin guessed.

"Then there'll be someone there to meet you." Mathias stood up and went to the door. He gave an unrevealing smile as he opened it for them to leave. As they filed past him, he stopped Dianne by lightly catching hold of her sleeve. "If you get any more calls from the Police Department please give me a call to check it out." He handed her a card.

"I will," she promised.

"By the way, you might like to know who was behind last night' fiasco."

"I thought it was obvious," she said.

"Oh, and who do you think it was then?"

"One of the Sicilian families of course."

Mathias shook his head. "Just that the advantage of your friend leaving a few of the men alive is that one of them has talked."

"So you knew the truth already," Benjamin exclaimed.

"The question is, do you?"

"You're talking in riddles," Dianne said vociferously.

"I'm trying to tell you that somehow your former boss got mixed up in something a little more devious than his usual behaviour. He made new enemies. Do you understand?"

"Not really," said Benjamin.

"What I'm trying to tell you is that those men, as far as I have been able to establish, had nothing to do with the mafia."

Dianne's jaw dropped. "Then who the hell were they?"

"Terrorists."

"Terrorists? What sort of terrorists?"

"Imported ones from Europe. And we do very well over here for murderers without that sort of shit oozing into our back yard."

"I get the message," Benjamin said. "I have to stay away and keep the flies away from the midden."

"Something like that, Mr. Carlisle, only I couldn't have put it as eloquently as you." He gave another of his impassive smiles and moved to one side to indicate that he had said all he was going to say.

*****

The three hardly spoke on their way back to Malterswood, and once they arrived, Carl left them. Dianne made some sandwiches and a coffee to share with Benjamin. As they sat and ate, Dianne began to discuss the morning's events. Neither could work out the terrorist angle. It all seemed a bit too far fetched to be real.

"And I was really convinced that the call came from the Police Department. The voice sounded so familiar and spoke as if the person knew me."

"What did the tape say?" He tried to recall what had been played to Mathias. *'Miss Barker, sorry to disturb you but we've had a call from Lomax that there is somehow breaking into the warehouse. We have a squad car on its way.'*

"That's about it," Dianne said. "They certainly knew our nightshift guard." She went to play the tape again. "Damn it!"

"What's the matter?"

"Mathias has the tape. I never made a copy."

"The tape!"

"That's what I said."

"No, I mean another tape." Benjamin walked over to the coat hanger in the cloakroom cupboard. He hadn't worn his overcoat since he had returned from the bank. He put his hand in his overcoat pocket. "The tape!" he shouted, waving it at Dianne.

"What tape?

"It's a tape Daniel left for me at the Bank. Where's that cassette player?" he asked as he looked around.

Dianne took the tape out of his hand and walked over to the wall cabinet. She lowered the door and out slid a hi-fi system. "There," she said, slipping in the tape and pressing the play button,. She went over to sit by Benjamin on the long couch and they both sat and listened to the message from Daniel.

*****

'Hello Ben. Do you remember me mentioning that I got involved with smuggling a long time ago and it led me to know a Bulgarian by the name of Pyotre Vlatsov? Well he uses an international terrorist organization to do his dirty work for him. It might seem strange that a country that works closely with Russia, a country that would crush terrorism at the roots, should sponsor a terrorist organisation. But they do, to further their own ends, in other more open societies.'

"That figures," said Benjamin. It fitted in with what Mathias had said when they were leaving.

The tape ran on: *'I've smuggled things for him in the past, usually in the field of technology, but two weeks ago I did a different job for him. It was getting a case of arms into India, into the city of New Delhi, or at least I thought it was arms at the time. I didn't supply the crate. I was just paid to deliver it. I had it x-rayed but nothing showed up, so either the case was lined with tin foil or it wasn't a hardcore type of weapon. I didn't see inside it, but whatever CHEF is, it is dangerous to even know the name.*

'When I got it to New Delhi I was to deliver the crate to a soldier. His men were heavily armed and I have no doubt that they intended keeping whatever it was once it had arrived. The man I am talking about is called Drim Balhi, a mercenary who I have found out since has fought in more wars than I knew existed. He has a small army of his own. Whatever it was that I delivered to him, he showed great pride in having acquired it and bragged about being the only person outside the United States to possess CHEF.

'I would never have given it any more thought only that Drim Balhi tried to kill me as soon as it been delivered. Otherwise I would have returned as usual to my legitimate shipping business and that would have been that; another deal concluded. But it was quite clear that there had to be no loose

ends lying about. It reminded me of Ivan the Terrible who killed all those involved in building St. Basils in Moscow to prevent another ever being made. It seemed that serious.

'I remembered a news bulletin that mentioned a top US scientist who disappeared from the top secret Granite Rock Weapons Research Centre. I made a couple of phone calls from France and asked some friends to make some discrete enquiries. The scientist's name was Edward Taylor and he disappeared at the time I was asked to move that crate out of the US. I asked them who he was and what he had to do with CHEF. The two men I spoke to knew nothing about it, but despite neither knowing about Taylor or of CHEF they disappeared.

'Meanwhile, back in France, I had a feeling I was being followed. Then, suddenly, somebody tried to frame me. First of all they set me up to be caught in possession of a stolen painting, but when I made enquiries about the man involved, a man called Diacre, I found out that he was supposed to be C.I.A. The people I asked to find out about him ended up dead. Nobody managed to get me on the painting rap because they couldn't catch me in possession of it, but it was definitely a setup and the French Intelligence Services were also involved. Only they, with ministerial backing could have pulled the strings they did. A minister by the name of Duvant wanted retribution for my exporting technology from his factory, but needed to keep his name out of it, hence the frame-up.

'I'd discovered something about Diacre that was even more dangerous. I presumed that if I could find out about Diacre, the French could do as well, so my conclusion was that Diacre was some kind of double agent.

'I decided to arrange to make a deal'

Benjamin and Dianne sat silently, hanging on every word of the taped message.

'At first I didn't think that any of my troubles had anything to do with the freight I'd moved to Delhi. I telephoned a man in the States who I had come to know quite well. He was a top man in the C.I.A. His name was Hart. He had let me carry on my business with very little interference from the police and in exchange I had given him and the F.B.I. inside information whenever I got it, especially about the mafia and their drug rackets. It helped

to keep them off my back. I knew about people I thought were double agents, but I never relayed any information over the telephone.

'Remember, I was still in France. Suddenly I was arrested by men who said they were plain clothed police officers, but they didn't take me to a police department. Instead they interrogated me in a derelict army base. A man called Colonel Bereman led the team of French interrogators but I didn't know if they had arrested me to find out what I knew about the C.I.A. agents or to ask me about the deaths of my two friends. I certainly didn't dare tell them about my illicit smuggling business or they would have locked me up and thrown away the key. But instead, they questioned me about Vlatsov. I had never mentioned his name to either the French or the Americans, but the French had definitely found out about CHEF. They asked me what I knew about CHEF, and I would have liked to tell them that I first heard the name used by an Indian soldier by the name of Drim Balhi and that the Bulgarians had shipped it to him; but I didn't dare.

'After what seemed like weeks but was in fact a couple of days, they released me just when I thought the real interrogation treatment was about to begin. I suspect Hart had more than a little to do with my release.

'On top of all this, the mafia is trying their level best to get hold of my companies. Up till now, their intimidation has fallen on stony ground but lately they have decided to kill me and make it easier for themselves. They have already got somebody on the inside working for them, someone who is helping them to set me up to be killed. Hart told me that. He got it from a reliable informer and he told me when I got back from France. But he said he had a sure-fire way of getting me out of the country with a new identity. It was my only choice really. There are too many people trying to kill me to consider mere protection. That is why I came to England to buy that house. The trouble is, Hart hasn't told me the whole plan, only the steps leading up to it I'm supposed to drive off in a car that has been left for me in the warehouse yard. I'm to meet him in the underground car park for instructions of where to go and what to do before I drive away into the sunset. The reason I am making this tape only hours after meeting you is that I have a feeling something is wrong. I don't trust him any more but I am relying on his plan. If it doesn't work out then you'll get this tape and you'll know he betrayed me.

'With the Bulgarians, the French and the mafia trying to get their hands on me, a deal with Hart seemed the next best option, but when the French released me it seemed obvious that Hart had some deal going with them. God help me if he's in with Diacre, I just don't know any more. All I know is that this is only the beginning. They already have somebody here on the inside. It's only a matter of time before they succeed in getting to me if I can't get out of the country fast. I've made plans, but if I fail then this tape is to warn you.

'I can only say how sorry I am for involving you in all this, but after my visit to England there is no turning back the clock. They will involve you now since they know I came to see you. So all I can do is warn you and tell you that you are in danger and to warn you to beware anyone bearing gifts in any form be it advice or packages. Either can turn out to be deadly.

'Good luck Ben. I love you.'

*****

When it was clear there was no more on the tape, Dianne rewound it, took it out of the player and placed it on the table in front of them. They both stared at it.

"Well, I have a plane to catch," Benjamin said and picked up the tape and placed it in his coat pocket.

"You mean that you are still leaving now that you have heard that?" Dianne said with panic in her voice.

"Well I can't see that I am any better off over here. They got Daniel so they'll ultimately get me." He put his hands on her shoulders. "My best bet is to go to England," he said softly. "There I can get this thing brought out in the open. I know a man, a journalist. He produces programs for the BBC. If I can get this into the public domain then they'll have to kill half the people on England."

"That sounds a bit drastic to me." She snuggled into his chest. "You might be better forgetting the tape exists."

"They've already had two goes at killing me. They aren't going to take any chances on my knowing nothing."

"All the same, I wish you'd think about it."

"Mathias is expecting me to leave. I haven't a lot of choice."

Dianne sighed and turned away. "Come on then. I'll have Carl waiting with a car."

*****

The 747 flight from New York was scheduled to leave at 4.30 pm. Benjamin went over to the booking counter, dropped his hold-all on the floor and fumbled in his wallet for his return ticket. Catching planes was worse than catching a bus in the centre of London. He sorted out his seat on the flight and was about to join Dianne when Lieutenant Mathias approached him. He held out the passport and Benjamin took it and zipped it in his bag. "Thank you Lieutenant," he said with a smile.

"Good luck," said Mathis and was about to walk away when Benjamin spoke.

"Lieutenant," he said. He was going to give him the tape, but at the last second he dropped his bag and held out his hand. "Thanks for saving my bacon yesterday," he said as Mathias shook his hand.

"Let's hope that this whole thing is sorted out before you return."

Benjamin turned and joined Dianne with only a few minutes to spare. The Flight had been called and the passengers were already filing onto the plane. He gave Dianne a kiss and they said their farewells to each other in the departure lounge. "I'll give you a call," Benjamin said as she gave him a little wave.

Dianne watched the flight take off and then turned to Carl and smiled. "Wait in the car. I just have a phone call to make."

Benjamin looked at his watch. "Oh well," he said to himself. "I'll be home earlier, that's one good thing." He watched from outside the terminal as the Jumbo Jet climbed into the clear blue morning sky; a huge ponderous bird weighing hundreds of tons thrusting itself away from the ground its four engines blowing out the dark grey smoke of exhausted fuel. It was the second time he had missed his plane because he hadn't got his bag with him. He looked around for Dianne but she was nowhere to be seen. He smiled as he thought about her. She would be back on her way to that massive house; a lonely place for anybody.

"Has anyone seen a blue sports bag?" he asked the young lady at the ticket counter.

"This one?" she asked and held up the hold-all from behind the desk.

"Yes, that's the one," he replied with a sigh of relief. "My passport's still in it I hope?"

"Could this be it?" she asked holding it in the air. "A lady spotted the bag. You nearly caused a bomb scare."

"Nearly?"

"Well it wasn't too hard for me to have a peep inside. I checked where you were going and I was about to have them flown on to you since you were supposed to be on the plane that has just flown out."

"Well, anyway, I'm here now. Can I book a place on the next Concord to London?" he asked. He collected his ticket and went to a book stall, picked out a thin novel, some envelopes and a letter pad and sat at the remotest part of the lounge.

*****

"Would you be kind enough to post these for me?" he asked the young lady at the desk as he went to board the flight to London. "Could you get the stamps for me?"

"My pleasure," she said, taking three envelopes and a $20 bill out of Benjamin's hand.

"For the stamps," he said. "Keep what's left for your trouble."

She smiled and watched the good looking Englishman depart. She looked at the addresses. Two were for England and one was for a Lieutenant Mathias of the New York Police Department.

CHAPTER 13

1st October.

Doc Emerson sat at his leather-topped desk looking out of the mullioned window of his study It wasn't a very big room. Book shelves filled two walls and a third wall was covered in water colours by Alfred Stannard and Frederick Miller and illustrations by Lawson Wood, three of his favourite artists. The mullioned window swallowed up the whole of the fourth wall and beneath it was a small table full of fossils.

Doc was approaching seventy years of age and spent the majority of his retirement studying and writing about recent events that would become of historical interest in years to come. However, he wasn't a writer by trade, having been a civil servant until the age of sixty five. It was an ambiguous title for an ambiguous job. Few people knew what that job entailed, He often wondered himself just what his terms of reference were for a position he held in MI5. There seemed to be no set boundaries, seemingly having carte blanche to be anywhere and do anything. His title of 'Doc' had nothing to do with medicine, but related to his years before the Second World War when he'd been a brilliant professor at a London University. The title had been pinned on him as being a boffin, working at Bletchley Park during the War and being engaged in debriefing agents and double agents as part of his mandate.

He looked out of his window at the birds on the bird table that his wife Laura had made the previous spring. She came into his office with a tray of coffee. She was a tall quiet woman with silver hair deep blue eyes and always immaculately dressed. She sat on the edge of his desk.

"Did you read the morning paper?" she asked as he lifted his head from writing.

"No, was there something I should have seen?"

"A man was shot at London airport last night."

"Anyone we know?"

"A man called Bernard Grant, a salesman from Burroughs. He was returning via New York from a meeting in Detroit."

"Sounds interesting but I've never heard of him."

"No, I didn't think you had."

"What makes you say that?"

"It's just that the police think he may have been mistaken for somebody else; a politician or something."

"Possibly. Dead is he?"

"Yes. Single shot. Sounds like a professional hit."

"I don't suppose that they caught the assassin?"

"Shot from a long way off apparently, and probably using a night sight."

"Well," Doc said with a chuckle and patting her on her leg, "That will save me having to read it now."

"Here," Laura said and handed the newspaper. "I thought you might want to read it yourself."

Doc glanced over the article. "Not a lot to say really. The reporter obviously got a degree in assumption and speculation."

"You miss your work with MI5 don't you?"

"Most of the time it was pretty boring stuff."

*****

Benjamin sat in his office reading the Daily Mail. '*Murder at Heathrow*.' It happened three hours after he arrived on Concord. The man was on the same flight as he would have caught had he not forgotten his hand luggage. The reporter spared none of the public's feelings, taking a picture of the dead man lying in front of the exit doors lying in a pool of blood. The neon lights made it look like a black shadow, a spirit flowing from the dead body. Benjamin looked a bit closer at the picture. The victim was wearing the same kind of overcoat that he had been wearing; behind the body lying on its side was a Puma sports hold-all. "Hell fire!" he shouted. His secretary, Mrs. Seaton, knocked on the door and came in.

"Is there something the matter, Mr. Carlisle?"

Benjamin had already got to his feet. "What?"

"Is anything the matter? I heard you swearing. You only do that if one of us has dropped a clanger."

"Ah, not always," Benjamin said, forcing a smile. The blood had drained from his face. "You also may have noticed that I also swear when I've dropped a clanger, Mrs. Seaton."

"Oh, yes, well I hope it isn't too serious," she replied and turned to go back out.

"Mrs. Seaton," Benjamin called after her. She turned to face him. "Has there been anybody looking for me while I've been away?"

"Several people sir. I just told them that you would be at your brother's funeral and would be back shortly."

"Did you tell any of them that I had gone to America?"

"No, I don't think I mention where the funeral was. Is there something the matter?"

"Nothing I can't sort out. I want you to tell Mark to hold the fort again until I get back."

"You've only just got back."

"Well I'll be away again for quite a while. Just tell anyone who asks for me that I've gone up to The Lakes on a week's holiday. That should put them off pestering you for an explanation. I'll be back as soon as I can."

"Yes sir," she said and went to relay the message to her stand-in boss.

It took Benjamin just ten minutes to get his things together and leave the garage. He gave a few instructions to Mark and then he left. He was going to give himself a bit of breathing space until he had figured everything out. He knew that if he thought things out carefully, the same way he had done in his early years at the garage, he had a better chance of foiling whoever it was that was trying to kill him. Twice now Concord had saved his life. He had no doubt in his mind that it had been sheer good luck.

By mid afternoon he had arrived at a little cottage in the Chilterns. He and Karen had bought a holiday cottage some eight years ago. Since her death he had not been to stay there, only to check it and remove odd items such as electricity bills. He'd never bothered to rent it out. The whole place held the lingering smell of neglect. "Ought to have sold this place years ago," he said out aloud. "Still, it will serve a purpose now."

3rd October

"Hello Ben," Doc greeted after picking up the phone. "Where are you?"

"On holiday," Benjamin replied. "Did you get my letter?"

"Arrived this morning. Are you still in New York then?"

"No, did you read it?"

"I usually do read my mail Ben lad. A bit of a habit you know."

"Well then?"

"Well all you told me was that your brother got blown up and you think the same lot is after you."

"What about CHEF?"

"Never heard of it."

Benjamin was quiet for a moment. "Oh, I just thought you might know the right people to ask."

"Been out of the system too long, I'm afraid. Best thing would be for you to tell the police. They can get to the right channels. Special Branch deals with things like that."

"Bugger channels. Can you help me or not?"

"I'll see if I can get you an interview with the right chap. Can't promise anything though. They probably won't like me sticking my nose in."

"Thanks Doc." He hung up. "Bloody hell!"

*****

That same afternoon, Benjamin drove into the local town and bought a couple of cassette recorders and some groceries. As soon as he got back to the cottage he copied the tape that had been left by Daniel. "One for Doc, one for Scotland Yard and one for Matthew," he said after completing the task. He switched on the television but there was nothing worth watching. It babbled away in the background while he made himself a meal. He sat down in an armchair with a plateful of sandwiches and a mug of tea. It wasn't until the news came on at six pm that he sprang forward and turned up the volume.

The newscaster was relating: '*A police hunt is under way for a London garage owner, a Mr. Benjamin Carlisle. He was last seen at Heathrow airport and is thought to be connected with the killing of Bernard Grant, the computer salesman, who was shot and killed at the main terminal yesterday. A police spokesman said he is extremely dangerous and should not be approached.*'"

"Bloody hell!"

*****

For the next few days Benjamin thought about the predicament he was in. He only ventured out to post his letters. His mind kept focusing on the facts. It was obvious now that the gunman was supposed to get him and not the Grant fellow but it puzzled him how the gunman knew that he was arriving on the Jumbo. He'd booked it only minutes before it set off, at the desk where he had left his bag. God, if I hadn't forgotten my bag, he thought. Somebody must have watched me depart. A shiver went down his spine. It couldn't have been Dianne. It might have been Carl, but he hadn't heard the tape and he was one person who was still trying to keep him alive.

It was late afternoon when Benjamin shook hands with Matthew Holden. He was a middle aged man with bushy grey sideburns and a nicotine-stained handlebar moustache cluttering up what was otherwise a hairless face and completely bald head. They met in a pub half a mile away from Shepherds Bush studios.

"What the hell have you been up to Ben?" he asked throwing Benjamin a welcome smile.

"Did you get the tape?"

"Of course I did. How else do you think I ended up here?"

"Oh, of course."

"Sounds like you've got yourself mixed up in something big. The police are looking for you everywhere. What did you have to do with Grant?"

"Nothing. Never heard of him till he got shot. His problem was that he looked like me, wore a similar coat to me, carried a similar sports bag and was on the flight I was supposed to have caught."

"But you weren't on it I presume?"

"No, I caught Concord. Twice as fast. Set off three hours later and arrived nearly just as far ahead again as the 747."

"Somebody got the word you were on the Jumbo."

"Only two people saw me off."

"Sounds a bit suspicious."

"I've wondered about that. But why now have the police got hold of the wrong end of the stick?"

"You haven't any idea, have you?"

"Look Mat, if you know what's going on then bloody well tell me. I'm fed up at playing charades."

"It's bigger than the police Ben. They only follow what they have been told. You are into official secrets and big time political chess."

"Well how did I get there?" Benjamin exclaimed.

"Someone in a powerful place wants you out of the way."

"That's ridiculous."

"It's true Ben. Whatever this CHEF is that your brother smuggled out of The States, it's political dynamite. Politicians play for high stakes. Everyone is dispensable except them."

"Can't you make it public? That way there will be no point in topping me."

"None of the TV stations will touch your story. The major newspapers will have already had a gagging order put on them. Exposing official secrets can land them in big trouble." He took a long draw on his cigarette. "My best bet is a newspaper with a heavy political bias and which wants to stir up the mud about the current government. It's a long shot but I can give it a try. I can't promise anything though. Don't hold out too much hope."

"Thanks Mat." Benjamin left as downhearted as when he had arrived at the pub.

6th October

"Whose is that car coming up the driveway?" Laura asked her husband.

"I don't recognize it," replied Doc. He waited until the red Mercedes pulled up and the driver got out. "It's Ben!" he exclaimed as he got out of his seat and rushed to the door.

"Hello Doc," said Benjamin as he shook the old man's hand.

"Come in lad. I see you've scrapped the Lotus." Doc showed him into the front room. "Take a seat my boy." He waved towards the comfortable settee. Benjamin sunk into it. "Laura will make you some coffee," he said as his wife said hello and then disappeared into the kitchen.

Benjamin just sat and waited for Doc to say something. There was an uneasy silence. "Well," Doc said eventually. "I had a word with an old colleague of mine, and I don't know if it was something I had said, but within an hour the police were hunting high and low for you."

"That worked well then."

Doc chuckled. "You know what happened, don't you?"

"No idea, Doc."

"Both the C.I.A and MI5 are in it together."

"I knew the C.I.A. was involved. Daniel mentioned them in his tape, and so did a woman over in New York, who took me under her wing, so to speak."

"How far under her wing?"

"Threw me to the floor when a crackpot took a crack shot at me."

"Very poetic," grunted Doc. "Can women usually throw you about as easily as that?"

"Seems so Doc. Or at least she seemed pretty adept at it. I did wonder about it myself."

"Who is she?" Doc probed.

"I'm not sure now. She was one of Daniels's security guards and a shareholder in his company." Benjamin didn't want to believe that Dianne had betrayed him. God please don't let it be Dianne.

"And now?"

"Well she heard the tape. And somebody over there gave my description to somebody over here along with the arrival time of my flight," he found himself saying without any hesitation.

"Yes, it seems like quite a coincidence that Grant chap being on the same flight. Didn't do him a lit of good though."

"I didn't catch that flight, that's the thing. Should have but didn't, and neither of the people who saw me off knew that. So who wants to shut me up?"

"Both sides really. The assassin obviously works for the people who wanted to keep you quiet about the export to India and the C.I.A and MI5 for state security reasons. Whatever that CHEF is that you mentioned, it must be top secret stuff."

But why was that Drim Balhi chap in New Delhi and why did he want to get hold of CHEF?"

"Could be a couple of reasons," said Doc leaning forward and resting his elbows on his knees. "Firstly he's an Indian and must work from that country as a base, "He could be taking delivery of weaponry ready for some action in that country."

"Such as?"

"Such as an assassination attempt."

"On whom?"

"It's my guess that it's the Prime Minister, Mrs. Indira Gandhi or someone close to her," said Laura as she came into the room with a tray of coffee. She proceeded to pass out the mugs.

"Thank you," said Benjamin. "But how do we get to know for sure?"

"We don't," said Doc. All we can do is warn the Prime Minister and let her take the necessary security steps. Security is her concern, after all."

"And are they going to tell her?"

Doc shook his head. "Ah, that I can't say. She has very close links with the Russians. If something top secret were to be found in her country there would be nothing to stop her turning it over to the Soviets."

"Well I sent a copy of the tape to Scotland Yard. Will they pass it on to our own Prime Minister?"

"It's more than likely that they will have passed it on to the Home Office for them to deal with. But that doesn't explain why the police have been given instructions to catch you."

"Or kill me. They are armed police looking for me."

"And it would solve their problems if the police did the job for them."

"So should I hand myself in?"

"And be handed over as the sacrificial lamb. Not such a good idea in my opinion."

"Handed over?"

"Look Ben, it isn't easy to draw definite lines when national security is at stake. Good and honest people are killed if they are a threat to the current political agenda. It's above the law; it shouldn't be, but we put people in the position of power and they take it. They can do what we would be sent to jail for and do it with impunity. Housebreaking, theft, murder; all done in the name of national security. Yes, there might be enquiries afterwards, but that doesn't help the people who have already been killed."

"That's great!" Benjamin said despondently. "I'm beginning to wish I hadn't set eyes on my long lost brother."

"Where are you staying?"

"I was staying at the holiday cottage Karen and I bought years ago, but the trouble is, too may people remember me from around there."

Doc looked at his son-in-law. He'd only ever once seen Benjamin in such a state of despair but his eyes showed it again now. "Come on, Ill tell you what we can do. We'll start by getting your car out of sight in the garage and putting you up in the spare bedroom."

8th October.

At nine thirty on Monday morning Doc drove into The City with Benjamin. "It's a long time since I've been inside this place," he said, looking up at the windows of the red brick and white limestone building.

"Do you feel nostalgic?" Benjamin asked to make polite conversation. He wasn't really in a chatty frame of mind. In fact he felt decidedly unchatty. His mouth had dried up, his heart boomed in his eardrums, and he felt like getting as far away from the place as possible.

"More like neuralgic lad," Doc joked. "It's as nerve-racking a business for me as it is for you, I dare say." He grinned at Benjamin and led the way into the building. "Don't worry, we have a few goods cards to play, believe me."

"Well I don't know about trumping, but I'm just about shitting myself."

"Good morning sir. Can I help you?" asked a dark-haired bespectacled woman in the outer office.

"Good morning Nancy," replied Doc.

"Oh, good heavens! It's Mr. Emerson. I didn't recognize you at first. What a nice surprise."

"I've called to see Whiting. I presume he still runs things around here?"

"Yes sir, but he didn't say anything about your calling to see him."

"No he wouldn't," Doc said evasively.

"He usually tells me when people have made an appointment."

"He hasn't told you because I haven't made one Nancy. But if you'd like to call him and tell him I have come to consult him on a matter of national security."

"Yes sir," she smiled and pressed a button on the intercom. There was a silence as she waited for a reply. Benjamin held his breath. With a bit of luck the man would be out and he could get out of that place at only slightly less than warp speed.

"Buzz him again Nancy will you?" Doc asked with a gentle smile.

She pressed the button again. This time a gruff voice answered. "Look Nancy, How many times have I told you not to buzz me more than once. If I don't answer it means that I don't want to be disturbed."

"I… I'm terribly sorry sir, but there's a Mr. Emerson to see you."

There was a long pause and then Doc said, "Doc Emerson here John. I've got to see you urgently."

"Well you don't work here any more so you don't warrant any special favours without an appointment."

"Same matter that I mentioned to Hastings, John. I don't want to shout it out all over the place."

This time there was no hesitation. "Show him up Nancy."

"That's all right, Nancy," Doc said. "I know my way up."

"What about the other gentleman sir," Nancy asked Whiting.

"What other gentleman?"

"He's with me," Doc answered for her.

"Does he have a name, Mr. Emerson?" asked Nancy politely.

"Carlisle," Benjamin answered before Doc could answer.

"I see," Whiting grunted. "Let them come up."

*****

"What can I do for you?" asked Whiting. His name did not portray his features, being dark haired and with a dark complexion to match his brown eyes. He sat on the edge of a large knee-hole desk.

"That's what I came to see you about, John. Since I spoke to Hastings about this CHEF thing, things have turned decidedly sour."

"Hastings is my operative now," Whiting proclaimed. "His duty is to inform me of anything that might threaten national security. It's a police matter now. Your friend here seems to be connected to some kind of terrorist organization."

"John," Doc said quietly. "I think you are forgetting I worked in this department. You can tell me to keep quiet about certain matters under The Official Secrets Act but the only person you are bullshitting is yourself." He paused, but Whiting showed no reaction. "Mr. Carlisle is my son-in-law besides being a personal friend of mine. The two don't always go together, but they do in this particular case." He threw Benjamin a proud glance and continued. "He's told me what connection, be it ever so slight, he has with the murder of the man called Grant. You know full well that Grant was killed by mistake. The target was Benjamin. It looks to me like you set that up and made a pig's ear of it."

"I couldn't care less what you think. I run this show now,"

"So why did you try to kill Ben?"

"The plain truth is that we didn't. Someone else is trying very hard to do that."

"For you," said Doc.

"You said that, not me."

"But it's in your interest to help them succeed?"

"Not at all. We want Carlisle so that we can get the full story. Only when we know how important CHEF is will we know who is behind it."

"Vlatsov," Benjamin said feeling he ought to be contributing to the conversation.

"I take it you haven't any connection with that man?" asked Whiting.

"So you know who I'm talking about."

"The question is, do you?" Whiting went around his desk and sat behind it. He waved the others over to the bentwood chairs. "You see, if you have had any dealings with the Bulgarian Peoples Army you are indeed in more trouble than your everyday parking meter offender."

"I've already explained how Daniel Carlisle was involved with him," Doc stated. "His involvement is probably the reason he's dead. What we have come to find out is why you want his brother out of the way as well."

Whiting drummed his pencil on the desk. "You never explained that Daniel Carlisle was a relative of yours," he said after a while.

"Would that have made a lot of difference?" asked Doc.

"All you said is that someone had leaked information to you about CHEF and that it was connected with the death of Daniel Carlisle. We didn't have a great deal to go on."

"And?"

"It's all official. I can't discuss the matter with people who don't have the necessary security clearance."

"Not even if we can help sort the matter out with you?" asked Doc.

"You are still bound by the Official Secrets Act. The trouble is that people like Mr. Carlisle seem to think that freedom of speech is freedom to tell everybody else's secrets."

"Bloody stupid sod," swore Benjamin. "All I'm doing is telling you why somebody wants to kill me. All I am doing is trying to spread the liability. I couldn't care less if it's an American secret, a Russian secret or your own personal skeleton in your cupboard. It's the people connected with Vlatsov and Drim Balhi whose secret I want out in the open. They were the ones dealing with Daniel and they are the most likely ones to have killed him."

"It isn't hard to see how your son-in-law has made enemies," Whiting said to Doc. "Not only does he insult people, he fails to grasp a firm understanding of what he is speaking about before he opens his mouth."

"So just what do you think I'm talking about?"

"A stolen secret doesn't become the property of the thief. Just because they want to keep it a secret doesn't mean that the people he stole it off want it publicizing either."

"Meaning what exactly?"

"Meaning, Ben," Doc broke in, "that American and British Security aren't about to let you publicise the matter just to stop Vlatsov and his cronies wanting to kill you."

"That, Mr. Carlisle," said Whiting, "is why we had to get you arrested as soon as possible."

"All that did was make matters worse," said Doc.

"Yes, well he's here now, that's all that matters."

"Meaning what exactly?" asked Benjamin.

"I mean we can't leave you running about out there telling every Tom, Dick and Harry about matters we don't wish to have made public."

"Couldn't he take the oath of secrecy?" asked Doc.

"Bugger you and your oaths," said Benjamin. He took a cassette tape out of his pocket. "This is a copy of a tape my brother left me. I've since made more copies and added my own postscript to them. My sending one to Scotland Yard and one to Doc just resulted in you chasing me with a big stick. Well your aggressive manner didn't do a lot of good because if I am not free to go then more copies of those tapes will be put in the public domain by people who don't give a damn about your Official Secrets Act."

"Yes I have heard the tape," Whiting confirmed, "but the matter of secrecy is still of the utmost importance."

"I'll make a deal with you," Benjamin said. "I'll collect those tapes and you can call off your dogs."

"And then what?"

"And then you give me armed police protection, not harassment, until something can be done to stop the people who are after me."

"It strikes me that they will realise that MI5 will have been told the story by now. "I should imagine that they have already called off their dogs." He turned to face Doc. "Can he be trusted to keep his word?"

"Provided that he and I are put in the full picture," Doc replied.

"That includes telling me what CHEF is," Benjamin added.

"Can't do that," Whiting said casually. "I don't even know what it is myself."

"But knowing what it is could be important. If we know what it is then we can possibly work out what it is going to be used for," Benjamin argued.

"That's no .longer your concern," Whiting said brusquely.

"It is if someone like Indira Gandhi is going to be killed with it."

"That's already been dealt with She has an excellent security service."

"You mean she's been told about CHEF?" asked Doc.

"I hardly think that was necessary," Whiting commented confidently. "So long as she is warned that the mercenary Drim Balhi is collecting arms together then she's in a position to have her own secret service keep a watch on him."

"From what I've heard lately she has a full time job stopping a full-scale civil war breaking out. Without specific information it is impossible to pin-point a single professional attempt at assassination," Benjamin stated. "This CHEF could me a guided missile or something. That would need a lot more than doubling her guard and keeping an eye on somebody. It would need an all-out search."

"I think I've explained the problems of that to you, Ben" Doc said calmly. "If CHEF is top secret, and the Americans certainly seem to be getting in a flap about it, then there are no guarantees that finders aren't keepers."

"Yes," Whiting confirmed, "Mrs. Gandhi has too many connections with Russia to have her hands on secret weapons belonging to The United States. She might even blame the Americans for importing it in the first place. God knows what would happen to her relationship with Russia if she thought that we or the Americans were plotting to kill her."

"But what about Vlatsov?" Benjamin asked. "Can't you tell her that he is behind the plot?"

"We don't even know there is a plot. You seem to be convinced that his plot is solely a plot to kill the Indian Premier. Drim Balhi could be going to use his army against the Russians for all we know. He is quite capable of popping over to Afghanistan."

"One weapon, perhaps only one incident. You really think that would hurt the Russians?" Benjamin argued.

"I am merely stating one alternative. You must get this whole thing in perspective."

"Perhaps I could if you told me what CHEF was or is."

"I've told you, I don't know, and even if I did, I wouldn't be able to tell you. I couldn't even tell Mr. Emerson. His security clearance is no longer valid."

"Then get it renewed," said Doc angrily. "I still have contacts you never even heard of, and I'll find out what this matter is all about, if only to keep Ben and myself in the clear from now on."

"Well when you find out, perhaps you'll tell me." He smiled, quite unconcerned. "But now I must really get on with my day's work." He stood up. "In return for my calling off the search for your friend, I expect to hear no more about CHEF from any other than my own sources; unless you stumble onto something that might interest me. No Publicity, understand?"

"What about protection?" Benjamin asked.

"I think 'the others' whoever they are already know that MI5 has got hold of the information," said Doc. "And if what you tell me is correct then I suspect that the woman in New York or her guard worked for them, otherwise there would have been no killing at Heathrow."

"Yes, perhaps you are right," Benjamin said with a resigned sigh. Suddenly he felt weary of the whole business. "Come on. Let's get out of this place. God knows how you could have stood for working in this place for as long as you did." He stood up and went out of the door.

Doc had a quick word with Whiting and then followed. "You aren't in as bad a position as we thought you were," he said as they descended a flight of stairs. "What Whiting says is probably true. Daniel's connection to the illegal export of an American secret to India is probably old news by now."

"All the same, I don't like the idea of them putting a bomb under *my* car."

"If you feel at all bothered, Laura and I will gladly let you stay with us until you feel sure."

"No, I'll get back to where my real business interests lie I think."

"Whiting has said that his men will go and check out your flat and your house for possible booby traps. If any were laid, the people who left them won't have bothered to come back and remove them."

CHAPTER 14

10th October.

"Come in," Benjamin greeted his visitor,

"Got you out of bed?" asked Doc with a chuckle, his eyes scanning over Benjamin's oriental dressing gown.

"Just ready for off. I'm an early riser myself, and I've had a couple of trying days. It will take me the rest of the week to catch up on my sleep."

Doc took off his overcoat and sat down. "Had a couple of hard days myself." He followed Benjamin into the kitchen. "Coffee for me Ben."

Ben rattled about in the small kitchen of his flat for several minutes before returning with a tray containing a coffee pot and two mugs. "I've made plenty. I know what you are like when you scent coffee."

Doc was leaning back in a comfortable chair. "Good lad," he said and waited for Benjamin to finish pouring. "When I was in MI5 I had little to do with chemical and biological warfare."

"I suppose you're going to tell me that that has something to do with something."

"The only thing I had to do with it was when I and several top men at my section asked the Prime Minister for details about what research and development was being carried out in the light of the death of one of the scientists at the Porton Down Microbiological Research Centre in Wiltshire."

"How did he die?"

"She, actually. It was a doctor Mabel Askins. Caught anthrax. A very unpleasant death if not caught soon enough with streptomycin. She had definitely missed her inoculation, but the precautions there are so tight that at the time it sounded impossible to have such an accident. Anyway, we wanted to know what we were involved in because it wasn't impossible that there had been interference from outside."

"Such as?"

"Such as the K.G.B. for instance."

"And?"

"Hit a brick wall," said Doc, finishing off his first mug of coffee.

Benjamin leaned forward and refilled his mug. "Come on, Doc, let's have it."

"The people at the top of the government say they don't know or are unwilling talk about C.B.W. But research goes on all the same. I was astonished by the cloak of secrecy surrounding the whole topic. So I drew my own conclusions."

"Go on."

"Well, there's a National Research and Development Corporation which was established to make commercial use of scientific discoveries in government research laboratories, on license. The fact that the Ministry of Defense still renews the Patents shows that here is an ongoing interest in them."

"Has this something to do with CHEF?" Benjamin asked patiently. "Or are we talking about something else here?"

"Oh, I'm talking about that all right!" Doc exclaimed and went on quickly. "You see, after the First World War, The Geneva Protocol in 1925 didn't classify napalm as a chemical weapon."

"Napalm?"

"Quite; taking into account that the carbon monoxide gas given off from these substances disables people so that they cannot get away from the ensuing fire, it should be classed as a chemical weapon, but the United States has used it on many occasion, first in Japan in the Second World War and later in Korea and Vietnam. Bomber Harris used it over Dresden and he was acting on the British Government's orders. Since then, however, Britain has maintained it doesn't manufacture or use it. That doesn't mean they don't have the facilities to make it if they want to. They soon came up with some when they needed to bomb the oil slick from the Torrey Canyon." Doc sipped at his coffee.

"However," he went on, "Because there's an agreement on the sharing of information between the United States and Great Britain, I presumed that someone over here would know what was going on behind closed doors in the research laboratories in America. Since my original probes into subversive activities at Porton, I made quite a few contacts. Although they were not bound by The Official Secrets Act they were still able to throw some light on the matter for me."

"So can you or can't you not tell me just what you are getting at Doc?" Benjamin asked impatiently

"Up to now I've told you nothing you couldn't find out yourself. The problem is you know the name of something that is top secret and the only way to solve your problem is to explain what I have now discovered."

Benjamin sighed. "That would be good, Doc."

Doc smiled. "At least it will stop you asking awkward questions all over the place."

"Precisely"

"The first thing I have to explain is that it isn't CHEF."

"Then what is it?"

"It's SHEPH. That is S.H.E.P.H. not C.H.E.F."

"And that makes a difference because?"

"It's a top secret development by an even more top secret U.S. Weapons Research Laboratory in Utah, called Granite Rock just east of the Nevada state boundary. It was one of the centres set up by President Kennedy to research alternative defense systems to the atomic bomb."

"Well that explains it then," Benjamin said sarcastically. "I could have guessed most of that just from the amount of killing there has been going on all around me. Look, you do know what it is, don't you?"

"The Ministry of defense is a river that flows dark and deep Ben." He put his hand on Benjamin's arm. "I didn't mention to my source where I had got my information from. All I said was that it was getting to be known publicly since a chap called Taylor disappeared from the Research Centre in Utah."

"Yes, Daniel mentioned him in his taped message. So what is SHEPH since it is becoming public knowledge?"

"SHEPH is a mnemonic. It stands for Super High Explosive Hydrocarbon."

"And that means what in plain English?"

It means that a pair of scientists in Utah combined their new discoveries. It was a man called Edward Taylor who invented a new explosive compound similar to but much more violent than nitro glycerin. It's also reasonably stable on its own. For a colossal sum, a company called Sanderson Chemical Refiners, who, as far as I know are not linked to the Dow Chemical Company which manufactures ordinary napalm, sold the contract of employment of a chap called Marvin Schiller to the US Government. Schiller invented a new refined hydrocarbon mixture at least ten times more inflammable than normal petroleum used in napalm." Doc screwed up his face. "If you can imagine instead of gelling petrol with the fatty acids from coconut oil for napalm, or using a mixture of petrol, benzene and polystyrene for napalm-B, imagine the two new components mixed together. Combined they make a *Platicine* that can be roughly handled, stood on or even rolled into balls and bounced. You can imagine then what a warhead of half a ton of that stuff can do."

"A warhead," exclaimed Benjamin. "You mean they've put it into missiles!"

"Well, the Americans possibly have, but as I say, Britain has reservations about this kind of thing, in public, at least."

"What would a hundred kilos of that stuff do? That's about what Daniel smuggled into India."

"I reckon that it would explode with enough force to obliterate an area over a quarter of a mile square and the fireball would not only incinerate everything in that area but set fire to everything for hundreds of yards beyond, The heat at the centre of the explosion, though not hot by nuclear standards would still melt rock."

"Hell fire!"

"I couldn't have described it better myself."

"A bit on the side of overkill don't you think?"

"Depends on how many people you want to kill. It wouldn't do to be in crowd, that's for sure."

"Well I was beginning to think there was going to be an attempt to kill Mrs. Gandhi."

"That might be so and as far as I know she's been warned. But she lives with the threat of assassination as do all heads of state."

"So what do we do now?"

"Well Whiting will have to know. He'll probably say he knew about it even if he didn't, simply because an old fart like me can still out-maneuvre his lot."

"And?"

"And we'll have to leave it with him. He'll tell the appropriate sections and they will do what they deem fit, but I doubt whether that will include telling Mrs. Gandhi. It's a job for diplomats now son."

11th October

It was six o'clock the following morning when the phone rang. Benjamin's hand fumbled for the telephone on the table at the side of the bed. "Hello," he said with a dry voice.

"Hello, is that Mr. Benjamin Carlisle?" a woman's voice asked.

"Yes," Benjamin said crossly as he pressed the button on his digital Timex to see what time it was. The room was pitch-black and it took him a second or two to focus his eyes on the LCD figures.

"Call for you from New York, Mr. Carlisle." There were the usual switch-over noises and then a man's voice came on the line.

"Hello," the Brooklyn accent said, "This is Cayley here… You know…"

"Yes, I know," Benjamin broke in. "How are you?"

"Fine, Mr. Carlisle. And you?"

"Asleep."

"Oh, sorry about that. It seems the best chance I have of catching you in. I've tried calling during the day and you seem to have been out."

Benjamin gave out an audible sigh. "Yes, I understand. What can I do for you?"

"Well, it's rather the other way round. You see, probate has been granted on your bother's estate and I thought you would like to come over and sort out some of the remaining details."

"Such as?" Benjamin asked complacently.

"Well I have buyer for your stock for a start."

"My stock?"

"The company, you know?"

"Oh, of course." Benjamin had no real ambition to return to New York. The last time he'd been there he's been used as a target for a trigger-happy sniper; he'd made love to a beautiful woman, and it was most likely she, for some reason he hadn't yet worked out, set him up as a target for yet another sniper. The Big Apple was, as far as he was concerned, rotten to the core. Any time he went back there would be too soon for him.

"Well, what do you wish to do with these?"

"Sell them if course."

"You aren't going to carry on in the business then?"

"No," Benjamin replied without hesitation. "I have my own life and my own business over here. In fact I'd quite forgotten about my little nest egg over there. I have been rather busy trying to stay alive."

"Yes, I had heard. I'm truly glad that you are all right."

"Thank you."

"What about the properties?"

"The properties? Oh yes. I don't really know what to do. What do you suggest?"

"I could sell them for you, but I suggest that you come over to see them first. There are lots of things in them that you may want to keep."

"Such as?"

"Well,there are one or two nice paintings, and there are quite a few valuable antiques that are much sought after by collectors, you know."

"I'll have a think about it."

"May I suggest you come over and see the properties? I'd enjoy showing them to you. Who knows, you might just like one enough to keep it as a holiday home."

"Holiday? I haven't had a holiday in the past four years." He thought back to the time he had spent with Karen in their cottage in the Cotswolds.

"Well then, use it as an excuse," prompted the lawyer.

"I might just take you up on that. When are you free for a day or two?"

"How about next week," Cayley suggested. "I could get the papers drawn up for you to sign over that stock to a purchaser. The rest of the property and the bank account can be signed over to you at the same time."

"Right then, I'll try to arrange to be over there sometime mid-week. I'll let you know for sure over the weekend."

"Excellent, Mr. Carlisle. I'll wait to hear from you then. Goodbye."

"Cheerio," Benjamin said and hung up. He lay back on his hands and stared into the darkness. Yes, perhaps a holiday was what he wanted after all. Things had certainly calmed down lately.

*****

"Hello Ben. Come on in," Doc said as he waived his visitor into the sitting room.

"I'll put the coffee on," said Laura as she got up and waited for Benjamin to pass through the doorway.

"You'll never guess who rang me this morning," Benjamin said.

"How about someone to do with Daniel's estate?"

"Huh, could you pretend for once not to know everything, Doc."

Doc chuckled. "What's happening over there then?"

"I'm going over to sort out the property and sell the stock that Daniel left me in the freight business."

"When?"

"Next week probably. It seems like things have begun to be less dangerous now. Over here anyway."

"Are you going to see that woman, Dianne What's- a-name?"

Benjamin frowned. "I can't see any reason to go looking for her."

"You can't tell me you weren't struck on her. I can tell the way you get bitter every time it occurs to you that she may have tricked you."

"I had my reservations," Benjamin insisted. "*Don't trust anyone*, Daniel said. Well it was good advice as it turns out. I'm pretty sure I'd have got that bullet that that Grant chap got if I'd caught the flight that she thought I was on."

"It might have been somebody else."

"And she might want me shot. I'm not sure I want to find out."

"Laura came in with a tray of coffee. "You don't mind if I watch the news with you?" She asked as she placed the tray on the occasional table.

"Not at all," Benjamin said hoping that Doc would change the subject.

They chatted and watched the program. There was no mention if India at all. Since the storming of The Golden Temple in Amritsar in June there had little news coverage. A few killings here and there didn't make for interesting news. The climax of the situation had gone and as far as the media were concerned Benjamin realised that he had probably over-reacted to the whole situation. His imagination was getting the better of him and perhaps Dianne did have an explanation. Perhaps it was somebody else who had set him up, or perhaps the bullet at Heathrow was meant for Grant after all.

12th October

By Friday, Benjamin had arranged everything at work to carry on in his absence. He'd booked a flight with British Airways to fly to New York the following Tuesday. He arrived at his flat in the early evening and rang Cayley's number in New York. The line connected almost immediately and an answer-phone message came on stating that the call was being transferred at no extra cost. Eventually Mrs. Cayley answered at the other end. "Hello, Moira Cayley, can I help you?"

"Hello, Benjamin Carlisle here. Can I speak to Mr. Cayley please?"

"Oh, hello Mr. Carlisle," she replied. "I'm afraid he's out at the moment. Can I give him a message for you?"

"Yes, could you tell him I'll arrive in New York on Tuesday and I'll contact him from the hotel, probably the Waldorf, and meet him at his office on Wednesday if that is all right?"

"No need to go to a hotel. Mr. Carlisle, You have a lovely penthouse apartment in Central Park South."

"I have? Curiouser and curiouser," Benjamin said pensively.

"Sorry?"

"Oh, I'm still trying to get used to the idea of owning property over there. Er, what about keys?"

"One of us could arrange to meet you at the airport if you like."

A shiver went down Benjamin's spine. The last time he'd arranger to meet at the airport things turned decidedly awkward tending towards lethal. He hadn't got over the way Dianne had so easily led him away from the terminal like a lost puppy. Then apparently she had saved his life again, gained his full confidence, made love to him and finally after gaining the information from the tape had set him up for a hit on his return home. The hit? If it wasn't for that the rest would have been real. His insides ached at the thought of not going near her to find out. He had to find out. "Right," he found himself saying, He didn't know why. Perhaps, deep down, he didn't like to admit that he was afraid or at least being seen to be afraid, "I'm booked on the Concord's 10.30 morning flight that arrives in New York at 9.30 your time. I was going to book in at a hotel and spend some time exploring the city." He'd given himself plenty of time to get up the courage to go and see Daniel's ex-partner, but he didn't want to say it. At best he was going to make a complete fool of himself, at worst he could end up in another scrap and not a well defined one at that. He could hold his own in most situations when he could see what he was up against and count the odds, but somebody was fighting dirty. Everyone was nice to his face, but somebody was out to kill him.

"That's perfectly alright, Mr. Carlisle. Bertram has given me strict instructions to take care of you and give you all the assistance you need."

"That's very good of you."

"Well your brother was a very important client, you do know that?"

Of course he would be with all his money and property. Few attorneys thrive on State Aid in the U.S. "I'm beginning to gather that. Was he a personal friend of Mr. Cayley?"

"Hmm, well more close friends on a business footing," she explained.

That figures. "Right, I'll see you at Kennedy on Tuesday morning then. "They said goodbye and hung up. He smiled to himself. Perhaps he was going to get the holiday he had needed after all. He was going to enjoy it if it was the last thing he ever did. Nothing was going to spoil it.

16th October

His flight was exactly on time taking off from Heathrow, and he was pleased that he had sorted things out better than the last time he had departed from there. No queuing, no rush, no hanging about in the International Departure Lounge. He'd had plenty of sleep to last him through the extra long day, going through the time zones and arriving before he set off. He had a light meal as he hurtled through the sky faster than a rifle bullet. Property or not this was not going to be a business trip. He laid back and relaxed. Occasionally he caught a glimpse of the expanse of blue ocean beneath the cotton-wool clouds parted in the weather zone below. The flight was smooth with no sensation of travelling thousands of miles at high velocity. Concord touched down at 9.22 precisely. It was like getting into a lift in London and stepping out at another level in New York.

He brought no more luggage with him than he had done the last time. He wondered if he would have the same problem of identity that he had when he was supposed to meet Weber, but Cayley had come himself. There wasn't going to be any mix up this time. "Hello, Benjamin," Bertram said and held out his hand.

"Hello Mr. Cayley," Benjamin replied, shaking his hand vigourously.

"Bertram, please," the lawyer offered. "Pleasant flight I suppose?"

"Supersonic," Benjamin said with a grin.

"Quite," Bertram said, not just picking up on the English sense of humour. "Come, I have a car waiting for us." Benjamin followed him and got into a Mercedes beside him.

"Good taste," Benjamin stated as he nodded at the car.

"Like it do you?"

"I sell them."

"Ah," Bertram laughed, "well you'll be interested in seeing one I have at home then. We'll have to pop by for you to see it."

"What model do you have there then?"

"You'll see," Bertram said grinning from ear to ear.

"Did you tell Lieutenant Mathias that I was coming?"

"No, should I have?"

"Not at all." Benjamin wondered if it was the police officer that had set him up. The less people that knew he was arriving the better as far as he was concerned. His head ached when he thought about the fact that somebody had betrayed him. "What about Dianne Barker?" Benjamin asked faint-heartedly.

"What about her?"

"Does she know that I'm coming?"

"I certainly haven't told her."

"I see, then who is offering to buy the stock if she has first option then?"

"Oh, that will be the same company that has offered to buy hers; a company called Frank Freight Incorporated."

"So she's selling her share. It might have paid her to buy me out first."

"She might be thinking of you. Not everybody is out to make a fast buck."

"Big company is it?" Benjamin said to change the subject.

"One of the bigger ones. Owned by a mail order company."

"With mafia connections?"

"Who's to say? These things are cloaked in so many subsidiaries and conglomerates that it's hard to find out who owns what any more."

"How long would it take to find out?"

"I could get a man to look into it for you, but it could take weeks, months even."

"If you could." He watched the road and noticed that they had turned off the main highway. "What will Dianne do when she's sold out?"

"Retire I should imagine. The company must be worth sixteen or seventeen million to her."

"I see."

"Like her do you?"

Benjamin wasn't getting drawn into that subject again. "I'm curious as to why she bought the stock in the first place if she's selling it again."

"Simple. Daniel was in a hurry to unload it."

"Unload?"

"Turn it onto cash."

"That's the money in the account then?"

"Not at all. The stock was worth sixteen million. He sold it to Miss Barker for half that. A nominal sum really.

"Where did she get the money?"

"Borrowed it probably."

"So she stands to make a big profit then. What happened to the money she paid him?"

"That went to Daniel's fiancée."

"So who was that?"

"He didn't tell me. He didn't even mention her in his will. Everything was done through Swiss bank accounts."

"Why?"

"Because he was in danger and tried to get out quickly. It didn't work, but he was taking no risks of anyone tracing him through her." Bertram turned into a driveway of a half-timbered house. He climbed out of the car. "Are you coming to see my car then?"

Benjamin jumped out and followed him to the garage. He watched as Bertram unlocked the door and slid it up over the car. It was a beautiful, pre-war sports car with the familiar Mercedes grill and silver manifolds pouring out of the side of the bonnet, a bonnet strapped down by a leather belt. "An SSK! Gosh I have never actually seen one in the flesh."

Bertram smiled broadly. "Worth more than my house," he said proudly.

"What does your wife think of it?"

"Why do you think I'm driving the 450SLC?"

They both burst out laughing. "Well, can I sit in it?"

"Come on, I'll let you have a spin. I'll just ask Moira if she'll throw us some grub together for when we get back." He disappeared into the house and emerged a couple of minutes later. Moira Cayley came to the door and beamed as she gave Benjamin a little wave. She looked twenty years younger than her husband with short red-brown hair pinned neatly behind her head, and a face full of freckles. "Right, off you go," he said and threw Benjamin the keys.

They were gone a good hour and a half. By the time they arrived back at the well-enclosed mansion Benjamin was in love with the fifty seven year-old car. He was in heaven. This was a real holiday.

Moira was a chatty young woman, slightly plump for her good looks but obviously enjoying the affluence of her successful husband. She made them a conventional American dinner and they finished off by sitting out on the patio and drinking cold beers.

"How come you have the time to play host to me Bertram?" Benjamin asked jovially.

"Because, my dear boy, I am retiring soon. I want for nothing. I've made some particularly good investments, and even now, I take off a couple of months from work when it suits me. On top of that, I promised Daniel that I would see that you came to no harm."

"That sounds as though he knew he was going to be killed and that I would have to come over here."

"In a way," Bertram said vaguely.

"In a way?"

"When he made his will out, he paid me a very handsome fee. He discussed what would happen if you ever did inherit his estate. He entrusted me with the letter that I handed to you and told me that anything did happen I was to tell Dianne Barker to contact you by phone immediately with the time of the reading of the will."

"Why Dianne and not you?"

"Usually I do contact beneficiaries myself but he insisted that I do it this way. Don't ask me why. He had peculiar ways but he always turned out to be right in the things he did. I can only presume that he wanted to make sure you attended the funeral as well."

"But…"

"Well we'd better be off to your apartment." Benjamin stood up and followed him to the 450. He got in and Bertram tooted the horn as he swung the car around to face the road. Moira popped her head around the door and waved as they drove away.

Benjamin just sat and thought while the miles flashed by. He wondered about the discussion he had just had and why Dianne had sent a telegram rather than make a phone call. It seemed like a good way for somebody else to find out which flight he was on. Or was it all some sort of ploy to make him feel safer with her. She had certainly made all the right moves to do that. He shook his head. It couldn't be Dianne. It just didn't make sense. She had been caught up in the ambush as well. He needed to see her if only to find out for sure.

"Here we are," Bertram said as he pulled up outside an apartment block. He got up and led the way to the foyer. A security guard saluted him.

"Good afternoon, Mr. Cayley," he greeted.

"Good afternoon Pearce. This is the new owner of the penthouse."

"Please to meet you sir," Pearce greeted.

"Hello," said Benjamin. "Do I need a key or anything?"

"I have it here," Bertram said as he led the way to the elevator. "I'll have to take you into the office later to conclude all the formalities. Nothing is done without paperwork."

They took the elevator to the top floor, the doors opened and they stepped out into a hallway. They were facing a heavy wooden door. Bertram took out the key and handed it to Benjamin. "Here, you let yourself in."

Benjamin unlocked the door and went inside. At first glance it was bigger than his country cottage, taking up the entire top floor of the tower block. It was tastefully decorated and there was a smattering of antique furniture and ornaments. "What do you think?" Bertram asked.

"Better than the Waldorf." Benjamin beamed and threw his bag on the bed. He didn't know if he should sell it or move in! He took his time looking around and eventually found a drinks cabinet. They both had a beer and then Bertram took him to his office a few blocks away. He already had everything on his desk laid out ready for signing. Benjamin sat up to the desk as Bertram went through each in turn. All the paperwork had been done for transferring ownership to Benjamin of two ships, *The Silver Ambassador* and *The Silver Comet* along with a lease to the freight company. A second set of papers were made out for their sale to the proposed purchasers of the stock, *Frank Freight Incorporated* for the sum of eight and a half million dollars. Bertram explained the contents of the documents and then handed him a pen.

"I'd better hold off signing the contract of sale for the boats until we sort out for sure whether they are buying the stock," Benjamin remarked.

"As you wish." Bertram carried on with the next set of papers. "This is to transfer to you the title of a house in Longbeach in California," he said and handed a document for Benjamin to read. When he had read it he signed it. "And this is for a beach house in Miami." Benjamin did the same.

Bertram looked at the next set of documents. "Ah, this one is for the bank account in *The Bank of America*. Much reduced I'm afraid due to taxes and disbursements. I've taken the liberty of taking my fee for the work I have done for getting probate and administering the estate. I hope that's all right."

"Yes," said Benjamin. "How much is left?"

"Just over two hundred thousand," Bertram replied and picked up the next set of papers. He glanced over them and handed them to Benjamin. "These are for the sale of the stock.

You might as well read through them so you know what the offer is and who has made it. It's a very good offer and they want the ships as well. Another customer might want to continue leasing. In any event, there's a likelihood that you'll not net as much by splitting them up."

"Seems like a good reason to sign," Benjamin said

"I think so, Benjamin. It is well worth considering before the offer closes."

"Oh they put a time limit on their offer then?"

"The offer closes tomorrow at noon."

"Why the time limit? They either want them or they don't?"

"Simply they are offering double the value of the stock to get the full holding in the company, but when they have bought the majority then acquiring Miss Barker's stock will be unnecessary."

"How come you didn't mention that to me when I asked you to check them out?"

"Quite frankly, I hoped that you would change your mind about that when we'd got down to sorting the matter out. I've done the normal checks on the purchasers and they all seem legitimate to me. I didn't want you to lose a good offer by me spending weeks of my time and thousands of dollars of your money on what, if you'll forgive me, is a whim of conscience. When one has dealt as close to human nature as I have and seen how the law discriminates against the poor simply because they simply cannot afford justice, you'll realise there is a certain stage at which one must draw the line between monetary reward and self gratification. Personally I made my choice a long time ago and don't regret it. It's up to government to sort out the moral issues, not individuals. I try to advise my clients what is best for themselves."

Benjamin could see what had made this man such a rich and successful attorney. He only picked clients that could afford his brilliant oratory and left the scruples to someone else. "I see," Benjamin said, and put the papers to one side. "What's next?"

Bertram shrugged. "Two apartments, the one on Central Park South and the one sub-let to a man in Grey Oaks." Benjamin signed for them.

"I suppose you have keys for all of these properties?" Benjamin asked.

"Of course, keys!" Bertram shuffled in a drawer and took out a tin box. It rattled as he placed it on the desk in front of Benjamin, and opened it up towards him as one would offer a quality cigar. There was a bunch of keys held together by a plastic-coated wire. "You will, of course require your documents of proof of ownership if you want the security guards to let you into the apartments."

"I'll keep them in the box if that's alright." He placed the tin in front of him.

"I can't persuade you to sign these contracts for sale while you are here then?" Bertram asked before placing them in a folder.

"I'd rather like to sleep on it. It's been a long day."

"Of course. You'll be much refreshed by the morning." He sorted the other papers into two piles. "One set for you and one for the appropriate records departments." He said and handed Benjamin his pile. He opened a drawer and took out a bank book and a folder and placed them inside. "You will need proof of identity and the papers and the book if they are to complete the transfer of the account." He hovered for a moment. "Now are you sure about these papers?"

"I'll let you know before the deadline, Bertram, rest assured." He still wanted to know who owned the company making the offer but knew he wouldn't have time to find out before the deadline. He also wanted time to see Dianne and see what she was going to do with her stock. Selling behind her back would virtually render her stock worthless. It was a good reason for going to see her. Hell, he thought as Bertram ushered him back to the car. I don't need an excuse to see her. She doesn't know that I think she might have set me up.

Cayley dropped him off outside the apartment. "I'll call for you at say 10.30? We need to sort out going to the properties."

Benjamin thought for a moment. "It would be better if I go the properties on my own. I'd rather like to spend a little time at each one to sort them out one at a time. I can come back to you once I have decided what I want to keep and what I want to sell. It might take me a while to decide."

"You'll sort out this other business with the stock and such before you go though, won't you?"

"Yes. I just need a little time, that's all. See you at ten-thirty."

Bertram gave him a friendly smile and drove away. Benjamin went into the apartment and had another good look around. It felt much better without somebody looking over his shoulder. Bertram was a likeable enough kind of guy but he couldn't have stood for him hovering around while he poked into every corner and examined everything in detail of each property. He hadn't realised before he came over to The States just how wealthy his brother had become. He put the tin of keys and the folder of papers in a drawer and then got undressed. He decided whilst he was having a shower that he would eat out. He tried to make up his mind if he was going to see Dianne. Right, he thought. He got out of the shower, dried himself off and got dressed. He picked up the phone. "Damn," he swore, placing the receiver back on the cradle. He threw on his jacket, picked up the keys and went down to the foyer. "Have you got a telephone directory?" he asked the security guard.

"Sorry. Best thing is to call Directory Enquiries. I presume it's a local number. Who do you want to ring?"

"Carlisle Freight."

"Oh, I know the number for that, Mr. Carlisle. I often had messages for your brother."

"Okay, er…"

"Pearce, sir."

"Yes of course. Can you write the number down and also the one for Malterswood Lodge?"

Pearce did as he was asked and wrote the numbers on the front of a newspaper. "There you are, sir. May I say how sad I was to hear of your brother's death."

"Yes, it was quite a shock."

"I liked him very much. Such a busy young man."

"Who else did you know?"

"How do you mean sir?"

"Well how about Carl and Dianne."

"Ah, his security officers as he liked to call them. He never liked to call them bodyguards. Not that they did him a lot of good in the long run."

"Did you ever see them?"

"Saw Miss Barker here only the other day. She came with some official to value Mr. Carlisle's belongings; said she'd been all over The States with the guy cataloging all his personal effects."

"What's she like?"

"A very nice young lady," he answered scratching his nose. "Far too young and good looking to be a bodyguard."

Benjamin smiled. Obviously the silver-haired, ageing guard liked her very much; much more that he liked to admit. "Why didn't she marry Daniel?" Benjamin asked outright.

"Miss Barker? Good heavens, they fought like cat and dog." Pearce chuckled and shook his head. "You know she gave him hell sometimes when he went out without a bodyguard. 'How the hell can I have a private life with a bodyguard in my bedroom,' he used to say."

"That bad was it?"

"Well, not really. I think she nagged him because she didn't want him to get hurt."

"I'll see you in a minute," Benjamin said and turned and got back in the elevator. In his room he went to the telephone and stabbed out the number for Malterswood. "Hello," he said as a man's voice answered, "can I speak to Dianne Barker please?" He waited several minutes before another voice came on the line.

"Hello, Mss Barker isn't available at the moment. Can I take a message?"

"Er, no, I'll try again later."

He was about to hang up the phone when the voice on the other end shouted out, "Hang on. It's Ben, isn't it?"

"Er... yes"

A man's voice took over the line. "Hi. It's Carl here. How are you doing?" Obviously he wasn't surprised that Benjamin was still alive.

"Fine thanks."

"When are you coming over to New York again?"

"Already have. I'm at Daniels penthouse. I thought I'd call and see Dianne."

"Well if you hang on there, I'll ring Dianne at the warehouse and she'll probably pick you up." He hung up before Benjamin could reply. He looked at the telephone receiver, put it down and went over to the drinks cabinet. He'd just poured himself a glass of bourbon when the telephone rang. "Hi, Carl again. I just caught Dianne as she was setting off. She should be with you in twenty minutes."

"Right, I'll wait here then. Thanks Carl."

"You're welcome Bud." He hung up.

Seemed friendly enough, Benjamin thought. For the next quarter of an hour he couldn't think of anything but Dianne and how he had felt about her when they had fought by the skin of their teeth against twenty-five hoodlums. It was a feeling he hadn't had for many long years; a feeling of wanting, not a feeling of lust that he usually got when he was downing Freddie Fudpuckers in *Mikes Cocktail; Bar*. It was the same feeling has had when he first met Karen, but now he had to be strong. He had to decide what to say to her and how to ask her if she had anything to do with the sniper at Heathrow. He just couldn't leave it as if it had never happened; never trusting her, waiting, wondering what was going to happen next. But he knew that if he confronted her with it then it would destroy the bond of trust they had had before he left last time. That spark of something might have kindled into a flame. And if she'd felt that spark then it couldn't have been her. What was he to do?

The telephone rang and he jumped up out of his dilemma. "Hello," he croaked down the line and then cleared his throat.

"Pearce here Mr. Carlisle. Miss Barker is here in the foyer," he said almost melodically. "Shall I send her up?" Benjamin could picture the glint in the old man's eye. His voice gave it away.

"Yes please," he replied and waited until Pearce had hung up. He braced himself and stood outside the elevator. The doors opened and Dianne stepped out, her thin cotton dress clinging to her body as it flared away in pleats. She beamed as she stepped towards him.

"Hello Ben" she said softly, "when did you get here?"

Benjamin could only answer, "This morning."

"You've seen Cayley to pick up your keys I can see," she said and stood right in front of him. She seemed cooler than before. That was good. He was dreading her throwing her arms around his neck and greeting him like a long lost lover.

She wondered why he hadn't told her he was coming over, why he'd waited a whole day before contacting her. "If Benjamin calls I want to know right away," she had told Carl. She drove to get there as fast as she could when he'd called her on her car-phone at the warehouse. She took a hold of his hand.

Benjamin stepped inside the door and she passed in front of him, still holding his hand. She stood and faced him. He hadn't answered her question, but then it hadn't been a proper question. "What's the matter Ben?" she asked as she pressed so close to him that the pores of her body breathed him in. Benjamin could feel it too, the aura, the personal feeling that two bodies feel when they are close to each other and only experience if the feeling is strongly magnetic. His heart began to thump as his mind struggled with the task he had set himself.

"Er… I don't know how to say this, but…"

"Yes," she said and stepped even closer so that the tips of her breasts touched his shirt. They were soft and radiated heat.

"I think..."

"You think what Ben?" she said softly, encouragingly.

"I think you and I are going to have to talk," He forced himself to say.

"Yes, what about?" Again her voice was soft and reassuring as she looked up into his eyes with her own dark grey pools. Her pupils were large, making them look almost black with the faintest grey corona.

"Well the truth is..." He paused to find the right words. He had to tell her he didn't trust her. What was it Daniel had said? 'Don't trust anybody.' "The truth is, I don't know who I can trust." There, he'd said it.

"You don't trust me, is that it?"

"A lot has happened and a lot has been said and none of it makes any sense."

"It's beginning to," Dianne said and pulled away indignantly.

"Then I need to know two things," he said and walked towards her. He placed his hands on her shoulders and turned her to face him.

"Yes?" her body still felt soft.

"Well, first of all, do you know anything about the sniper that was waiting for me when I got off the Jumbo at Heathrow?"

"Yes," she said abruptly. She felt a slight jolt run through his body.

"Oh, I expected the answer to be no."

"I thought you might," she said and pulled away again.

"What do you know about it then?"

"I guessed there might be some danger to you but you insisted on going. So I just didn't remind you that you had left your bag."

"You knew about that?"

"Yes, and I saw you turn back for it. But Mathias didn't see you. I knew you would catch Concord like you did before. I handed your bag to the girl at the counter, and then looked around and spotted Mathias."

"Mathias?"

"He was still there on the background so I had to lead him away. I knew he would follow me once you had left. I knew you would rebook on Concord and I knew it had worked a treat the last time you caught it. I told Carl to pick me up outside the airport and Mathias followed me. It was quite a nice day for a walk really. Then I got in my car and he had to walk all the way back to the car park."

Benjamin chuckled. But then his face became serious again. "You are saying that Mathias had something to do with the sniper?"

"I wasn't sure about him. Both Carl and I thought that something didn't ring true with the man. Something just didn't fit."

"What didn't fit?"

Dianne gave a deep sigh. "I wasn't too sure," she said and walked over to the drinks cabinet. "It was more of a feeling I had at first." She poured herself a whisky and then poured one for Benjamin and handed it to him.

"Thanks," he said and took the glass from her hand. Their fingers touched and he realised that he hated himself for what he was doing to her. "But you are sure now?"

"I was when I heard about the killing at Heathrow. That sort of news travels around the world fast. She pointed to *The New York Times* lying by the telephone on the table.

"Is that all you have to go on?" Benjamin seemed less convinced.

"Mathias had said that the ambush we repelled was conducted by terrorists."

"Yes. That fits with what Daniel said on the tape."

"But does it though?" Dianne said, waving her glass at him. Does it? That telephone call was for me that night. I answered the call I believed it to be from the Police Department."

"Meaning what?"

"Meaning that nobody knew you would be in the car. Even I didn't know you were coming until you tagged on behind us."

That makes me sound like Bengo."

"Bengo?"

"Some pet dog drawn as a cartoon on the television when I was a kid, before my mum and dad got a colour television, actually. Programs weren't like they are today."

"Oh, I see. Well I didn't mean it to. And anyway, we were pretty glad you did tag along really." She gave him a grateful smile. "Anyway," she continued, "I thought that the Bulgarians that Daniel mentioned would have been as keen to get you as they were to get me. They'd had plenty of chance to get me before if they'd thought I knew something I shouldn't."

"Yes and that messy brawl wasn't exactly their style of doing things. Poison pellets or phials of nerve gas are more in their line."

"Messy! That's the exact word. It was too amateurish for words."

"I thought so at the time, but we were lucky it was. There were a bloody lot of them."

"Terrorist are devious and cunning men. Some of them have brilliant planning minds, and they wouldn't have planned to send the anti-tank rocket at us at the road block."

"No, they'd have used it without any road block at all."

"So?" Dianne prompted.

"So they were just a bunch of gangsters hired to kill me."

"No. They were gangsters but they were after me, not you."

"Why?"

"Because it had been announced at the attorney's office that I had been offered the major share in the stockholding. I was the one the mafia wanted out of the way."

"So you think that they were hired by the mob?"

"And given a weapon that would make it look like a terrorist attack. The trouble is, they fudged it and it ended in a car chase and a gun battle. It wasn't what they had expected, especially coming up against someone as proficient with sub-machine gun as you."

"Mathias knew I'd been a soldier. I mentioned it outside the bank."

"Then he either didn't rate you very highly or he didn't expect you to be there."

"Couldn't Mathias have just made a mistake about the gunmen? If he wanted to have me killed why did he save my life outside the bank?"

"I thought about that as well. That hit was obviously set up before the reading of the will. My only way of thinking is that he had to make sure that the assassin didn't live to tell any tales. I already had my gun leveled on him when Mathias fired."

"So why was that hit set up for me. They couldn't have known I would be outside the Bank."

"They would if Cayley had read the letter and told them what was in it. Did the letter mention the tape?"

"It said there was a message for me to listen to at the bank."

"Then it was a fair bet that you would go to the bank. Karlten would have killed you, Mathias would have picked up the tape and he would have handed it to the Bulgarians."

"But you were too fast for him." He smiled. "So you reckon Cayley is involved?"

"We certainly shouldn't trust him."

"So why haven't they tried to kill you since?"

"Because I told Cayley that I was going to sell my stock in the company anyway."

"Cayley told me that you'd been instructed to telephone me about Daniel's funeral."

Dianne frowned. "He told me to send you a cable. Why would he have said that I wonder?"

"To build up mistrust, perhaps."

"Did it work?"

"Didn't trust you already," Benjamin said with a shrug and taking hold of Dianne's hand. They both chuckled.

"You really meant that, didn't you?" Dianne looked hurt.

"Why do you think I'm holding your hand?" They laughed again.

"I can still reach you with the other." They both laughed again.

"You know, Cayley said something to me that made me wonder about his motives."

"What did he say?"

"Well he kept pushing me to sign a contract to sell the ships and my stock in the company to a firm called *Frank Freight Incorporated.* I thought it rather strange that you hadn't taken up the option on them. He said once they had Daniel's stock then your holding would be pretty worthless. I didn't like that."

"Despite the clause allowing me to buy his stock, I'd agreed to release the rest to you if anything happened to him."

"Cayley said that the owners of the company would take a lot of tracing."

"*Frank Freight* are the mafia. The President of the company is the son of one of the New York Families. Nobody would have wanted my share in the company once they got it. They are the people who killed Daniel and they were the ones that set up the ambush on me. Cayley knew full well who owned that company. He was pushing you to make a deal for them. He would have raked off a fat see, probably more than a million, and settle in his retirement."

"I thought that Daniel seemed determined to stay alive in his taped message."

"Yes, so did I."

"No," Benjamin corrected. "That's what I was thinking when I was talking to Cayley. Then he said Daniel had given him the letter at the time he had made out the will. Looking back on it, if he read the letter he would have known it wasn't dated, but what he didn't know is that Daniel had written that letter between seeing me in London and getting killed the same evening in the warehouse. He must have gone to the bank first, then, probably posted the letter which Cayley resealed in one of his envelopes."

"It's all beginning to make sense now," Dianne said quietly. She sat on the edge of the table and looked at the floor. "Did you sign the contract?"

"No, I wanted to see you first," She nodded at him "You see, I really had begun to believe that it was you mixed up with the baddies."

"I know; I could tell that the moment I stepped out of the elevator."

"I'm sorry," Benjamin said and squeezed her hand. She squeezed it back and raised her head to look into his eyes.

"What are we going to do?" she asked.

"I thought you had all the answers," Benjamin said with a smile.

"I mean, what are we going to do? We are no better off than Daniel was."

"And we live three thousand miles apart." He sighed.

"What does that mean?"

"That if I have to, that is if there is no alternative, I can live without you," he said, letting his voice dry up before he'd finished. She let a smile escape from the corner of her lips and carried on looking at him.

"Do you have to?"

"That depends on whether you can live without me."

"What if I told you I could?" Benjamin's heart sunk. Of course she would be able to, the same as he could. "If I had to," she added.

Damn it. He couldn't ever say what he wanted without fumbling and making a mess of it. He knew Dianne felt the same. There had been something from the very start. He knew that feeling and he never thought he would feel it again. But he was feeling it and it was real.

"Yes," Benjamin said sadly. "Our lives, our way of living are completely different."

"That's no problem, not if we both sell our share of the company and get out."

"You mean you are willing to sell your stock to the mafia?"

"Only if we sell our stock together, for the full market price."

"But would they buy them?"

"Oh yes. When I explain why, you'll see." She smiled at him again and he knew she meant it. She took hold of his other hand and pulled him closer. "Mind you, I can live without you if I have to." Her eyes seemed to be asking rather than telling him this time, as she tilted her head to one side ever so slightly. "You said that you needed to know two things. What was the other?"

"Have you ever been to London?"

"Never."

"Concord is much better than Jumbo," he said with a grin as he pulled her up close to him.

"You'll have to take me on it then, won't you?" she said and then kissed him.

*****

Something about their conclusions didn't fit just right yet. Something at the back of Benjamin's mind kept gnawing at him, eating away at his self-satisfaction. He'd been happy he'd been able to sort it all out. He and Dianne were back together in her bed at Malterswood. They'd had a lovely evening talking and planning for the trip to visit all the properties that he still had to sell. But it all seemed too neat. "You know," he said to her as he looked at her head on the pillow next to him, "we're better off than Daniel in that the French aren't after us."

"Hmm," she said sleepily. Benjamin couldn't sleep. In fact he was more awake than he'd been all day. He'd got some of the facts and they fitted nicely into the theories they had worked out over in the apartment,, but his mind was racing, churning over all that had happened from the time Daniel had visited him over in

England. 'I'll live for ever,' Daniel had said ever since he was a boy. He was nobody's fool. He was the sort of person to avoid scraps but he'd ended up getting killed; killed by the people that had given up trying to kill Benjamin and Dianne because they were going to buy them out.

"And the Bulgarians seem to have forgotten about us as well," he stated as he looked up at the ceiling.

"Hmm," Dianne acknowledged in a muffled groan.

"So why didn't he just wait until things had settled down a bit and then sell his company like we will?"

Dianne didn't answer. She was fast asleep.

"Perhaps he was tired of swimming up stream?" he put to himself as he slid out of bed. "Perhaps, but I don't really know. He must have known that the mafia would get the company in the long run. He couldn't have expected me to take over." Dianne didn't hear him talking to himself. Neither did she hear him leave the room. Middle of the night or not, Benjamin had some telephone calls to make. He went into the part of the mansion that had been Daniel's living quarters. He switched on the table lamp and settled into a comfortable chair with the cordless telephone. He looked at his watch as he stabbed at the first number. It took a long time to connect, but when it did, a disembodied voice answered almost straight away.

"Emerson," it grated.

"Not got you out of bed have I Doc?"

"Just getting up son. The alarm has just gone off." He sounded more cheerful when he heard Benjamin's voice. "How are things over there, getting it all sorted out, are you?"

"Slowly," Benjamin answered as truthfully as he could. "Listen Doc, can you find out if all that buggering about over there was to do with SHEPH or could it have been about somebody else?"

"Somebody else?"

"Like the mafia." Doc laughed. "It's not funny Doc. They are in it over here up to their necks."

"Sorry Ben. I didn't mean to laugh, but I know the answer to that already. No doubt about it. It was somebody trying to stop you talking about SHEPH."

"How can you be so sure?"

"I couldn't tell you that over the phone. Let's just say that since all this blew up, if you don't mind the expression, my sources have revealed quite a lot to me."

"I see. Well thanks Doc. I hope you have a good day."

"I will do if I can drag myself out of bed. You obviously don't know the meaning of the word sleep."

"Oh, I've been to bed. I got up early to sort out a few things ready for the day ahead."

"Early? It isn't as early as it is over here!"

Benjamin chuckled.

"Well take care, do you hear," Doc said affectionately.

"Okay. Benjamin hung up and thought for another ten minutes. No answer to his problem yet. If Mathias wasn't in with the Mafia, then who was it who set him up in London? And what about Kalten? Mathias knew him so was he working for the mafia or for the Bulgarians? A hit-man from out of the country. Then he was more than likely working for the Bulgarians.

He walked through to the office. A short search revealed a stack of telephone directories. He looked up a number, scribbled it down on a notepad and returned with the top leaf to his chair in the lounge. Quickly he prodded the numbers on the phone. An answer phone was waiting for his message. "This message is for the president of *Frank Freight Incorporated.* I would like you to call me back before 9.30 this morning. If he doesn't call back then say goodbye to the *Carlisle* companies. He gave the number of the apartment on Central Park South. He needed to be there when Cayley called. If Cayley was in the pocket of the mafia then he would know about it before the morning was out.

CHAPTER 15

17th October

Benjamin was eating breakfast at 6.00 am. Howard the cook had been knocked out of bed and he'd given him strict instructions to make an early meal so that they could travel to Manhattan before the traffic became ulcer-inducing. Benjamin woke Dianne softly. She rolled over and saw Benjamin fully dressed and sitting on the side of the bed. "We've got a busy morning ahead of us. I need to be at the apartment before nine."

"Why?"

"I'm expecting an incoming call and we have a couple to make."

"What's wrong with here?"

"Cayley is picking me up at ten." He kissed her on the nose. Before she could say that Cayley could go boil his balls, Benjamin had already got up and left the room.

Benjamin explained everything to her as she forced down some black coffee. It had been a hell of a good night. She wasn't so sure about the day. Carl drove them into New York in the Lincoln. They arrived at the apartment at 8.45. Benjamin instructed Carl to be ready to pick them up outside Cayley's office at 10.30. Dianne and Benjamin went up to the apartment.

Benjamin had hardly said a word on the way. "Is everything alright?" Dianne asked him.

"Great now were alone together," he said and gave her a big hug. He took his piece of paper out of his pocket and started to prod the numbers on the phone.

"New York Police Department," a woman's voice answered.

"Could I speak to Lieutenant Mathias please?"

"Who's calling?"

"Carlisle."

"Please hold." There was a silence broken only by an occasional static crackle and then Mathias came on the line. Dianne stood and listened. He hadn't mentioned anything about ringing Mathias.

"Lieutenant Mathias," he stated.

"Benjamin Carlisle here, Lieutenant."

"Ah, Carlisle. Now where have I heard that name before?"

Benjamin smiled. "Perhaps from the telephonist," Benjamin chided. "Not worried about my being in New York then?"

"Carlisle! Good God, I'd better ring the mortuary and warn them to expect another pile of fresh corpses!"

"You seem to have got over it very well," Benjamin said, smiling.

"Well I knew you were here. Went to Cayley's, had a spin in his old banger, then you went to an apartment in Central Park South, on to Cayley's office and back to the apartment again. I don't think I have missed much out. No idea what you did after that though."

"Bang on Lieutenant, you seem very well informed."

"Not much I don't know when I have somebody watched."

"Yes, I thought that as well."

"Well what can I do for you?" he asked pleasantly.

"I think you've already answered my question, Lieutenant."

"Forgotten where you'd been then?" he could hear him chuckling.

"I thought you would want to talk to me."

"What about?"

"You mentioned a few dead corpses."

"Corpses are usually dead, young man. Hence the name."

"All right, well can you tell me anything else about them?"

"Such as?"

"Such as did any of the half dead tell you anything different to what you had been told before I left?"

"Oh, well you have realised yourself that they were just a gang of hired hoods. It wasn't an assassination attempt, so much as attempted murder. Two of them confessed that they had been told they were doing it for the I.R.A. There's a lot of support for the I.R.A. over here you know."

"Yes, I know."

"What is it Lenin called such people: *useful idiots*?"

"No, I didn't know that."

"There are a lot of them about unfortunately; easily talked into doing things that they have been told is a good cause."

"Who hired them then?" Benjamin asked, wondering if Mathias had got any of it right. What happened to the Bulgarians in his theory?

"Well not the I.R.A. that's for sure. If they had wanted you out of the way they would have been a bit more selective with the people they sent to do it."

"Like Kalten?"

"Good God, no. They would have sent one of their own to do their dirty work. There are enough of them."

"So two questions then: Who hired them and who hired Kalten?"

"I've come to the conclusion that it was our local mafia that was trying to have your Miss Barker bumped off."

"Not after me then?"

"From your statement you only decided to go along at the last minute."

"And Kalten?"

"That's different altogether. He was definitely sent to kill *you*."

"Well, perhaps if I give you a call you'll see me off again when I leave. Thanks"

"They seem to have lost interest in you don't they?"

"Who?"

"The people that hired Kalten. Was it because of what happened in England?"

"What happened in England?"

"Come now, surely you remember getting involved with your MI5?"

"Is there anything you don't know?"

"Try me?"

"Who set me up for the sniper at Heathrow?"

"Probably had a man tailing you. I've had you tailed and you never noticed."

"Yes, I realise that. I just wanted to know for certain."

"Not getting suspicious of me, are you Mr. Carlisle?"

"Must go now," Benjamin stalled him. "If you need me I'll either be at the apartment or at Malterswood." He heard Mathias chuckle. "Cheerio," he said and hung up without waiting for an answer.

"Well," Dianne asked. Did that clarify anything?"

"Quite a lot. It supports all our reasoning except for him being a part of it."

"He would, wouldn't he?"

"He knew my every move since I landed at Kennedy. "

"Does that surprise you?"

"It doesn't surprise me to realise that somebody could have done the same when I was on my way back to London."

"He didn't see you return to the lounge, I know that. If there had been anybody else then they would have known you missed the 747 flight."

"Not if they had been following you *and* Mathias. Your actions would have indicated that I was on the flight. Another thing that doesn't fit is that Mathias tried to get a copy of the letter that Daniel left for me. He thought I'd asked Cayley to shred it.

Dianne was about to admit that she might have been wrong when the telephone rang. "Benjamin Carlisle," Benjamin said as he picked up the handpiece.

"Antonio Batalli. You wanted to speak to me?" The voice was confident and assumed an air of authority.

"Yes?" Benjamin replied in the same tone.

"You want to make a deal, eh?"

"If that's at all possible." Benjamin looked at his watch. It was 9.28. By 9.54 he'd finished talking with Batalli. "It's a deal then?" he asked.

"It's not what I expected. I will have to think about what you have said. Your implications are quite damaging."

"Ring me with your answer at Bertram Cayley's office at 10.30." He hung up.

"Well how did I do?" he asked Dianne.

"I'm beginning to think that you meant it," she said and looked directly into his eyes. "Did you mean it?" She asked.

"I meant it."

"You're a pirate!"

The telephone Rang again. "Pearce here, Mr. Carlisle. Mr. Cayley is waiting here for you."

"Okay, tell him I'm on my way down." He hung up. "Better not keep him waiting," he chuckled.

Cayley looked disturbed when he saw Dianne emerging from the elevator with Benjamin. "Hello," he said as cordially as he could. "I see you two have got together."

"Got quite a bit to thrash out this morning," Benjamin said with his friendly smile. "I thought it best if we all got round a table and worked it out once and for all."

"Suits me," Cayley replied and escorted them out to his car. They got in and he drove them the few blocks to his office. Nobody uttered a word. No doubt, the lawyer was working out his plan of action for when they got to the office. He no doubt had a fat fee at stake. He led them through to his desk. "Will you take a seat?" he said, eventually. He sat opposite them and said, "Now, down to business."

"Down t business," Benjamin nodded with his pleasant smile once again.

"Now then, things are changing all the time with the offer to buy your stock."

"Right."

"It appears that *Frank Freight Incorporated* wants to buy all the stock." He said and pinned his half moon gold-rimmed spectacles to his face.

"I see," Benjamin said. Dianne just sat and listened.

"No, Mr. Carlisle, since yesterday they have decided they only want to buy all the stock that you have. That, of course, means that Miss Barker should wait in the other office." He looked at her and she remained seated like a stone statue. Even Benjamin wouldn't have liked to move her.

"There's just one thing I'd like to ask," Benjamin said to lighten the tension. "You told me that Miss Barker has no right to buy my stock under the preemption clause. Is that correct?"

"Quite correct. She contracted out of it when your brother sold her the holding she had now."

"Why?"

"Because he asked her to. It was a good deal for her and he wanted to make sure that you got a shareholding in the company." Benjamin was trying to work out what the reason for that was.

"Did Miss Barker understand the contract?"

"She signed the paper to that effect."

"Did Daniel read the document and understand it?"

"I'm sure he did, Mr. Carlisle." He was suddenly being very formal.

"I was told he always left the reading to you. He couldn't be bothered with paperwork if he was paying you to do it for him."

"I'm sure whoever told you that had misunderstood." Benjamin knew that with Daniel dead he couldn't refute what Cayley was saying.

"But the preemption clause still stands, doesn't it?"

"I've told you, it doesn't apply now," Cayley said patiently.

"Not to Miss Barker, but it does to me."

"To you?" Cayley looked disconcerted.

"I have first option to buy her stock, do I not?"

"Er, well yes, if you wanted to but…"

"But I don't wish to. That's not what Daniel wanted, and I'll tell you why, shall I?"

"I have a feeling that you are going to, Mr. Carlisle."

"Because he knew that Dianne wouldn't be able to make any better deal with them than he could."

"What does that mean?"

"It means that when they tried to kill us they got the measure of me and played right into Daniel's hands. He knew I wouldn't let them push me around. He'd seen people try it before and fail."

"So what do you intend doing?"

"I refuse to let you sell her stock to anybody outside the company until I have been offered them at the same rate as Miss Barker was offered them. And I will insist on buying them all. I have signed no contract relinquishing my right to do that."

"But Ben," he said condescendingly, "You don't know anything about the business. Do you really want to be burdened with all the problems that weighed down your brother?"

"His only problem was the mafia."

"I don't think you understand the facts here, if I may say so."

"Well, maybe so, but I have a proposition to make to you."

"Yes?"

"First Dianne and I pool our stocks and sell them at a fair market price to *Frank Freight Incorporated*."

"As I have said, they don't want a full stockholding now."

"When did they tell you that," Dianne butted in.

"Late yesterday evening."

"Funny, Mr. Batalli didn't mention that when I spoke to him this morning," Benjamin stated.

"This morning?" Cayley pushed his spectacles up his face. Beads of perspiration were making his nose slippery.

"I offered him a deal."

"What kind of deal?" Cayley asked rather faintly.

"I offered them all the stock at the full market price."

Cayley shook his head. "They won't do it."

"Why do you say that? Is it because you really know who they are and that they will do to me what they did to Daniel?"

"All I can say is that if they are the same people you would be advised to sell to them. I have already explained to you that you shouldn't get caught up in moral issues."

"I should if it affects how much we get for the shares."

"Perhaps I can make a better deal with them than the offer they made before."

"That isn't all," Benjamin added.

"Oh, what else do you wish me to do?"

"I also want to know how much you creamed off the company by abusing your trust."

"That's an outrageous slander."

"What did you do with his money from the sale of his stock to Dianne? And what did you do with his Swiss bank accounts?"

"Are you seriously accusing me of taking that money?" He was seething with anger, his voice bouncing off the office walls like a recording studio echo chamber.

"Then perhaps you can tell me?"

"I can tell you nothing," he hissed.

"Then I will tell you what the rest of my deal was with Batalli."

"Oh, there's more is there?" Cayley shouted and stood up, pounding his fist on the desk. "Well let me tell you…"

"No," Benjamin broke in. "Let me tell you first Sit!" He stood up, pointed to Cayley's chair and hovered over him. The attorney stood his ground for a moment and then lowered himself reluctantly into his seat.

"The deal is this," Benjamin began. "First they buy the stock at full market price, and then they buy the ships at the offered price. You draw up the necessary contracts for the transaction and you also draw up a contract for the sale of your SSK."

"You're mad!" growled Cayley, his face turning a bright red. There is no way I would sell that."

"Yes there is, for a nominal sum to make up for the money you have embezzled from Daniel."

"I embezzled nothing."

"I know you did and that's the price you will pay."

Cayley suddenly became calm. His eyes narrowed and a spark of defiance glinted in each one. "As I said, you're completely mad. There is no way I will agree to your demands. You might find yourself out in the cold. Antonio Batalli will eat you alive like he did with your brother."

"He already had the measure of me. He knows I'm not like my brother and I proved it a couple of weeks ago. He knows that Daniel only put up a passive resistance but he knows that if comes up against me he will be sucked into a bloody war. He would rather see me out of New York before try to kill me again because I have told him who will get hurt next."

"You overate yourself boy," Cayley grated, now as calm as ever he had been. The cool headed lawyer was rising from the ashes of doubt and his anger had turned to reason. "Batalli is a very cunning and devious man. Fighting him would be like pissing into a gale."

"You over-rate Batalli. He doesn't give a shit about you and he knows exactly what you are. He must have a dozen things he can pin on you. Once you have slept with the mafia you are married to them forever and the mafia will end your marriage with them abruptly if you are going to bring them problems. And by abruptly I mean they will simply make you disappear. They have you by the balls Cayley and you know that; and I'm betting your old banger on it."

"You're all talk I would be obliged if you would both leave my office this instance." He stood up, no longer afraid of his opponents. He brushed past Benjamin, opened the door and stood beside it waiting for them to leave.

Benjamin nodded through to the open space beyond. Cayley turned to see what he was indicating and froze when he saw three men standing next to receptionist's desk. One was a tall thin man with short cut black hair and a small Clark Gable moustache; the second, obviously a bodyguard was shorter, fatter, and half bald, heavily sunburned and carried a bulge in his jacket where his pistol pushed out against it. The third man was Carl. He was standing next to and slightly behind the armed man and smiled at Benjamin reassuringly. Benjamin knew who would be the quickest if the fat man went for his gun.

The receptionist turned and spoke. “Mr. Cayley, Mr. Batalli is here to see you,” she said nervously.

“Show them in,” Benjamin said. The tall one smiled and stepped forward, followed by the other two. He grinned and held out a hand to him. Benjamin took it and shook it firmly.

“Glad I’ve had the chance to meet you. I’m Antonio Batalli,” he stated.

“I expected a phone call,” Benjamin replied.

“I wanted to see who I was dealing with.”

“So there is a deal then?”

“I think we can work something out.” He smiled again as he looked across at the lawyer. Cayley stood as if he had had a spell cast over him, neither moving nor speaking. Beads of sweat had turned into globules that were running down his temples.

“Good,” Benjamin said and turned to Dianne. He took her by her arm and led her past them and out of the office. “If you get everything drawn up I’ll see you in three day’s time, at your new warehouse shall we say? I’ll call to confirm the time.”

Batalli let a small chuckle escape from his diaphragm, and unable to hold down his relief of having concluded what was really not too bad a deal he began to laugh. “My new warehouse,” he chortled. “I like it.”

“Make sure your attorney crosses all the t’s won’t you. I’ll be reading the contracts very carefully and I expect them to be in plain English.” He walked Dianne to the door. “Oh, by the way,” he said as an afterthought.

“Not something else?” Batalli said still in rapture.

“While you’re doing the paperwork how will you be fixed for drawing up a contract to ship my new car over to England at the same time?” Batalli laughed even louder. Cayley turned purple to the point of near apoplexy, and Dianne and Benjamin left the office with Carl at the rear.

"I can't get over the fact that you would have stayed on in New York to spite them all if they hadn't agreed," Dianne said as they walked to the car.

"I wouldn't have had much choice. Now I realise just how Daniel was beginning to feel. He was forced to stay or give in to them. He would possibly have made a deal with them if he'd had something to bargain with."

"Such as guns, you mean?"

"Daniel used his head, not his muscle. He said when he visited me in London that I was always the scrapper in the family. He was right."

Dianne looked at him as he got into the Lincoln. She knew now what it was about Benjamin that attracted her so much. He had a mind as good as his brother but he wasn't passive like Daniel had been when it came to defending himself and his property. To Benjamin, attack was the best means of defense.

"Malterswood?" Carl asked as they cruised away.

"Yes," said Dianne. "And then when we've had dinner we'll get on the first flight to Miami. We have some properties to put on the market."

CHAPTER 16

20th October

Edward returned to the apartment at Grey Oaks. It seemed the safest place to be, where everybody had already looked. It had been a risk, but he knew if Hart hadn't found Janine or himself, the Matthew Roland story would be considerably weakened, and Hart wouldn't, with a bit of luck, believe a single word the 'crazy scientist' said.

The day he'd been to New York to find Janine had ended in total chaos. He'd been gazing from the window and laughing at the fleeing Matthew, watching intently as Hart's men bundled Matthew into their car when suddenly, out of the corner of his eye, he saw Janine disappearing out of the door of the apartment. He spun on his heel and ran after her but he only got as far as the elevator doors when he realised that he had no pants on. He cursed for being so confident of himself and went back inside. By the time he had decently clothed himself and followed her out into the street, she'd gone. He swore at her and after getting a few things together, including the bag of money, he left.

It didn't take Janine long to realise that knowing what she did about Edward, and having betrayed him once, he would not trust her again. Edward would expect her to either rob him again or kill him in his sleep, or do something just as unbecoming of the gentle looks and pleasant nature she portrayed. She took her chance and ran, taking no more than her coat and the clothes on her back. She hadn't dared grabbing the bag of money from his hand. For that he would have surely followed her into the street in the centre of New York wearing nothing. Fortunately for Janine, penniless though she was, she carried the tools of her trade with her everywhere she went. She was more than able to secure and rent an apartment by the end of the week.

It hadn't taken Edward's brain much effort to work out his alternatives either. He could leave Janine out there, walking about free, in which case, knowing who he was and what he'd done, she could blow the whistle on him yet again. He could stay at the apartment and wait for Hart's men to return, as they were forced to do if they suspected there was a witness to what happened in the street beneath the window. They would also return to check out Matthew's story. He would undoubtedly tell them that Janine could verify everything he said and that he could point out the real Edward Taylor.

He didn't trust Hart either. Hart suspected him of stealing the highly secret explosive compound but he treated him like a little child, allowing him to have the drivers license he couldn't use, following him all the way to New York when obviously his men had seen him leaving the safe house in San Francisco, play-acting that he wanted Edward to do a job of impersonating someone when they had a hundred people in their organization already trained and capable of doing just such a thing. If they really believed his story about being kidnapped they would have asked him to return to work at The Granite Rock Research Centre, not play at modern-day cowboys and Indians with somebody with a brain as valuable as Edward possessed. "And what the hell would they want to set me up with a new identity for!" he said out aloud as he looked in the mirror. "If they don't want me then they will sure as hell not want to give anybody else the chance of buying what I know." No, he saw Hart for the clever and devious man that he was. He had seen through Edward but he couldn't prove that he was a liability to the safety of the United States. They couldn't lock him up but they couldn't ask him to work for them again either. The research Centre was the last place that would want him now. Hart had seen through Edward alright, but Edward had seen through him.

Like Janine, he went into the city. First of all he took his money to another safety deposit box at the airport, keeping back enough to see him through a couple of week's inexpensive living. Then he booked in at a cheap hotel, knowing that if Hart did believe Matthew they would expect Edward to be living in a more up-market kind of accommodation.

After two weeks during which he had spent most of his time looking for Janine, he returned to the apartment and asked the security guard what had been happening in his absence. He hadn't been on duty at the time, but the log showed that, after an initial visit from men, who, according to gossip from the guard that was on duty at the time, flashed badges like judges flashing cards at an ice-skating rink, no further visits were made. He knew they would be looking for Janine if they hadn't already got her.

Edward had thought it a reasonable investment to give one particular security guard named Teisen, a heavy bribe to let him know if any of Hart's men came back looking for him. He was the guard that had sent Edward up to the apartment the first time he visited. In his way, the guard liked the man he knew as Matthew Roland. He'd seen him return unshaven and not a little inebriated many times after a long night on the town. Edward soon realised that his appearance at the apartment had been a perfect character impersonation. And Teisen was still none the wiser.

Teisen had direct orders to warn him if Hart's men came visiting again. With Teisen's persuasion, the other two guards agreed to do likewise for a much smaller bribe. Edward had evolved a plan whereby he was to let the phone ring. If it rang three times and stopped before ringing again, he would be forewarned of danger downstairs. With such an alert signal he would remove himself to an empty apartment on the same level, an apartment for which Teisen had lent him the key. The other guards knew nothing about the contingency plan; all they knew was the procedure to warn Edward and the instructions if he didn't answer the second call to indicate to the visitors that he was out.

For two weeks now, Edward had been back at Grey Oaks. He had gambled that is conclusions about Hart were right. He had guessed that Hart had plans for him that didn't include extending his health and he had gambled that Hart would not involve the police in the search for him. The odds were in

Edward's favour. He had gone over all the facts again and again until, with the precision of his academically honed mind he was almost a hundred percent sure that only Hart or his two men would be the ones looking for him. Antonasi was out so the police were out.

He lay back on his armchair and smiled to himself. Nobody had come looking for him. That could only mean that they hadn't found Janine. By now, Matthew Roland must have fulfilled his role that they had in store for him, but he had never found out what that role had been. He chuckled to himself and wondered if he had agreed willingly to do Hart's mission. Probably not but Hart had a way of persuading people to do his bidding.

He pulled himself lazily from the chair, poured himself a small whisky and checked his watch. It was just after noon. He picked up a letter that lay next to the telephone and read it again.

Malterswood Lodge
Long Island
New York
15th October 1984.

Matthew T. Roland,
Apartment 7,
Bourneville House,
Grey Oaks, Westchester Co.

Dear Mr. Roland,

As you may have heard recently, Mr. Daniel Carlisle, the owner of Apartment 7, at the above address, which you lease half-yearly from him, was killed in an unfortunate accident. It is for that reason therefore, that it is necessary to make an appointment for his brother, the beneficiary under his will, Mr. Benjamin Carlisle, to see the premises with a view to their sale. May we suggest an early date, the 20th of October at 1.00 pm? We hope that this is satisfactory and that it does not put you to any inconvenience.

We will assume the appointment time to be agreeable if we do not hear from you to the contrary in the meantime.

Thank you for your assistance in this matter,

Yours faithfully

D Barker, pp Benjamin Carlisle.

Edward put down the letter, went over to the window and looked out at The Thomas E. Dewy. Thruway, his mind still on other things. Janine was still up most in his mind. He had looked and not found her. She was his Achilles Heal, the only person who could blackmail him or destroy him by revealing who he really was. He breathed a sigh of relief. He knew that there was no way he could have silenced her without killing her, and despite what she had done, he knew he couldn't do that. True, there were plenty of people he could kill if he wanted to, if he were angry enough, but not Janine. He still loved her despite all she'd done. "If only she had loved me," he said quietly into his whisky glass. He frowned and sighed again. It still hurt. "Dammit, I'd have given her everything. Dammit and damn her!"

His mind wandered over what had been and what they might have done together. With Janine he could have turned his million into many times that; he knew he could have. He knew enough to patent discoveries that would have sold to any of a dozen firms, discoveries he had never even hinted at whilst he was working at the Research Centre, things he had worked on in his spare time, things entirely out of the range of terms of reference of his work, all sorted and filed in his head for just the right chance to be hatched out into the world. But now, what had he got? He had nothing; no incentive to work, no incentive to live life to the full, nobody to share his money or his life with. All he was doing was existing, and while he still held inside him the feelings he had held for Janine, there was no spark of enthusiasm to go out and find somebody else to share his life.

He glanced at his watch again and saw the grey Lincoln pull up outside in the main road below. It was 12.57.His glass was still full so he emptied into the back of his throat and swallowed the warm liquid as he watched the occupants of the car get out. A reasonably good-looking man with fair, curly hair and wearing a royal blue suit stepped out of the back. He helped a brunette out after him and slammed the door. The chauffeur remained in the car. "Obvious a wealthy man," Edward remarked to his empty glass. He was impressed by Benjamin's business-like appearance, smart, well dressed, carrying himself confidently. The woman was also smartly dressed; probably a prospective buyer.

He waited for the telephone to ring and when it did he automatically let it ring more than three times before answering. "Mr. Benjamin Carlisle to see you sir; the gentleman you said you were expecting," Teisen said in his best official voice.

"Send them up," Edward replied and hung up. He went to the door to meet them from the elevator. He gave them a friendly smile as the doors opened.

"Dianne smiled back. "Hello Mr. Roland," she said. "This is Benjamin Carlisle." Edward managed to keep a fixed smile on his face as he shook hands with Benjamin. The brunette was obviously not a purchaser, or Benjamin would have introduced her. She must be the agent Edward thought.

"Pleased to meet you Mr. Carlisle. I was sorry to hear about your brother."

"Yes, it was a shock to me," he replied politely.

"Come on in then" Edward said and turned to lead the way through. "I suppose you'll want to have a good look around."

"Dianne scowled. "No, I'll leave that to Mr. Carlisle," she said. "You don't mind if I take off my coat?"

"Not at all Miss…"

"Barker," she said, knowing full well that he hadn't said it as a leader.

"Ah, yes," Edward replied and took it from her as it slid off her shoulders. He had a feeling he should have known the name.

"I presume you want to renew the lease?" she asked him.

"Edward shrugged his shoulders. "I'd thought of doing," he answered vaguely He hung up he coat on a pinewood stand behind the door.

"You've changed your mind about the offer you made to Mr. Daniel Carlisle I suppose?"

"Offer?" Edward asked nervously "Oh the offer, Hmm, I hadn't given it a great deal of thought. I didn't know he was seriously considering it."

"You didn't know? I see," Dianne said and changed the subject. "I will have a look round if you don't mind." She got up from her seat and looked around each room in turn, locating Benjamin in the bedroom. Edward stayed near the drinks cabinet. He thought he was going to need some fortitude.

Benjamin was looking out of the bedroom window when he heard someone come into the room. He turned and was surprised with her insensibility when he saw Dianne looking in the wardrobes. He watched, saying nothing as she ran her eyes over the contents of each of the cupboards and closed the sliding doors when she had finished. She glanced up at him as he watched her in bewilderment. She threw him a plastic smile and he followed her out into the living room.

"Well, have you seen everything you need?" Edward asked tentatively.

"I think so," Benjamin said. "Does the offer you made my brother still stand?"

"Er, the offer. Well I'd like to think about it again if I may."

"I see," Benjamin said before Dianne could say the same. Well, do you realise that we are looking to sell the place, and I should imagine that your offer was not as high as we could net if we put it in the hands of an agent."

Agent! Then who the hell is this woman then? "What do you think it will make if you do?"

"About six hundred and eighty to six hundred and ninety," Daniel said as he gave another cursory glance around.

"I see," Edward said and rubbed his chin. His eyes flitted from Benjamin to Dianne and back again. "And you'll still accept my offer?"

"We had decided to if it was still open. It would speed things up for us."

Edward hadn't planned on this. Buying the place was too permanent. But then he could always let it again or even re-sell it at a profit. He wondered what the offer was and what the profit would be. "Alright, I'll have it. Can you have the papers drawn up for me?"

"That is already being done," Dianne said and walked over to the door. "Can I give you a call when we are ready to complete the deal?"

"Great," Edward said. Dianne picked her coat off the hook and led Benjamin out onto the landing. Edward followed them to the elevator.

"Goodbye," Benjamin said and held his hand out to shake hands.

Edward took it. "Goodbye," he replied.

Dianne just smiled politely and pushed the button to close the doors.

Edward went back inside and poured himself a large whisky. It had been an ordeal. He had expected a casual visit from someone he had never met and it had been sheer hell. He downed his whisky and slumped into his armchair. He had something to do.

*****

"What the hell were you playing at in there?" Benjamin asked as they went down in the lift.

"Later," she said and stepped out quickly into the foyer. She strode outside as fast as she could. Benjamin thought it reminded him of the day she'd picked him up at Kennedy airport the time she thought they were both in danger. He followed her the same way this time. She got in the car and he climbed in beside her.

"Where to now?" Carl asked.

She was silent for a moment and then said, "The warehouse. We have another appointment this afternoon with Batalli, remember?"

"Not until five," Benjamin replied.

"We've got something to discuss and sort out before then," Dianne stated.

"Such as? We've seen all the real estate, arranged for the contents to be shipped to London or to an auction room, and arranged for all the properties to be put on the market. I was hoping to have a relaxing afternoon. This evening is going to be hectic."

"Do you believe in doubles?" Dianne asked outright.

"Benjamin thought for a moment. "Doubles? Tennis doubles or scotch doubles?"

"Like identical twin doubles, actually," Dianne said patiently.

"I suppose you have a reason to ask that question, or is it just casual conversation?"

"I'm asking you a serious question. Can I have a serious answer please," she said, compressing her lips.

"There's a possibility of somebody looking like somebody else I suppose." He thought for a moment. "You know in Britain they had look-alike competitions for people looking most like Princess Diana?"

Dianne just stared straight ahead.

"What's so important about that now?" Benjamin asked, seeing that she was getting irked.

"That wasn't Matthew Roland."

"What?" Benjamin wasn't sure if he had heard right.

"It wasn't him. He didn't recognize me when I walked in."

"Should he have?

"Yes, I went to discuss his offer to buy the apartment with him and his live-in girlfriend just before Daniel died. He said that since they were living together and she had inherited enough money, he would offer to buy the place."

"So he forgot who you were."

"I've seen him before that when I took the lease for him so sign a renewal. He recognised me when I returned before, so why not this time?"

"Perhaps he's just had a hard night," Carl suggested.

"He didn't even know about the offer he was supposed to have made. I asked if he'd decided to renew the lease and he replied that he had thought of doing. That wasn't what he'd said before."

"So you had a flick through his wardrobe. I suppose there was a reason for that?"

"His live-in girlfriend is called Janine Westcott. All her clothes were there. There's something very funny if she's still living there and he'd had second thoughts about buying the place. It was her money and they were going to buy it together. If he has the money now then I am wondering what has happened to her."

"Perhaps they fell out?"

"That man is not the one I have spoken to before. I would bet my last dollar on it. What I want to find out is who he is and what he has done to the girl."

"Haven't we got enough problems of our own without getting involved? If he buys the place it doesn't matter if they have fallen out or not. Make out two contracts, one in their joint names and one in his alone, who cares?"

"I do. I don't like being duped. Call it professional pride, call it sheer stubbornness, but I like things to be neat and tidy and until I find out what's going on I won't be happy."

Benjamin sighed. "Well, I suppose it's the warehouse then Carl."

"Sort of guessed it would be," he replied and smiled.

At the warehouse they drove through the special security radio-controlled gates and parked in the private basement car park. "Just think, after today we won't be able to do this anymore," Carl said to his two passengers as they got out and walked to the elevator.

"That reminds me, I meant to ask you something," Benjamin said to Dianna. "Who will own the Lincoln when we have signed over the company?"

"Batalli of course. It's a company car. Does it matter?"

"Then we'd better sort the paperwork out first," he said as he pressed the button for the office level.

"Sort it out? Dianne gave him a questioning glance. "All the paperwork should already be sorted out."

"We need to keep the Lincoln for a while," he stated.

"But you are having them bring that vintage car here for you. I heard you tell them when you fixed the time for the meeting. I thought we would be using that until we got all the loose ends tied up here."

"Not necessarily. It all depends on how friendly we all are at the time of the deal."

"There's something you aren't telling me isn't there?"

"Just let's say we might need a bullet proof car till we get back to England." He gave her a broad grin and patted her on the shoulder as he put his arm around her.

They walked into the president's office. Dianne hadn't moved any of her things in there out of her own suite of offices. She hadn't had the time. It seemed bare and unused apart from a pile of accounts books and folders stacked neatly in the middle of a large desk.

"Looks like the auditors have been working out all the relevant facts and figures for their new bosses," Benjamin said as he flicked through the accounts. "Where's the balance sheet?"

"In the blue folder at the bottom," Dianne replied as she picked up the hand phone and pushed in the numbers. "Hello, can you get me Grayson from accounts up to my office," she said. "And get Hardy with my security team to assemble in the main security office."

"Of course, when Batalli takes over," Benjamin said, "your team will be surplus to requirements."

"If you are still thinking we need a bullet-proof car then my security business will still be in work. You do realise that it's an independent company within *Carlisle Importers* don't you?"

"I do now," Benjamin grinned.

"In fact I have given Carl and Hardy the option to buy me out and set up their own security business five blocks away. All my equipment has already been moved out to the new premises including six of my own company cars, an I.B.M. computer and all my files."

Benjamin nodded. "The last thing we would want Batalli to see is your files, I imagine. I have to say, you have a very loyal staff. I just hope that the warehouse staff are safe in their jobs."

"Should be. They ran the company with very little interference from Daniel and at a good profit too. But I expect some of them will leave for pastures new after today. They have put up with a lot of aggravation because of the mafia."

"Batalli is no fool. He has wanted to take over the company for a long time but he must have known he would get it in the long run. He hasn't intimidated the staff as much as he could have done. He didn't just want to take over the order book. It still had to be a working company. He needs it and its licenses as a front for his own activities."

"Like Daniel did, you mean?"

"Only, he'll use it for smuggling drugs, I bet." Benjamin stopped and thought for a moment. "I wonder…" he said as a short, square-bodied man entered the room. His bald patch in the centre of his short-cut brown hair made his head look flat.

"Ah, Grayson," Dianne greeted him. "Mr. Carlisle has a job for you."

"Yes?" he said politely.

"He wants you to get the value of the Lincoln off the balance sheet and sell it to him at that price."

"It's worth much more than that, Miss Barker. The value on the books is merely the write off value."

"So he's got a bargain then," she replied. Grayson grinned.

"Yes ma'am. I'll do it before you see Mr. Batalli."

"There's no problem with that then?"

"Not if I can do anything about it." He strode purposefully out of the office.

"I can see him getting employment somewhere else before Batalli has been here a week," Benjamin prophesied as the square-set accountant went out of the room.

"He already has had a job offer," Dianne stated.

"Let me guess: at an up and coming new security business?"

"Are you coming," she said to Benjamin and Carl, who had just stood by and listened. Benjamin noticed how he was always there when he was needed without getting in the way, like at Cayley's office when Batalli arrived. He was good at his job.

Dianne went through into her own suite of offices and they followed.

All, except a few crucially placed security staff, were assembled in the centre of the main office. Until that moment, Benjamin hadn't realised what a large workforce she led in her work to protect Daniel and his company from the mafia.

"Right," she said and stood on a chair and began to address them. "Everything is ready for a deal to be signed for the transfer of Daniel's company to be sold to another purchaser." There was a general chant of acknowledgement. "And as you know, you have a new set of offices to go to." There was another chant, this time with cheers. "And you'll have been through a drill to evacuate these premises on my signal." There were more cheers.

"It remains for me to thank you for loyal service. We have worked well together but the time has come for me to take another path," More melancholy sounds this time. "Finally, I have put enough money aside for your new bosses to set up and maintain your new company until new clients can be found. I have no doubt that you will all be very successful. Thank you all." She stepped down amidst a loud applause, and then turned to Carl and Hardy. "I suggest you look no further than the sales staff that Daniel employed to put your new company in the spotlight. They worked well for him and they will do the same for you." They both nodded their agreement.

"I've waived any fee for the sale of my business so you can perhaps start your new business with me as your first client. I want you to find a woman by the name of Janine Westcott and I want tabs keeping on a man called Matthew Roland. It will do until you get yourself some good contracts." She turned to join Benjamin but he was already standing at her shoulder. "Right, Carl. I leave you to ensure Benjamin and I get safely out of here after the deal is done." She began to walk away with her man.

"Thanks Dianne," she heard Carl shout after her.

*****

Benjamin was looking out of the window when an entourage of three vehicles drove through the security gate. The front was a Cadillac with darkened glass. The second one was Bertram Cayley's 450SLC with Cayley at the wheel, and the third was Cayley's SSK with a single driver.

He watched them all park in the yard where Dianne indicated and saw the people get out. The man in the SSK jumped out first and opened the door of the long limousine. He looked heavily armed. Seven men got out from behind the dark glass, four of which were definitely armed. The other three were Batalli and probably another partner in *Frank Freight Incorporated* and a banker. Cayley was the last to emerge from his car. Reluctantly he followed Batalli, and the other two men brought up the rear, their guns obvious but still holstered.

Benjamin turned to a young man called Vic Beecham. He had arrived an hour ago. One of Dianne's security men had recommended him as an attorney who was red hot on contract law. No doubt if it all went well, the newly established security firm would have some work for him. Vic knew Cayley and was dismayed when he heard how the brilliant old lawyer had fallen under the spell of the mafia.

Carl ushered the buyers into the board room and signaled for the bodyguards to remain outside the closed doors, and then he left. Benjamin followed him out. "Carl," he said aside, "have somebody check out the old SSK. You never can tell what these guys have in mind for afters.

"Will do, boss," he said and grinned before leaving his army of guards watching Batalli's men.

Benjamin went back into the board room. Batalli was sitting next to the end of the table and Cayley was by his side. The other two men were sitting at the same side of the table. Vic and Benjamin sat opposite with Dianne at the head of the long mahogany table.

"Good evening gentlemen," she said and folded her hands on the table. Despite being nervous she kept her voice calm and level. They all nodded and mumbled a return greeting. The meeting was definitely going to be formal. "I would like you to tell me, Mr. Batalli, if you've drawn up the contracts that Mr. Carlisle listed three days ago and if they are exactly as discussed?"

"Sure," he said in a loud confident voice, the voice of a victor at the end of a long battle. "They are all here." He held out his hand to Cayley and he handed Batalli a folder. He, in turn, handed them to Dianne. "There are three copies so that you can study them at the same time as your attorney."

Dianne took out the copies, handed one to Vic and one to Benjamin. Then she began to read hers. She placed it to one side when she had read it and picked up a similar contract for the sale of the two ships. She read it and handed the copies to Benjamin and Vic. Then she handed out the contract to buy the SSK.

"It's alright," Vic said, "But I'd make sure that you have all the documents with it when you hand over the money."

"Right, Gentlemen," Dianne said, assuming the chair, "If all the contracts are in order I would now like to confirm the payments for the transaction will be made by banker's draft.

"Batalli nodded. "This is my banker," He introduced the man next to Cayley.

Dianne turned to the intercom behind her and pressed a button. "Is Mr. Dreyfus here yet?" she asked.

"On his way now, ma'am," a voice replied.

She released the button. "Thank God for that!" she said. It seemed to lighten the air a little. Batalli grinned as did all the others around the table except Cayley. His face remained solemn as he pushed his spectacles up his face. Within a couple of minutes Carl ushered a tall, thin, grey-haired man into the board room.

"I do apologise for being late," he said over his horn-rimmed spectacles. He looked flushed with exertion. "I had to arrange for staff to stay on until your banking business is complete."

"We shouldn't be long now," Dianne said to him as he sat next to Vic. "This is Mr. Dreyfus, by the way," she said to introduce him.

It took less than half an hour to complete the exchanging of the contracts and handing over the relevant bankers drafts. Benjamin held his hand out to Cayley for the documents for his car before he handed over his contract. He knew it was robbery at a mere ten thousand dollars but Cayley had embezzled more than the real marked value of the vehicle before and after Daniel had died, so he felt no shame. "And the keys," Benjamin said.

Batalli shouted out as loud as he could, "Stephan."

The man who had driven the car came into the room and handed over the keys. He placed them on the table in front of Batalli and stood back from the table. Batalli slid them over to Benjamin and then all the rest of the business was concluded. "I see you haven't signed the contract for shipping the vehicle over to England, Mr. Carlisle." He pointed to a remaining piece of paper on the table. Benjamin smiled and picked it up as Dianne pressed the intercom buttons again.

"Carl, could you see that Mr. Dreyfus is escorted safely to the bank?"

Carl entered the room with four men and escorted Dreyfus out of the building.

"Well, I think that concludes all our business," Dianne said as she stood up. "All that remains to be done is for us all to leave along with my own staff."

"Which staff are those?" asked Batalli. "You mean your bodyguards do you?"

"I mean the security staff, of course."

"They'll no doubt take their orders from me when you leave the building."

"Your Mr. Cayley is slipping. He should have told you that my security company is independent of the companies you have just purchased. None of he staff of my remaining company are on the payroll of *Carlisle Imports and Forwarding Agents*, and I rented the suite of offices from that company and operated it from within the warehouse. I suggest you hire your own security staff if you deem it necessary to keep out undesirables. That's if there are many more people about like you." Batalli flushed pink. "And besides," she continued before he could answer, "until you are elected to the chair at a proper meeting of the shareholders, called in accordance with the procedures laid down, I retain the position in the company you have just bought."

"I see," he said looking at Cayley." The lawyer just shrugged his shoulders. "Why didn't you point that out?"

"You should know what you are buying," he said bitterly. "I suppose that you never even looked at the accounts!" Their bullying him into practically giving away his pet car, a car he would never have let go at any price, had won them no favours. His manner was decidedly worn. "And I'm not *their* Mr. Cayley," he said to Dianne bitterly.

"I assume that the accounts are in order?" Batalli asked Benjamin.

"We've tried to be fair," replied Benjamin. "I think you ought to know that we have bought Lincoln from the company, but all the other capital has been left intact."

"Bought at a fair price, I suppose?"

"Book value. Fairer than the old Merc."

Batalli laughed. "Ah well, it hasn't been too bad dealing with you. I think I have learned a thing or two. I will remember never to underestimate you, that's for sure."

"I hope you'll never have to Antonio. I intend to live peacefully from now on. That is why we have made a bargain and stuck to it." He stood up and walked around his chair to Dianne. He took hold of her arm and walked over to the door.

"Come and see me when you want your car shipping, he grinned as he walked after Benjamin. He held out his hand. "I have a contract ready."

"That'll be the day," Benjamin said and ignored the hand. "I've done my last deal with the likes of you." He turned his head to Dianne. He was proud of her, proud of the way she was not fazed by Batalli's superior attitude nor by the men she was dealing with, and proud of the way she had put the gangster in his place. "But just in case I do want you to ship it," he said over his shoulder, "the contract already exists and is binding on your new company. It's a contract to ship and insure at full value with a penalty clause for failure to deliver for any reason. Come on darling," he said to Dianne as they walked to the elevator, "I haven't eaten all day. I'll give Howard a call and tell him to have something ready for us."

Batalli watched as they disappeared into the elevator along with Carl and five armed guards. Ten minutes later Benjamin drove the SSK out of the main gate followed by Carl in the Lincoln and an exodus of other cars from the car park beneath the warehouse. All belonged to Dianne's security staff. He realised that he had made the best deal that he could with Benjamin Carlisle. He was a clever and dangerous man and worth buying out. He could proceed with his plans without a battle that would undoubtedly have led to intervention from the F.B.I. But because neither Benjamin nor Dianne shook hands with him, and instead openly showed their revulsion, somehow, he still felt cheated. He folded his arms and watched the last of the cars depart and then, after scratching his chin, he smiled to himself.

BOOK THREE

CHAPTER 17.

New Delhi, Saturday morning, 20th October.

General Drim Balhi descended the stairs of the Boeing 737. The Pakistan International Airlines' flight from Karachi was half an hour behind schedule, but he knew he would have plenty of time to meet with Winder Singh. He knew a car was already waiting to whisk him away from Palam International Airport, around New Delhi to the old township of small streets and crowded stalls. Drim Balhi was a dark skinned thick-set man, dressed in white western style trousers and jacket to match. He wore nothing on his head, but darkened *Reactolite* sunglasses hid his bloodshot eyes from any passing glance. He carried a slick of jet black hair cut short at the sides, and his face was clean shaven, giving prominence to a heavy jaw that sagged like that of a Bengal tiger as he padded past the customs barrier. Only a selected few knew he was still an active general, not in the Indian army which he left more than twelve years ago, but over his own private army of mercenaries. And only he knew how many he commanded at any one time, recruiting and dismissing personnel as appropriate to the particular job in hand. But at all times, he still maintained and commanded a hard core of war-hardened combatants.

Lal Shah knew not to salute his General in public. He was equally the height of Drim Balhi, but even broader in the chest. Like his master, he wore a white cotton suit, but not nearly so well-tailored to his massive block-shaped body. In contrast to the man he was meeting, his head was shaved, giving him the awful appearance of the executioner of the legendary fanatic Aurangzeb, a man who had deposed his own father Shahjahan in 1650 to take over the Mogul dynasty that had ruled India up to the middle of the eighteenth century. He waited for the passengers to disembark, and as soon as he saw Drim Balhi, stood up and went towards him with an expressionless face.

Drim Balhi walked up to his lieutenant, his face blank. He stopped and let his hand-stitched valise drop to the floor. Their eyes locked for a moment, reading each other's thoughts, and then as if given a silent cue, held out their right arms and shook each other's gorilla-like hands. Their left hands clamped onto the other's shoulder like two wrestlers about to clinch, and then, they both smiled, the true smile of camaraderie as their eyes lit up with their ritual contest.

"Mohal is waiting in the car," said Lal, speaking first.

Drim Balhi looked at his Seiko watch. It was 1.42 p.m. "Right," he said, "Let's go." They turned towards the exit together and went out to the car. The driver knew the roads well, avoiding the long queues of bullock carts and cars that Drim Balhi usually associated with this city. It was a normal hot dry October afternoon, but the General was used to much hotter days. He had travelled the world over several times, from desert to swamp, mountain peaks to ice-cold tundra, and nowhere had he found it impossible to exist comfortably. Here he loved the familiar smell of oriental cooking, and languished in the heat of the Indian autumn.

Half an hour later the car drew up outside a small shop, and the driver got out and opened the door for his passengers. The thick muscular thighs of the general were the first glimpse Winder Sing had of his guest, as he stood at the door and waited for him to get out of the car. His thighs were as thick as Winder's own waist; tree trunks compared with his own saplings. He shook hands with Drim Balhi and led him into a gloomy back room. The driver stayed with the car, while Lal followed.

To the soldier, this Delhi policeman had not been what he'd expected. It was three years since he'd recruited him for his task and he'd exceeded all expectations. At their first meeting, he was in uniform, but he posed no threat to Drim Balhi. Unlike him, Winder was physically a slightly built man with almost feminine hands. Drim Balhi had concealed his surprise at the contrastingly male voice as he greeted him, the same voice that was now friendly and familiar. Winder was no longer a policeman.

Despite the feeling of physical superiority, as a backup Lal kept his hand on the Ingram Model 10 sub-machinegun, concealed under the flap of his jacket, to safeguard against any surprise use of weapons. The General never took chances when he was meeting someone. He had seen too many good men die simply from lack of caution. He trusted no one until they were inextricably bound to him. Money was not such a tie.

"Things are beginning to hot up again," said Drim Balhi. "Zia is claiming Mrs. Gandhi has been plotting to kill him."

Winder pointed to a chair at the table. Drim Balhi sat down and unfastened his jacket, and Winder sat opposite. "Is this anything to do with my mission?" asked Winder bluntly, "I'm sure the feelings of hatred between them will never be healed." He gently and calmly stroked his beard. He was a direct man to deal with; no innuendos or half references. Straight talk was all he was capable of; straight talk to mask a cunning and devious mind, a mind not unlike Drim Balhi's, the mind of a strategist, a planner. Most men were overawed by Drim Balhi's presence, nodding agreement in a wish not to offend him. But not Winder. He was cool and calculating. Drim Balhi liked him.

"Indirectly," replied Drim Balhi as he instantly assessed the reaction of the man he was dealing with. "Only indirectly." He grinned self assuredly, more inwardly than outward. "Tension with Pakistan is always a good thing for us, being so near the border town of Amritsar," he stated. "Wily old Fox is Zia ul-Haq. You mark my words."

"Not wily enough, so it seems," remarked Winder in an almost off handed manner.

"Oh, and how's that?"

"His Embassy staff are always being thrown out of the country for spying."

"Yes, I had heard." Drim Balhi grinned again. "But then, what are embassy staff for if not for spying!" He burst out into a raucous laugh.

Winder barely smiled, his long fingers locked both hands together as he leaned his elbows on the table.

"You've done well for me these past three years. All our planning is beginning to reach a head. You understand what it is you have to do?" Drim Balhi asked him.

"Oh yes, I have no doubts about that. Everything will be as we have stated."

Drim Balhi passed a flight bag over the table. "The rest of your money is being put into a Swiss account for you," he said.

Winder unzipped the case and began counting out the cash for his expenses, whilst a young girl served up a biriani.

"You will of course be able to draw on that account after the job is done."

"I understand," replied Winder. "There will of course be no need for us to be in touch again. All the work has been done. All that remains now is the final act."

"You'll not let me down, I'm sure," Drim Balhi confided.

"Have no fear. This means as much to me as to you."

Drim Balhi smiled. "Your money in Switzerland means a lot to you, I'm sure."

"More than you can imagine," smiled Winder, not lifting his eyes from his task of counting. He always counted cash, never taking it for granted that the amount was as stated by the big man. He did it, not because he didn't trust him, but because he wanted to show that Drim Balhi's size did not intimidate him in the least.

The General tasted his meal. "Your food is good," he said, and regarded the top of the policeman's head as he counted, noting how his turban hid most of his greying hair.

"The best," Winder replied in between wads.

"Good. Very good," were the soldier's only words until he had finished eating.

When Winder had finished counting, he just sat back quietly and watched his guest. Finally Drim Balhi took out a large white handkerchief, wiped his mouth, grinned and stood up. "Farewell my friend," he said and shook Winder's hand fiercely before going outside to his waiting car.

Winder did not follow him. He stayed in the shady room and sat back down at the table. He had enjoyed his task and now it was nearing its end. He'd enjoyed the risks, he'd enjoyed the plotting and he had enjoyed the travel. He thought about his trip to a foreign embassy in the December of 1981.

*****

* Western Europe was a cold place at that time of year in stark contrast to the warm city of Delhi. The weather didn't bother Winder Singh, though. He wore a thick black overcoat to keep out the wintery breeze. His cold soulless eyes narrowed as he looked around. Binder Singh was waiting in the airport lounge to meet him. They knew each other from previous meetings, and greeted each other warmly. Binder, a tall well built man, had athletic features rather than those normally expected of embassy staff, and dwarfed his guest as his tall frame did most other mortals. He too wore a thick overcoat to shield him from the European winter. Instead of the turban worn by the majority of Sikhs, he wore a thick woollen hat. Nor did he have a beard in tradition with the Sikh religion. They chatted cordially as they left the airport, and laughed at mutual jokes as Binder drove along the snow-lined streets of brick buildings to the Indian Embassy, where he worked.

Winder looked around the walls of the vast reception room, studying first the pictures painted by western artists, and then, the French furniture. Nothing of the orient was to be seen. "You've picked an inhospitable country to live in my friend," he said ruefully as he took off his coat and handed it to his host. "You should have stayed at home." He could not help thinking that this man was no longer connected in any way to the Sikh faith.

"Not so," Binder replied, disappearing into a closet, and coming out swinging his arms into a light jacket. "I have a very warm relationship with the government here. It makes up for the cold winters." They both laughed. "Besides," he continued, "where else could I work from in total safety and under the umbrella of diplomatic immunity?"

"I'm not sure whether diplomatic immunity will save your skin if anything goes wrong. We have a long slow task ahead of us, and only success will guarantee our survival."

A servant came into the room carrying a tray. He placed it on the table in front of them. "Tea?" asked Binder as he grinned, showing a chipped front tooth. Then, "Don't worry, I have every confidence that Beant will come in on this," he stated. His eyes watched the servant leave. "Have you arranged the finance?"

"Banker's draft. All arranged. It will be in your private account already."

"Well then, I can see no problem. Once you've succeeded in agitating the Sikhs to the right stage of insurgency, he will willingly do it," Binder proclaimed. "He's a loyal Sikh."

"Especially if you pay him, heh?" laughed Winder.

"Especially if he can be convinced of the importance of his role in the future of an independent Sikh nation."

It had been only a month later when Winder Singh arrived at a clandestine meeting in Pakistan at Islamabad. General Drim Balhi was there, but he kept well out of the main run of the conversation. In the beginning he left all the talking and arguing to his Sikh friends, although friends were not what he considered them to be. They were weapons of war, and as such were used and positioned for achieving the best results. Only Winder knew his identity. Everyone else at the meeting assumed him to be just another heavyweight used as Winder's bodyguard.

Winder turned his attention to discussion with Jasbir Singh. "You're sure that we can take full advantage of the position in Punjab?" he asked the rotund Sikh.

"I'm absolutely sure," Jasbir confirmed, waving his hands in the air and revealing fingers like so many sausages. He perspired profusely, stopping to wipe his mouth and his forehead every couple of minutes, with a handkerchief that he kept in his hand ready for that purpose.

"And how are you going to incite enmity between the various religious groups, sufficient to cause the necessary shift in feeling against Mrs. Gandhi?" Winder asked him.

"Simple," replied Jasbir. The others there looked at him. "Very simple," he repeated, patting his handkerchief against is sweat-beaded forehead. "My uncle knows a man who is an expert in guerrilla warfare. Together, they can intensify the unrest that has already built up in our country since the war in East Pakistan, and with them we can undermine the stability between the Sikhs and the Hindus in Punjab. With a little help from our friends over the border here, we should have caused civil war in no time at all. If that doesn't lose Indira Gandhi the support of her own officials, then I'm not the nephew of Sant Jarnail Singh Bhindranwale," he stated proudly.

"And just who is this friend of your uncle?" asked Winder.

"Well, he's Major-General Shubegh Singh, of course," replied Jasbir."

"I know him," Drim Balhi broke in. "He was thrown out of the Indian army for corruption ten or twelve years ago. A good man."

"Sounds just right," said Winder with a smile.

"Since the bomb in my uncle's temple last month," continued Jasbir, "he has already reiterated the demand of the Akali Dal for an independent Sikh state."

The Akali Dal, led by Sant Harchand Singh Longowal, was the organization to establish a free Sikh community within India.

"Khalistan," stated Winder.

"Khalistan!" beamed Jasbir with a gleam in his eye.

The gleam of a fanatic, thought Drim Balhi, who had noticed it even from the back of the room. "Who planted the bomb?" he asked out of the shadows.

"The Hindus of course. Who else?"

Drim Balhi didn't reply to the question. He didn't need to enlighten this man. He knew the answer before he asked his question. His men had done their job well. He just wanted to make sure of Jasbir's reply. "What about the killing of the newspaper editor, Lala Jagat Narain?" he asked.

"He was against the Khalistan movement," stated Jasbir. "But it wasn't my uncle who had him killed, I know that for sure." Drim Balhi suppressed a smile this time. His two masked men on a motorbike, who had fired the fatal shots, had led to the arrest of Sant Jarnail Singh Bhindranwale, a further spiraling of unrest and more killing. It ended in the hijacking of an Indian airliner before his eventual release.

"The Sikhs must defeat the Hindus," added Winder, emphasising the point by pointing his long finger at Jasbir. "You must stand out for the granting of all your demands, including the declaration of Amritsar as a holy city."

It wasn't such an impossible demand in itself, but the declaration of such, would ban the use and sale of tobacco in the city, a step many Hindus would resent, causing more alienation and unrest.

"Furthermore," Winder summed up, "our friends here in this country, will help the pro-Pakistan forces in Kashmir to cause insurrection. They will help the Kashmir Liberation Front to demand the release of their president, Magbool Boot." *

*****

The meeting had gone to plan, thought Winder. From those first meetings three years ago he had steered the unrest that was necessary for the blame of the assassination of Indira Gandhi to fall squarely on the Sikhs. They alone would stand condemned by the world. At that same meeting, Drim Balhi had assessed the strengths and weaknesses of his recruits. He had been able to see if his strategy and long term planning was having the required effect. He could see that, by teasing the already glowing embers of intercommunal unrest in the border states of Assam, Sikkim, Mizoram and Tripura, he could kindle them into an inferno. But only by seeing the insurgents for himself, could he guide or alter his master plan. Guided by the ambitious Vlatsov, he would himself steer India into the anarchy and discontent that was necessary for the acceptance of communism. "Revolution will only be born out of discontent," Vlatsov had told him. "Without it, a united India will remain a powerful and free democracy, a threat to our very own existence."

CHAPTER 18.

25th October

“What's worrying you?" Dianne asked Benjamin. He was sitting eating his egg breakfast and staring blankly at the door. She was standing beside him and watching him, quite unnoticed.

"You know, I was just thinking how easily all this matter has been sorted out."

"Makes for a simple life doesn't it?" she said and put her arms around him.

"I remember playing golf once when I was in Scotland."

"Didn't know you played golf," Dianne remarked.

"Never did get the swing right," he replied with a grin. "I was just up there on holiday and played a few rounds with someone from the hotel."

"And that's worrying you?"

"There was a golden eagle there you know."

"That sounds nice," she said and kissed the top of his head.

"Fearsome creatures, they are, really."

"How do you mean darling?"

"Well they prey on weaker animals, that's what I'm trying to say."

"Isn't that a fact of nature? Big animals prey on little animals, and they in turn prey on tiny ones?"

"It wasn't that I was really thinking about though," he answered. "You see, when I was up there, I saw a rabbit on the links. It was a pet black and white rabbit that must have escaped from somebody's back garden. The eagle went after it. As it ran over the brow of the hill the huge bird swooped down to catch it."

"Oh, poor little thing," Dianne said sadly.

"Yes," Benjamin continued, "poor little thing; but not poor because the eagle had got it. I thought it had, but it hadn't. When I was returning to the hotel I saw the rabbit again. There was no mistaking it, the same black body and white head."

"So it escaped then?"

"It did and it didn't. It was dead, but it was in the talons of a hawk, not the eagle."

"I see," Dianne stated. "And how did the hawk get it off the eagle?"

"It didn't. That's what I'm saying."

"Is it?"

"The eagle must have missed it somehow. Perhaps it managed to dive for cover. I don't know. But being a pet rabbit, it was unaware of the dangers of being out in the open, and the hawk must have got it the next time it came out."

"Must have." Dianne agreed.

"And that's what happened to Daniel," Benjamin said as if it explained everything.

It didn't.

"What exactly are you talking about Ben?"

"I'm saying that the eagle was after him but the hawk got him instead."

Dianne gave a sigh of frustration and pushed herself away from him. "You're talking in riddles, you know that?" she said as she went around the table and sat opposite him. "Spell it out for me will you?"

"It's the tape from Daniel that worries me. He said that the French were after him, the mafia was after him, and some soviet-backed fellas were after him. Finally he made a deal with a bloke called Hart in the C.I.A. who he suspected was somehow linked with the French, since he helped him get back from France."

"Right, I see now!" Dianne exclaimed. "What you're saying is, who looked to be the ones to kill him, and who actually did it? Who was the eagle and who was the hawk?"

"That's it exactly. Up to now, we've been thinking that he was killed by the mafia, agreed?"

"Agreed. Who do you think did get him then?"

"Now *that's* what's worrying me," Benjamin said, waving his fork at her. "Everything you've told me about the night he was killed points to a set up. There was Anita Holt and the car she was supposed to have driven to the warehouse yard earlier and parked for him, a car that was subsequently booby trapped. Who besides her knew he was going to get in that car? And there was all his talk about a plan, and the telephone calls he was making when you left him, which obviously had something to do with the plan he'd set up with Hart and the C.I.A."

"You know what I'm thinking, don't you?" Dianne said with a frown.

"The same as me, I imagine."

"The problem is, unlike your little fable, it was the hawk we've been thinking was after him, when all the time the eagle was hovering in the background."

"Right," Benjamin confirmed. "The Mafia is the small fry in this, and, although we suspected them of killing Daniel, I think there might be something a lot bigger involved."

"You know something?"

"What?"

"I think you've got *me* worried now," Dianne said and took hold of his hand. "You dealt with the mafia the way they were used to dealing with other people. They weren't expecting that. That was your strength and their weakness. But where do we begin to deal with the C.I.A., the Soviets, or the French?"

"We don't. Daniel tried to, and I'm sure they were involved in killing him. The business with the Bulgarians and SHEPH had something to do with it, it must have. The French knew about SHEPH, which means they knew Daniel was linked with it. The C.I.A. must have known he had something to do with it as well. The deal he made must have involved not only his getting out of the hands of the French, but his absolution from his involvement in the theft of a military secret."

"Could he have made such a deal?"

"He might have thought he could."

"You think the C.I.A. decided to kill him rather than bring him back for trial?"

"Such a trial would have mentioned a deal. Such a trial would have involved discussion of military secrets. I think it's highly possible they took the easy way out."

"That worries me even more," Dianne frowned. "I'm beginning to wonder who was behind the attempts to kill you."

"I'm afraid we might never know for sure now," he said and stood up. He'd heard a car outside. "My contacting MI5 seems to have got whoever it was off my back. I'm not sure if we shouldn't let sleeping dogs lie." He looked out of the window and saw Carl draw his car up to the steps by the front door. He waved to Benjamin and sprang up the stone flags as the door was opened for him by one of the guards.

Carl beamed as he burst into the room. "Morning folks," he said jovially. Benjamin tried to look as carefree.

"Hi Carl. What's making you so happy?"

"Shouldn't I be happy?" he asked. "Got my own partnership in a security firm, got the mafia off our backs, what other reason should I have?"

Dianne and Benjamin looked at each other and shrugged their shoulders in a negative response. "Want some breakfast?" Dianne asked him.

"No thanks. Already eaten. Got to look after my figure," he grinned. Benjamin cracked out laughing. He remembered thinking of Carl as a thin streak of bacon. He hadn't fattened up since either.

"Coffee then?" Dianne asked and picked up the pot.

"Go on then," he replied. "It'll give me chance to discuss this Westcott woman."

"What about her?" Dianne asked and handed Carl a black coffee the way he always drank it.

"Located her in the Bronx."

"Oh good. It didn't take you long."

"Had all thirty of our office staff out on it. Stroke of luck we found her really."

"Well, anyway, I'll be able to tidy that problem up before we go and see our Mr. Roland next week."

"There's something you ought to know," Carl said tentatively.

"About Janine Westcott?" asked Benjamin, "or the fella at the flat?"

"Flat?"

"Sorry, apartment."

"About Miss Westcott," Carl announced. "She's a hooker."

"A what?" Dianne scowled in disbelief. "Did I hear that right?"

"Sure did," Carl replied. "That's how we found her. Paul Tattley was checking the hotels and it seems she was known to a few desk clerks. He said that somebody recognised the name and that she was a high class prostitute. Used to work the rich guys in the big hotels. Had a guy pimping for her in all the best ones. She didn't come cheap if you'll pardon the expression."

"I bet she didn't!" Dianne exclaimed. "She was about to buy Daniel's first apartment. She'd have to be screwing some big knobs for that kind of money."

"If you'll pardon the expression," Benjamin broke in. Carl grinned and Dianne suppressed a smile. She knew what he was saying.

"So where does that leave Roland?" she said more to herself than to the others. "If she's back at work then she's obviously still trying to make some money, and what about the money that Roland still has to buy the apartment with?"

"You're not asking us are you?" Benjamin asked.

"No, but I think you'll perhaps do a little job for me."

"Job? I was just getting ready to retire. Hell Dianne, why do we want to get mixed up in this?"

"Neat and tidy. That's my motto. That's why I'm not happy with your decision this morning."

"Decision?"

"To let sleeping dogs lie."

"Laissez-faire seems a good principle to adopt in both cases as far as I'm concerned," Benjamin protested.

"All I need is for you to book in at a hotel for a couple of nights and arrange for a visit."

"Me! What the hell are you trying to do to our relationship?"

"Might be fun visiting you in your room," Dianne chuckled.

"Oh, I thought you meant this Janine Whatsername for a minute."

"I did. But you don't think I'd leave you alone with her do you? I'm not that desperate to sort this matter out."

"Neither am I," Benjamin said quickly. "So let's forget it shall we?"

Benjamin booked in that afternoon at the hotel where Paul Tattley said he'd discovered Janine to be working. He booked in as Benjamin Carter, and paid in advance to save them asking for his passport. It was expensive. It was the only suite that was available. 'The Presidential Suite.'

"Beats the Bridal Suite," he sniped at Dianne as he reserved it over the telephone just before noon. Let's hope she's worth it."

"Don't get your hopes up Trigger," Dianne squinted at him.

"Can't I stay here?" he asked with a wicked smile. "I haven't had my oats today."

"You'll get your head in a nose bag for sure if you don't shut up and face this job seriously," she said, trying to keep her face from cracking into laughter. "Anyway, you've done enough bucking for a dozen broncs lately."

"You don't fancy another ride before I go do you?"

She slapped his shoulder. "Out!" she ordered and picked up a suitcase full of Daniel's old clothes.

Benjamin had suggested taking one to make his appearance at the hotel more authentic. "I'll take that if you like," he grinned.

The Presidential Suite was magnificent. "Almost as good as the apartment at Central Park South," he said to the bell boy as he placed Benjamin's case in the bedroom.

"I beg your pardon sir?"

"Just right for a couple of nights away from the wife," he said and winked at the youth.

"I see sir," he said and smiled. He waited for a tip. "Tell me, who does one see about fringe benefits?" Benjamin asked as he handed the boy a ten dollar bill.

"I take it you mean a girl sir?"

"My friend told me to ask and I shall receive."

"I know nothing about such matters, sir. Your best bet is to ask Morton on the desk sir."

"I'd rather ask him in private if it's all the same to you," he said and held up another note.

"I'll ask him to pop up and see you," the bell boy said and held out his hand. Benjamin handed over the money and watched him scurry away on his mission. He must have mentioned the rich Englishman in the Presidential Suite straight away because Morton was at the door before Benjamin could examine the place completely.

"Come in," Benjamin shouted as he heard the knock on the door.

"You wanted to see me sir?" Morton asked. "I shan't have to be long sir, the desk is unattended." He was plump, dark haired with a parting like a footpath and very well groomed. He was a young man in his early twenties.

Benjamin got straight to the point. "My friend who stayed here a while ago told me you might be able to fix me up with a girl."

"He may have rung a number from the hotel sir. Whether there is a 'girl' at the other end is none of my business." He gave Benjamin a knowing look. Benjamin wondered just how many lecherous old - or not so old if it came to a poll - men had had that look from him before.

"He said to mention Janine," Benjamin said as he busied himself about his unpacking. He didn't want to look like he was particularly bothered who he got. He certainly didn't like people thinking what Morton was undoubtedly thinking about him.

Benjamin saw him go to the note pad by the telephone and write down a number. "There seems to be a number on the note pad here," Morton observed. "Why don't you try ringing it and see who answers?" Benjamin gave him ten dollars. "If you don't get any answer ring me at the desk. I'll be there till eight this evening, sir."

Benjamin smiled and carried on with his task of discovering what Dianne had packed for him. Five suits, a shirt and two pairs of shoes! "All too small," he muttered to himself. He went to the telephone and picked up the hand piece. "Could I have an outside line?" he asked.

"Yes sir," came the reply. The voice sounded very much like Morton's. What's the betting he listens in, Benjamin thought as he dialed the number. The line was engaged and he hung up. He decided to try again in half an hour. It gave himself time to look around and see what he'd paid for. It was forty-five minutes before he tried the number again, having got caught up in a cable television quiz program that looked very much like strip poker. There was nothing shy about any of the contestants on that channel. He asked for a line again and dialed. This time a female voice answered. He wasn't ready for it. He'd expected her to be out.

"Yes," a soft voice said to him. Did they always sound like that over a telephone, he wondered. Possibly he'd dialed the wrong number. Possibly Morton had given him the wrong number.

"I wonder if I could speak to Janine please," he said awkwardly.

"Speaking." There was a long pause while he picked his words. She was used to dealing with up market clientele.

"My name is Ben." Hell fire what *do* you say?

"Hello Ben. What can I do for you?" she asked cheerfully.

Christ Almighty! How do I ask her if she's free to have a good screwing this evening?

"Hello," she said politely. "Are you still there?"

"Yes. I was told you might come round and..."

"Ben Carter is it?"

Morton the sod! He must have told her to expect the call. "Yes."

"I can come this evening. Is that all right?"

"Great!"

"What time do you want me to call?"

"Let's say around seven." If she turns up before Dianne gets here it'll be difficult stopping her getting undressed!

"Booking me for the evening then?" her girlish voice said to confirm the arrangement.

"Yes please." He thought he heard a little chuckle.

"I'll call at seven then."

"You know where, don't you?"

"Yes, a little bird's told me all the details already."

"Right then, see you at seven." He hung up, his heart pounding as if he'd run up a flight of steps. As long as he lived he'd never be able to go through that again. "Hell!" he swore to himself. "I've heard of rent-a-dic, but dial-a..." He shook he head. "Perhaps she enjoys it," he concluded and looked at his watch. It was 5.15 p.m. He decided to call Dianne and tell her the arrangements, then he remembered Morton would probably be listening in. He would tip Janine the word and she'd never turn up. He put on his jacket and went down to the desk. "Where can I get a newspaper?" he asked Morton.

"Just down the street sir," he replied. "The evening papers will be here in about half an hour if you want to wait."

Benjamin nodded his appreciation. "The exercise will do me good," he said and walked outside. The air was cool and a fresh breeze was beginning to blow the first spots of rain that would set in for the evening. He walked quickly to the end of the block and found a pay phone. There was a long haired, scruffy looking man already using it and he had to pace about for ten minutes or more before the booth was vacated. It was coming on to rain. He dialed the number for the apartment at Central Park South and Dianne answered almost immediately. "Couldn't we just call at her apartment?" he asked her.

"No way of getting her exact address. She'll obviously not make it public knowledge. Anyway we'll know if she's a hooker then."

"Despite your ideas about me, I don't intend proving it."

"Glad to hear it. What have you arranged?"

"She's coming at seven. It'll give you time to get to the room before she comes." He heard Dianne laugh. "What's so funny?"

"Nothing," she answered. "I suppose you're calling from a pay phone because the telephonist listens in?"

"Right. The fella on the desk set it up. Don't want him hearing anything that might spoil your fun now."

"Right then, I'll be in your room before seven," she said cheerfully. She hung up and he did the same. He pulled up his collar and walked as fast as he could back to the hotel, stopping only once. He bought a newspaper.

Benjamin answered a knock on his room door at two minutes to seven. She's cutting it a bit fine, he thought as he walked over to the door. "Only just made it," he said as he swung it open. But Dianne wasn't there. Instead, a different young woman stood facing him. She had sparkling blue eyes, dark long wavy brown hair and she wore a long silk evening gown that clung eagerly to the curves of her body. A cape draped casually over her arm. She looked surprised, but no more surprised than Benjamin.

"I thought it was a woman's prerogative to be late," she replied.

"Yes, of course," he said to her and regained his composure quickly. "My little joke."

"Hello," she smiled graciously and held out a hand. "You *are* Ben I presume?"

"Yes," he replied and took hold of it.

"Janine," she said and looked him straight in the eye.

"Yes, of course." Certainly not the material he'd seen pacing the London streets. But then, she wasn't the street type, more the escort agency type. It didn't matter what she was so long as it was who he'd asked for. But there couldn't be any mistake, he thought, with a glimmer of relief. A real high class hooker!

"Well, aren't you going to ask me in?"

"Come in," he said and stepped back from the door. "I'm sorry, but you're not what I expected." She wasn't even who he expected!

"Oh," she said in a disappointed tone.

"No, I don't mean you're not good enough," he tried to explain. "It's just that I expected somebody more, well..."

"I understand," she said and smiled.

"Here, let me take your coat." He took the cape off her arm and hung it in the closet.

"Right, make yourself comfortable," he said and caught her arm lightly to point her in the direction of the lounge.

"I won't break you know," she teased and held her arm out for him to latch onto properly. He linked up and headed to the door. Her body brushed against his as they walked into the large sprawling interior of the suite. Her hip felt soft through silk, and it tried its best to distract him from his mission.

He realised he didn't know what to say. Without Dianne there the whole exercise seemed pointless. He was going to have to ask this woman questions to which she had no reason to reply.

"You're married aren't you?" she asked. It sounded as if she'd already been told by Morton.

"Yes."

"Not used to this sort of thing are you?"

"Oh, I travel about quite a lot," he replied.

"I was thinking a bit further ahead myself."

"Were you?" He was trying not to think of it

."Is your wife back in England?"

"With the children," he lied.

"Oh that's lovely, how many?" How many! What the hell does she want to know that for?

"Six, three girls and two boys."

"That's five."

"So it is! Shows how long it is since I counted them up. They run around so much it's hard to get an accurate count of heads."

Janine couldn't prevent herself from laughing. She put her hand to her mouth and brought it under control.

"You aren't the type," she said outright.

"Now how the hell can you tell that?" he asked as if he was affronted. He was quite pleased she thought that. She got full marks for human observation at least.

She just smiled and wandered about the room.

"Why don't you tell me a little about yourself?" Benjamin asked eventually.

"I'd rather talk about you," she said and changed the subject.

"I know all about me," he grinned. He was paying so he'd call the tune. "I really do want to know about you," he said, but despite his efforts to get her to talk about herself, he knew she wasn't likely to divulge her personal secrets to a customer. The argument eventually ended in a stalemate and they chatted for several minutes about New York and London instead. It didn't matter. This had been Dianne's idea, she could ask all the questions when she arrived. Then, Benjamin would just stop Janine from leaving until she'd told them about Matthew Roland.

"Gosh it's the best room I've been in for a long time," she said as she walked around, finally stopping to look at a pair of oil paintings over a semi-circular side table. Both had Arabian horses on them. "I like riding, do you?" she asked seriously.

Benjamin looked around as well. Where the hell's Dianne? "Never been on a horse in my life," he confessed. Dusty smelly awful things. Give me a good car any day."

"There were no cars when these were painted," she remarked.

Benjamin took off his jacket and threw it over the arm of a chair. He picked up the hand phone and rang room service for a tray of coffee. Janine went into one of the bathrooms whilst he was talking on the telephone and didn't emerge until the coffee had been delivered to the door. He went back into the lounge, sat on a deep purple chaise-longue and poured himself a black coffee. He checked his watch again. 7.35. Despite his efforts to pass the time, Dianne hadn't turned up.

Janine stepped over from beside the bathroom door and came and sat next to him. "What's the matter?" she asked. She could see he was tense.

Benjamin realised it was down to him now. He rubbed his forehead and turned towards her. "Look Janine," he said, looking straight at her. "The simple truth is that I've asked you here for nothing more than a chat."

"Whatever turns you on," she replied with a smile.

"All I asked you here for tonight, is so that I could have a talk with you. No sex, just a talk."

"Anything you like," she said and smiled again.

"You haven't asked me what we're supposed to be talking about."

"Most people like to do their talking afterwards," she answered derisively. "It's normal to talk later. Much later."

"Get it straight will you," Benjamin said firmly. "I don't intend doing anything but talk. You and you alone have the answers to some questions, and I intend getting them before you leave."

"I see," she said, and then, "Well if you insist," She crossed her legs and reclined Salomi-fashion on the chaise longue. It was her turn to look slightly tense.

Benjamin's eyes followed her. "You used to live at Bourneville House in Grey Oaks, didn't you?"

There was a silence, a space in which their eyes locked, hers searching for a reason for the question, his, forceful and demanding of the answer. "Yes," she said tentatively.

"And you lived with Matthew Roland."

A shorter silence this time, but a definite vacuum. "What about him?" she scowled as a look of suspicion filled her large eyes.

"You were very fond of him weren't you?"

Even with he scowl she looked as beautiful as ever. "Yes," she answered immediately and without the slightest flicker of her long eyelashes. "In a way I was."

"In a way? Well you liked him enough to give up this...this profession of yours?"

"Perhaps."

"Perhaps?" What sort of answer was that? He'd expected an outright yes. "You mean you prefer this life to what he could offer you? Is that it?"

"No."

"What then?"

"Is this all you want to know, all about my past?"

"Only the part about the man you were going to share your life with." Janine sat up. He thought he saw her hands tremble as she folded them on her knees. "I want to know," he insisted.

"Why do you want to know?" she asked sharply. "What has my life got to do with you?"

"I have my reasons for asking, and I wouldn't ask if I didn't need to know."

"Have I any choice?" she asked defiantly. Her manner had turned decidedly sullen.

"No," Benjamin lied. "I've been sent to find out. Whether you make it easy or hard is up to you. I've shown you I can be kind and considerate. To keep me that way all you have to do is answer a few questions."

"Who sent you?" she asked. "Was it Edward?"

"You aren't afraid of him are you?"

"I'm not afraid of little men like him. He's sent you to get me has he, the little rat?" She remained motionless in her seat, no panic, no attempt to run out.

"No." Benjamin replied and waited for a response. She lifted her large blue eyes up to his.

"He sent you though, didn't he?"

"Did I say Edward had sent me?"

"Then why are you asking all these damned fool questions? What damned business is it of yours anyway?" She tried to sit upright but Benjamin's firm grip on her upper arm pinned her to the seat.

"It wasn't Edward you were very fond of was it?"

"Who sent you here?" she shouted as her eyes filled with rage.

"What happened?"

"What happened when?" she hissed.

"Why would he send me after you?"

Janine shook her head. "It doesn't matter why. I've been expecting him to do it. If it isn't you then it'll be somebody else."

"So what were you doing, getting an apartment with Matthew Roland?"

Janine's head jerked up. "What the hell do you want?"

Benjamin put his hands on her shoulders and looked down at her. "I want to find out about Matthew Roland."

"Edward wants you to kill him as well does he?"

"Where is Matthew Roland?" Benjamin pressed.

"I don't know, and I wouldn't tell you if I did."

"It's Edward at the apartment, isn't it?"

"Don't you know?" She gave Benjamin a curious glance through narrowed eyes.

"So how did he get your money?"

"My money?" She burst into laughter.

"The money you were supposed to be sharing with Roland to pay for the apartment."

"It was Edward's of course," she snapped.

"I see. That's why he wants to kill you is it?"

"That and a dozen other reasons."

"What other reasons?"

"Since you must already know, why do you ask?"

"I want it from you."

"I betrayed him, robbed him and left him for dead. Is that enough reason?" There was no remorse in her voice.

"Sounds adequate, I must admit," Benjamin said and smiled as he straightened up. Janine gave a little grunt as she realised the humour of it. "How come he looks like Matthew?"

"Why do you ask such stupid questions?" Her eyes were mere slits now and her contempt for her interrogator was climaxing.

"There must be a reason for it."

"Plastic surgery, perhaps?" she said with a full injection of sarcasm.

"If I promise not to harm you, will you tell me where Matthew is?"

"Why is he so important to you?"

"Because my name is Carlisle not Carter."

"Is that supposed to mean something?" she asked sharply.

"The apartment belonged to my brother, Daniel Carlisle."

"Yes, of course!" she exclaimed. Her tone softened. "I read about him getting killed. It's your apartment now is it?"

"Not if the man, who says he's Matthew Roland, buys it. What I want to know is, what happened to the real Matthew?"

Janine relaxed. She knew now this man had nothing to do with Edward Taylor. "All I know is that some men who were after Edward came and bundled Matthew into a car by mistake. He's never been seen since."

"What men?"

"I'm not sure. Have you got a handkerchief?"

Benjamin passed her his, and she wiped her hands. "Edward said they were his friends, but I think he was joking," she went on. "They didn't treat him like friends."

"What exactly did he say?"

"He laughed as they grabbed Matthew, and said he bet they would escort him to their car. He said one was called Chester and the other John or David, I can't remember."

"And?"

"And he laughed when I asked who they were. He said they were friends of Edward Taylor. I said friends of yours? And he said no, he was Matthew Roland now." She looked up at Benjamin and saw his face. It was ashen and as grim as death

"Thank you," Benjamin whispered and sat down beside her again.

"You're perfectly safe and you may go if you wish."

"Thank you," Janine said and tossed back his handkerchief as she stood up.

"However," Benjamin added. "I'm willing to pay you for the full story."

For a thousand dollars Janine omitted nothing. Benjamin wished that Dianne had been there to listen as well. It would take some effort to retell it properly. She explained how Marvin Belk had been looking for a woman to do a particular job when he interviewed her personally in a hotel room. She had a business and a personal relationship with Matthew Roland. He'd been her agent in a prostitution business run by the mafia. He'd set up her contract with Belk. She explained everything about Edward and the operation on his face. She told him about his escape, about her leaving him to die at the airport, and how he subsequently arrived at the apartment, an apartment she'd told him about before she realised he was going to put his money in a safety deposit box. It was like something in a novel, but she was neither exaggerating nor playing it down. She was proud of her scheme. Benjamin was well pleased.

"I'll see you home if you wish."

"No thank you," she said and went towards the bathroom to remake her face. "Just one thing," she added as she got into her cape. "Don't tell Edward where I am, will you? I don't want him trying to find me."

"I promise," Benjamin said, "provided you remain silent."

"I promise," she said convincingly. She took a cab to her apartment and Benjamin checked out of the hotel and returned to Dianne at Central Park South.

"Where the hell were you?" he shouted at her as he walked in.

"Had the cops round for a cosy chat," she answered solemnly.

"Police, what did they want?"

"You, would you believe."

"Mathias?"

"Don't think so. I have a feeling we're going to be getting another call from them shortly. There was something about their attitude that was too casual. I had them show their I.D.s but they all seemed genuine."

"Did they say what they wanted me for?"

"No. Just wanted to talk they said. They were here from six until ten. Then they went home. I think I convinced them you were in California looking at your property over there. I was praying you wouldn't turn up until they'd gone."

"You wouldn't have said that if you'd seen Janine."

"I know what she looks like," she said passively. "How did you get on?"

"Like a house on fire."

"Oh great. That was the next thing I was praying for!"

Benjamin laughed at her and gave her a big hug. "I nearly panicked when you weren't in the room."

"You managed all right though, did you?" she said and twisted his hand. "And don't say anything that might endanger your life."

"The hardest part was arranging an appointment over the phone, would you believe?"

"No, but go on."

"Then things smoothed out a bit after that. We talked for a while and then I came home.

Dianne checked her watch. "It's past ten now," she said pointedly.

"Gosh doesn't time fly when you're enjoying yourself?"

"So what happened?" she pursed her lips at him.

"I told her I only wanted to talk but she wouldn't believe me and... Ouch!"

"What happened I asked?"

"I don't think you're ready for it," he said seriously and went to the whiskey bottle.

"Are you going to tell me or not?"

"Do you want one?"

"We have to drive back to Malterswood tonight. One of us had better stay sober."

"She told me that the money for buying the apartment belonged to Edward, who she robbed and left for dead."

"Sounds like a parable about a good Samaritan."

"At first she was afraid Edward had sent me to kill her."

"What did she do?"

"Just sat there like a pillar of salt. She would have just let me do it as well."

"No fight?"

"Nothing. She obviously still expects him to reap vengeance on her some day."

"And the man at the apartment has the money now?"

"They're both one and the same."

Dianne nodded she understood. "If he wants to kill her when he has his money back, it must be because he's afraid she'll say he isn't the real Matthew Roland."

"More than that. She can say who he actually is."

"What?"

"She can positively identify him."

"How do you mean? Is he wanted for something?"

"You tell me. His name is Edward Taylor."

Dianne sank onto the arm of a chair. She was visibly shaken. "I think I'll have that drink now," she said. "A big one!"

CHAPTER 19.

26th October.

At first, Benjamin had not been eager to go running around New York for the sole reason of answering Dianne's curiosity about Matthew Roland, a man who undoubtedly had the money to buy an apartment off them. He was glad they had now. "People are always saying it's a small world," he said to her when they arrived back at Malterswood in the small hours of the morning.

"You could have knocked me down with a feather," Dianne replied.

"Thought you were going to fall down."

"There he was," Dianne observed. "Right in our own back yard."

"Are you sure you haven't got some sort of mystical powers of foresight?"

"If I had, I'd have been able to save that globe trotting brother of yours."

They fell into their bed for what remained of the dark hours until Dianne's wrist watch alarm awoke her. "Come on," she said, and heaved him out of bed and onto the floor. It wasn't yet daylight. "He'll probably not want to discuss the contract without going through a lawyer anyway," Benjamin protested.

"He was supposed to have done all that before."

"He still might not see us without an appointment."

"It's the only excuse we have for getting in. If you don't like it I'll go on my own," she shouted and walked out of the bedroom.

"I'll go with you on one condition," he shouted back at her. She put her head back through the open door. "Tell me," she said with a look of resignation.

"We call Mathias and go and see him straight after we leave there. Those coppers must have wanted something."

"Is that all?" she said with a grin. "I was going to suggest that myself."

Benjamin grunted and pulled himself upright. "Are we having breakfast?"

"I thought we'd eat out between calls."

"I'll be with you in a few minutes then," he said and struggled to his feet. The late nights and early mornings were beginning to get on top of him.

It was 8.00 when the walked into the foyer of the apartment at Grey Oaks. The guard greeted them cordially. "Good morning Mr. Carlisle," he said and touched the peak of his cap. "Called to see our Mr. Roland have you?"

"Yes," Benjamin replied with the best smile he could muster.

"About the apartment is it?"

"That's right. Hope he hasn't changed his mind."

"I'll give him a ring. Is he expecting you?"

"No, we just wanted a quick word while we were passing," Dianne said irritably. "We have other business in town as well." She looked at her watch to indicate that time was of the essence, and he dialed the apartment.

"Hello Mr. Roland. There's a Mr. Carlisle here to see you again."

Benjamin heard Edward speaking but couldn't hear what was being said. "Right you are sir," Teisen answered and put the receiver down. "You can go up, but would you mind taking your time? You seem to have caught him still in bed."

"Right," Dianne said and paced towards the elevator. "We'll knock on the door and he can answer it when he's ready."

They didn't have to wait long before Edward opened the door and asked them to step inside. He was still in his dressing gown. "You certainly don't like wasting much of the day," he said with a smile. "Got to admit, I've got a bit lazy lately what with one thing and another. Used to be up at the crack of dawn at one time."

"Before you came to New York I suppose," Dianne suggested.

"Yes, before I came to New York," he said with a sigh and offered them a seat. They both sat down on the sofa nearest the door.

"Can I get you a drink or something?" he asked as he went towards the kitchen. "Got some coffee on."

"That would be nice, thank you Edward," Dianne said and smiled pleasantly as he swung his head around. His eyes were suddenly narrower and he looked at her suspiciously.

"Right," he said and turned back to the kitchen. "Won't be a moment." They could hear the rattling of cups and shortly he emerged with a tray with a percolator full of coffee and three mugs. He placed it on the table in the middle of the room. "Would you like to help yourself while I get dressed?"

"Fine," Dianne smiled again and got up and started pouring as he disappeared again. "Do you take milk Edward?" she shouted to him.

"No thanks," he replied as he emerged at the door again, still in his dressing gown. He held Matthew Roland's .36 Smith and Wesson in his right hand. He craned his head to look past her at Benjamin and then felt a hand close on his wrist. Benjamin wasn't behind her. He'd placed himself behind the pillar that stood out into the room between an arch leading to the kitchen and a similar arch to the bedroom.

Edward tried to struggle but it was no use. They had him now. The game was over, and he knew he'd lost. Benjamin skillfully twisted the revolver out of his hand and put it in his pocket. "Shall we have that coffee now?" he said quietly and calmly.

"Do I have to?" Edward asked defiantly. "I know what you've in store for me. Why waste time on trivialities and games."

"Games?" Dianne asked and raised her eyebrows.

"They must have sent you here," he stated.

"Or we wouldn't have known your name?" she nodded.

"Quite."

Dianne just looked at him and he just looked back calmly. "Coffee isn't bad at all," she said eventually. "I can recommend it."

"Must have known you'd be found eventually," Benjamin said as they both sat down beside Dianne.

"I just calculated wrong that's all," he replied, "just calculated wrong. I took a risk and lost."

"You calculated that you wouldn't be found," Dianne stated.

"Thought I'd got away with it, I must admit."

"Why were you so certain of that?"

"You seemed pretty keen to get it over with a month ago. When you got Roland, I had hoped you'd think I'd cracked. You believed him after all did you?"

Things were working out well, Dianne thought. She was teasing the information out of him. "What makes you think that?"

"What are you going to do with me?" he asked without answering her question.

"What would you like us to do?"

"I could pay you to let me go."

"How much?" Benjamin asked.

"Half a million dollars." He looked into Benjamin's eyes to see what response he was getting.

"Benjamin looked at Dianne as she looked at him.

He turned back to Edward. "And what would that buy?" he asked. "We found you once. What makes you think anybody else won't?"

"Anybody else? There's only...Why are you asking all these questions?"

"Just being polite," Benjamin stated and sipped his coffee.

"And what's an English guy doing working for them?" The look of suspicion was back in his eyes.

"Who said I had anything to do with Chester?" Benjamin asked calmly. Edward's face sank visibly. For a fleeting moment he'd thought he'd made a mistake, spoken out of turn. But he knew for sure now.

"Stop playing games. If you're going to kill me then do it."

"Kill you?" asked Benjamin. "Who said anything about killing you?"

"Don't screw around with me. I know you never intended letting me go. I know too much for your safety, or should I say the safety of our gallant country?"

"Would you have killed Janine?"

So they'd found Janine! "She wasn't worth the sweat," he replied bitterly. "I'd have shared everything with her. Now I wouldn't give her the snot off my handkerchief."

"You loved her that much did you?"

"We all make stupid mistakes. I made plenty in my miserable life, but I reckon she was the biggest," he said sourly.

"Yes, she told me all about betraying you and leaving you for dead," Benjamin admitted.

"Why did she do it?" Edward pleaded. "Couldn't she have just laughed at a foolish old scientist and taken the money?"

"You wouldn't have minded that then?"

"I'd have given her most of it if she'd asked. I could have made it all back in a couple of years."

"Could have? You mean you aren't bothering now?"

"Wasn't going to rush into it. Had enough for my frugal needs to last me for years."

"Would you have killed her if you'd found her?"

"Dumb stupid question."

"You would then?" Dianne came in.

"I could have killed you to save my own life. I doubt if I could have ever killed Janine." He shook his head and stared at the floor.

"You still want to buy my apartment then?" Benjamin asked suddenly. Edward just stared at him with a bemused look on his face. Benjamin stood up and put his empty cup on the table. Dianne scowled at him. He'd spoilt the deception and she'd been enjoying it. He looked back at her and shrugged his shoulders. "You'll get your answers," he said to her.

"Will I?" she said angrily.

"I've told you Dianne, I'm not interested in getting involved with anybody else's affairs. We have enough on our plate trying to figure out our own problem. He obviously hasn't harmed the woman. In fact they seem a damned good match! They both expect the other to be out to kill them."

Dianne turned to Edward. "Who did you think we were?" she demanded.

"I was trying to work that one out myself," he said and got his coffee.

"You said *they* had got Matthew Roland. Who were you talking about?"

Edward didn't answer. He didn't want to give any more away than he already had.

"Who was after you, the Mafia? Or who was it that you escaped from?"

Edward looked at her defiantly. "Why are you so interested?"

"I want to know what happened to Matthew Roland," she said again firmly. "Since you're impersonating him I have a right to know."

"Have you?" he replied angrily. "Have you? What rights do I have, tell me that?"

"I'll tell you what rights you have," Benjamin said sternly. "The police will read them out to you when they arrest you. I've offered you the apartment in your assumed name. That means, whether you accept it or not, I was willing to forget all I know about you, but I'm running out of time and patience."

"What do you want to know?"

"I want you to tell me everything from the beginning."

"Sure, and then you can tell everybody else."

"Please yourself Edward. If you don't start talking about SHEPH then I am telephoning the police. They'll no doubt be interested in your whereabouts."

“Not the police. They couldn't prove I took anything. That's why they handed me over to the C.I.A. It's they that want me. The police will just hand me over to Hart and..."

"Who?" Benjamin broke in. "Who?" he shouted and grabbed Edward's shoulders.

"Jack Hart. He's C.I.A. That's what I'm telling you."

"What did he want with you?" Benjamin said, still holding onto Edward and shaking him.

"I'll tell you what he wanted. He wanted to dupe me into thinking that I was going to be some secret operative doing an important job for my country, and then give me a new identity and set me up somewhere safe."

"Dupe you?" Dianne pressed.

"Sure. He has an army of men trained to do his impersonations. Why would he want me?"

"No idea," Benjamin shrugged.

"I'll tell you," Edward went on. "He was just biding his time until he got the order to kill me. I was too high a risk to keep alive and free. The Bulgarians wanted me for my brain. The Americans knew I'd taken some SHEPH, but couldn't prove it so they didn't want me. That's why they handed me over to Hart." He looked at Benjamin. Benjamin had let go of him and was staring at the wall. "So, what's it going to be?"

"What?" Benjamin said as he broke out of thought.

"What's it going to be? Are you going to turn me in or let me go?"

"Neither," Dianne answered. "Turn you in and I'm convinced you're right. Hart will kill you. Let you go and they might get you anyway. We found you easily enough through Janine Westcott. If they stumble on her, she'll sing like a bird."

"We can't keep him prisoner," Benjamin protested.

"Right, but we can help him."

"Why would you want to help me?" Edward asked skeptically.

"If you help us," Dianne explained.

"What use would I be to you?"

"Well we can't sell you the apartment that's for sure. You're sitting on a time bomb. The safest place for you is out of New York."

"I still don't see why you'd do this."

Benjamin pulled a bentwood chair over from beside the table and sat astride it with his elbows on its back. "When I explain," he said, "you'll know why I need to know everything I can about SHEPH, the Bulgarians, and Hart."

"Especially Hart," Dianne asserted.

*****

Lieutenant Mathias was out when they rang him from the apartment. It was important to talk to him about the visit Dianne had had from the police, but he was the only one Benjamin was prepared to talk to. Instead, Benjamin and Dianne decided to pack up Edward's things and get him to safety. It took the best part of an hour. Benjamin helped Edward while Dianne made some breakfast. It was going to be a long day, and if they couldn't reach Mathias, then the sooner they left the better.

"Where are you taking me?" he asked his benefactors.

"Have you got a passport?" asked Dianne.

"Here," Edward said and went to a drawer. I have all of Matthew Roland's things. His passport, his social security card, and his driving license."

"Great. Then prepare yourself for England."

"Can I take a spare travel bag?"

"What for?"

"I have something I would like to pick up at the airport."

"Not cash is it!" Benjamin exclaimed.

"I don't want to leave it behind."

Benjamin sighed. "You'll have to trust me. I'll take it through customs for you. You'll be arrested and brought back for sure if you're caught, whereas I'll probably get my knuckles wrapped for trying to export my brother's cash."

"No need to take the risk of losing it or your liberty," Dianne said confidently. "I have a contact of Daniel's who's going to ship his collection of bronzes for us. He'll bring the money over for you." It would be Andre Kercheval's last job for the partner of his old smuggling friend. "He's also arranged with the ship owners to move your car at the same time. If we want to get out of here, Carl will see to the assembly of all the freight. He'll see to the real estate as well if we don't want to return in a hurry."

"What it is to have friends in all the right places," Benjamin quipped.

"What it is to have friends," Edward said with a smile.

27th October. New Delhi.

"Where are you taking me?"

"Your enthusiasm for your mission begins to wane once more," Kehar Singh stated to Beant as he opened the door of the car, outside Government Buildings. "Since your visit to Europe with Mrs. Gandhi, when she negotiated the deal with the French for those war planes, you've shown little enthusiasm for your task. Now we must go to Amritsar."

The car cruised away silently along the Rajpath. As an assistant in the Directorate General of Supply and Distribution, Kehar was not afraid to be seen with the bodyguard of the Prime Minister.

"Where's Satwant?" he asked Beant.

"He was called to duty by Gandhi," he replied. "He says he will ring you to arrange another time."

"I hope your young friend isn't going to let us down. You know what it means if a solitary link breaks in our chain."

"He's all right. I swear. He's been called to work."

"Good," smiled Kehar, and mentioned him no more. He knew how the young Satwant feared for his life as did most of the other people caught up in the plot. It wasn't a fear of punishment for being caught, although such a fear would always be hanging over them like an ominous cloud of water ready to burst upon them, but fear of failure for which there was no hope of going unnoticed. The organization had eyes everywhere, a threatening presence which guarded against flapping tongues and idle gossip.

"Why do you wish us to go to Amritsar?" asked Beant.

"I need to be sure of your loyalty. Come what may, we have a duty to perform, one we are destined to carry out. We cannot afford to fail."

The pace of traffic slowed to that of the slowest oxen-pulled cart in an early morning traffic jam a mile long. They seemed unperturbed, for that was the way in that city. A slow tranquility grows over all but a few natives. The pace of life outside their places of work was little more than that of a snail. It was going to be a hot day, and they were glad to let the cool breeze from the open window wash over them. Once on the outskirts of the city, progress was faster, but it was still a long and tiring journey along the Great North Road from Delhi to the 'Pool of Nectar,' the holy city of Amritsar.

They passed the oblong tank of water at Kurukshetra, a four hundred yard long bird sanctuary and bathing ghat treasured by the Hindus because of mythical battles; through the ancient city of Patiala, a former capital of the Punjab; and past the magnificent palaces of the Maharajah. It was late afternoon when they arrived at their destiny. They removed their shoes and walked up the marble causeway that passed by the pool. The sunlight reflected off the gold-covered plates, sending daggers of light into the shimmering water. They approached the Akal Takht.

Beant knew the Akal Takht. It was the holiest place within the Golden Temple, sacred, and never empty of people. "Have you ever been in here before?" asked Kehar.

"Never," replied Beant as he gazed around the magnificent place.

"Then this is an auspicious occasion for you." He took a hold of Beant's shoulders and pulled him around to face him. "I want you to swear, by all that is sacred, that you will kill Mrs. Indira Gandhi."

Beant's eyes were wide, his mouth was dry and his palms were wet with sweat. He knew that he was in a corner. He knew he could not back out now. He had to swear on oath to do that which he had already been paid to do, but which he dreaded doing. He looked into Kehar's eyes, eyes of authority, strong eyes, telling, no ordering him to confirm his oath that he had taken when he had received the money from Binder two years ago.

"I...I swear by all that is holy," Beant said in a whisper.

"Go on," ordered Kehar.

"I swear to kill Indira Gandhi," he said in a voice that was barely audible, but he knew Kehar had heard.

CHAPTER 20.

27th October. 10.30.

Kennedy International Airport bustled with the constant contra-flow of people. It was as if every nation in the world had consciously made a contribution to the cosmopolitan whirlpool. The three figures waiting to board the 09.30 Concord flight to London were invisible against the background currents. They laughed and talked like pensioners on a coach trip, their worries soon to be left behind them.

There was a definite glint in Dianne's eye. She'd never been to England, and never been on Concord. Her new life was about to blast off from the launch pad.

Edward looked the same, as excited as a child about to go on an old steam train. He too, had never been to England. He'd never been outside the United States. "You'll love Concord," Benjamin said to them. "You'll never want to go on an ordinary airliner again. The British and the French have at least managed to get a world's exclusive with this one."

"What about the Russians?" Dianne said. "They have their version of it."

"Withdrawn," grinned Benjamin. "Couldn't sort out a few measly technical problems. If it weren't for Western technology they would still be flying kites."

"I think you're understating them," Edward argued. "They've advanced in many fields in which we're merely scratching the surface."

"True," Benjamin conceded. "It will take the West some time to catch up on labour camps and chemical warfare."

"You know about that sort of thing do you?" he asked with a marked sarcasm.

"Only what I've been told," Benjamin said evasively.

"I think I can tell you a thing or two that you've never even dreamt of," Edward bragged. He was on his own ground when Chemical Weapons were being discussed. He knew there were few people in the United States knew more than he did. "And the most interesting thing is that many of these chemicals either already have a commercial use or have the potential for it."

"Is that what you meant when you said you could make your fortune again?" asked Dianne.

Edward's eyes gleamed. "With the right incentives, yes."

"I take it money isn't the main incentive," she stated.

"It helps. But it's nice to have another reason for working. You can only spend so much money, and then you have to start accumulating it or giving it away. That's what happens with all these multi-millionaires. They enjoy making the money more than anything else. And to do that, they have to enjoy the way they make it. After a while the actual money becomes unimportant."

"I think the power it gives them might have something to do with it," Dianne commented.

"Finance gives power and power has to be financed," Edward stated profoundly.

"Meaning what exactly?" Benjamin asked.

"Politics."

"Who mentioned that?" Benjamin asked him with a frown.

"Politics is power," Edward pronounced.

"Quite," Benjamin agreed. "And by that, I presume that power isn't your incentive to become rich?"

"No."

"What is it then?"

"Recognition as a human being helps for a start."

"And to finish?"

Before Edward could answer that he hadn't worked that out yet, Benjamin turned to listen to the flight announcement. Five minutes to go. "Excuse me, I've a call to make," he said and walked to the nearest empty telephone booth. He was glad to get away from political argument. He dialed New York Police Department.

"N.Y.P.D." a voice chimed.

"Could I speak to Lieutenant Mathias? My name is Carlisle."

"Will you hold please sir?" He waited for only a few seconds before Mathias came on the line.

"Hello, Mathias."

"Benjamin Carlisle here, Lieutenant."

"Good morning," he replied cordially. "What can I do for you?"

"I was wondering what I could do for you, actually."

"Such as?"

"Well, why were the police looking for me on Thursday evening?"

"That's news to me. But then, you have to remember that I'm only in homicide. I'm not really involved with any other crimes you're mixed up in."

"Mixed up in? I thought I was absolved from all the blood letting!"

"Might be so, but I can't answer for other departments."

"Such as?"

"You'd better hold on and I'll have a quick word." Benjamin was beginning to get anxious. His flight had been called and Edward and Dianne looked at him in anticipation. He waved them to go on ahead at the same time the lieutenant came back on the line. "Hello?"

"Yes, I'm still here."

"Can't tell you anything. I suggest you ask your MI5 when you get to London." That sounded like he knew something and wasn't supposed to tell. "You'd better go or you'll miss your flight," he added.

Benjamin chuckled. The old fox knew his every move. "Thanks Lieutenant."

"Good luck," he replied. "Take care of Miss Barker."

"I will," Benjamin said but Mathias had already hung up. He ran over to the others and they joined the parade of passengers.

Benjamin wondered what Mathias had meant. Why should MI5 know what the police wanted with him in New York? It had to be because of Hart and the C.I.A. They were the only ones that would deal directly with MI5. He sipped at his champagne as they hurtled through the stratosphere toward England.

"Well," Dianne broke into his thoughts, "are you going to tell us what you're thinking?"

Benjamin explained what Mathias had said to him over the telephone. "So Hart was still after me," he said to Dianne as she reclined in her seat and looked out of the window. Outside, the sky was clear and blue as they travelled faster into the day. The cotton wool clouds below gave their movement a slow unreality. It was some time before they spoke again.

"And Hart knew Edward," Dianne stated eventually. "But they won't have circulated his picture over in England. Nobody knows he's with us. They think they've got him already."

"All the same, I think he'd be safer going through Heathrow on his own. Nobody will think twice about a stranger even if they do stop us for questioning. He'll be just another holiday maker."

Apart from the discussion, the flight was uneventful. They landed at Heathrow in the early evening, three and a half hours flying time but eight and a half hours later in the day, and contrary to their fears there was no sign of either police or British Agents.

They all assembled again at the car park, where, by arrangement, Mark Stevens had the 450SL already to drive away. He dropped them off at the apartment in Kensington Palace Gardens. As Benjamin ushered them inside they could hear the telephone ringing. It rang off just as Benjamin got to it. "Can't be important," he said and turned to go back out again. "Nobody knows I'm back."

He told them to make themselves comfortable and then drove Mark home. "See you in the morning Mr. Carlisle," Mark said to his boss.

"I'll be late in mind," Benjamin said with a chuckle. "You'll be able to manage without me for an hour or two I suppose."

"I'll try," Mark grinned. He watched as Benjamin drove away and then he stepped into his little terraced house.

Dianne had already found the kitchen by the time Benjamin had arrived. "Some food on its way," she shouted as she heard him come in.

"Just got a phone call to make and I'll be with you," he shouted through to her. He dialed Doc's number and was surprised when he picked up the telephone straight away. "Hello Doc, Benjamin here. Got the phone under your cushion have you?"

"I was just about to ring you. I've been ringing you every half hour, waiting for you to get back to London. A bloke called Carl said you'd be here this evening."

"You rang over did you?"

"He rang me. He told me to tell you that a man called Hart wanted to see you urgently."

"I bet he does," Benjamin grated. "He's the one that killed Daniel, I'm sure of it."

"That Carl chap said for you to ring him back at Malterswood whatever time you got back."

"Okay, but before I do that, have you any objections to my paying you a visit first thing in the morning?"

"Not at all. It will be nice to see you again. Laura will be pleased."

"I'll be bringing Dianne with me."

"Ah, so she's over here as well!"

"Must be."

"I wonder why?" Doc said with a definite hint of mischief in his voice.

"Since you're the only parents I've got we thought we had better tell you first."

"Tell me what lad?"

"We're going to get married."

"That's wonderful, Ben! Wait till Laura hears the news! I'll wait and let you break it to her when you come over."

"Thanks Doc."

"For what son?"

"For understanding." He had a particular soft spot for Doc. Since Karen's death, he had still treated him like his own son. He hung up and went through to the dining area. "Not as big as we've been used to, this place, is it?" he said as he joined Dianne and Edward. "Didn't think it was small till I saw the one's in New York."

"Ready for some grub now?" Dianne asked.

"Came to tell you that Carl's called. He said to tell us that Hart wants to see me urgently."

"Sounds about right with the police business and what Lieutenant Mathias said to you."

"I'll call him now. Do you want to have a word?"

"Better have," she replied and went through to the telephone. She dialed and waited for it to connect. It didn't ring long before Carl answered at the New York end. It was early afternoon. "Carl, Dianne here. You've heard from Hart then?"

Carl chuckled. "Yeah. He came to see Benjamin personally. Ranting and raving he was, because he'd missed you."

"How many were there with him?"

"Nobody that I could see. He said he'd asked the police to get hold of Ben because he didn't want to scare him off before he'd had a chance to talk to him."

"What did you tell him?" Benjamin came in on the other line.

"Hi Ben. Told him you were in Miami. He'll have found out I lied by now I should think."

"What did he want?"

"Wouldn't say exactly. Just said it was about Daniel. Apparently he'd got hold of the tape recording that Daniel made."

"That figures," Benjamin said. "MI5 will have asked the C.I.A. what part they've been playing in all this. The tape could be pretty damning."

"Well, I can't see him wanting to just explain his murdering Daniel to you," Carl commented.

"God knows what he wants," Dianne said bitterly. "Surely he knows everything's blown over by now."

"Well that's all he'd tell me, but he did leave a number for you to ring if you felt that way inclined."

"Well he'll know I'm in England by now I expect," Benjamin surmised. "No harm in giving him a call. Might be able to put him off hounding us."

Carl dictated as Benjamin jotted down the number. "Okay then," Carl said, "I'll get what's left of a day's work done, now then. I'll let you know when to expect your cargo."

"Thanks Carl," they both said together.

"Solong then," he said and rang off. Dianne put the receiver down and looked at Benjamin. They both shrugged their shoulders.

"Beats me," she said.

"And me," Benjamin answered.

Benjamin dialed the number Carl had given him. It was afternoon in New York, best time to catch him if he's going to be in. He listened to it ringing and then a man's voice came on the line and said, "Hello, Hart."

"Benjamin Carlisle," Benjamin said just as succinctly.

"Oh, you got my message did you?"

"No, I dreamed I was ringing Father Christmas," Benjamin said sharply.

"Then I've a Christmas present for you."

"Another car bomb! Gosh I am excited."

"I must talk to you," Hart said tersely.

"You are doing."

"I don't mean over the telephone, idiot!"

"That's the safest distance from you."

"I can't say anything over a public telephone line. What I have to say will not be unpleasant."

"It's what you'll do that worries me, Mr. Hart."

"I've had a chat with our friendly Lieutenant. He's very impressed."

"Hooray!" Benjamin said in a monotone.

"This isn't getting us anywhere Ben."

"What do you really want, Jack?" Benjamin asked sarcastically.

"I've told you. I want to talk to you privately. If you don't understand what that means, it means meeting somewhere, and talking face to face."

"And it's too private to say over the telephone?"

"Too damned right it is. But I assure you, you'll not be harmed. And I assure you, I've some news to tell you that will not be at all unwelcome."

"You'll have to come over here then. I'm too busy running my own life to get mixed up in your games again. No doubt your friends in MI5 will be pleased to hear that you're friendly. They couldn't do enough to help me make up my mind the last time."

"Went off half cock as usual," Hart commented accurately. "They sent me a copy of your brother's tape."

"Don't tell me, it's to play at Christmas instead of carols!"

"Jesus, you never give up do you?"

"I don't intend giving up staying alive either. You heard the tape. You know that I know."

"You know fuck all! That's why I want to talk to you. Then I can explain first why MI5 sent me the tape, and secondly what I was going on it in the first place."

"Tuesday morning. I have a lot to catch up with here, and I don't intend wasting any of my time until I've got on top of my work and caught up with my sleep."

"But..."

"Tuesday morning," Benjamin persisted. "I'll meet you off the first flight in from Kennedy."

"That'll be eight thirty at Heathrow."

"How will I know you?"

"I'll be carrying a crocodile skin hand-case."

"Might be hundreds of them. I don't want to be picked up for importuning. You'd better wear a bright yellow tie as well."

"It'll make me look damned ridiculous!"

"Good."

"I'll see you then. Goodbye." He hung up and smiled to himself. As he turned around he realised Edward was sitting listening.

"He's coming over here?"

"Yes, but don't worry. You can stay at my house until he beggars off back to his own hole. I'll drop you off there on the way to pick him up. In the meantime, I'll have a word with someone about some new identification for you."

"I didn't think you'd be into that sort of thing," Edward remarked.

"I'm not. That's why I'll have to find out about it."

Edward grinned. "I'm going to have to go to elocution lessons if I'm to pass as English!"

"Well, we'll see," Benjamin smiled. "See what we can find out first shall we?"

28th October.

Benjamin found it hard to sleep. His body was bone weary but his mind kept going back to Hart. He tried to work out what it was Hart wanted but still came up with no real answer. He pressed the light button on his digital watch and looked at the time. 4.45. "Right," he whispered. Dianne was fast asleep beside him. She slept on as he eased himself out of bed and tiptoed out to the lounge, closing the door behind him. Edward was snoring beneath a pile of blankets on the sofa. He stirred when Benjamin went out for an early morning walk, but didn't wake up. The fresh, cool air helped Benjamin to think.

Benjamin and Edward made breakfast for Dianne, but she didn't eat it. She slept until eleven, burst out of the bedroom and swore. "Why the hell didn't you wake me?" she said as she steadied herself against the door jamb. She'd come out of a deep sleep, seen that Benjamin had gone, glanced at her watch and jumped straight out of bed. Her hand caught one of his dressing gowns, and she fell into it as she opened the door.

"Enjoying the holiday?" Benjamin asked. He looked fresh and clean shaven the same as Edward. Edward was sitting opposite Benjamin and explaining the finer details of the new discoveries made by Russian scientists in the field of chemical gases, gases against which there was no protective clothing issued to Western forces. They were both chain drinking coffee.

"Have you decided what to do about that Hart guy yet?" she asked.

"If he says he must talk to me, then I'm ready to listen. He's coming over on Tuesday to speak to me personally, so who am I to refuse such an audience?" There was more than a hint of sarcasm in his voice.

"Will you be safe darling?"

"That's why I've given myself a couple of day's grace. It gives me time to get something worked out."

"By that, I presume he wanted to come earlier."

"He'll make me angry if he tries gate crashing any earlier."

"If he does that I think he'll be the one in danger," Dianne said with a hopeful grin.

"Here," Edward said to her. "You sit down and have some coffee, and I'll make you something to eat."

"Great! I could eat a horse."

"I'll look in the fridge and see if he has a fresh one in then," he said and went through to the kitchen with a motivated spring in his stride.

Dianne and Benjamin were more than a little impressed with his cuisine. "You ought to have been a chef," Dianne said seriously.

Edward beamed and watched her eat her cooked breakfast with relish "You know," he said with a pensive look on his face, "I think you might have something there."

It was nearly lunch time when Benjamin and Dianne cruised up Doc's drive in the red Mercedes. He opened the door and walked out to them. "Hi Doc," Benjamin said affectionately, "This is Dianne."

"Pleased to meet you dear," Doc said to her and held out his hand. Dianne offered her hand, and he took a firm grip on it and led her into the house. "Come in young lady. Laura has been dying to meet you." Dianne looked over her shoulder at Benjamin and shrugged her shoulders and smiled at the same time as Doc led her eagerly inside the house. "Look Laura," he shouted. "This is Benjamin's new lady friend. Isn't she just a beauty?"

Laura emerged from a kitchen that was full of cooking smells, and rubbed her hands on her apron before holding one out to Dianne. "He'll fuss over you like a prize puppy until he's got used to you. Then he'll just talk you to death," she said about her husband. He looked dejected when he had to release her hand so his wife could greet her. "I'm so pleased you've been able to come over," Laura said with a smile.

"She might be staying for quite a long while," Benjamin said diplomatically.

"Ah, do I hear...." She prompted him by shaking her hand by her ear.

"Wedding bells. Yes mum," Benjamin said with a shy smile.

"Well that means only one thing then," she said and turned to go quickly into the kitchen. She emerged with a bottle of Moet et Chandon. "Champagne!" she cried with a beam on her face. "You know," she said to Dianne, "it's the best thing that's happened to him for years!"

"Quite right," Doc substantiated. "He's been like a dog with no master since he lost...Oh, I'm sorry; I never thought to ask if he'd told you."

"Oh yes he's told me all about Karen. If she was as nice as her parents then he was a very lucky man." Doc and Laura beamed with pride. "But one thing I have to say is that I've no intention of treating your son like a dog!" They all laughed and

Benjamin cracked the champagne and poured it into long glasses conjoured up by Laura.

Laura had anticipated her guests would be staying for Sunday dinner, and it was well into the afternoon, while she was showing Dianne around the garden, that Benjamin decided to ask Doc what he wanted to know. They had gone to chat in his study. "You said on the phone that you knew for sure that it was the Bulgarians that had arranged to have me killed," he prompted as he sat in Doc's arm chair. Doc sat by his desk and leaned his back against it.

"What I did say, is that it wasn't the mafia."

"Yes, I found that out."

"Right," he said. "Ever since we made our enquiries about SHEPH, I've had a constant stream of information fed back to me. It seems that all these things your brother was mixed up in culminated in his deal with the C.I.A. to get him out and extricate himself from any involvement with the Bulgarians. A little bird across the Atlantic, however, has told me that he made a deal with the C.I.A. on more than just that issue. My source didn't say what that was, but I presume it was the French connection that he mentioned in the tape. However, he did say that the man who was shot in New York called Kalten was hired by a foreign government agency. The mafia had nothing to do with him and I presume the gunman at Heathrow was hired by similar people, since an ex-colleague of mine in MI5 has said they know who that sniper was but neither they nor MI6 were to apprehend him for political reasons."

"Meaning what? Why are they so friendly with the Bulgarians?"

"I said that one was hired by similar people. I didn't mean the same ones," Doc corrected.

"Meaning?"

"Meaning a deal of course."

"Who was he then?"

"They didn't tell me that. What I do know, is that since you sent the tape to MI5 your life has no longer been in danger. Either they failed to silence you, or you showed the C.I.A. and hence the people they made a deal with, that you didn't know what they thought you did."

"What do you mean?"

"Simply this, either the Bulgarians were afraid Daniel had given his secret away, but realised as you hoped, that the cat was out of the bag, or someone else thought he had something else to tell and thought he might have told you all about it. What I do know is that when the C.I.A. got a copy of the tape, somebody breathed a sigh of relief in Washington and the pressure was off you. That was my informant's very own words."

"So whoever tried to kill me were in touch with the C.I.A., is that what you're saying?

"If you want my opinion, and it is only an opinion mind, I think the sniper in New York was working for the Bulgarians, and the one at Heathrow was working for, dare I say it?"

"The French!"

Doc shrugged his shoulders and pushed out his bottom lip in a very French manner. "It's only an opinion mind," he emphasized.

"An informed one," Benjamin added. "Well then," he said after a moment's thought. "What would you say my chances of survival were, if I told you I'd arranged to see the C.I.A.'s man on Tuesday?"

"I'd say he's harmless. If they wanted you dead they'd have done it without an appointment. As I've said, their getting a copy of your tape took the pressure off you, so they might just be on your side."

"But Daniel said that Hart might be the one who killed him."

"I think he might know something about it, but whether he did it, is another matter. There were a lot of people after Daniel. You see, it could well have been any of them, including the mafia."

"Dianne and I don't think Daniel was that careless to be lured to a car and be blown up by them," Benjamin stated. "We think he was supposed to get in the car because it was part of a pre-arranged plan, the plan he mentioned he'd fixed with Hart, to drive away to a pre-arranged rendezvous for his new life to begin. It would be the only way he'd have been so careless. After all, he suspected that he was being set up by someone connected with the mafia on the inside of his own firm. That would have made him even more cautious."

"Well, as I say, you should be all right meeting him. If he wanted to kill you, they'd have done it by now. And it wouldn't have been a sniper. They're expert in killing people and making it look like an accident, believe me. I say meet him and ask him yourself. Bring him back here if you wish and I'll ask him."

"Thanks Doc. I know you would, but I don't want you involved any more than you are already."

"Bit late to think about that now son."

"Incidentally, Doc, how do they set up a new identity for somebody?"

"Depends who they're doing it for. If they're going to give the man a bank account that reaps him a living through paying interest on the capital sum bestowed on him, then it's easy. If he wants to get a job though, he has to get a social security number. That's a little harder. Not impossible for government agencies that, even then."

"How would you go about it," he asked as off handedly as he could, "forgetting that you have any connections with government agencies of course?" he added.

Doc gave him an askance look. "Well, basically, to exist comfortably you have to have an income. That means, as I've said, either a bank account or a social security number."

"Say a bank account."

"Well even then, it's got to be set up. The Inland Revenue would ask questions otherwise. And then you wouldn't have everything. You would still need a medical card for treatment by a G.P. or a hospital."

"I see," Benjamin said despondently.

"Of course, getting over the money problem, then you only need a birth certificate," Doc went on. "With that, you can get a passport, and take a driving test to get a license. No use getting stopped for a motoring offence and not having any identification. Basically, if you're a vagrant, you need nothing, but if you wish to drive and travel then the birth certificate is the real necessity."

"Go on," Benjamin prompted him.

"Well, that, I thought was common knowledge. Even in this day and age of computers they still haven't mastered keeping tabs on birth certificates."

"How do you mean?"

"Well, let me say that it's all listed step by step for you in a book, *How to get a birth certificate in a different name.*"

"I don't believe it," Benjamin said as he watched Doc get up from his seat and walk over to the bookshelves.

"Now let me see," Doc said as he glanced along the shelf of paperbacks. "Ah, here it is; a reference book for you." He pulled down a book and handed it to Benjamin.

"*The Day of the Jackal!*" Benjamin said in disbelief.

"Here," Doc said and took the book back. "If you aren't a reader, it's, let me see, about chapter three or four." He thumbed through the book. "There," he said and prodded the page. "Nothing's changed. See, page sixty eight." Benjamin laughed. "You will have your little joke won't you?"

Doc just chuckled back and put the book back on the shelf. "It's not the professional way of course," he said finally as he returned to his seat. "The real professional takes the identity of someone else, someone who's alive and has all the necessary documents to start with."

"You mean he takes over from somebody." Like Edward, thought Benjamin.

"Exactly," Doc agreed. "Either that, or he gets the necessary documents issued and copies filed in the right government departments."

"That's the MI5 way is it?"

Doc chuckled again. "There's one other way of doing it with a birth certificate of course."

"Tell me then," Benjamin said interestedly. "Change your name."

"You mean by deed poll?"

"Or getting married."

"That's all right if you're a woman."

"No law states that the man cannot take the wife's name. It's just a custom that saves a lot of misunderstanding when two people live together."

"Never thought of it that way," Benjamin conceded.

*****

"Well, what do you think?" Benjamin asked Dianne as they drove back to the apartment. It was late in the evening and they hadn't out-stayed their welcome at Doc's.

"I think I'm going to like it over here," she answered. "What are you going to do?"

"How do you mean?"

"Well, what about the garage?"

"Probably leave the running of that to Mark. He certainly seems to be coping. I'll find out for sure this week."

"Where are we going to live?"

"I was hoping you'd want to stay in England," Benjamin said and pulled the car to a halt.

"I mean where in England, silly."

"Oh, I haven't thought about it. I'd prefer to have a new place, a new start, you know? The house I have has too many memories. That's why I've never bothered living there. I should have sold it years ago really."

Dianne smiled at him and gave him a kiss on the cheek. “Come on; let's see how Edward's coping on his own."

Edward looked up from the table where he was writing. "Hi there," he said with a smile. "How did it go?"

"Beautiful," Dianne beamed.

"You writing a letter?" Benjamin asked him.

"No, I was working some figures out that's all. I realise it isn't going to be easy, but I really would like to get some sort of business going. I'd thought of buying a hotel or something to do with catering."

"What happened to the scientific brain waves," Dianne asked.

"Nothing, but they wouldn't take me a week to write down. I wouldn't want to manufacture them, just patent them."

"Hardly a lifetime's work, I must admit," she said.

Benjamin sat down and explained what he had said to Doc, and what Doc had told him. Dianne seemed unconvinced that Hart was harmless. Edward was definitely unconvinced. He explained the facts about new identities to Edward, and they concluded that he'd already used the right method to change his identity. The trouble was, to be safe, he would have to do it again. If Janine ever talked to Hart, he would be traced through his passport. He knew the real Matthew must be dead or he would have returned with a vengeance. He cursed Janine. If only she didn't know about him taking Matthew's identity, he could have set up a business in Britain legitimately. "Not a satisfactory position to be in," Edward remarked.

"Never mind," Benjamin consoled. "We'll sort something out, you'll see."

"What are we doing tomorrow?" Dianne asked, to try and get onto a more solvable problem.

"What do you want to do?" asked Benjamin.

"How about taking us to see your house, or the cottage in the Chilterns?"

"Got it!" Benjamin exclaimed. "We'll let Edward have the flat until we solve his personality problem. And we'll buy a new house!"

"Eventually, yes," Dianne said patiently. "But in the mean time, can we do a tour tomorrow or not?"

"I can do better than that, I'll take you around them first thing tomorrow, and then in the afternoon I'll pop you over to see the house that Daniel was going to buy. If it's still on the market, and if you like it, perhaps we can buy it?"

"Am I invited?" Edward asked.

"Of course," Dianne said and patted him on his hand in a motherly manner. "It's going to be a marvelous day; I can feel it in my bones."

CHAPTER 21.

New Delhi, Monday 29th October, early evening.

"There are many ways for you to accomplish your goal," explained Balbir. "It is just a question of preparation and planning." They were in Balbir's little office at the back of the police headquarters' building. Balbir Singh, a police sub-inspector, was the official assigned to help and direct Beant to carry through his task. Now, only hours before the task was to be finished, everything depended on Beant.

"But how do I do it so that no one knows it was me?" asked Beant. He flicked a fly from his eyebrow and stared intently at his adviser. Once again he had become gaunt and thin from lack of sleep and inadequate meals. The responsibility he carried on his shoulders weighed heavily on his soul.

"It's difficult to say exactly. If you plant a bomb in her house you will be found out either through forensic tests on your clothes and skin, or through interrogation. You know what the secret service men are like when it comes to questioning suspects. And her body guards will be the first to be suspected. You would eventually be forced into telling the truth. That would endanger *everyone* connected with you. It would certainly endanger me."

"I'd be as well blowing myself up at the same time," Beant observed

"Quite. That would solve the problem of a following purge. But it wouldn't help you a great deal," said Balbir, his sympathy growing for Beant slightly. On the other hand, it was an admirable suggestion. He was trapped in the same sprawling net that had caught Beant up, a net of an organization whose tentacles reached far and wide into Indian security. He had wondered just how big the machination was, and just who precisely was behind it. He had been drawn into the net like so many others. He wished he could turn the clock back. He even had sleepless nights worrying about it. That was something he had never done when he was in charge of his own fate. But now somebody else held the strings and they were beginning to pull tighter and tighter on them, drawing them in like the strings on a purse. Now there was no way out but forward. "You're not in an impossible position," he stated so convincingly and sincerely that he almost believed it himself.

"I'm beginning to wish I'd never agreed to do this now."

"You're in too deep to get out now my boy. If you defaulted on your agreement they would kill you the same as they would kill me."

"But *who* are *they*?"

"That, my boy, I don't know. In fact I have a feeling it would be best never to know. Knowing that, could cost us our lives more surely than the mere risk we are taking now."

"So what can I do?"

"You must think." replied Balbir "You must be cool. Above all, you must be prepared to take any opportunity that arises now the organization says it's time to do your job. It must be accomplished before the end of term of the present Lok Sabha,"

The Lok Sabha is the Lower House of the Indian parliament, elected for a five year maximum term of office. It had been last elected in January 1980.

"That means having more than one alternative up your sleeve," he added.

"So what are my alternatives?"

The stocky policeman leaned back in his chair, making it creek back at him in protest. "Well, as I have said," he went on, "a bomb is difficult. So is cyanide gas in her bedroom. You really need some method where you cannot be automatically connected."

"How about a car bomb?" asked Beant.

"That is a possibility, but I would have to make it appear to be one of the other guards that planted it. Such a guard would have to be killed before he was interrogated." He looked up at the ceiling. "Hmm, tricky but a distinct possibility."

A flicker of light came into Beant's eye. He knew now what he was to do to accomplish his task and survive. He knew he had to do it before his resolve vaporized again.

London, Monday 29th October.

It wasn't a particularly early start for Benjamin, Edward and Dianne. The fact that Dianne couldn't sleep after the break of day, didn't seem to deter the men from slumbering on another hour and a half, with the plea, when they awoke, that it takes time to adjust to jet lag. "That's no excuse," she said and wagged her finger at Benjamin, in mock anger, as she catered for them. "We've a very busy day ahead of us."

"Only be able to see the outside of the place in Surrey," Edward said. "I doubt if even the real-estate guys will be able to meet you there at such short notice. Monday will probably be their busy day."

"Monday!" Gosh yes of course!" Benjamin exclaimed. "You know, I've lost all track of time. Well, we'll have a look at the outside first before we do anything strenuous like calling at an estate agent's."

"Jet lag?" Dianne commented.

"Must be," the men said in unison over their coffee.

Benjamin took great pride in exhibiting his properties, meager though they were compared with those he had inherited from his brother. Even his own house was too large for him. He was a single man, and in a large house he would have rattled around like a ball on a pin table. Up to now the apartment had suited him fine, handy for work and handy for getting out for a drink. .Now his whole lifestyle was beginning to change. He wasn't just well off, he was wealthy. He was going to be married, and he was going to run his car business from a distance while he and Dianne decided how they were going to invest their money.

They ate out in a small restaurant on the way back to London and then Benjamin ushered them into the car for the final trip of the day. It seemed a long way, much further than when he had gone with Daniel, but then he hadn't been in a hurry that day. Now he wanted to go and see the house as soon as possible and talk Dianne into wanting it.

As they drew up the tarmac drive the house still looked dark and empty behind the leylandii hedge. There was still no placard with a for sale sign on it so Benjamin pulled up beneath the yew tree and stopped the engine. All three got out and admired the double fronted building as it stood majestically amidst the well cut lawns and landscaped garden. The sun glinted on the water of a small -pond, and the finches, sparrows and tits chattered around the top of a bird table, taking turns at flying away and returning for another peanut. “Somebody's keeping the place neat and tidy," Edward commented. "They've left some food for the birds."

"That might mean it's been sold," Benjamin said with a sinking feeling. "Come on, lets go and knock on the door." He led the way up the steps and thumped the heavy door with the large brass knocker. "Seems like we've missed the boat," he said as he heard noises in the passage way behind the door. They all heard a bolt being drawn and then the door opened slightly.

"Yes," a young and attractive young woman said. She had long rolling dark red hair that fell past her high cheek bones, and she looked at Benjamin curiously as if she knew him from somewhere. He'd never seen her before. He would have remembered that face.

"I'm terribly sorry for bothering you," Benjamin said politely. "We thought the house might still be for sale." He turned to leave. The others took his cue and did the same.

"Wait," she called after them. "Forgive me but you look very much like Daniel's brother. Can it be?" she asked with a heavy French accent.

The mention of his brother's name froze him to the ground. He turned around to face the woman again. "You knew Daniel?" he asked.

"You look very like him," she smiled. Her beam caught everybody. It was stunning. "He told me he had a brother," she went on. The others still stared at her, speechless. "You're better looking than he said."

"Thank you," Dianne replied for him. "Are you the lady he was going to marry?"

"That's right," she said, still smiling brightly. "Would you come in please?" She pushed the door wide and stepped aside while they filed inside. Benjamin realised she had done a great deal of work to the house on the inside. It had been decorated from top to bottom in soft pastel shades. She flicked a switch as she walked past it, a wall light came on and it lit the colours to perfection. "What a nice surprise," she said and showed them into the massive lounge.

"Yes," Dianne answered as she looked at the bronze and ivory ornaments around the room, "What a surprise." On the centre table stood a magnificent bronze and ivory figure of lady being helped off her horse by a gentleman. "Daniel would have liked that," she stated.

"Yes, I think that is why he asked me to marry him. It was the only way he could get his hands on it."

"Marry you!" Benjamin exclaimed.

"Yes," she replied, "Why not?" She seemed offended.

"Good heavens, why not indeed," Benjamin soothed. "So you're the lady he was going to marry?"

"Still am, I hope!"

"But..." She'd obviously moved into the house and had been waiting for her future husband to return. He had arranged the purchase and everything. But she hadn't been told about the bomb. God! Benjamin thought. How can I tell her? "My name's Benjamin," he said. "This is Dianne..."

"Oh you are the lady from America, no?"

"Yes."

"And you looked after Daniel so well. He has told me all about you." I bet he did! thought Dianne.

"And this is a friend of ours, Edward," Benjamin introduced.

"I am happy to meet you," she said and shook hands in a jolly manner. "Isn't this exciting?" she said and put her hands to her mouth. "Daniel will be so pleased!" She turned to go down the passage. "Would you like to come in?"

"Look, I think there's something you ought to know," Benjamin shouted after her as she disappeared into the back kitchen. He followed her through and signalled for the others to stay behind. She had to be told. She went out of the French windows onto a lush dark green lawn. Ahead of her was a table with a parasol sun shade and several reclining chairs around it, facing onto a miniature lake. Benjamin kept after her and was just in earshot when he heard her speak.

"You'll never guess who has come to visit, cheri," she said to the back of a chair. Benjamin was nearly up with her now, and suddenly he could see the back of a man's head, held back as he sipped at a can of beer. "Your brother Benjamin and Dianne are here!"

"Hell, why didn't you say?" Benjamin heard a familiar voice answer her. The man got up and came face to face with Benjamin. "Ben! Hey when did you get back?"

"You little bastard," Benjamin shouted and grabbed a hold of his shirt. You faking little shit!"

"Steady on, Ben. I can explain everything," Daniel tried to appease as he was pushed backwards.

"Steady on? Steady on!" Benjamin screamed at the top of his voice. "I'll bloody well kill you!"

Edward and Dianne came running out as Daniel sprawled backwards on the lawn. He got up and held his hands out to stop the onslaught. "Do you know what I've been through on your account during these past few weeks?" Benjamin shouted.

"Wait Ben, I know you're mad, but I can explain," he cried as Benjamin picked him up bodily and flung him backwards once again.

Marietta screamed, "Stop them," with her hands to her mouth, "Please stop them."

Her words were no sooner out of her mouth when Dianne shouted, "Give him one for me the no good twister."

This time Daniel sprawled across a rose bed and was visibly pained by the thorns as Benjamin bore down on him once more. He struggled to get to his feet to make his escape, tearing his shirt as he did so. But Benjamin had a hold of his belt and hoisted him, legs and arms flailing like paddles, into the air once again. "I'll bloody murder you, you little shit!" Edward couldn't make out just how two brothers behaved in England when they were reunited. Moreover he couldn't understand the younger brother calling the other little when they were of equal size. He watched as Daniel sailed through the air, flapping his arms desperately, in a fight to reduce the pull of gravity, as he hurtled into the lake. There was a big splash and Daniel surfaced amidst a cacophony of abusive yells and splutters of panic. Benjamin was about to go in and finish him off when Edward stepped in front of him.

"Enough!" he shouted at the top of his voice. "He's alive, what more do you want?" Benjamin resisted the urge to brush him aside as Edward pushed against him with all his strength to stop him going into the lake after his brother. Benjamin shook his fist and swore again before turning and marching back towards the house.

"You animal!" Marietta screamed at him as he went past. Edward and Dianne followed. He was going and they thought he might be best with someone with him to calm him down. His chest heaved as he brought his rage under control, still heading around the house to the car.

Daniel scrambled to the shore of the lake and ran after his brother. "Ben," he shouted as he trailed mud and water behind him, "For God's sake let me explain!"

Benjamin ignored him and climbed into the Mercedes. Daniel ran around to the driver's side and yanked the keys out of the ignition. "You hand those back!" Benjamin said threateningly.

"Bloodywell listen you big ape!" Daniel said and grabbed his hair, jerking his head back against the seat. Benjamin responded with an uppercut that sent Daniel sprawling across the tarmac drive on his belly. He jumped back out of the car to get the keys that had gone ahead of Daniel and stopped when he saw no movement from his brother. His anger evaporated as suddenly as it had flashed to boiling point, and he bent over and lifted Daniel over to lie on his back. His eyes were closed and his body limp and lifeless. Edward and Dianne ran over to see what had happened.

"Danny!" Benjamin said loudly. "Danny, are you all right?" He felt at Daniel's jugular and suddenly Daniel's eyes flicked open.

"Thought you'd hurt me then didn't you?" Daniel chuckled as a trickle of blood ran down his chin.

"I thought I'd killed you," Benjamin said with a sigh of relief and let him drop back onto the hard surface with a thud. Daniel winced.

"I thought that's what you said you wanted to do. Knew you'd be happy once you'd finished the job." He looked at the spectators as Marietta ran up to attend her wounded champion. "He never could stand to see me get hurt you know," he grinned with a display of pink teeth. Marietta dabbed his burst lip with her handkerchief and cradled him in her arms.

"If this is how you treat your brother then you are not welcome here," she shouted.

Benjamin turned to the others and nodded to the car. Without saying another word he retrieved the keys and went over to the Mercedes. Daniel pulled the pampering hand from his mouth and shouted to them.

"She didn't mean that, Ben. Stay and let me explain," he called in vain as the three visitors piled back into the car. "Ben! Come back you young idiot!" Benjamin gunned the Mercedes back onto the lawn and then did the same in a forward gear, skidding at first, and then bolting forward onto the tarmac and away down the drive.

"Damn you Ben," Daniel shouted after them. He turned to Marietta. "Look at my blasted lawn!" he said and prodded his heel on the side of two black groves in the otherwise flawless velvet turf, in an attempt to flatten them out. "If only he'd let me explain!"

Marietta put her arm around him. "Never mind mon cheri. You don't need them any more." She looked down the empty driveway and pursed her lips. "They don't deserve you," she said bitterly.

30th October.

Benjamin watched as the passengers disembarked from the Boeing 747 that had just arrived from New York. He had dropped Edward off to settle in his house for the time being. With Hart about, there was no use in chancing an accidental meeting.

It wasn't difficult to pick out a man carrying a crocodile skin suitcase and wearing a bright yellow tie. Benjamin worked his way upstream to meet him, and as he came face to face with him, Hart smiled and held out a friendly hand. Benjamin took it, less nervously than he would have if he hadn't known Daniel was still alive. "Mr. Hart?" he said with a suppressed chuckle.

Hart still managed to hear and pulled the tie off. "Good idea, bad taste," he said and threw it into a waste bin.

"Call me Jack won't you?"

"Now I know you didn't top my brother, I reckon I can be a bit friendlier," Benjamin said and smiled. "Let's get out of this place." Hart showed no surprise at the fact that Benjamin had found out the news he had come over to break himself.

"Where are you going?"

"You hungry?"

"A beer would go down well," Hart grinned.

"Have to be back to my place then." He led the way to the car. They both seemed relaxed as Benjamin cut through the traffic.

"You know Daniel's alive then?" Jack asked.

"Only by a stroke of sheer luck," Benjamin replied. "Or bad luck, if you look at it another way."

"Oh, why bad luck," Jack asked seriously concerned.

“Just getting used to the idea of being rich," Benjamin grinned. "Have to hand it all back now."

"Does it bother you?"

"Not really. He'd do the same for me. But what I regret is falling out with him when I saw he was alive. I was so angry that I'd been shot at and nearly killed at least three times, all on his account. It was only sheer luck that kept me alive!"

"That's not what I heard," Jack grinned. "You sound to be better at looking after yourself than three of my men."

"Coming from you, I'll presume that's some kind of complement, but I don't know what your sources of information are. If it weren't for catching the wrong plane, I'd be dead now."

"I was talking about the shoot out at O.K. Coral. It seems like you were grossly underestimated."

"So were Carl and Dianne. They were brilliant." There was a long silence while Benjamin negotiated the traffic lanes. He thought of what he wanted to say to Hart. He'd had plenty to say before he found Daniel alive and kicking, and now there was even more to talk about. Benjamin still had to know the answers to a lot of questions, questions that would never go away until they were answered.

Dianne was waiting for them as they went up to the apartment. She smiled amiably and asked her guest in.

"He'd like a cold beer," Benjamin said to her as he took Jack's coat. She got some drinks on a tray and joined them in the lounge.

"Well, are you or aren't you going to tell us what happened?" she asked.

“I had to let you know I hadn't killed Daniel. I realised what you'd be thinking."

"It took us some time to come around to that conclusion even then. We're a bit slow over here," Benjamin said modestly.

"How about telling us how he still happens to be alive," Dianne suggested.

Jack grinned. "Now that, believe it or not, will take some doing!"

"I might say that we know more than you could possibly think we do," Dianne warned.

"Oh," Jack said with a skeptical glance. "Well, I don't think you know it all. That's why I've been trying to contact you in the States. Then I tried ringing you at home and there was no reply. Finally, the guy that sent me the tape told me your pop used to be one of their lot, and gave me his number to tell him to give you a message. I couldn't even tell you over the phone. Security on these matters has to be tight. Even MI5 don't know Daniel still exists. I couldn't contact Daniel and tell him to contact you, or we could have even blown his cover that way. But it was important that you didn't still connect me with his death."

"Why did he need a cover?" Dianne asked.

"No doubt Daniel will tell you when you make up," Jack observed. "But, I can tell you what he knows. All off the record mind."

"Absolutely," said Benjamin.

"Well I knew Anita Holt was a plant. A man in the Mob told me so when we put the pressure on him. He spilled the whole can of beans about a plot to kill Daniel and enable Anita to inherit the shares of his company. What the mafia didn't know is that Daniel had sorted that lot out nicely in his will. I'd warned him about an insider, and I think he realised who it was. I gave him strict instructions not to let it out that he knew as that would spoil my plan to get him away clear. I didn't even tell him what my plan was to get him out with a new identity, because I think he was too soft to go through with it if I'd told him everything.

As things turned out, I was right not to tell him, and he ended up dead as far as everybody was concerned. I couldn't afford for a single person to know about him or the way I did it!"

"So why are you telling us now?" asked Benjamin.

"Because Daniel will tell you anyway, and I had to tell you he was alive to stop any problems with you in England. If you kept pushing, it's likely it would jeopardise his new identity.

"How did it happen?" asked Dianne.

"I arranged to meet him below the warehouse and he was told he was to get in the Cavalier and drive out of everybody's lives. I told him that, but what I didn't tell him was that the reason I had to see him first was so that I could switch him for somebody else."

"You mean you killed somebody in his place!"

Jack ignored the question and carried on with his explanation. "All he knew was that he was to drive away so that if he told the wrong people about the plan, it wouldn't matter because after the explosion, they'd think he was dead anyway. I said he had to drive away and be picked up where I told him to stop. But when he got down to the underground car park I told him to strip off and change clothes with another guy. He was to drive away in the car, and Daniel was to disappear with me. The trouble was, he was struck dumb when the bomb went off and blew the other chap to pieces. He was in such a state that we bundled him into the trunk of our car and left him there until we got him well away. Eventually, after a long drive, we released him.

"So you didn't know there was a bomb in the car," Benjamin surmised.

"Oh yes," Jack explained. "I knew all right. That other guy was meant to get blown up."

"What!" Benjamin shouted incredulously.

"He was set up for it. As I say, I knew the mafia had rigged the car, but I had an assignment to remove the other guy, so I used it as an opportunity to kill two birds with one stone. These things just have to be done." Hart looked proud of the way he'd carried out his plan.

"I had no idea the C.I.A. were so ruthless," Dianne lied. "Did Daniel know the other man?"

"I don't know. It was hard for Daniel to see in the gloom. The other man had his face sideways on to him and he was nearest the daylight, so he really only got a silhouette of him."

"His name then?" Dianne pressed. Jack shook his head. "I could never tell you that." Benjamin had gone pale. He already knew the name and he knew now that the real Matthew Roland would never return. It all fitted into place. Edward had known what his fate would be, and if it hadn't been for Janine and her photograph, his end would have come just as he'd predicted. He had something to thank her for after all.

"Why did Daniel make the deal with you?" Benjamin asked.

"Because he could tell us about SHEPH, about Vlatsov, about the mafia, and about two men in France who were active C.I.A., agents that were acting as double agents. He realised that if the men he'd set on to investigate could find out Diacre was C.I.A. then the French must know. But they'd set Diacre up in a huge villa in Versailles, so they obviously weren't bothered about his affiliations. Then, when a couple of the people that were helping investigate got killed, he knew they would be after him next. You see, Diacre was doing a job for a powerful industrialist politician. He was to frame your brother for stealing a national art treasure, but he played too clever and made Daniel suspect him."

"Why the set up?"

"Revenge for Marietta stealing technology, and to silence her for good about what his up-and-coming politician son had done with her money. He embezzled a fortune off her. He could never have afforded it to be made public. So they arranged to tie her in with the robbery and, voila!"

"So you helped Daniel out of France?"

"Only with a bit of hard dealing. But he was never safe from them. To avoid an all out political scandal we eventually reached an agreement. You see, the French have agents in America the same as the United States have them in France. France is really a non-aligned independent power, and with the present movement of European countries towards left wing and communist governments it has at least justified Washington's reasoning for long established secret agents in them."

"I've no doubt they have them in *all* the Allied countries in case there is a shift in politics," Dianne suggested.

"You mean in Britain?" Hart smiled. "Don't worry, I don't doubt the British do the same," he continued. "You'd be surprised how right wing your Ministry of Defense is, irrespective of the government of the day." He paused only for a second. It mattered little to justify the actions of the C.I.A. "Anyway, getting back to what I was saying, to avert an international scandal, we decided to brush the matter under the carpet, and in exchange, I agreed to remove Daniel and his future wife."

"Permanently?" asked Benjamin.

Hart nodded. "So in effect I killed three birds with one stone because the French think they're dead as well. They don't know Marietta left the country, because we faked her death in the South of France. I arranged for them both to have a new name and identity." Benjamin looked at Dianne. It all sounded familiar.

"I think I owe you an apology," Benjamin confessed. "I accused you of killing him."

"Daniel did the accusing first," Jack admitted. "That's why, when I got a copy of Daniel's tape, I wanted to get hold of you to tell you the truth."

"So the sniper at Heathrow would be French I bet," Benjamin stated. That's why politics were mentioned after a copy of the tape arrived at MI5 head quarters."

"Yes," Jack said seriously. "The problem we haven't worked out is how did they know about the tape? I don't think they would have tried to kill you just on the odd chance that you'd been told something by Daniel while he was in England. Somebody must have known about the tape.

"I think you're wrong there," Benjamin said. "I think the French did just that. The Bulgarians of course are another matter. Cayley was the leak there of course," Benjamin explained. "He opened the letter, read that it mentioned a recording, and told the mafia. They're in thick with the Bulgarians with the heroin run, so they in their turn passed the information on to them."

It all seemed to make sense, but the fact that Jack Hart had come over signified that the C.I.A. wanted to be seen by Benjamin to be free of involvement in any of the attempts on his life. Benjamin still couldn't work out what Jack Hart was afraid of. He wondered if the C.I.A. would go to such lengths just to protect Daniel's anonymity. He didn't ask.

Jack left after lunch. Dianne and Benjamin went to the garage to sort out work that had been left uncleared. It seemed such an anti-climax to the way their lives were turning now.

CHAPTER 22.

31st October 1984.

There was a glint in Beant's eye as he walked with Satwant outside the guards' quarters. "We'll have to blame it on the other guards," he said, waving his hand at Satwant. "We must shoot Mrs. Gandhi, and then shoot the other guards and say they were caught red handed but refused to throw down their guns. We say we had no choice but to shoot them in self defense."

"My friend, you're right," Satwant grinned. "That is exactly what we must do. It's our only chance. Come, we must not be late to accompany her."

Mrs. Indira Gandhi walked in the grounds of the Presidential Palace every morning. Today was to be no exception. She always had two of her bodyguards with her at any time, and this day her guards were Satwant Singh and Beant Singh.

It was still cool, the sun hadn't risen more than a fraction above the high walls. Satwant walked behind Mrs. Gandhi, a sten-gun under his arm, whilst Beant walked nearly alongside her, glancing around in all directions as any good bodyguard should. Only, today his motive for doing so was not to look for would-be assailants. It was to see whether there were any people around that could witness the deed he and his friend were about to carry out; a deed that would never be forgotten in the history of the Indian continent, a deed for which he hoped to transfer the credit to someone else. It was now or never. She was already half way back to the Palace. He tightened his grip on the handle of his Smith and Wesson. It felt wet against the stock. The air was still cool but he was soaked in sweat.

"Are you all right?" asked Mrs. Gandhi. "You look ill." Her eyes locked onto Beant's. His eyes were wide and stared at her without blinking like those of a deer before the lion finally pounces onto its back. He opened his mouth but found no words. "Are you all right?" she asked again, and stopped and turned to face him. Then she knew. Something instinctively told her what that look on his face meant; a look of fear, no, a look of regret, a plea for forgiveness. No words. His throat was as dry as the desert sands; just a panic-stricken look in his eyes, and streams of sweat running down his face and dripping onto his already sodden shirt. No words as his hand pulled out the revolver.

"Oh god!" whispered the Premier. "God forgive you!"

His gun was already clear of the holster and leveling at her breast. It was slippery in his wet hand as he fought to squeeze the trigger. His arm veered away at the very last minute and the shot went within an inch of her shoulder.

Satwant followed on behind Mrs. Gandhi. His Sten-gun was already cocked to fire. As he walked along the bottom of the high perimeter wall his eyes were locked on Beant. He was ready to shoot when his comrade did. They would both fire at the same time. Both would do the assassination as they had sworn to do, carrying it out for their beliefs. He thought about the money. That helped. But it was for his friend Beant that he was prepared to do the deed most of all. He would not let him down, but the money would help him go away and forget what he had done in the misguided cause of an independent Sikh nation. Yes the money would be good...

Suddenly he saw the look in Beant's eyes. A wild staring look. He noticed his friend was perspiring profusely. He gripped the handle of the Sten-gun and got ready to fire.

"Are you all right? You look ill," he heard his Mistress ask. She got no reply. It looked for a moment as though Beant was going to reply but Satwant heard nothing when his friend opened his mouth. He could hear the sound of his heart. It was going to burst out of his chest at any moment.

"Are you all right?" he heard her ask again, as she turned to face Beant. Satwant raised his Sten-gun as he saw his friend level the revolver at the Premier. Everything moved in slow motion, his finger on the trigger, squeezing further and further, his heart beat like a base drum in his ears.

"Oh God! God forgive you!" he heard her say as the recoil of his Sten-gun broke the trance and he saw her falling to the ground, her body soaked in blood.

*****

"Halt, throw down your arms," a voice ordered from the palace gates. Three heavily armed guards ran up to them. Satwant saw Beant drop the revolver and he did the same with his Sten-gun. They'd both been caught. Too late to do anything about it now.

"It was him," Beant pointed accusingly at Satwant. "He shot her before I could get my revolver out to stop him. He's gone completely mad."

Satwant stared at his friend. He had heard wrong. Beant would not betray him now. He fired a shot. He *had* fired it, he'd heard it, and he'd seen the smoke discharge from the barrel.

"Take them both inside, and bring round the ambulance," the guard shouted at his men.

Within a minute the Prime Minister's car - not the ambulance that was always on standby near the Prime Minister for emergencies, - was whisking Mrs. Gandhi to the hospital, whilst Satwant and Beant were escorted away by their fellow guards. Arun Mohal, the chief guard, a huge man with a leaden face and hands like dinner-plates hustled the assassins into the guardroom and with one hand on each of their shoulders compressed them into two chairs at either end of a small table.

"Watch them," he growled and went out to the scene of the murder, for murder it was now. He had been told immediately, that the Premier had died without regaining consciousness. "Pick up all the discharged rounds of ammunition and their weapons. I want them in my office," he commanded two more of his men. He returned to the guardroom. The two guards armed with Sten-guns still stood watch over Beant and Satwant. They looked up at the giant as he stepped sideways through the doorway. "Right," said Arun in a whisper. He looked directly into Beant's eyes. "Now talk."

Beant had stopped sweating now, but his shirt was soaked with pungent smelling perspiration. Steam rose from his body in the increasing heat of the guardroom. His eyes were no longer wild and full of panic. He gazed back at Arun. "Satwant did it," he stated bluntly and in a calculated tone.

Satwant's eyes were wide with disbelief. For the second time in the space of five minutes his friend had passed the blame onto him. He did not speak, but let Beant go on.

"I only managed to get my revolver out and fire one shot at him before you came to my assistance."

"And you missed at a range of fifteen feet," remarked Arun.

"I was in a state of shock," pleaded Beant.

"You're a liar," Satwant shouted, erupting from his passive silence and drumming his fist on the table. "You fired the first shot at her." He turned to the huge guard. "We had a pact, an agreement that we would do it together."

"That's not true," protested Beant. "He did it alone. I had nothing to do with it."

"Is that why you are sweating like a hog?" asked Arun. His face showed no sign of belief or disbelief. "Answer me, why are you nearly shitting yourself?"

"I'm afraid," protested Beant. "I'm afraid you will accuse me of being involved in the murder of Mrs. Gandhi."

"Murder? Who said it was murder?"

Beant's eyes widened again. He hardly breathed as he felt the feeling of panic well up inside him. Like a trapped animal, he began to feel the pangs of despair creeping upon him. His mouth suddenly went dry as he tried to speak. "She isn't dead?" he croaked.

"She will be able to tell us what really happened soon," said Arun.

"She cannot possibly be alive!" Beant replied after pulling on all his resources of energy to bring control over his thoughts. "I tell you Satwant was responsible."

Satwant had sat opposite Beant motionless. He had listened to the man in front of him betray him and his cause. He leaned forward with his hand over his face, and then, as if resigned to his fate, slowly put them down by his sides. Without a flicker of warning, using his hands on the sides of the chair to help propel himself backward, he jumped up and grabbed at the Sten-gun off the guard who stood behind him. In a split second he had gripped the gun barrel and pointed it towards Beant. The guard clung onto his weapon frantically, his hand still gripping the pistol grip, his finger still wrapped around the trigger. As the weapon moved away from him, the Sten-gun spurted out its deadly load, ripping across and opening up Beant's chest like an axe would do to a melon. The other guard fired at Satwant, making him fall backwards and release his grip on the gun. He smiled. No longer did it matter that he had been caught. No longer did it matter that Beant had thrown the blame on him. He knew that Beant was dead, his chest ripped wide open by a burst of 9 millimeter bullets. Now he didn't mind if he died.

"Holy shit!" shouted Arun. The two guards stood mortified, looking down at the two prisoners. Arun bent over to feel at Beant's jugular. "He's dead, as if I needed to tell you that," he scolded. "What about Satwant?"

Just then, Satwant raised his head. "He *was* in on it," he stated and then passed out."

"Right, get the ambulance round here for that traitor, post a round the clock four man guard, and just pray he doesn't die," ordered Arun. He looked at the two guards. "You did all right," he said to the one who had shot Satwant. As he went to the door he turned back to face the other. "We'll probably all be sacked anyway!" he consoled.

Already more than a dozen soldiers had gathered outside the guardroom. He pointed to the one nearest him. "Get some men to clear up in here," he stated and went to break the news to Rajiv Gandhi, Indira Gandhi's only surviving son.

*****

After working late at the garage, it was well into the Wednesday evening when Benjamin and Dianne reached his apartment in Kensington Gardens. They'd had a long afternoon at the garage trying to catch up with all his paperwork. Mrs. Seaton, his secretary, and Mark, his stand-in manager, had done a good job whilst he'd been away over the past weeks, but there had still remained a mountain of work for Benjamin to scale. Today, with Dianne's help, he had finally conquered it.

He could hear the telephone ringing as he unlocked his door. He wasn't particularly bothered if it rang off before he got to it. He held the firm opinion that if somebody rang and didn't get through to him, then, if it was important, they would ring again. It didn't stop, and he strode over to the lounge, picked up the telephone receiver, and sank into his favourite armchair. “Hello," he said with a sigh of relief from getting the weight off his feet.

"Benjamin?" asked a voice at the other end of the line.

"Yes, hello Doc. How are you?"

Doc Emerson didn't reply to Benjamin's question. Instead he asked another. "Have you heard the news?"

"Just got in Doc," Benjamin replied. "Should be on in half an hour," he said, looking at his watch. It was eight thirty.

"It's happened."

"What has," Benjamin asked. He was feeling a little too tired to play at guessing games.

"They've killed her," Doc shouted down the line.

Benjamin held the receiver away from his ear. What the hell was Doc shouting about? "Who has killed who?" he asked as patiently as he could.

"Indira Gandhi. She's been shot by two of her own bodyguards."

Benjamin sat silently for a few moments. "Let me get it straight, Indira Gandhi has been assassinated?"

"Yes," Doc broke in.

"Shot?"

"Yes."

"By her own bodyguards?"

"Yes."

"That doesn't fit in somehow," Benjamin proclaimed.

"Not with your theory perhaps," Doc stated.

"So what do you make of it?"

"Well," Doc hesitated. "I think perhaps you were barking up the wrong tree."

"But she's been killed," protested Benjamin. "Don't say that I'm prone to premonitions."

"No, I'm not saying that. What I am saying is that those men over there didn't want SHEPH for it. They had their own inside men to do it."

"So what about SHEPH?"

"Probably Drim Balhi had it for his own personal activities in some other country."

"Perhaps he stole it for the Russians," Benjamin suggested.

"I can't think that's at all likely, Ben. If the Russians wanted it they would have, after stealing it, just put it in a diplomatic bag and shipped it out. That's how they get much of their equipment for their experts to copy; saves them millions."

"Typical," Benjamin remarked. "I think their communist society would collapse without capitalist American grain and Western technology."

“Yes, well that's as may be, but Vlatsov and Drim Balhi are unlikely to have gone to the trouble of paying Daniel to ship the stuff if it was merely for analyzing. Remember, they probably got the formula out of Taylor anyway before they got rid of him.”

"You reckon he was killed then?"

"I have no doubts about that at all."

"Well it fits," Benjamin commented, before getting back to the subject of SHEPH. He was pleased. If anyone had thought Edward was still alive, Doc would have heard, he was sure. "So what do you think all this killing and secrecy was for?"

"I honestly don't know, Ben. I have a terrible feeling that the owners of SHEPH had something to do with it."

"Meaning?"

"Meaning governments," stated Doc without elaborating further.

There was a pause as Benjamin thought of Hart. "Christ Doc, won't they stop at anything?"

"I'm not forced to be right, Ben. All I'm saying is that the SHEPH thing is over and out of our lives. They're leaving us alone, and it's none of our business now where it went. Your theory that they'd imported it to assassinate Mrs. Gandhi was wrong, and that's that. From now on we should keep our noses out of the matter; otherwise we're likely to get clobbered for interfering with national security."

"I'd better ring off then," Benjamin said. "I'll get in touch later, but I want to watch the Nine O'clock News."

"Okay. Ben lad, we'll look forward to your calling. Cheerio." He hung up.

Benjamin sat with the receiver in his hand for at least five minutes. He thought about Daniel and how he had almost got his come-uppance for dealing with international terrorists. He thought about a mercenary called Drim Balhi importing a top secret explosive into New Delhi. He thought about a Bulgarian terrorist. What was he up to, he wondered? He thought about the Indian Prime Minister, and then glanced at his watch. One minute to nine. He banged down the handpiece, jumped up and switched on the television. Dianne came through from the kitchen where she'd thrown together some tea and sandwiches. She looked at him and smiled, but then realised something was wrong. "What's the matter darling?" she asked and put her hands in his.

"You'll see," he said and pointed to the television. He had just enough time to pour Dianne and himself a whiskey before the familiar sound of the music, that preceded the Nine O'clock News, rang through the lounge.

The news headlines were predictable. *'Assassination of Indira Gandhi.'* He listened to the documentary about her, how she had strived to unite India; how she had close military and economic links with Russia; how she had intervened in the war in East Pakistan which broke away from West Pakistan and formed the new country of Bangladesh; establishing India as one of the main forces in that part of the globe; how she had recently overthrown Sikh extremists in the Golden Temple at Amritsar; a whole breakdown of events leading to two Sikh bodyguards killing her in a fit of religious extremism.

"I don't believe it," Benjamin exclaimed. "Two religious fanatics!" Dianne stared speechlessly at the news bulletin.

The newscaster went on to say that Rajiv, the son of Indira Gandhi was sworn in as new premier later that afternoon, along with four cabinet ministers, and he had announced a twelve day period of mourning for his mother. Benjamin shook his head. "There's something wrong somewhere," he told Dianne. He had been convinced that SHEPH had been intended for the job of killing Mrs. Gandhi. Now, well he wasn't so sure.

"Perhaps the Indian security forces have found it and so the assassins had to find an alternative way of carrying out their plan. After all, it was a sledge hammer to crack a nut. The assassination has succeeded just as well with two fanatics and a hand gun, without any need to blow up anybody. It was probably just a last resort in case all else failed," she said to try and stop him worrying.

"Yes, that's it," Benjamin tried to convince himself. He put down his glass and turned off the television. "Come on then," he said. "Let's have something to eat and then I've a visit to make." Fifteen minutes later they picked up their coats and went out of his apartment.

The television was already on when they arrived at his father-in-law's house. Laura had just made some fresh coffee "You're just in time for the Late Evening News," she said to Benjamin and Dianne. "Cup of coffee?"

"Yes please," they both said together.

She poured them each a cup and then turned up the volume of the television. The newscaster was already describing the events in India. He told of the violence in the union territory of Delhi. Hundreds of Sikhs were being set upon and killed by angry gangs of Hindus, with apparently little or no attempt on behalf of the police to protect them. In Delhi a curfew was declared and the army was out in force. Trains and Sikh temples were being attacked and there were many other incidents of arson and looting, in particular in the commercial area around Connaught Place, where entire blocks of buildings were being razed to the ground. There was a general wave of riots throughout the northern states of India.

Rajiv Gandhi was reported as trying to calm the inflammatory situation. "The Sikh community is an inseparable part of India," he said. "The Sikhs played a glorious role in the freedom struggle and in the building up of an independent India. To subject Sikhs as a whole to violence and indignity for what a few misguided individuals have done, however heinous their crime, is most irrational and not becoming of our heritage of tolerance."

"Sounds a sensible sort of chap," Benjamin remarked.

"Well, I think he's right. The majority of people don't want anything to do with all this agitation and violence. We get it the same in Britain where a minority of extremists infiltrate a community and break it apart by setting otherwise peaceful people at each other's throats."

"You mean Northern Ireland?"

"That for one," said Doc. "It ends in civil war. But you get agitants who go wherever there is a likelihood of trouble. Take the riots in Toxteth with black against white in a community where most people get on all right together until someone puts a petrol bomb through your letterbox. Most of these agitants are never seen. They mingle in with a crowd. Nobody knows they don't belong there, so they let them lead them into an irreversible head-on collision."

"I suppose that sums up most of ordinary people like you and me," said Benjamin, pointing to the news program which was now covering the miners' strike. "We're all too willing to let somebody else do the leading for us."

"That's because most of us are happy to get on with what we're doing," Laura butted in. "That's why, when people like you get mixed up with international terrorists, you're out of your league. I think you were damned lucky not to get killed the same as your brother. I'd have disowned him long ago I'm afraid. He was a no good crook that got out of his depth."

"Now now," Doc placated. "Benjamin had nothing to do with that side of it."

"I didn't say he did. But Daniel nearly got him killed. I wonder what sort of brotherly love that is."

"He was trying to leave Ben a fortune. Hardly a sign of a brother who hates him," Doc scolded. Benjamin felt he should tell them about Daniel, but something stopped him. He thought Daniel would not appreciate going through the whole facade of being killed and leaving everything he had to his brother and his close friend Dianne, if his brother then told everybody he was still alive. Dianne said nothing, she just watched him as if to let him make up his own mind.

“He's still my brother, Laura, whatever he's done," Ben began defensively. "I could have asked him to risk his life for me," he explained, "and he would have."

Laura sat and studied for a moment then she sighed deeply and stood up. "Oh, I'm sorry Ben love, but it just seemed so outrageous to get you involved with his stealing top secret weapons. If he were still alive I'd have said he'd done it to..."

"To what?" asked Benjamin.

"Oh well, to draw everybody's attention away from him."

Benjamin chuckled. "Well it might just have worked if he'd thought of it that way. It's a pity they blew him up first."

Dianne smiled. She realised that Benjamin's anger was abating. "I think, sometimes you show definite criminal traits in your character, Ben," Doc concluded.

Benjamin shrugged. "Well, I wouldn't have done the things Daniel is supposed to have." He drank down the last of his coffee. "Goodness knows what I'm going to do with the money he's left me," he said, thinking about giving it back to Daniel somehow. "I'm quite comfortable enough off doing my own thing," he added to convince himself he didn't need it. "I've built my business up from nothing and I enjoy being able to say I did it on my own. It won't be the same with money I haven't earned."

"You'll get used to it my boy, don't worry," said Doc.

"You'll have to get used to my money anyway," Dianne said seriously. She knew what her future husband was thinking. "I bought those shares we sold. I didn't have them given," she reminded him.

"There you are then Ben," Doc said. "She's worked for her money the same as you. You can hardly decide not to share each other's money if you're getting married."

Benjamin nodded. He would feel more rational tomorrow.

They left Doc's late and weren't in their beds before 2.00 a.m. Dianne was asleep before her head hit the pillow. Benjamin was wide awake. There was something wrong, something not what it should be. His mind cast back, doubting his fears. With all that had happened he had turned out to be wrong. He remembered how he applied his story of the eagle and the hawk to what he thought had happened to Daniel, and instead of Jack Hart being the eagle he had turned out to be a dove. Some dove!

It was four o'clock when he finally succumbed to sleep and it was five thirty when he suddenly jumped awake, his eyes staring into the darkness of the room, and the continental quilt clinging to his body which was soaked in perspiration. "You all right?" Dianne said wearily and lifted her head off the pillow.

"I am now," he replied and jumped out of bed. The cool air made him shiver as he struggled to pull on his dressing gown over his damp body. "I am now sweetheart. I have to see Daniel."

"Why?" she asked in a sleepy drone.

"Got to get hold of Hart," Benjamin exclaimed as he tied the belt of the dressing gown with a determined jerk. "It's got to be the eagle and the hawk this time!" he shouted.

"What on earth are you going on about?" Dianne asked wearily.

"I am going on about what we see and what we think we see," Benjamin answered tersely. "Vlatsov may or may not be behind the assassination of Mrs. Gandhi, but her killers were only the hawk. The eagle hasn't drawn blood yet!"

Dianne gave a baffled shrug. "Can't you ring him?" she asked.

"Have you got his number?"

"In my coat pocket," Dianne muttered. "I always make a note of telephone numbers when I'm at someone's house."

"I don't know how I could manage without you," Benjamin said affectionately. He gave her a kiss on the forehead and disappeared into the lounge before she could ask him any further questions. She could hear him dialing a number.

"Hello," a weary voice said at the other end of the line.

"Benjamin here. You all right."

"Nothing wrong with me," Daniel replied indignantly.

"I saw Hart yesterday morning."

"Yeah, so he told me."

"You saw him as well?"

"Sure. Anything wrong with that?" He was still angry at Benjamin, not for losing his temper with him, but for upsetting Marietta. She'd said she would never forgive Benjamin and Dianne for the way they'd treated Daniel.

"Do you know where I can reach him?"

"What do you want him for?"

"I have something to discuss with him, all right?"

"Sure, I'll get him for you."

Benjamin grinned. So Hart and Daniel were good enough friends for him to stay the night as a guest! The extension line opened and Hart spoke.

"What can I do for you?" he asked in a not too unfriendly tone.

"It's about SHEPH," Benjamin stated.

"Well, what about it?"

"Not meant for Mrs. Gandhi at all!"

"Obviously. Is that what you've called me for in the middle of the night?" he asked patiently.

"I know who it's for."

"Oh do you? Well pray tell."

"You won't believe me."

"So what the hell are you ringing me for man?" Hart shouted.

"Do you have any idea what it was taken over there for?"

"No damned idea," Hart said with an unconcerned air.

"Vlatsov is a Soviet agent, isn't he?"

"Sort of. The Bulgarians do a lot of the dirty work for the Politburo so that the Kremlin can deny having any connection with whatever foul deeds they may carry out."

"Exactly! No connection with the murder of Mrs. Gandhi."

"Now there are some things we can't pin on the Politburo as much as we'd like to," Hart scolded.

"But just say for a minute that the insurgency and the terrorism that's been going on have been stirred up by an outside power?"

"It's possible. It's a common Trotsky type of strategy. Communism can't thrive where there's strong democracy. It can only feed on discontent. That's what revolutions are made of."

"It would take a lot more than that though to allow the Russians into India," Benjamin observed.

"A lot more," Hart confirmed.

"How much more? Total civil war? War with other nations? What?"

"God knows." Hart was being very patient.

"What if a load, say a hundred politicians and heads of state were to be killed in one assassination attempt? The turmoil would be enough to allow a ready power to slip in the back door."

"Impossible. If they could do it then all hell might break out in many countries that are sensitively balanced. But it would be impossible to co-ordinate all that many all at once. The timing would have to be to the minute."

"Even if they were all together."

"Well that would be easier," Hart began to say. "Hold on, are you thinking what I think you're thinking?"

"What's the best way to kill the heads of state of umpteen countries all at once? What's the best way to get them all together? What sort of device could be used to do the job correctly, other than a nuclear bomb? And what device could the Russians say was planted by the Americans?"

"Jesus! You have a warped mind," Hart shouted down the line.

"I see," Benjamin said and was about to tell him to go to hell.

"But so have those damned Reds," Hart exclaimed. "With their infiltration into the media, it's more than likely that it would be reported as an American plot to move into an independent nation that is friendly with Russia."

"And what would Russia do?"

"Probably move in to protect it like they did in Afghanistan!"

"So what do you think?"

"As I said, I think you have a warped mind. I'll let you know if you're on the right trail." He rang off.

*****

It was seven thirty when Daniel rang back. "I'm going to India with Hart," he announced.

"What the hell for? Don't they have operatives over there? It'll be the only place they don't if they haven't," Benjamin complained.

"I can identify Drim Balhi. They know who he is but nobody ever got to meet him first hand."

"And you did of course! Well you know what you're letting yourself in for if that thing blows up anywhere near you, don't you?"

"That's why I'm calling. To ask you to take care of Marietta if anything happens to me."

"Since when did you start to fight their battles for them?" Benjamin said angrily. "What have they ever done for you?"

"I shouldn't have to answer that. *You* nearly killed me because you found out *they'd* helped me escape instead of blowing me up."

Benjamin fell silent for a moment. "When are you going?"

"Morning flight in about two hours."

"Not long to make up in then," Benjamin said sadly. "You realise Marietta will probably hate me for you going as much as she hates me for hitting you in your own home?"

"I'll explain it to her. Hart has asked me to thank you for everything."

"Least I could do."

"Same goes for me. Solong, see you later." Daniel hung up leaving Benjamin with so many things to say. So many things he wanted to say because something in his bones told him that if Daniel went, he would never come back alive, so many things that he would never have said any other time. He stabbed the cradle and got a dialing tone. He dialed and waited for what seemed like hours and then Edward answered.

"Hello," he said sleepily.

"Edward. Benjamin here. Can you tell me if there's any way to disable SHEPH?"

"How do you mean?"

"I mean, if someone found it, could they make it safe?" There was a silence for a minute and then Edward grunted.

"They've found it then? You know what that means?"

"What?"

"That they have proof I stole it. The only reason the police weren't able to hold me was that they couldn't prove any was stolen in the first place."

"It hasn't been found. They think they have some idea where it is and who has it, but they think it's to be used at a particular time and place. What I want to know, is if it's about to be detonated, how can it be made safe."

"It would be better for me to let it be exploded."

"And deadly for Daniel. They've taken him with them to identify the man who has it."

"Then all I can do is tell you to keep away from it."

"No way of doing it at all?"

There was another long silence and then Edward answered. "It has to be detonated."

"Why, just to save you? They don't know you exist! They think you're dead."

"How do you know that?"

"Because they blew Roland up in the car that Daniel was in. Hart had orders to kill you and had agreed to save Daniel. He had to look to have made sure Daniel was dead to appease some French idiots. It's all very complicated, but you're Matthew Roland now. Edward's dead."

"Well, that's nice to know. But I meant what I said. It has to be detonated. If it is set alight it just burns like any other hydrocarbon incendiary."

"Like petrol you mean?"

"Right. So if it were found and the detonators removed, there would be little risk to anyone if it were set alight."

"Does the American know this?"

"Doubtful. I hadn't produced my final report on it, only some of the more successful test data. I made a point of never showing the powers that be the deficiencies in my products until I'd sold them on the advantages. Helped keep me in a good salary. By the time my final reports were due I'd already agreed with the guy called Belk to get the stuff out to him."

"But detonated, it would do what we said it would do?"

"Oh yes. Every bit of it."

"Can you give me any idea how it will be detonated?"

"Ordinary detonators."

"From a long distance, of course?"

"Yes, Radio controlled I should think."

"But you've no idea what device or signal code they would use?"

"It would be a group signal to prevent accidental detonation. That sort of device is fairly standard for covert operations you know."

"A jammer, wouldn't that stop it?"

"Would have to be a damned good one to make sure."

"Right. Now you stay there Edward, and Dianne will be in touch. I'll see you in a few days." He was about to hang up when Edward shouted.

"One other thing. If you find it and do want to burn it, all you have to do is leave a trail of something inflammable to it. You'll be safe fifteen yards away until it gets hold."

"Thanks Edward. I'll see what we can do for you, I promise."

CHAPTER 23.

1st November.

Reluctantly, Dianne dropped Benjamin at the airport. She hadn't wanted him to get mixed up in any more of the C.I.A.'s shady goings on, but he'd persuaded her that, if Daniel had gone to India to identify Drim Balhi, then he was, indeed, in very grave danger, not only from the man himself, but from the effects of the explosion should SHEPH ever be used.

He caught up with Daniel and Jack in the international departure lounge. "Come to see us off?" Jack asked sarcastically as he looked at the sports bag Benjamin was carrying.

"I fancied a trip to India," Benjamin said in an off handed way. "I think it's about time I saw a bit more of the world."

"Didn't you see enough in the army?" Daniel grinned.

"Didn't stay in long enough," Benjamin said. "But I'd have thought you'd have seen enough of India to last you a lifetime."

"I'll tell you something," Daniel replied. "I could never see enough of that place. It would take a lifetime to see everything that country has to offer."

"Sightseeing trip is it then?" Benjamin said.

"I reckon I owe Jack one. And besides, somebody has to care."

"The difference is, Jack and his gang are paid to care."

"If it's money Daniel wants, I'll arrange for him to be paid what I get." Jack chuckled. "That'll be a real come down!"

"Well as far as I'm concerned," Benjamin said indignantly, "it was my theory, and I reckon I should be allowed to tag along to see if I was right."

"You don't seem to realise how dangerous this SHEPH stuff is," Jack argued. "If it goes up, it'll take us all with it."

"It isn't forced to go up," Benjamin replied.

"True, but if we locate it, SHEPH will have to be detonated whether we like it or not. We can't afford to let it fall into the hands of the Indians. They would accuse us of every killing that's gone on in India since their independence."

"What you have to do, is stop somebody else from detonating it first," Benjamin emphasized. "You'll need a radio jammer."

"That's a long shot isn't it?" Daniel broke in. "They could use a timing device."

"Not with any accuracy. How many funerals do you know that have run on time. There would only be a few minutes to play with even at walking pace. A quarter of an hour's delay and you've missed your target even with something as powerful as SHEPH."

"We'll get one don't worry," Jack said and smiled pleasantly. "Welcome to the team."

Benjamin shrugged his shoulders at Daniel. "Seems like you've got me along whether you like it or not," he said to his brother.

"I wasn't complaining," Daniel stated. "In fact, I feel a damned sight safer now, for some reason."

The flight to Delhi was long and tiring; with three more stops before finally landing at Palam International Airport. All three travelled as reporters. Since Jack Hart had already got all the necessary papers for himself and Daniel who was travelling under his new name of Jason Hamilton and he got a last minute visa for Benjamin and pushed a camera bag into his hand. He was to travel as a photographer. "I just hope you don't expect me to use this thing, that's all," Benjamin remarked. "I never got the hang of the Polaroid." The disguise worked well enough for him to get into India with little difficulty. The hotels were not fully booked at the time of year, and since the rioting, custom was flowing away rapidly. They all booked into the *Oberoi Intercontinental* for three nights. Daniel and Jack had already booked ahead and got adjacent rooms. Benjamin was one storey higher, but it mattered little. The rooms would only be used separately for sleeping in. The rest of the time they would be working together.

"Stayed here before I suppose?" Benjamin said to Daniel as they assembled in Jack's room.

"Didn't have much time to enjoy it then," Daniel complained.

"Nor will you now," Jack emphasized. "We've one day to find that bomb, one day and then it's the day of the funeral."

"Have you got a timetable?" asked Benjamin.

"They don't issue bloody timetables," Daniel scolded. "They don't work like that over here. Everything's planned by the day and they fit as much as they can in at their own pace."

"What pace is that?"

"Boringly slow most of the time. The Indians have a relaxed way of going about their lives."

"Yes, I heard they meditate a lot."

"There'll be nothing boring for us," Jack interrupted. "After we've eaten, we'll have to get some sleep. There is a curfew once it's dark and we'll need all the daylight we can get. On top of that, Rajiv Gandhi has brought in the army and tanks to quell the rioting and has ordered that looters and arsonists be shot on sight."

"And we're supposed to be going to go out and find somebody in all that!" Benjamin exclaimed. "We'll be lucky if we aren't killed before we've gone fifty yards."

"For God's sake Ben," Daniel yelled. "Where's your backbone!"

"Connected to the rest of my body," Benjamin replied. "Which is more than it will be if they get their kirpans on us."

"It isn't the Sikhs that are of any threat to us," Jack explained. "It's the enraged Hindus. Whatever your theory, and despite the fact that Washington has given me the go ahead to investigate it, the Sikhs are being lumped together and squarely framed for the death of their leader. Whether it was Sikh fanaticism or a well executed incitement to riot, they're all being hounded for what has happened."

"How will we get a radio jammer?" Benjamin asked.

"I have a man who has connections with the Indian air force. He says there's a possibility that they can borrow one from them if they think there's any truth in the story we tell them. He's already put it to the Indian Security Service, and they're thinking about it."

"And has he got a map of the route the funeral procession is going to take?" Daniel asked.

"He'll bring that first thing in the morning. After we've studied that, we might have some idea what we're doing."

"That sounds unlikely," Benjamin quipped.

He was back at Jack's room at six in the morning. Daniel was already there and there were two other men there as well. One was an obese American called Walter Basset who perspired perpetually, the other was an Indian Secret Service man whose first name was Ram, but Benjamin didn't catch his last name. "Ram's been assigned by the Indian Security to give us all the help he can. We've told them why we're here, and they respect our motives, irrespective of the fact that they think we're a load of loonies," Jack announced. "He's told us the funeral route will be the normal route taken for state funerals, and it will pass through the centre of the city."

"Hell fire," Benjamin shouted. "That means that anybody could have planted a bomb in any of a thousand buildings. The entourage will trundle past at the traditional Indian pace. They'll be sitting ducks!"

"Unfortunately, we don't fully accept your theory that you think some one has planted a bomb to kill the visiting heads of state," Ram said in a Cambridge accent. "First of all, the bomb would have to be so great that it would have been found by the search force already." Benjamin felt he should remain quiet about the actual type of explosive. "Secondly," Ram continued, "even if it were hidden well, we have sniffer dogs and sniffing apparatus for detecting explosives."

"Well, how about a radio jammer then?"

"We can get you one of those. If the device does exist, then I agree that they would use a radio signal to detonate it."

"How will it be operated?" Jack asked.

"It will be installed in one of the tanks in the city centre. It will be powerful enough to jam all radio signals within half a mile. The tank will go ahead of the procession so as to give it a covering blanket beam."

"And what about our best clue?" Benjamin asked.

"I'm going to take you to where I saw him," Daniel asserted. "Otherwise there's not much chance of finding him."

"We've already circulated his description," said Ram. "Unfortunately I should imagine the man we know as Drim Balhi will be keeping a very low profile. Only if he realises the jammer is working, then he might just come out to detonate the bomb less remotely." Nobody bothered to explain to him the unlikely possibility of that.

They all set off, soon afterwards, to the house where Daniel had delivered the crate. They were accompanied by six armed soldiers in an armoured truck, whilst they led the way in a Ford Transit. The house had been burned to the ground along with a row of other houses next to it, during the riots. "Oh well," Daniel said apologetically, "I didn't expect him to hang about waiting for me to return."

"What now?" Benjamin asked Ram.

"I already have men patrolling the route as part of the peace keeping operation. Another four pairs of eyes won't hurt."

"If that's the best we can do," Jack said despondently. They paired off with Daniel and Jack and Benjamin and Ram together and spent a fruitless morning driving back and forth along the funeral route. Walter Basset went his own way. The only people anyone saw were soldiers going in and out of houses searching for explosives and arms. They met again for a meal at the hotel and discussed their failure to turn anything up with little conclusion how to get any better results. In the cool autumn afternoon they carried on the same boring routine until daylight faded and Ram escorted them back to the safety of the hotel.

"I'll meet you again in the morning," he said and left the three Westerners to discuss their theory again. His orders were to help them, but he knew they were crackpots, every one of them.

"Well, what do you think?" Jack asked them when they regrouped in his room after their evening meal.

"I think, if I'm stuck with Ram again in the morning, I might as well stay in bed," Benjamin said disparagingly. "He doesn't know what we're looking for so how the hell can he help us?"

"Drim Balhi would stand out in any crowd," Daniel stated.

"Well I saw a dozen soldiers today who could have been the size of a gorilla under all their gear."

"My God!" Daniel exclaimed. "I wasn't looking at the soldiers!"

"What the hell do you think Drim Balhi is?" Benjamin asked. "You don't expect him to be waltzing around the centre of Delhi in his Savile Row suit do you?"

"Well I still didn't see any soldiers resembling him," Daniel said defensively. "I'm sure I would have recognised him if I had."

"And what's more, we're looking in the wrong place," Benjamin claimed.

"Why?" Jack asked. "The planned route is the best place to look."

"Well, if I were going to plant the explosive, and I knew its potential I'd not plant it there."

"Then where the hell would you plant it?" he said impatiently.

"About three blocks back from the route. Near enough to reach the target with the explosive force, and well inside the fire circle, but far enough away for anyone who thought we were looking for conventional explosives to miss out of their area of search all together."

Jack and Daniel looked at each other and then Daniel spoke. "Why the bloody hell didn't you say that this morning?"

"He couldn't," Jack stated. "Ram wouldn't have believed us unless we explained exactly what kind of explosive we were talking about."

"Then we either have to tell him or get him out of the way," Benjamin said coldly.

"The only way we can drive down the back roads is if he's accompanying us," Jack stated.

"Then I vote we tell him something he'll believe."

"What I want to know Ben," Jack said patronizingly, "is how come you know so much about this damned explosive."

"Well it's a super high explosive plastic hydrocarbon isn't it?" he asked as if it were common place.

"Oh, well yeah," Jack said with a deep frown. "I didn't know that you Brits knew about such things."

"Only what I learned at school," Benjamin said with his poker face.

"Jesus," Jack said after a moment's thought. "You sure do know how to take the piss!"

"You don't believe me do you?" Benjamin asked, his feelings seriously hurt.

"You're damned right I don't."

"Oh well, it'll all be academic by this time tomorrow," Benjamin said with a yawn. "See you at breakfast." He got up and walked out.

"There's something uncanny about that brother of yours," he said to Daniel as he also got up to leave.

"Don't ask me what," Daniel smiled. "I never could fathom him properly."

3rd November.

"Ram," Jack said sincerely, "we've something to tell you." Ram turned his attention to the American. "We haven't told you that Benjamin is an explosives expert." Benjamin stared at Jack in disbelief. "He hasn't told you the reason we suspect this plot is hatching is because he knows that a new explosive was stolen from a French factory."

"Why do you wait till now to tell me?" asked Ram.

"Because he didn't explain how dangerous it was. It can reach the main route of the funeral from three streets away." We need to look along the other roads that run away from and behind the main road."

"You think that I believe that do you?"

"We aren't here to play games with you Ram," Benjamin asserted. "I only realised the seriousness of it yesterday when I heard what kind of explosive had been stolen. If we could borrow your men we could find it I'm sure. It probably won't be all that well hidden because the people who stole it will not expect anyone to search for it so far away."

"If you are having a joke with me, I warn you, I can have you shot," Ram stated.

"And knowing that, do you think we would have risked our arses coming over here?" Jack demanded. "Do you think we have no wives and family to sit at home with? What the hell else other reason would we be here for, tell me that?"

"You will have to excuse me," Ram said suddenly and stood up. "I will have to report this to the Chief of Security." He stepped quickly out of the room stating that he would be back shortly.

"Why me?" Benjamin asked Jack as the door closed behind Ram.

"Because you know a damned sight more than I do and I was in touch with the Research Centre from where the stuff went missing. I reckon that you haven't played all your cards yet either," he added.

"I liked the French bit," Daniel grinned."

"Sure," Jack chuckled. "If that damned thing does blow then we want the attention turned away from us don't we!"

"You slimy old sod," Benjamin laughed, but then became serious. "You must also tell them that I must be the one to disarm it if it's found," he added.

"Hell, you'll blow yourself up!" Daniel shouted. "If it's to be destroyed, let them do it."

"Wrong. I know what I'm talking about. If it's found, then the jammers must be brought nearby and I must be taken to it, right?"

"Okay I'll go along with you," Jack agreed. "Up to now you seem to have been ahead of us anyway. Why not let you get killed first as well?"

"Seriously Jack," Benjamin said, "will you do that or not?"

"Seriously Ben boy," Jack stated, "you're welcome to the fucking thing if it still has the detonators in it."

Five minutes later Ram knocked and entered the room. "We have four patrol vehicles and two hundred men at our disposal. One of us in each truck to keep in radio contact at all times. The jammer will not be used until the procession is on its way."

"What're we waiting for?" Jack shouted and jumped up. The sooner we get looking the sooner we find it."

"We rendezvous at noon," ordered Ram. Each of them was accompanied in their truck by two armed soldiers. No doubt the soldiers had their orders, but nobody asked what they were.

After the first hour each had done one pass of their chosen area. The foot soldiers methodically started searching the houses from the beginning of the route.

"Nothing here," Benjamin said to the others over the radio.

The others came back with the same answer. "We'll do another run the in the opposite direction," Ram ordered. Again, there was nothing but a few hiding residents and several smoldering burned-out houses. The presence of armed soldiers and tanks had suppressed the looting and the violence. They passed back through the areas being searched. Again there was no sign of success. It was nearly eleven o'clock, less than an hour to the beginning of the funeral procession. The searching soldiers had covered less than a third of the route. They were running in and out of the houses like ants. The search was hardly thorough. It would have taken them three days at least to do their task properly.

"Let's try again shall we?" Jack asked. "Time for one more pass."

"All right," Ram agreed and they began again. They heard Ram speak to his Commanding Officer. He suggested that all visiting heads of state be driven separately and at intervals to the funeral site. The answer came back that the order had already been given and was being implemented. His final instruction was that a detour of the procession should be made. That order he sent by personal messenger. Nobody was to know the route had been changed until the leaders of the procession were actually directed up Mathura Road.

By 11.30 the four patrolling trucks were well away from the scurrying foot soldiers. "Hart here, I've just seen soldiers leaving a house where no soldiers have reached yet."

"How many?" Ram asked.

"Four, two big ones and two little ones." Benjamin and Daniel were heading towards his section before he'd stopped talking.

"Give your exact position," Ram ordered. "Jammers proceed to location." Jack read out the street signs as he approached the four men. They were getting into an army jeep when they spotted the truck coming towards them. They stepped back out and waved the truck down. Jack slammed on his breaks to keep as much distance as he could between himself and the four men. He could see plainly now the face of the man they had all been seeking. There was no mistaking the description Daniel had given them. He had thought Daniel had exaggerated, but now he'd seen the man himself, he knew that the superlatives Daniel had used were right. "Got a positive I.D. on Drim Balhi!" he shouted and threw the truck into reverse as their automatic weapons began to come up level with the windscreen. The guns rattled and the windscreen shattered. Jack threw himself across the front seat as the two soldiers returned fire. They both fell bleeding on top of him and pinned him down.

Drim Balhi and his men began to run towards the truck when they saw another truck coming in the opposite direction. They turned and fired, causing it to veer wildly and crash into a shop front. The driver was killed outright. The two soldiers followed shortly after him. Drim Balhi ordered his men into the jeep and they ran towards it as a third truck came from nowhere and slammed into it, throwing the four men out onto the road. Two soldier opened fire but too late to hit Drim Balhi's fleeing men. Now they were on foot. Daniel pulled out the keys and jumped out of the opposite side of the truck. The two soldiers followed and took cover behind the front wheels as a spray of bullets hit the tyres. He kept his head down. The two soldiers were the only armed men on his side. They returned fire and almost immediately one of them fell hard, face down, on the concrete road. He didn't feel it; he was dead before he dropped his gun. It had tumbled out onto the open road. Daniel knew that Drim Balhi was a real professional. He would pick him off as soon as he tried to get at it. "For God's sake keep your bloody head down!" he shouted at the remaining armed soldier. He didn't understand and peeped over the bonnet as a hail of bullets took the top of his head clean off. Daniel grabbed the Sten-gun from his hands as the soldier collapsed in a bloody heap beside him.

“Right you bastard big fucking gorilla!" he shouted and swung the gun over the bonnet as it sprayed bullets at the four mercenaries. They'd moved and were ready to rush out at the back of the truck, using it for cover. But then, suddenly, a burst of gunfire came from across the road behind Daniel. It was a short controlled burst, a professional attack. It cut one of the big men down and lamed a smaller man as he rebounded with the shock of an unseen enemy. Daniel knew who was behind him when he heard a second controlled burst. He ran to the back of the truck and fired around the back the same way. He was remembering now. All his training in the army. He had never really taken to it, but now he wanted to. Now he knew he had to. There were still two highly trained soldiers facing him and his brother, and their remembered skill would decide the outcome.

Then the men in the shop opened fire again, and again a soldier fell. Daniel glanced behind and caught a glimpse of the Indian falling forward into the road. He thought it had been Benjamin. "Where the hell are you?" He shouted in despair as he realised he was alone again. "You're never around when you're most needed," he shouted as he gritted his teeth. He had to move or they would rush him. He fired another burst blindly around the corner of the truck before there was a sickening click. "Jesus Christ all bloody mighty!" he almost sobbed as he realised the magazine was empty. He had to get to the other gun that had fallen clear of the truck. Not much chance, but he had no choice. He ran back to the front of the truck and crouched ready to spring for it. His eyes fell on the soldier whose gun he'd grabbed. He knew the mercenaries would cut him in half before he touched the fallen weapon. He searched the soldier for a spare magazine but to no avail. "Oh well," he said quietly and prepared to try for the other gun. "Here goes." He sprang forward as his ears were filled with the sound of automatic fire again. He landed on the Sten-gun and rolled over expecting to be torn to pieces at any moment, when he realised he could hear the same familiar controlled bursts of fire from behind him. Drim Balhi was firing but not towards him. He rolled back without a single bullet coming his way. Those soldiers knew how to draw fire thank God. They knew how to use a Sten-gun as well. It was the other one from the remaining truck. He was giving Drim Balhi hell.

Daniel swung his gun over the bonnet and fired as he saw the other small man thrown back into the dark interior of the shop. He fired again as he saw Drim Balhi flick lightly from one side of the opening to the other. There was no return fire as he emptied his gun at the moving target. He couldn't tell if he'd hit or had missed until out of the darkness loomed a huge creature that looked like a man but was the size of a bear. It growled like a wounded bull elephant as it sprang at him with the agility of a tiger. There would be no stopping that, he thought as he braced himself to take the impact.

Benjamin's gun was empty too. He had got the message from Jack Hart just as the second soldier in his truck had gone to relieve himself. He hadn't waited, but drove away in the direction of his American friend as fast as he could. He arrived to see one truck stopped in the middle of the road with no sign of life from the occupants slumped in the front. A second truck was steaming as its nose rested inside a shop front. Again the occupants had been killed. Daniel was pinned behind the third truck and was about to be out-flanked by all four mercenaries. "Not a single one!" Benjamin swore at the Indian soldier. "They haven't got a single one!" He grabbed the spare Sten-gun and ran to the cover of a street corner, firing a controlled burst as he went. He hit a big one squarely in the chest and a small one in the backside as he scrambled back inside the shop.

The soldier with him stood clear to open fire and was hit immediately without firing a shot. "Bloody hell fire!" he swore as he saw Daniel swing his gun around the back of the truck and fire on an empty magazine. He watched as Daniel moved to the front of the truck again. He watched him search in vain for more ammunition and then, as he was about to go for the gun in the road, Benjamin saw Drim Balhi and his remaining man get ready to open fire. They hadn't seen him. His first burst of gunfire had taken them by surprise, and when they shot the soldier who was with him they must have thought they had got the man who had done the shooting. Benjamin opened fire as he saw Daniel spring forward. He hit the small man in the face and killed him outright. Drim Balhi spun around and returned fire to cover his retreat into the shop. Benjamin fired his last four rounds after him. He went to find the other soldier's gun but it had jammed. "No wonder he didn't get a shot off!" he said aloud and then saw the awful figure of a giant beginning his run at Daniel. He was out of ammunition as well then!

Without thinking he found himself running forward and closing the gap between himself and his brother. The giant was doing the same, only he was slightly nearer Daniel as he rounded the corner of the truck. Daniel's foot stopped Drim Balhi's genitals but the rest of the huge wall of bone and sinew bore down like a fleshless tank. His fist hit the huge chin of his attacker and he felt every bone crumble in his hand. The death-like eyes stared at him in anger but the plate-like hands hesitated for just a split second when the eyes recognised the man that was about to be torn to pieces. It was him! He had a second chance to kill this pestilent little Englishman. It was that split second of hesitation that saved Daniel's life.

Benjamin was at full speed as he neared the big man. He took off in one big leap as Drim Balhi leaned over his prey, and he brought his leg through with all its momentum of the take off. The heel of his shoe stopped dead against Drim Balhi's temple, and as the pain shot up Benjamin's leg he saw the giant topple sideways away from him and his brother. He landed on his knees knowing he'd broken his ankle, and fought the pain as he pushed himself upright. Drim Balhi was stunned, his eyes stared forward angrily, fixed in their sockets and gazing where Daniel would have been if he hadn't toppled sideways. The pain in Benjamin's leg slowed him as he staggered forward to deal another blow.

Daniel took his chance when Drim Balhi fell away from him. He had learned his lesson, not to hit Drim Balhi in a bone. The man was made from solid granite. He swung the edge of his one remaining good hand against the jugular of the stunned man again and again in a frenzied anger until he thought he had no more strength left. He saw Benjamin as he watched through sweat drenched eyes until the life seeped out of the man. He was no longer a big Indian soldier.

"I think that will do it," Benjamin said as he caught a hold of Daniel's arm. Daniel broke out of his trance and sank to his knees in sheer exhaustion. He looked up at his brother.

"I thought it was you behind me," he grinned as he gulped at the air. "Never known anybody as disciplined as you with machine guns."

"Never knew you knew how to use your hands in anger," Benjamin remarked as he balanced on his good foot.

"A friend called Carl showed me a thing or two," he said as he controlled his breath.

"I know him well!" laughed Benjamin. "Not a man to be underestimated is he?"

"Not if he isn't on your side, that's for sure!"

"How's your hand?"

"Bloody broken I think. How's the foot?" he asked as he looked down at a shoe with its side ripped open and grinning as broadly at the two brothers.

"What do you think?' Benjamin laughed painfully.

As they recovered from the relief of survival, they heard the sound of approaching vehicles. "Quickly," Benjamin said, "which house were they coming out of?"

"This shop I think. They parked the jeep outside it."

Benjamin limped inside and frantically searched for the explosive. "Where the hell is it?" he shouted desperately. "Is this what you're looking for?" Daniel asked and pointed to the familiar wooden crate. Benjamin came over and looked at it.

"Is it in that?" he asked skeptically.

"It was when I delivered it," Daniel answered.

Benjamin was already pulling at the lid. Daniel handed him a screwdriver and he prized off the top. In the bottom of the crate was a metal lining and within it was a blue substance that reminded him of *Plasticine*. He pulled out a small box and that, in turn, pulled out three long thin detonators attached by wires. He pulled the detonators off and threw them as far away as he could, tossing the radio device into the back of the shop. He gathered a bundle of packing papers and laid them by the crate, and then spread some on top of the plastic explosive. Daniel just stood beside him and watched in bewilderment. "Match," Benjamin demanded.

"What the hell? You'll kill us and everybody for hundreds of yards around! Have you gone mad?"

"Trust me Daniel. It'll only explode if it's detonated."

"I just hope you're right!" he said and handed his brother a book of matches. Benjamin grabbed some wrapping paper and screwed it up, tore off three matches, struck them and lit the paper. He watched for a second or two and then turned.

"Right, let's get out of here!" The plastic had already caught fire. With Benjamin clinging onto Daniel, they both hobbled out as fast as they could, into the open street and leaned against one of the army truck where Jack had been. He gasped for air as they pulled him from under the fallen soldiers just as four more trucks full of soldiers pulled up and pointed their guns at the potential looters.

CHAPTER 24.

3rd November.

Dianne sat in Benjamin's apartment watching the funeral. It was morning in Britain when the funeral began in India. At a few minutes after India's mid-day the entourage set off from Mrs. Indira Gandhi's childhood home, the home of her father Pandit Jawaharlal Nehru, to travel the seven miles past the Presidential palace where she had lived and died, to the India Gate War Memorial and through the city to Shanti Vana on the banks of the River Yamuna. The Presidential Palace was the place where she had spent much of her life as her father's helper, and later in life as the Prime Minister of India. A gun carriage bore the body, covered in pink and white and red rose petals but leaving her face fully visible. The three scarlet ropes of the gun carriage were each drawn by a line of servicemen, one for the army dressed in red, one for the navy in dark blue, and one for air force in light blue. Ahead marched platoons of juans, the ordinary airmen soldiers and sailors. The family mourners followed on behind in cars, and behind them followed the dignitaries and heads of the Indian states. The visiting Heads of State were driven to the funeral site separately without procession. At no time did they assemble until they reached the fenced enclosure erected specially to keep out the rest of the crowds. There, they waited patiently for the funeral procession to arrive.

So many presidents and prime ministers had gathered to pay their last respects to a leader of a non-aligned government. They had come from the four corners of the globe friend and foe alike.

President Zia of Pakistan, he had been at war with India over Kashmir in 1965, and later over East Pakistan, now Bangladesh. Both times India had shown military superiority, but now, despite rumoured attempts by each leader to have the other assassinated, he paid his last respects.

President Nyerere of Tanzania was there, a president who was dogged by the embarrassment of the tyranny that overtook the Spice Island of Zanzibar in the Indian Ocean, an Island freed of colonialism and immediately taken over by Karume in the name of socialism, and after his assassination, by the Chinese communists to use as a springboard to the African continent.

Yao Yilin the Chinese Deputy Premier, stood there proudly representing yet another country with whom India had been at war in 1962 over border disputes, a country like Russia, now embarked upon the policy of annexation.

Tikhonov the Soviet Prime minister sat quietly waiting for the procession to arrive. He wore a confident expression, for his was the one country that had held hands with and courted India's leaders so successfully. Attending a foreign religious ceremony could only add strength to Russia's atheistic elbow.

George Shultz, the Secretary of State for the United States, a country desperate to woo the Indian continent, if only to prevent its democracy falling under the wing of the communists that surrounded her, a country incapable of seeing that India with its own nuclear weapons and modern strike forces, was quite capable of making its own way in the world. His face was sad.

Even Yassir Arafat was there to represent the non existent state of Palestine, an advocate of terrorism for the minority cause, a Lybian-backed killer of innocent people to bring publicity of his grievance to the world, a man who killed dispassionately, an extremist like Sant Bhindranwale.

Nearly a hundred leaders were there, President Jayawardene of Sri Lanka, Ali Keshtmand the Prime Minister of Afghanistan, President Kaunda of Zambia, Obote of Uganda, Mugabe of Zimbabwe, Djuranovic the President of Yugoslavia, the Prime Minister of Czechoslovakia Lubomir Strougal, Gareth Fitzgerald from Ireland, and Mrs. Thatcher the British Prime Minister. Princess Anne, who had already been in India as president of Save the Children Fund, was there to represent her mother, the Queen, and there were more, many more. Some had come to mourn.

"God, they're all there, Communists, democrats, terrorists and dictators," Dianne exclaimed to herself. "Could Benjamin have been wrong?" A thin wisp of uncertainty threaded itself through her mind. Benjamin had been certain, but now she was no longer sure if he'd been right. They had all diligently avoided the procession, and even gathered as they were at the funeral site, it would have been take one take them all with an explosive like SHEPH. What organization of anarchists would be prepared to kill that many? What cause would that further? Dianne began to believe that Benjamin had been completely wrong. "Bloody hypocrites, the lot of them. Most of them hated her!" she grumbled.

The crowds that gathered along the route, hours earlier, lined the way, and although only three or four deep, the bodyguards of the leaders from ninety four nations of the world realised that it posed a massive security problem. Anyone approaching too near was quickly turned away. The army was out in force, shooting arsonists and looters on sight, following the previous days of rioting and killing in the city. Houses were still burning and the community was still split. The numbers in the crowds were only a fraction of those at her father's and grandfather's funerals, but a policy of stopping all trains and buses, in and out of the city, to prevent more unrest and more killing, seemed to diminish the crowds to a manageable size. The curfew was relaxed only hours before the funeral began. The entourage proceeded past the elegant Rashtrapati Bhavan along the Rajpath, between the two Secretariats, to India Gate.

It was as if the wide open tree-shaded parks and avenues designed by Sir Edwin Lutyens in the Renaissance style were created for just such events, for parades and funeral processions, the dignified spectacle of heroic scale and splendour. The Rashtrapati Bhavan, now the Presidential Palace, and the Secretariat, built by Lord Hardinge, the Viceroy during the 1920's, in the contrasting Oriental style, were obscured by the mid-day haze, giving out an atmosphere of calm, solemn tranquility befitting the occasion.

Dianne hoped that it would remain that way. Her heart beat wildly, expecting the unexpected.

Suddenly and without warning, at India Gate, the procession changed route, avoiding the main shopping area in the centre of the city and heading straight up Mathura Road, parallel to the River Yamuna and through the open fields of Old Delhi. The television cameras showed a pall of black smoke rising from the city in the direction which the procession would have followed. Dianne's heart leaped. If it was diverted for the reason suggested on the news to avoid the burning city centre, a much graver threat had possibly been averted. Her only worry now was what had happened to Benjamin and Daniel?

Even then the bodyguards of the visiting Indian state leaders and dignitaries were still in a state of extreme agitation. Some of them seemed alarmed that they were all travelling together at the back of the procession with the crowds running alongside to follow the new route. The gun carriage was showered with garlands of flowers. As soon as any landed on it, for fear that there may be grenades in them to endanger the following family, they were removed by soldiers, and handed back to the followers who chanted Indira Gandhi kee jai, long live Indira Gandhi. Nobody was heard to shout out the threats to kill Rajiv, the threats that had already been received before the funeral.

Dianne felt edgy. She got up from her seat, switched off the television and went out. She got into the Mercedes and drove over to Doc's.

"What do you think of it so far?" Doc asked after Dianne explained that she had been watching the funeral procession.

"Seems like you and Benjamin had a fit of worrying over nothing," replied his father-in-law. "I told you, they've an excellent secret service over there."

"So good that they let their Prime Minister get shot to death by extremists."

"Dianne love," Doc soothed, "the problems of being a head of state is that you're a target for all sorts of unstable attacks.

They represent an authority, a figurehead, that's all. The chap who shot Spencer Perceval liked him. He just got so unbalanced that any person in authority would do to vent his frustrations on. The world is full of them; all have-nots, all seeking recognition. The President of the United States gets more than two thousand crank threats a year. In Britain the threats are there though most of them are not voiced. The I.R.A. are amongst those wanting to bring society to its knees. It's a full-time job averting their attempts. It's the same in India. It's a huge country and there are a lot of people not happy with their share of power."

"They detoured. That says something."

"It says there was danger in the centre of the city, nothing more."

"Well we aren't likely to know are we?"

"No, so I suggest you watch the funeral and just be happy that whatever it was that Daniel got mixed up in was not the cause of it."

She went through into Doc's sitting room and sat in front of the screen.

"*Mrs. Gandhi was born a High Caste Brahmin, and the funeral ceremony and cremation was carried out in accordance with the scriptures of all Hindus*," the newscaster was saying.

Dianne took it all in.

The cortege took four hours to arrive at the site of the funeral pyre at Shanti Vana, The Forest of Peace, but even then it was one hour ahead of schedule. The risk of planned attack or time bombs had been thwarted, the diversion had worked. A fence had been erected in order to allow the officials and guests to be nearest the fire, and although the fire was on the top of a two tier platform, the ordinary Indians, being only allowed to stand at the back with no terraces and no seats, were prevented from being able to get a perfect view. That applied, equally well, to any potential sniper.

The family carried the body up the steps onto the platform and placed it in position on the ceremonial cremation mound.

The Indian flag that adorned her body was removed, and the funeral pyre built around her. Rajiv Gandhi adorned the dignity of his mother, his face expressionless and serene as he walked around the body with a lighted flame before touching it to the sandalwood logs. The sound of trumpets filled the air as the cremation began. Ghee, a clarified butter was added to the fire to increase the heat and so speed up the burning process. Around the funeral fire, security men outnumbered mourners, although they discretely kept their weapons out of sight, and dressed as professional body burners or in the same fashion as the visiting leaders who had come from all corners of India. In their own good time, they walked up the steps of the two tier platform and poured on their contribution of incenses. Then, backing down the steps, they returned to the audience.

The public address system rang out with the prayers the attributes and the commemorations in respect of the deceased.

Rajiv stood back and folded his arms, as he listened to the prayers. He meditated and watched people approach with camphor and incense to scent the thin pall of smoke that rose. His face portrayed the composure and strength of mind of a true leader, a man of high Indian class; no emotion, the simple calm qualities inherited from his mother.

As part of the Hindu ritual the skull of the deceased was broken by a blow from a stick in order to release the soul. Her soul was shed of its body ready to inhabit a new one. The ashes were to be taken to the Ganges and scattered in the river to be cooled calmed and given peace. The mixing and returning of the elements, fire, earth and water would be complete. A period of twelve days of ritual, ridding of pollution, would follow, after which the family would be able to return to their everyday lives.

Sonia, Rajiv's wife and mother of his two children, the undergraduate whom he had met at Cambridge University in 1965, and whom he had married two years later, stood by his side. She had held her husband back from politics for a whole year after the death of his brother Sanjay, but had finally relinquished her hold and from then on had helped him fulfill his role in politics. Now she knew there would be no turning back. Congress had voted to support him with an overwhelming majority. He was the only person who could step into his mother's leadership. Congress had known it, his wife had known it, and despite the threats to his own life, he knew it. He had taken a firm hand with the rioters. The police had been given orders to open fire on them if they broke the curfew, whatever their religious following. Ordinary Sikhs who had nothing to do with, nor gave any support to the Independent Sikh movement, were being butchered by the outraged Hindus in blind retaliation. He was determined to bring the massive Indian community under control, and to do so, had stationed columns of tanks in the city centre where violence was likely to erupt.

None of the visiting heads of state or their representatives had approached the fire. They stood and watched. Theirs was a ritual duty, to many a political event. None felt so close to the dead Prime Minister that they could join in a totally alien ceremony.

It had been reported in Izvestia, the Soviet newspaper, that the C.I.A. were behind the plot to kill Mrs. Gandhi, and George Shultz took the opportunity to complain publicly and forcefully to Nikolai Tikhonov who simply replied that the Americans had mis-read the article. With the skill of an experienced barrister, the mere mention, by the Russians, of such a plot, meant the seeds of doubt had already been planted in the minds of the world. All politicians took the opportunity of speaking publicly and being seen to praise Mrs. Gandhi.

"It's a pity they couldn't have done that when she was alive," stated Doc as he munched on a sandwich. Mrs. Gandhi had dominated Indian politics for eighteen years. She had taken it from a country of famine and pestilence into the age of nuclear weapons and rockets. She established her own Congress Party after dismantling the old one. She intervened in East Pakistan in 1971 in the second war with Pakistan in six years, (the former in

1965 over Kashmir), establishing the new Bangladesh, and establishing her country as one of the major powers in Asia. Yet she had been killed so easily. No bomb, no SHEPH. Few knew the years of patient plotting that had gone into the assassination. Even fewer knew the real reason behind it.

"Do you realise that in India the sight of a dead body is an omen of good luck?" Doc said to Dianne as they watched last of the funeral on the box.

"Other people's bad luck is always good luck," she replied. "Good luck that it happened to somebody else."

CHAPTER 25

8th November.

Benjamin hopped down the airliner's steps and looked over towards terminal building. Daniel offered to lend him his good hand but it was refused politely. Jack Hart walked on behind and smiled at them both, one with a plaster cast on his foot, the other with the same on his hand. Both squabbled like young siblings, both glad to be with the other, both too proud to admit it.

Dianne picked them out from within the crowd and worked her way towards them. She threw herself into Benjamin's arms and gave him a huge kiss, and then, after pulling away from an embrace she could have held forever, she turned to Daniel. "I hope this is the last time you're going to get mixed up with crooks," she said with surprising aggression.

"Don't know about that," Daniel grinned. "I had thought of keeping in touch with you and Benjamin from now on."

"You can rely on us not to help you out again if you do go astray," she ordered. "Benjamin and I are due to have a bit of peace and quiet from now on."

"If it weren't for me, you'd be both as miserable as ever," Daniel retorted. "I did you both a favour."

"That's true," Benjamin agreed and leaned on Dianne. "Where are we off to then?"

"My place," Daniel stated emphatically. "Marietta will be expecting us any time now."

"All of us or just you and Jack?" asked Benjamin.

"Have to sort it out sooner or later," Daniel smiled. They walked out to the car park and Jack tagged along, reluctant to intrude in the family reunion.

"Is this the car you sold me?" Daniel asked as he climbed in beside Jack.

"Come to think of it, it is!" Benjamin exclaimed. "I'd clean forgotten about that between all the flying bullets. I only started using it so I wouldn't be recognised."

"Not mine now anyway," Daniel admitted. "I don't intend asking you for the few bits back that I left you."

"Few bits!" Benjamin shouted. Daniel chuckled. Dianne and Jack just sat and listened to their banter as they drove to the house that Daniel had bought. Marietta saw them coming up the driveway and was waiting at the door by the time they had all alighted from the car. She came down the steps to meet her man.

"Oh darling!" she cried and grabbed his arm. "I was so worried about you when the cameras showed all the smoke rising from the centre of the city."

"That was some stuff they gave us to eat," Daniel chuckled. "It's called frithath and it's for rubbing on lumbago."

"I'm serious. I was worried sick, no news about the bomb, no word from you. I'm telling you that smoke scared me."

"Yes, it made quite a good blaze, didn't it?" Daniel grinned proudly.

"That's something I have to discuss with you two," Jack came into the conversation. "How the hell didn't it blow us all up?"

"Quite simple really," Daniel bragged. "I just took my instructions from Ben. He knows all about these new fangled explosives you know." Jack turned to Benjamin who was looking away towards the big yew tree. He had to decide what to tell him.

Marietta acknowledged Benjamin and Dianne with a nod. She knew Daniel would want her to forget what happened a few days ago. Dianne followed her to the house, leaving the three men standing on the path. "Hey," Daniel called out. They turned to hear him as they were going to the door. "Put the kettle on will you if you're going inside."

Dianne gave a sigh of relief and looked at Daniel. He looked back as she shrugged her shoulders at his two companions and walked away to the house. "I'll serve the tea on the patio," Marietta said to Dianne with a welcome show of friendship. "If you'd like to go on through."

"I'd rather stop and talk," she replied with a smile. "I think there's something I should explain."

"No need," Marietta insisted. "Here, take these through will you?" She handed her a tray with cups and saucers on it. "I'll bring the tea."

"Come on then," Jack insisted as he put his arm around Benjamin's shoulder "I want to know how you know more than me about SHEPH. And don't tell me you learnt it at school!"

"I don't know how to begin," Benjamin parried.

"Then start by telling me who told you about it."

"A dead man," Benjamin replied. Jack just sighed with frustration. "It was the man you thought you blew up in the car," Benjamin said outright. There was no other way but to take the bull by the horns.

"You mean Taylor!" Jack exclaimed.

"If it weren't for me finding him, you would have either had a bloody big bang or a diplomatic scandal to wipe your hands of."

"If it weren't for him all this would never have happened," Jack insisted.

"Don't kid yourself," Benjamin scolded. "If they hadn't had SHEPH, then they'd have had gas or bacteria, or a dial-a-kill nuclear bomb. They'd already plotted for this event years ago. If I'm right, much of the murdering and rioting has been stirred up by them."

"We'll never be able to prove it," Jack asserted. "Even now, there's nobody going to believe the Bulgarian plot ever existed. It might have meant the death of some of their friendly heads of state."

"Most of the soviet representatives had made their way to the funeral site before the instruction went out to go ahead of the funeral. And what the hell, what's a few friends when it comes to world dominance."

"Even so, we'll never be able to mention it, you do realise? Without hard evidence they would gain more political acceptance from our wild allegations than we do."

"Well getting back to Edward Taylor," Benjamin maneuvered. "What would you do if he was still alive?"

"He can't be. If he's alive, then who got in the car?"

"Matthew Roland of course."

Jack studied for a moment. “What kind of arrangement are you working up to?" he asked cautiously.

"Arrangement?" Benjamin asked naively. "What makes you think I want to make an arrangement?"

"I know damned well you do Ben. So cut out all the bull-shit and give me the bottom line."

"The bottom line is that Edward is alive and well. I know where he is, and I want your help to set him up with the same kind of new identity that you have for Daniel. I have to say, I would regard it as being most indelicate if you were to kill him again," he warned. Jack knew there would be even more trouble if this matter wasn't sorted out amicably.

"So what name is he using?" he asked.

"Matthew Roland of course."

"Then why does he need a new identity? He already has a complete package."

"Except for one person who he knows will blow the whistle on him sooner or later."

"And that is?" Jack asked, expecting Benjamin to say Jack Hart.

"Janine Westcott," Benjamin stated.

"Well we did a check on her and she turned out to be a high price prostitute who has connections with the mafia. What harm can she do?"

"Merely mention his name," Benjamin said. "That's all it takes. And Edward wants to just forget it ever happened. As I say, it's just as well it was his brainchild that was involved with the plot. We came out better than we might have."

"I'll see what I can do," Jack said and began to walk to the house. He turned to Daniel who had been listening with interest. "Your young lady should have made us that tea by now."

Daniel led the way through the house to the patio where the tea cups were already being laid. He told them all to be seated and went though the French windows into the kitchen. Marietta came out soon afterwards with Daniel and the tea. She didn't speak as she poured the brew out into the cups. "This by the way is Marietta," he said and put his arm around her waist.

She turned away to go back to the kitchen. "Marietta," Benjamin called after her. "She turned to face him as he got up and walked over to her, her eyes looking straight into his. “I love him as much as you do," he said and held out a hand. She stood her ground for a moment and then, when he continued to hold his hand out, she touched it lightly.

”I know," she said and turned back to the house. Benjamin went back to the table and sat down and Marietta re-emerged with the sugar bowl.

"I don't think he realises what an affect all that macho image of his has on women, do you?" Daniel said to Dianne. Benjamin looked puzzled.

"She's all right now," Dianne said, "that's the main thing."

"Well it's broken the ice, I think," said Benjamin as Marietta walked over and stood between the two brothers. She put the sugar bowl on the table and placed a hand on each of their shoulders.

"I'm making some sandwiches," she announced. "If you wish, I'll bring them out here." She looked around the table for an answer, and Dianne was first to speak.

"That would be lovely, but I think it's suddenly getting a bit chilled. Could we have them inside?" Marietta smiled and they all followed her inside, Daniel carrying the tray and Benjamin quipping that he suited domestication.

*****

Daniel looked bemused. "What's all this about snipers?" he asked. Benjamin looked at Dianne and they both burst out laughing.

"God," Benjamin said as he caught his breath, "have we a few things to tell you!" They discussed the events of the past two months over again until finally the question of Daniel's will came up. It amused Daniel that Benjamin had got the better of the mafia.

"That was a better deal than I'd have got," he admitted when Dianne explained about the shoot out on Long Island.

"You realise we've sold practically everything you had over in the States don't you?" she said. "There's only a couple of properties left," she explained.

"Just as well. No good to me over there," he said impassively.

"So we won't be so well off after all," Benjamin said to Dianne, and squeezed her hand.

"Don't get me wrong," Daniel broke in. "I'm dead, and what I left you is legally yours. I have no intention of asking for any of it. The stocks Dianne had was hers anyway. I managed to put a considerable amount away for a rainy day, including what she paid me for them."

"How much?" Dianne asked bluntly.

"More than you have anyway," Daniel said with a grin. He tapped his nose indicatively.

"Bloody hell," Benjamin swore. "That means that I accused Cayley of stealing your money for nothing!"

"Serves him right," Dianne said dispassionately. "He wrote in that clause about the sale of shares for his own benefit. If it hadn't been for you standing up to him he'd have halved the offer on mine."

Benjamin grinned. "We make a good team don't we?"

"I think you do," Daniel said.

“I mean all of us," Benjamin asserted.

*****

As they sat and ate, they discussed the Bulgarian plot in every detail trying to analyze what the motives behind it were. "What I didn't understand at first was why they asked me to take the explosive over to India. That was what made me suspicious of their intentions in the first place," Daniel explained. "If they'd wanted, they could have done it with diplomatic packages. That was why I took precautions to keep myself from getting killed by that big fella."

"You know why they asked you to move it now though don't you?" Jack asked.

"The only reason I can think of, is so that they could point to American involvement."

"Exactly. And I should imagine they cursed themselves for losing Edward Taylor. They would have made him back up their cockeyed story. What's more," Jack added, "the allegations that the Americans were somehow involved in the death of Mrs. Gandhi were already being circulated for the press to get hold of. Two caches of American arms were uncovered near the airport to add emphasis to that theory. With many of the Indian leaders dead, including Rajiv, the Indian army might just have followed a Russian command to prevent a non existent American landing. With a few soldiers, they could have taken control of the airport and landed an occupying force in a matter of hours, to protect India from American aggression. In the turmoil nobody would have been worrying about India. It would have been as easy as their takeover of Czechoslovakia. The Indian nuclear deterrent would never have had to be aired since the aggressor never got off the ground!"

"How near to the truth are we though?" asked Dianne.

"Only the Russian's and their Bulgarian friends will know for sure. One thing Washington has learned is never to be complacent about other democracies. Russia will always exploit other political systems. That's why America has secret agents in all of them," Jack said as he looked at Daniel. "Even France," he added with a grin. "And they have their own agents doing likewise. They have no inhibitions about killing anyone who might find them out, that's why your two friends got killed."

"I hadn't noticed the Americans having any qualms about blowing people up in cars," Dianne said sarcastically.

"Most countries are hardened to the realism of survival," Jack said defensively. "Only the British seem to find killing distasteful. Someday they'll realise it's a fact of life."

"And you complain about the Russians!" she argued.

"All taken on balance," Jack retorted.

"I still don't see why Russia would want to take over India," Daniel said as he offered more tea. "They were bosom buddies anyway."

"Not at all," Jack contradicted. "Indira Gandhi was friendly with Russia, but then she started to sway towards the West. She bought planes from France, while Zia bought from America. Western weapons means reliance on Western maintenance and usually the weapons you buy are not too bad an indicator of your political leanings either. And what a prize India would have been. All that Mogul magnificence! A new hub from which to rule the rest of the world. A warm one at that!" Dianne smiled at his manner. Now he *was* getting carried away!

"And what about your theory about the Sikh bodyguards being backed by the Russians?" she asked Benjamin.

"The Indians have already got confessions that there were other influences at large. The only trouble is, nobody knew who was supplying the money. Those conspirators that have been rounded up have all received massive sums of money from somewhere, even the two bodyguards. That rules out a frenzied religious brain storm I think. It had been planned a long time ago and by better minds than those of the men who have been caught."

Dianne nodded. Some of it seemed real, some too much to believe.

At the end of the afternoon, she still had her doubts.

CHAPTER 26.

15th December.

Doc gave both brides away at the little register office wedding. Jack Hart couldn't make it to the double wedding, but he sent two telegrams to wish Benjamin and Dianne, and Daniel and Marietta all the peace and quiet in the world. Of course, Daniel was not known as Daniel but as Jason Hamilton, the name he had travelled under to India. So one telegram was to Jason and Marietta Hamilton, and the other was to Benjamin and Dianne Carlisle.

Matthew Roland got a telegram as well, but there were no good wishes, just some news of bereavement in his family. It wasn't signed and it didn't sadden him noticeably as he made his speech, as Best Men always have to. He glanced at it once, read the message that Janine had died from taking an overdose of heroin, crumpled it up and let it drop beneath the table. He grinned at the few selected guests that were gathered at the table like they were all his own family. Perhaps he had more in common with them than most brothers and sisters do.

The limited numbers were simply because it was difficult to invite any of Dianne's friends from New York since they knew Jason as Daniel. But Carl was there, and he was sworn to secrecy. Benjamin's few friends and acquaintances were there including his staff at the garage. Instructions that no photographs were to be taken, by any other than Mark Stevens, suggested that they intended a monopoly on sales.

The climax of the afternoon was when Carl went outside and drove a gleaming white Mercedes S.S.K. to the front door followed by Andre in the red 450, ready for the two couples to go on their joint honeymoon. The 450 was loaded with seventeen boxes of different sizes.

"What's all this?" Daniel asked.

"A few presents for you," Dianne grinned.

The next hour was spent opening sixteen red parcels and one white one revealing Daniel's collection of bronze and ivory figures. All had arrived safely from New York with the sports car. Of course, Andre Kercheval delivered them all personally. His retirement meant getting used to land once again. He'd enjoyed driving the supercharged sports car. The last parcel to be opened was the white one. It had to be the last on pain of death, according to Dianne. Daniel could have sworn he had all his figures unpacked already and the contents of the last parcel proved him right. It was a bronze figure all right, but a modern one. "Hey that's great!" he shouted much to Benjamin's and Dianne's delight. They'd had it made especially for the wedding, a present for Daniel and Marietta.

"I'm glad you like it," Dianne smiled. "No ivory of course."

"Good, I never did like the idea that the other ornaments had been the result of an execution," Daniel proclaimed. "And I like it because it has my favourite bird on it."

"Which one?" asked Benjamin.

"The eagle of course!" Daniel replied.

"How come the hawk has the rabbit?" he asked. Benjamin and Dianne looked at each other and laughed.

"By the way," Daniel said seriously, "you don't know anybody who wants to buy a cheap Cezanne do you?"

"He'll never change you know," Dianne said and shook her head.

THE END.

Printed in Great Britain
by Amazon

23996746R00270